THRILL TO A TUMULTUOUS ROMANCE!

As the romantic epic of Celia Skerritt unfolds, the
reader is gripped by the power of a rapturous tale
filled with adventure and peril, splendor and scandal. For Celia is a woman with a destiny, and as she
reaches toward i
GREGORY HO   r
out of schoolgi   f
unexpected sens
FRANCIS DEV   l-
lant, handsome exterior masks his true nature, a
willful, young hellion, never satisfied with what he
has—not even with Celia . . .
GWENN KATON, known for her beauty and her
cruelty, jealous of women like Celia—who possess
men like Francis . . .
OLIVER CHADWICK, whose love for Celia fol-
lows her from India to England—and persists even
after her marriage to Francis . . .

*These are the men and women who share Celia's
tempestuous journey through affairs, marriage, secret liaisons, and adventures, unfolding across a
broad, bright landscape of passion and drama!*

CELIA

CELIA

Marilyn Granbeck

PYRAMID BOOKS 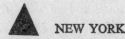 NEW YORK

CELIA

A PYRAMID BOOK

Pyramid edition published June 1977

Library of Congress Catalog Card Number: 77-5223

Printed in Canada

Pyramid Books are published by Pyramid Publications (Harcourt Brace Jovanovich, Inc.). Its trademarks, consisting of
the word "Pyramid" and the portrayal of a pyramid, are regis-
tered in the United States Patent Office.

Pyramid Publications
(Harcourt Brace Jovanovich, Inc.)
757 Third Avenue, New York, N.Y. 10017

for Arthur,
and the end of summer . . .

COME, MY CELIA

Come, my Celia, let us prove
While we may the sports of love;
Time will not be ours forever,
He at length our good will sever.
Spend not then his gifts in vain;
Suns that set may rise again,
But if once we lose this light,
'Tis with us perpetual night.
Why should we defer our joys?
Fame and rumor are but toys.
Cannot we delude the eyes
Of a few poor household spies?
Or his easier ears beguile,
So removed by our wile?
'Tis no sin love's fruit to steal;
But the sweet theft to reveal,
To be taken, to be seen,
These have crimes accounted been.

Ben Jonson

"Ah, but a man's reach should exceed his grasp,
Or what's a heaven for?"

Robert Browning
Andrea del Sarto

CHAPTER ONE

June 1838, London

Celia leaned against the cold casement and stared down at the wet street. Marley Row was a dreary thoroughfare at best, anything but the bright, tree-lined avenue she had expected of a London street when she arrived at Miss Claredon's School for Ladies ten months ago.

London was both more and less than she'd expected; mostly it was different. Although it was far more fascinating than tiny Renfield parish where she'd spent most of her life, it had not given her the excitement she had dreamed of. Oh, there were people—she'd never seen so many people!—and houses and shops with intriguing wares in the windows; there had been a few marvelous parties and occasional school outings in the city or along the river where she'd glimpsed fishermen, tradesmen, street dancers and so many curious things. But her life had remained dull and uninteresting for the most part, not much different than it had been at home, with an adult watching over her almost every minute. Her dreams of romance were unfulfilled. She had not been swept off her feet by some gallant young man who found her irresistible and drew her into the dim shadows of a garden to press his lips to hers and make her swoon with passion.

She shivered and hugged her arms about her, wondering what it would be like to experience such emotion. When she'd first arrived at Miss Claredon's, another of the girls

9

took her into her confidence and told the most marvelous tales of romance. Dorena was the eldest girl at the school and nearing the end of her year, having been in mid-term the previous year when her father packed her off to London after catching her in the hayloft of the stable with the strapping young son of a local farmer. Dorena had giggled and sighed in telling the story to Celia, detailing each step of the young man's lovemaking—how he petted her and called her sweet names, then kissed her quite boldly until she could not resist his embrace. He'd pressed her to his hard body, and she'd realized very quickly that it was not a childish game he played but a man's need that drove him. And she had been unable to refuse him even then, except that her father appeared like a demon, raging up the loft ladder and clouting the lad a blow to send him reeling. The next day Dorena had been sent to Miss Claredon's to learn proper ladylike manners and to find herself a decent husband.

And Dorena had met and enchanted an eligible young count. From the stories she whispered to Celia after evenings spent with the count, he was most ardent and managed to find numerous ways to get Dorena alone. She responded eagerly to his caresses and quickly became involved in an affair that was limited only by the excuses she could find to get away from the school. Shortly, Dorena was suffering from morning queasiness, and when Miss Claredon called a physician to examine her, the diagnosis caused a hurried note to Dorena's parents. Dorena left the school a week later to prepare for her forthcoming wedding, and Celia had not heard from her since.

Celia sighed deeply and watched the hurrying figures on the street below. It was drizzling and people were scurrying from one overhang to another, a few dodging across the street heedless of the hacks and carriages. She could make out her own wavering reflection in the streaked glass, an oval face with large eyes that dominated her features, blonde hair pulled back and caught in a ribbon—a style that made her look younger than her eighteen years but which required little care for routine school days. Somehow she had expected the year in London to change her; it had not, and she felt strangely discontented.

The day had started out overcast and by midday the

rain began, a series of downpours that made swirling waters rise above the curbs in places along the street, but finally settling to a light mist.

She knew Joseph would not come. It was understood between them that inclement weather on Saturday ruled out the walk they usually took in the nearby park. She sighed again, feeling the loneliness of a stranger in a huge metropolis. But she was not sorry that Joseph had stayed home. Being with Joseph did not dissipate her loneliness to any great extent.

Joseph was so like her own father, not in appearance or demeanor but because of the church. Her father, a country parson in the village of Renfield, spent days preparing his sermons. Early in life she had learned to sit perfectly still in the pew with a fixed expression of concentration on her face as her father droned on. She was able to let her thoughts wander far afield, and later when her father asked for opinions, "How did it go today, lass?" she would tell him the sermon had been inspiring and helpful. Those two words never failed her.

She had never heard Joseph preach, and sometimes she found herself biting her lip with a quickening heartbeat— what would she do if he asked her to the services? But as Joseph knew, the girls at Miss Claredon's attended St. Stephen's church, and the headmistress would excuse no one from daily chapel or Sabbath services. No one except a girl who might find herself engaged and wish to be with her betrothed's family . . .

Celia blew her breath against the window and watched it steam. She was not engaged, nor did she have any prospects of becoming so. Joseph was the only young man who had called on her during her stay in London, and although she had fervently hoped for romance, wanting him to sweep her into his arms and crush his lips to hers, Joseph had scarcely touched her hand—and that to help her in or out of the carriage, no more. Her dreams of romance faded slowly, leaving her more discontent than before. In a little more than a month's time her stay in London would be finished . . . and if she had no prospects of marriage, she would return to the tedious life of Renfield.

"I'm so sick of parsons and parsonages I hope I never see one again!" she whispered to the blurred face in the

11

glass. Her heart seemed to break its rhythmic stride and she clutched her hands to her throat, whirling about to make sure no one had heard. She was alone in the long room, and she let out her breath in a sigh, silently asking forgiveness of the God she had blasphemed.

Was it so wrong for her to want more than a dull existence? She was of marrying age, and except for these past ten months, she'd seen nothing of the world outside Renfield. She had only dim memories of the time when her family lived at Dunwaithe and her father seemed destined to be vicar of the vast estate which his family held. But his strong opinions and sharp tongue had brought about a disagreement with his brother and uncle, and they had withdrawn their support, throwing the Reverend Skerritt to the mercies of a bishop who took issue with his views. He'd been sent to Renfield with a stipend of four hundred pounds a year—barely enough to keep his family fed and clothed. And even in the tiny village parish, he had managed to all but alienate the families who might benefit him most.

Reverend Skerritt would not have sent his daughter for schooling in London except for his wife's insistence—and her scrimping to put away the money to accomplish it.

And now the year was at an end . . . and it had not provided her with a suitable match for marriage.

She frowned at the room that had been her home these past months. It was stark, walls painted brown and ceiling grey, relieved only by the tall windows at each end and by the dozen narrow beds and black wardrobes, one for each girl, with three short shelves beside them for books and school equipment. The room was damp and chill, unheated even in the depths of winter, and dimly lighted by four gas lamps which Miss Claredon was careful to turn down far enough to burn as little fuel as possible and still give a meager light.

As one of the older girls in the school, Celia had an end bed. She sat on it and opened the wardrobe doors to take out a small wooden chest which held her most treasured possessions. Fishing for the key on a ribbon about her neck, she unlocked the box and took out a slim volume of Shelley's poetry which she had borrowed from Miss Janeau, the dancing mistress, several days ago, promising to return it on the weekend. Celia read and reread the poems, dreaming of some magic in her own life that would cause such emotion to thrill her. She'd forgotten her promise to return the book until Miss Janeau had reminded her this afternoon.

Celia snapped the tiny catch on the box and returned it to the wardrobe, then sat with the book clasped in her hands, lost in dreams of what life might have been if—if what? If her father had been born other than fourth in the line of Skerritt sons so that he might have inherited Dunswaithe or perhaps had a military or diplomatic career? If he had found new support from the more affluent of his flock in Renfield? If—but her father was what he was and nothing would change him.

She sighed, thinking of Renfield. She did not miss the parsonage or her life there. Mama a bit, of course. Mostly she was lonely for Kevin, her laughing, teasing brother who always managed to raise her spirits and brighten her life when it seemed darkest—and who had been not only to London but to Paris and Africa! Kevin, who filled her head with dreams of distant places and adventure.

But she had not missed Renfield and its endless succession of dreary days with nothing to occupy her time except tending the sick, paying calls on parishioners with Mama and listening to her father's endless prayers and sermons. Her only refuge was to walk alone among the green hills or to stand at the foot of the long drive that led to Aylesford, the huge estate that belonged to the Devy family, and to pretend it was Dunswaithe and she lived there. She watched carriages draw up to the front portico where footmen helped down ladies in gowns of silk, with tight waists and yards of ruffles and lace, men in high-collared coats with spreading lapels, satin waistcoats and tapered trousers. She'd listened to the distant sound of orchestras and watched moving shadows against the big windows as people danced. But Aylesford was much farther away than the mile or so of fields that separated her from the house. Aylesford, like Dunswaithe, was another world ... another life.

The sound of running feet on the bare wood steps brought her up with a start. She had no desire to be

13

caught mooning by one of the younger girls who would giggle at the sight of a book of love poems.

It was not one of the younger girls but Mathilda Arbough who ran into the room, her dark green gingham held high so her racing feet would not tangle in it.

"Celia! It's happened! It's a dream come true!" Mattie grabbed her hands, sending Miss Janeau's book thudding to the floor. Mattie danced her about in a joyous circle between the beds.

Too surprised to worry about the book at the moment, Celia gasped. "Cecil asked you to marry him?"

"Yes! I'm so wildly happy I think I'll burst!" Mattie hugged her, laughing and babbling.

"Oh, Mattie, how wonderful! I'm so glad for you. When is the wedding to be? Will you live at Ponsby Hall? Will he . . ."

Mattie giggled and fell across her own bed next to Celia's. She flung her arms over her head, sighing. "Cecil is on his way to speak with Papa this very minute." She sat up abruptly. "Papa will say yes, of course," she said with mock seriousness.

Both girls giggled. The thought of any parent refusing a match such as Mattie had in store was comic. Hadn't both girls been sent to Miss Claredon's for that very reason—to catch good husbands, better than they might expect in the small villages from which they came?

And Mattie had succeeded . . .

Celia pushed away the encroaching depression. She would not let herself think of her own problems now—not when there was Mattie's happiness to share. She sat on the edge of the bed and hugged her arms over her firm young breasts, feeling her heart pound beneath her ribs as though romance had touched her as well as Mattie.

"How did he propose? Did he get on his knees?"

Mattie shook her head, dark hair flying. "We were sitting on a sofa and he simply took my hand and looked at me very seriously. I knew what he was going to say before he had the words out, and I couldn't even pretend surprise. I simply said yes, it would mean very much to me to marry him if Papa gives his consent."

Celia's blue eyes were shining. "Did he kiss you?"

"Not then, of course. Mrs. Holmsby and several of the

14

others were in the salon—not close enough to hear but certainly keeping an eye on us. But he did in the carriage coming home." She closed her eyes and pressed her hands to her face as though remembering.

Celia felt a twinge of envy but forced a smile when Mattie went on. "I wonder how I shall like living abroad? Cecil says there is talk of his being sent to France to an embassy there. Paris . . ."

A sigh escaped Celia's lips and Mattie took her hand quickly. "You mustn't feel sad." She slipped her arm about Celia's shoulder and hugged her close. "I've so much to do . . ." She leaped up, so caught in her own delight that she could not sit still.

Celia bent to retrieve the book that had fallen to the floor. Dusting it off, she said, "When will you be leaving?"

Mattie settled again. "Cecil wants the banns posted as soon as possible. He's planning for us to honeymoon the summer in the south of France. I'm sure Papa will send for me tomorrow."

"You shan't stay out the term?" Celia worked hard to keep the disappointment from her voice. Mattie was her dearest friend, her only friend really. Most of the girls at Miss Claredon's were several years younger, and Celia had found little in common with them. The thought of even a few weeks without Mattie was unbearable. Her smile felt heavy. "I'll miss you."

Mattie's face sobered. "I'll miss you too, Celia. I don't know what I would have done this past year without you." She smiled. "You shall be invited to the wedding, of course. I'll insist that Cecil send a carriage for you. Unless you have a wedding of your own to think about." She looked serious. "Do you think Joseph will propose?"

Celia's gaze returned to the rain-covered window, and once more she felt the day's wet chill. "I don't know . . ." Did she want Joseph Cole to propose marriage? There was scarcely any way she could refuse him if he did, and she was still so unsure of her emotions. Certainly she did not feel Mattie's ecstatic joy. Joseph wasn't the catch Cecil was, but even that wouldn't bother her if she felt *excited* about the thought of spending a lifetime with him.

Mattie was rummaging for a brush to smooth her dark hair. "I must tell Miss Claredon and the others. I wanted

15

you to be the first to know." She smiled, and Celia nodded, turning the book over in her hands.

"I have to return this to Miss Janeau. I'll walk down with you."

The rain had ceased by morning and the sky was a rich blue with only fragmented clouds stretching along the horizon. The news of Mattie's engagement had spread, and the entire school was buzzing. Miss Claredon smiled throughout the morning meal as though she were responsible for the match by allowing Mattie to attend the school. The meal was barely over when a message came from Mattie's father that he wished his daughter to return home at once.

Celia had only a few moments alone with her as the porter carried out the trunk Mattie had providently packed the night before. The others had trooped downstairs to leave for Sunday services at St. Stephen's; Celia lingered for a final goodbye.

"I wish you all the joy possible, Mattie. Be happy . . ." Celia took the other girl's hands in her own and squeezed them.

Mattie embraced her. "Yes, and you shall be too—I know it! I will keep in touch, I promise. If I come to London before the wedding—to shop or perhaps to a party— I'll visit, even if it's in the middle of lessons and Miss Claredon has a fit!"

Celia smiled, knowing Mattie was trying to cheer her. "Surely Cecil will return for the coronation?"

Mattie nodded, as though the coronation of Queen Victoria, only a few weeks distant, was insignificant beside her own forthcoming wedding. "I suppose we will. He has many friends at court." She hugged Celia again. "I must run, the carriage is waiting. Goodbye, dear Celia." She kissed her quickly on the cheek, then ran the length of the room and down the stairs.

Celia stared after her, feeling pain, loss and envy. She knew that despite Mattie's promises, they would never see each other again. Mattie had already become part of a different world.

Mattie's carriage was gone when Celia joined the others for the walk to St. Stephen's a block away. She was only vaguely aware of slipping into the pew and holding the hymnal, kneeling, rising, sitting on cue. She didn't absorb a word of the service but sat numbly waiting for the time to pass.

When the group was once more on its way back to the school, Celia became aware of the warm day, the abrupt change in the weather. She wanted to push off the stiff straw Dunstable bonnet and throw aside the shawl that covered her shoulders. She wanted to run and feel the spring breeze on her face, unfasten her tightly plaited hair and let it whip about. She longed to be free of the restraint of heavy petticoats and skirt—and of the watchful eye of Miss Claredon. She wanted to *feel* life.

The other girls were still chattering about Mattie as they went up to the third floor to change from their Sunday garments to the grey calicos Miss Claredon decreed more suitable for school wear. The only ones excused from the uniform were girls who had outside activities planned for the day.

Celia retreated to her corner of the long room and slipped out of her blue muslin, carefully hanging it on a hook in the wardrobe. With her back to the others, she studied herself in the small glass hung inside the door. Was she pretty? She thought her eyes too wide-spaced, but she had good features. Kevin called her a beauty, and Father forbade such talk lest it fill her head with vain notions. But she saw the look of approval in Mama's eyes each time she glanced at her daughter or spoke to the fact that she favored the Cumberland fairness.

She sighed. If she was pretty, why had she not found a suitable beau these past months? She was shy and awkward when first in London; her sheltered life at the parsonage had not prepared her for social activities on any great scale. The year at school had taught her social graces, how to meet people, contribute to a conversation and how to seem at ease in almost any situation that might arise.

She'd attended parties arranged by Miss Claredon but met no one who seemed impressed enough to call. Young men flocked to her at first but drifted off to be with others who flirted openly, and Celia was left alone to watch and

17

envy. The only one who had sought her out was Joseph Cole.

She glanced down at her slim body. She'd grown to full womanhood, and the cotton chemise was tight across her firm breasts. Her waist was slim, her hips gently rounded. The clothes she'd brought from home had grown snug and she'd had to let out the seams in order to make them do.

She turned and impatiently selected a brown merino with lace at the throat and cuffs. The dress was plain and unflattering but it would pass Aunt Henrietta's careful scrutiny. There were times when Celia wondered if spending Sunday afternoons at the school might be more enjoyable than tea with Aunt Henrietta and Uncle Samuel.

Henrietta was Emma Skerritt's sister; it was she who had located a proper school for Celia in the hope that Celia might marry well and thus erase some of the disgrace of William Skerritt's failure. Henrietta, childless herself, felt no warmth for Celia and considered her duty done by having the girl to tea each week. Every Sunday at precisely two-thirty, Samuel Bridgeman came for his niece in a hackney cab. The fact that the expense doubled because he made the trip both ways was a perpetual source of complaint with him but he did not consider it proper for young ladies to be gadding about London alone, even though the distance was but a few blocks.

Celia caught up her bonnet and ran downstairs. It didn't do his temper good to be kept waiting ... she'd learned that her first week.

Several of the girls were sitting in the parlor, talking quietly in groups or reading the Bible—the only pastimes allowed them on the Sabbath. Through a window, Celia saw several others enjoying the warmth of the garden, but looking exhaustively bored. Cakes and tea with her aunt and uncle at least gave her a change of scene, and it spanned the time until Joseph came.

It was his custom to arrive at the Bridgemans' home just as the plates and cups were cleared away. He would sit and chat with Samuel and Henrietta for precisely half an hour, as if there were a clock inside his round head that ticked off the seconds. Celia found herself timing him, and he never varied more than half a minute, which was a remarkable thing since he sat where the hall clock was not

18

visible. Then he would smile and say it was time he was getting Celia back to the school.

On pleasant evenings he drove the carriage the long way around, through the green and shadowy park so they could fill their lungs with God's air—as Joseph put it. But their Sunday outings were limited to the drive. Like his father, Joseph considered the Sabbath set aside for the Lord and allowed himself nothing in the way of frivolity or entertainment. Celia often wondered if he had convinced himself that the ride with her was somehow part of his Christian duty.

She saw the hackney rounding the corner and hurried out, waiting at the top step until the driver halted the carriage before she walked down to meet her uncle who alighted and held out his hand to her. "Ah, my dear. You're looking well, Celia."

"Thank you, Uncle Samuel. I trust you had a good week ..." It was always the same, the exchange of meaningless words as he helped her into the carriage and climbed in beside her, signaling the driver.

"Is Aunt Henrietta well?"

"Yes, indeed, and anxious to see you, my dear." He leaned back in the cab, staring out the window. His thin face looked gaunt under the heavy brows that were beginning to go grey like his sparse hair. His dark frock coat and top hat did nothing to relieve the somberness of his appearance. His blue jowls matched the color of the hat.

She turned to watch the streets, hoping for more activity than she saw—a few strollers, a running child and several dogs. Old women sat at windows of some of the houses they passed; occasionally there were young people her own age standing in doorways, laughing and playing with balls.

Samuel noticed these, grunting in displeasure and muttering to himself. "No sense of decency ..."

The middle class section of the city in which the school was located was composed of families who did not always observe the strict Sabbath. Celia, completely bored at the school because there was nothing to do, could not help noticing that these people had even less. She'd remarked on it once to her uncle and received a scathing reply which had sealed her lips thereafter. They often sat in the rocking, clattering carriage, silent throughout the entire trip.

19

She sometimes composed conversations in her mind. "Why must we sit with hands folded in our laps on the Sabbath, Uncle Samuel?"

"Because it is seemly."

"Does God want it thus?"

"My child, you must not be blasphemous!"

"Why is it blasphemous to ask questions?"

"Because it *is*."

Her father had given her such answers too, a thing is so or it is not so—but the reason was seldom mentioned. Long ago she had learned that no one could tell what she was *thinking*; the trouble began when one opened one's mouth, though she had done that too on occasion, gaining her the appellation of spunky—a term she abhorred.

She concentrated on the houses, most of them growing shabby though still well kept. There were bright flowerpots at windows and here and there small swatches of gardens bordering paths. Celia missed the open greenness of Renfield. The cobblestones and hard-packed dirt of the side streets, the rows of grey houses depressed her. They were far different from the more affluent neighborhoods she'd glimpsed on rides with Joseph.

The carriage had stopped. She came out of her reverie; Uncle Samuel was climbing down, rapping on the side of the carriage to hurry her along.

The Bridgeman house was in a row of eight almost identical buildings; they varied only in small details, a shutter here, a row of potted plants there, a window framed in blue or dull green. Georgian brick, they were all plain and cold looking, with only bits of white stucco fancywork at doorways and cornices. Each building had two storeys, with square windows, and had no space at all between them to give access to the miniscule gardens where wood fences afforded a measure of privacy between the privies. Celia thought the houses might once have been impressive, but now they were beginning to decay.

The Bridgeman parlor was austere, papered in dark stripes with heavy velour draperies over ecru lace at the windows. Two small sofas faced each other over a low table; several spindle-legged chairs with tapestry seats and backs formed a barrier at one end and the stone hearth and fireplace completed the square. The corners of the

20

room, dim with shadows, were occupied by small tables and stiff chairs that were never used.

Aunt Henrietta sat on one sofa, hands in her lap, the tea tray before her. Celia knew she had instructed the maid to bring the tray the moment the carriage stopped in front of the house. Tardiness was a sin of omission to Henrietta; she seemed to rush through life from one breathless task to another. She was thin and stern-faced, with none of the Cumberland comeliness, her brown hair drew up into a tight knot at her crown. The severe lines of her mouth bent upward into a polite smile that might have been painted on. Celia went to her immediately and took the proffered hand.

Henrietta's dark, prominent eyes indicated the chair Celia was to take as she poured tea into the three cups set out on the tray. Celia sighed inaudibly and laid back her wrap. Henrietta's eyes went at once to her bustline and a tiny frown appeared.

"Is that your usual dress, dear? You *are* growing fast, aren't you?"

"Yes, Aunt . . . I suppose I am." She saw Uncle Samuel's eyes flick toward her breasts and her cheeks became warm. She had let the dress out, but it would have to be let out again. Now that attention had been directed to her body, the dress seemed to constrict her even more.

Henrietta's lips tightened as she handed Celia the cup and saucer. "There are but four weeks left of the term, child. Have you heard from your mother? What are their plans for you?"

"Mama expects me to spend the summer at home," she said, rounding her shoulders slightly to make her chest more concave. She had a sudden suspicion that Henrietta was about to mention Joseph. It was not unfounded.

"What about Joseph?" Henrietta's bright eyes searched every curl of Celia's head. "Am I to understand that he intends to propose marriage? Have you discussed it with him on your solitary rides?"

"No, we haven't spoken of it." So far she had been able to turn his thoughts to other things, but how long could she go on doing it?

"I have spoken to his mother."

Celia's head came up so abruptly her hand shook and

21

she felt hot tea splash on her flesh. How could her aunt presume!

"I did not pry, child," Henrietta said harshly, reading the look correctly. "I have been acquainted with his parents for many years as you know, since it was I who introduced Joseph to you. Naturally I am interested in his intentions."

Celia looked into her cup, lips tight. Her pulse was a roaring drumbeat in her temples. She did not want to talk of Joseph, and she resented Henrietta interfering in her life. She sat very still, knowing her face was flaming, and once again words crowded to her lips but she managed to swallow them. Henrietta leaned forward in the sudden silence, lifted a tray of tiny sugar biscuits and passed them to her husband, then to Celia who took one with trembling fingers.

"Mrs. Cole is quite sure Joseph intends to speak for you. He would, of course, drive to Renfield to discuss the matter with your father first. It's only proper."

Celia looked at the tea, afraid to lift the cup lest it slip and spill. She was being pushed into marriage—a marriage she was not sure she wanted.

"I must say," Henrietta remarked, "you might look more delighted at the prospect. Joseph is a fine young man, and in a year or two he will undoubtedly have a good parish of his own and will need a wife to help him. Joseph is not one to speak hastily, you may be sure."

The remark was two-edged, inferring that Joseph would have better sense than to voice opinions that might jeopardize his career as William Skerrit had, and also that Celia might not be worthy of sharing his life. The thought of Joseph weighing her worth like a sack of meal infuriated her. She knew it was important that she should marry—spinsterhood was worse than a crippling disease. But she would not be bartered. She *would* not.

Henrietta calmly nibbled a biscuit and sipped tea. "You'll not do better in Renfield, my dear. You'll be the envy of many."

Perhaps it was true but Celia resented hearing it. Or was her mind too full of Mattie's marvelous fortune? In comparison her own lacked luster.

Uncle Samuel cleared his throat. "I don't see the girl has any choice if her father gives his consent."

He had the annoying habit of speaking to his wife as if Celia were deaf or mentally defective and unable to understand the words.

Henrietta agreed. "It's only proper and decent." She nodded to Celia. "Is your tea getting cold, dear?"

"No, Aunt Henrietta." She barely got the words out. Her throat had tightened to a dry cord and it was difficult to breathe. Good manners would not permit her to engage in an argument—besides, what would she say? What did it matter that she did not love Joseph? She looked at her uncle placidly swinging his leg as he sat to one side. Did he and Henrietta love each other? She could not imagine it.

At any rate, they were right and she knew it only too well. What had love and happiness to do with marriage?

Celia nibbled the biscuit and closed her mind to her aunt's droning words. From time to time she smiled or made some small gesture when Henrietta seemed to expect one. Her aunt was quite capable of running on for hours if not interrupted; Samuel seemed to sit with glazed eyes, the words washing over him like waves on a beach. Henrietta was fond of chronicling the folly of sending young girls to school and the merits of early marriage and settling down. She never spoke of her own childlessness, and she seemed lacking in any of the instincts that might have made her a good parent. Celia could not help comparing Henrietta to her own mother.

Henrietta spoke of a wife as a helpmate, a source of moral and physical support for her husband in his work and leisure. It was her favorite theme; her own life, she said, was devoted to furthering Samuel's position and welfare. But to Celia it seemed she was the driving force and Samuel the follower. It was almost impossible to imagine Uncle Samuel accomplishing anything away from Henrietta.

But at last Henrietta rang a small tinkling bell and the maid came to clear away the tray. The front door knocker sounded, and moments later Joseph was ushered into the parlor.

He was a smiling man of medium height and frame,

and at twenty-six his shoulders already had the rounded look of a man who spent most of his days poring over books. He wore steel-rimmed glasses and his blue eyes peered intently, slightly magnified and owlish. His dark suit and basque, relieved only by the white clerical collar that made his neck seem longer, emphasized his pallor. Did he ever wear anything else? He had strong features, she thought, looking at him as though seeing him for the first time, but he was so plain. So very plain. He bowed to Henrietta, then to Celia and smiled at Samuel.

"How nice to see you . . ."

Henrietta said, "How good of you to come, Joseph."

"My pleasure, my dear Mrs. Bridgeman." He inclined his head. "And you too, sir."

"Hello, Joseph." Samuel got up and shook hands briefly. "Please sit down."

"Thank you." Joseph dragged a chair forward and perched on the edge of it, smiling at Celia. "You're looking remarkably well today, Celia."

"Would you like tea?" Henrietta asked.

"No, thank you."

It was a weekly charade, her offering and his refusing. Celia murmured thanks at his compliment and tried not to let her eyes wander to the hall clock. Henrietta was already drawing Joseph into conversation concerning his father's parish, of which the Bridgemans were members.

Folding her hands primly in her lap, Celia prepared to get through the next half-hour. She had met Joseph at a church affair two months after her arrival in London. It had been a large gathering, held outdoors since the weather had remained mild through fall. Celia recalled vaguely that it had been an occasion to raise money for some worthy cause—a school for poor children? She could no longer remember.

It had been a time when she'd still been enraptured by the sights and sounds of the great city and knowing she was to live in it for the coming year. The social had been held in the parklike gardens adjacent to St. Mark's Church. By London standards, she was to learn, the church was far from imposing, but compared to Renfield's Ascension Chapel to which her father ministered, it was quite grand indeed. The sculptured towers, the aisled pres-

24

bytery between the apse and nave and the ring of smaller chapels opening from it gave St. Mark's an awesome appearance. Celia had been sure the rector and his family must be very well off; she was much surprised to discover the Cole family lived quite simply.

She had met Joseph, one of several young men, and Celia had given him scarcely a second thought. Following her aunt about the garden, she made little attempt to remember the dozens of names she heard. Henrietta kept up such a voluble running account of each person's position, background and prospects for the future that Celia found she got them all mixed up anyway.

When Henrietta finally drifted off to chat with a group of women sitting in the shade of a yew tree, Celia was freed. She moved about, feeling awkward in such a large group of strangers. Joseph had fallen in step beside her and attempted to put her at ease ... for which she was grateful.

There were other girls her own age, some of them flirting outrageously with the young men, chatting with heads close together and laughing. But Joseph only asked her about school and how she liked London, and soon she found her attention wandering again toward the more lively groups.

The following week she was surprised when Joseph came to call just after tea, a happening so precisely timed that Celia could not help wondering if Henrietta arranged it. He chatted and drove her back to the school ... and a pattern had been established.

She sometimes thought of it as a trap into which she'd fallen. A trap set by Aunt Henrietta, baited by cakes and tea, and with Joseph as her reward. She glanced at the clock and realized with a start that the half-hour was up.

Joseph said, "It's getting late and the skies are clouding again. It might be best if we are on our way." He rose and Celia got to her feet dutifully. If she married Joseph she would be dutiful all her life.

"Please remember me to your mother when you write," Henrietta said, as always. "We'll look forward to you next week."

Celia managed a smile.

The one-horse landau was tied to the hitching ring;

Joseph helped her up to the hard seat, untied the reins and sat beside her. She breathed a deep sigh of relief, drinking in the fresh air as he slapped the reins and urged the chestnut into motion.

"The rain will hold till morning I think. Would you care to ride through the park?"

So predictable! Normally she would have welcomed the longer ride but today she was anxious to be alone with her thoughts. "I am feeling tired, Joseph. Do you mind taking me straight home?"

He turned to her, eyes owllike with concern behind the round spectacles. "Are you ill? You should have mentioned—"

"I'm not ill, only tired."

"I see." The clip-clopping of the hooves and the rattle of the metal tires on the cobblestones filled the quiet street. She laid her head back and closed her eyes momentarily, knowing that Joseph was glancing at her. Would he speak of his intentions? She hoped not . . . not today.

He said, "Your term will be over soon . . ."

"Yes, in a few weeks."

There was a long silence. He held the reins loosely, allowing the horse its head. "I've enjoyed these past months."

She did not shift her gaze from the rows of houses they were passing. When she did not answer he said, "May I hope that you have too?"

"Yes, of course I have. Being in London has been the most marvelous time of my life."

"I rather meant—"

"Miss Claredon's school has been wonderful too. London is such an exciting place. Of course you've always lived here."

"Would you like to stay?"

He was looking at her, eyes wide behind the rims. His words startled her for a moment; they could almost be construed as a proposal. "I—I'm not sure." She regained her composure. "I am looking forward to going home, yet I hate the idea of leaving."

"I do hope so, Celia." He fiddled with the reins. "May I presume to ask if I would be welcome if I visited Renfield during the summer months?"

She turned her head, studying his profile as he gazed at the street. She didn't want to hurt him, yet how could she give him any encouragement? She chose her words carefully. "I'm sure my father would be delighted to have you pay a visit to our parish."

"Your father?" He sounded astonished.

She felt her cheeks flush. "I too. I would be pleased to show you the countryside the way you've shown me London."

He fell silent, saying nothing till they reached Marley Row and drew up in front of the school. Twisting the reins over the seat rail, he jumped down and came round to help her.

"Will I see you next week?"

She stepped to the street and for a moment they were eye to eye, only inches apart—and she wondered what it would be like if he kissed her. Hurriedly she said, "Yes, of course, Joseph," and stepped away.

He caught her hand, stopping her short. "Until next week then," he said softly. He bent and kissed her fingers.

She was so shocked she gasped. She felt a mild tremor but it passed so quickly no blush warmed her cheeks. The kiss was no more stirring than his hand helping her over the wheel.

She nearly ran into the school, exhausted by the interminable visit and Joseph's fawnlike eyes.

CHAPTER TWO

The early weeks of June passed with alarming swiftness, faster than Celia had thought possible. She had scarcely any time to dwell on thoughts of Mattie, save to wonder for moments before sleep how her friend was managing. The gnawing loneliness was forgotten in the rush of tasks as her year in London drew to a close.

London was agog and vibrant with preparations for the new Queen's coronation. The event was on everyone's tongue, the newspapers were full of it and placards along the street never let one forget, for shopkeepers were doing all they could to sell mementos and trifles bearing Victoria's image and highly glorified representations of the crown, some with ribbons and gilt.

The upcoming coronation would be nothing like that of Victoria's uncle seven years earlier, that was obvious, and everyone was making the most of it. William IV had been crowned in rather dull ceremonies, shorn of pageantry and the traditional splendor, and the mood of the occasion had been austere. There had been celebrations by the populace to be sure, but they had lacked the spontaneity and genuine rejoicing the lovely young Queen induced.

The coronation was to be held on the twenty-eighth and public fervor seemed heightened each passing day. Bunting was raised and strung from windows and across doorways; flags appeared in shop and house windows. There was something in the air that signaled change; the Queen was young and the entire country seemed to look forward to a new golden age as the old order was laid to rest.

The girls at Miss Claredon's School had been promised window seats from which to view the grand procession, and their excitement could hardly be contained. Miss Claredon had arranged with the mistress of Colby's, a larger and more elegant school near Northumberland Avenue, to allow the girls space in one of the halls. The procession would pass along Northumberland on its way from the palace to Westminster Abbey. From Colby's upper floors, the girls would have a good, if distant, view of the entire pageant.

Miss Claredon announced they would set out immediately after breakfast and morning prayers, arriving at Colby's early to avoid, she hoped, the crowds that would gather later.

Celia had never seen such festivities. The noise and color mounted till the eve of the great event when it seemed that every person in the city must be engaged in the celebration one way or another. There was laughter and shouting in the streets till well after dark. They were jammed with carriages and hacks; it was said that thousands of people from outlying districts were in London for the coronation day.

Celia slept fitfully, awakened repeatedly by the merriment outside and then toward morning, the booming of far-off guns. She sat up groggily, seeing that every girl in the room was awake and crowding to the windows. She jumped up to see what it was all about, peering over the heads of several smaller girls. She was astonished to see the usually gloomy and silent street bright with torches as people straggled by shouting toasts to the new queen.

One of the girls pointed. "What's he doing?"

A man had climbed a lamp post and was tying one end of a banner under the glowing gaslight.

"Can you read it?"

"It says something about the Queen—Long—live—"

"There's another one at the corner!"

They babbled with glee, pushing and shoving to vie for a view until someone called, "Miss Claredon's coming."

They scurried for their beds. Celia slid into her own cot as Miss Claredon appeared in the doorway, a long woolen robe over her nightdress, feet thrust into slippers, a frilly white nightcap on her grey hair. She held high a hooded lamp. "Girls!" She was very annoyed. "It's past four in the morning. Whatever are you thinking of?" She stalked down the aisle, looking about. "I will not have this. You are to stay in bed, all of you, no matter what noises you hear from the ruffians outside. I will not have you exhausted before the day begins."

There were a few murmurs and Miss Claredon swung around, looking sharply and shining the lamplight into the corners. "Lie quietly even if you can't sleep. You must get your rest." She stood in the center of the room like a sentinel until the girls finally subsided. Celia held the blanket close to her chin and stared at the ceiling. As the light came her way, she dutifully closed her eyes, resenting being made to feel like a child but not daring to disobey. Miss Claredon walked the length of the room and back again, pausing to fasten the windows. Her footsteps receded on the stairs at last and Celia took a long breath. For a few moments the room was hushed, then whispers and giggles erupted. A vacant bed, Mattie's, separated Celia from the others, and she was content to lie silent with her own thoughts. She was looking forward to the holiday. She did not attempt to plumb the special excitement inside her, it was enough that it was there. She wondered if Mattie and Cecil were in town—hadn't Mattie said Cecil had friends at court? Would Mattie be attending some of the gala balls and parties that would mark the historic day?

She wished passionately that she might somehow be allowed at least a glimpse of one of the glittering affairs. She sighed at the impossibility of it. Even in the privacy of a dream it was difficult to envision herself in a silken gown, with her hair piled atop her head in a mass of blonde curls, smiling and dancing on the arm of a tall, handsome stranger who found her attractive and said so. She would dance until dawn, or until she dropped with exhaustion—but such a thing would never happen. If only this past year had worked out differently! If only she had met someone as dashing and charming as the man in her dreams ... Why was reality always so much harsher and bleaker than illusions?

She tried to shut out the street noises, but sleep would not come. Other thoughts crept in. She had asked Joseph about his plans for the coronation day, hoping by a miracle that he might receive an invitation to *some* kind of festivity and take her along, but he and his father were conducting special services both morning and night to pray for the long and joyous reign of the Queen.

She turned her face toward the small window that overlooked the garden behind the school. The sky was greying slightly with the coming of dawn and she watched it change slowly. It became saffron, then rose, and the long room began to lighten. The bell at the head of the stairs pealed sharply to waken the students, only everyone was already awake, surging out of bed in a mad rush as the girls vied for the washwater the maids brought up in huge pitchers. Celia put on her best grey calico, smoothed the skirt, combed her hair and went down to breakfast and morning prayers sedately.

But the day was somewhat different in that the air seemed charged; there was a low current of whispers and fidgeting that even Miss Claredon's pertinent glances could not quell, and by the time the girls were walking down the front steps, they were openly chattering and giggling. Miss Claredon contented herself in guiding them with an occasional, "Young ladies—do not forget you're young ladies . . ."

Marley Row was thronged with people moving toward the palace but the carriage drivers had managed to bring the coaches around and the girls climbed in, pushing and laughing, vying for places by the windows so they would miss nothing. Celia was quite astounded by the air of general merrymaking. People jostled along the walks and spilled into the streets so the hack and coach drivers had to shout for passage, and horses stomped and whinnied in fright. The carriages were forced to halt more than two blocks from Miss Colby's, unable to force a way through the packed crowds. The streets surrounding the palace and Westminster were jammed. The big guns in St. James Park thundered and new waves of cheering rose. "God save the Queen! Long live Victoria!"

Viewing the mob, Miss Claredon realized the futility of trying to shepherd eleven young girls through in any kind of group. It had been foolhardy to attempt to reach Colby's this particular morning yet offered the chance, she had been unable to turn it down; she was almost as excited by the great event as the girls though she took extreme pains to avoid showing it. What should she do? It was distinct madness to go ahead on foot, yet the carriages could not turn to go back.

She conferred rapidly with Miss Dreyfus, the music instructress, who shared the first coach with her and five of the girls. Miss Janeau and Miss Tollinger were in the coach behind with the remaining six girls. "Perhaps," Miss Dreyfus ventured, "if we band together we might force a way ..."

Miss Claredon tapped her finger thoughtfully on the window ledge, then leaned out and spoke to the driver. "Does that alley cut through to the next street?"

The man craned around and nodded. "Yes'm, but them's narrow and the carriage won't make it through."

"Very well, then we shall walk." She frowned at the entrance. It should be possible to herd the girls across and gather them inside. She communicated her decision to the others, warning them to hold hands and stay as close together as possible. Once across the jammed street, the going would be easier, and the alley would bring them out to the street behind their destination. With luck they would be able to get through the school gates safely and into the courtyard that surrounded the building.

Celia was assigned to convey the plan to Miss Janeau and Miss Tollinger, but the effort was doomed from the start. Celia had no sooner set foot out of the carriage when a laughing, bearded man scooped her up, one strong arm about her waist. He swung her from the carriage step and held her high for a moment before he set her down, forcing a space with his elbows. Grinning, he bent and covered Celia's mouth with a sudden kiss that held the stale odor of spirits. She cried out and struggled to free herself from his grip.

"Let me go!" She turned an agonized face toward the carriage. "Let me go!" Conscious of his laugh, she pounded his chest with small fists. She could see Miss Claredon leaning from the coach, her face white as she shouted. The crowd surged as the man released Celia and she was swept along. Near panic, she wanted to scream but stifled the sounds in her throat. She could not see over the heads of the people about her—who paid her no attention at all. She was pushed and shoved, and she clutched her bonnet and shawl lest they be torn from her and trampled. In moments she was no longer sure where the alley was, and as she was carried past the next corner she despaired of getting back. The mood of the crowd was jubilant, even the drunken man who had lifted her from the carriage had meant her no harm, she was sure. It was a day for rejoicing . . . and she was part of it.

Quite suddenly the crowd fell away and left her against the side of a building; the rough stone felt cool on her flesh; her chest was heaving as she caught her breath. Gasping, she put a hand to her breast, thankful to be still. Where was she? Even on tiptoes she could see no landmark she recognized. Miss Claredon's carriage was far behind and to think of breasting the throng was folly. She would have to wait until the mob thinned—but then she would miss the coronation parade!

It was no consolation to think that this was the first time she'd been truly alone in London as she'd fancied being many times. There was no one to make decisions for her or tell her what to do. So—if she wanted to see the parade, she could see it and brave the consequences later. She could let herself be carried along . . . everyone was going that way . . .

She stepped boldly out and was caught up at once. Near her a pretty dark girl in a dress cut daringly low said something to the soldier whose arm was about her. Celia felt herself blush as the man promptly responded by kissing the girl, not caring who saw. How wonderful it must be to enjoy this glorious day with someone you loved!

Immediately she bit her lip, appalled by the thought. Imagine Joseph kissing her in the street!

The day was growing warm. Ahead, she could see the glare of the sun above chimneyed buildings. The river could not be far—yes, she glimpsed the grassy slope of a hill in one of the small parks that dotted the embankment. She gave a brief guilty thought to Miss Claredon and the others, knowing the head mistress would be frantic with worry about her, but there was really no way she could get back. Her only course was to wait then later ask some kind policeman how to get to Colby's.

She felt exhilarated as she neared the next corner. The crowd was carrying her to the right as it neared the embankment, turning south again toward Parliament Square. She could not see the river but she heard the tooting of boat whistles. Pulse racing, she jumped slightly in an effort to see over the shoulder of a stocky man in front of her. A burly woman pushed and Celia was thrown off balance, twisting sideways and falling against the steps of a house that faced the street. A sharp pain shot through her ankle as it wrenched under her. She cried out, grabbing at the steps to keep from falling. A strong arm caught her and held her up.

"There, miss—mind the steps—"

She held on to the arm and let the man pull her to safety. A groan escaped her lips—what a time to turn an ankle!

"Such a fragile butterfly as you would be crushed by the crowd, and a great waste too."

Celia stared into the smiling face of a youngish man clad in a dark green jacket. Hatless, he had dark glossy hair, grey eyes that seemed to be laughing at her, and a tanned well-shaped face. Celia felt a blush creep upward. "Thank you," she said, allowing him to pull her to the top step into the shelter of a deep doorway. Her ankle throbbed and sent fiery darts up her leg.

"You're hurt!" The man frowned and bent as if to examine her foot and she pulled away quickly in alarm.

"It's all right," she insisted, "just a bruise—"

He shook his head. "You're limping. You can't get about like that."

"Please ..." She didn't want him to concern himself. She sagged against the doorway hoping the pain would go away in a moment. She could see down the long road that flanked the river and led directly into Parliament Square. She could actually see the towers of the Abbey!

He said, "You are out to glimpse Her Majesty ride past?"

"Of course." What did he imagine? That she was out on such a day for the air?

He laughed at her tone, still holding her arm. When she moved he saw her wince and held her more tightly. "You *are* hurt. Do you have friends nearby?"

"I—I became separated from them." She glanced back, trying to make it seem matter-of-fact, as though they'd be along any second. But she saw at once that he had not been fooled.

"You need something for that foot—and I've just the thing for it. You're lucky I came along when I did."

She looked at him again. "Are you a physician?"

"Well, very nearly. I've attended any number of ailing patients." He said it with such assurance that she found herself believing him. Perhaps he was a medical student on holiday. "Allow me to introduce myself," he said with an amusing little bow. "I am Gregory Houghton, at your service, Miss—"

"Skerritt." She said it without thinking.

"Miss Skerritt. I am in the employ of the Duke of Arbel, on whose steps you happen to be standing, and I was about to go inside when you came calling."

She nearly laughed at his merry little speech. He was still holding her arm but with his free hand reached around her and opened the huge studded door. It swung outward and she moved to let it past, glancing inside with wide eyes. She saw a large darkened foyer with gleaming tiles, a few silken chairs and a vast hanging tapestry on the opposite wall.

Houghton led her inside and she went like a sleepwalker, amazed that she should be entering such a house and afraid the owner would come blustering out from behind one of the closed doors demanding by what right she ventured here!

"I was about to go upstairs to view the royal procession from the south balcony," he said in her ear, ". . . and you shall join me."

She swung around, biting her lip as she put weight on her ankle. "No—I can't stay here!"

"Of course you can! Didn't I tell you I'm in His Lordship's employ? I'm in charge here and can do as I please. I please to invite you to join me." He made another mock bow.

She stared at him, hearing the words "view the royal procession from the balcony." What harm? Gregory Houghton was charming and he was being kind, trying to please her. It was patently impossible for her to go

35

stumping about the city on a hurt ankle, tugged and pushed by strangers, and never to see the parade at all. It was cool in the foyer; with the heavy door closed the sounds of the street were blotted out. In front of her, under the tapestry, was a marble table with a four-foot alabaster statue of a nude woman. To the right was a gilt-framed mirror, and Celia blinked at her own surprised pink face under the wind-blown bonnet. She straightened it automatically and pushed errant strands of hair back into place.

Sight of herself seemed to spur thoughts of Miss Claredon's white face shouting at her from the carriage. What was she thinking allowing herself to be brought into this house?

She turned. "The o-others will be looking for me—"

"Nonsense! No one will be able to find you in that mob. At any rate, you're safer here than outside, and I must look at that injury." Before she could exclaim he swept her up, lifting her from her feet. She felt a rush of dizzying emotion as he carried her across the hallway and up wide clacking stairs.

"I've promised you will see the Queen," he said heartily, "and see her you shall."

She was frightened yet excited, even if he was taking far more liberties than a gentleman should. Her heart raced uncontrollably as he held her against his lean, muscled body, his arms tight about her. He ran up the circling stairway, smiling down into her face; she felt her breath quicken and her flesh seemed to come alive.

In the upper hall he moved to one of the closed doors and opened it without releasing her. They entered a large bedchamber, far more spacious and elegant than any she had ever seen. She was so awed by the room she did not think to protest Houghton bringing her into it nor think what his intentions might be. She stared at the huge post-ered bed, resplendent with a deep blue satin spread. A massive carved wardrobe of rich wood dominated one corner, a carved chest near it, and several gold-brocaded chairs stood about on the patterned carpet.

Houghton moved at once to one of the wide double windows covered by blue velvet draperies that had been drawn back to show soft curtains of the finest lace. He put her down gently, smiling with solicitation as he released her. He unlatched the windows and flung them open; the noise from the street filled the room. Celia looked out over the city just as one of the big guns in St. James Park boomed again.

Bringing one of the gold chairs, he positioned it on the balcony outside the windows. "There you are, my dear, the seat of honor." He smiled, turned the chair a bit, then approached her and swept her off her feet again as though it were the most common thing in the world. He sat her in the chair, fussing with it to make sure she could see the street below. "Are you quite comfortable? A pillow perhaps?" He went back into the room and returned with a small silken stool which he placed beneath her injured foot, then knelt to examine the injury.

His hands were warm on the ankle, gingerly feeling the extent of the swelling. She was conscious of a pleasurable glow but realized he was being exceedingly bold, using the excuse of her ankle for all it was worth—or was he? One hand moved to the calf of her leg, lightly massaging, but his face, when she looked at it, was solemn and concerned. How could she protest his behavior when all he was doing was for her good?

"It is only a slight strain," he said in an almost professional tone. "You must keep off it as best you can for awhile." He turned, cocking his head. "Listen to the shouts. The procession must be nearing." He got up and leaned over the rail. "Yes, here it comes!" He looked at her with such a joyous expression that she could not keep from smiling in return.

Celia craned her neck to look as the street below erupted in wild shouts and cheers. She watched the crowd press back to make room; uniformed men lined the streets, holding the throngs at bay.

"Here come the Horse Guards," Houghton said excitedly. His hand closed over hers and at first she did not notice—there was so much to see!

The street was filled with prancing horses and soldiers. Line upon line of mounted soldiers clattered by, the morning sun flashing on gold and burnished steel breastplates. Bands were playing and more mounted men, holding naked sabers and glittering lances, rode past with a steady rhythm of hard-sounding hooves. Each unit rode horses of identical colors, from creamy white to shining black.

Celia found herself clutching Houghton's hand, her eyes fastened on an approaching coach—it must be the Queen! Her heart was pounding as the crowds cheered louder than they'd ever done. The roar drowned out the sound of the guns and the boat whistles. Houghton was speaking—she saw his lips move but could not distinguish the words. He bent over her, his fingers warm on her flesh where the neckline of her dress met her throat. His touch was so casual she felt no fear. He was no longer a stranger and the caressing fingers only seemed to heighten the excitement of the moment.

His lips were very near her ear as he said, "The others in the carriage with Her Majesty are the Duchess of Sutherland and Lord Albemarle."

She nodded, accepting it without question though she had never heard of either. The coach was magnificent, red and gold with ornate carvings on the top posts and outlining the windows and doors. It was drawn by eight postillion-ridden, cream-colored horses in red leather harness with gold fittings; a groom walked beside the head of each animal, and a Yeoman of the Guard marched in line with each wheel. Celia strained to see inside the carriage where silhouetted figures moved and a hand fluttered from time to time. The Queen!

As the coach passed another roaring cheer came from the multitude, hands waved, flags made brilliant splotches of color. Celia felt Houghton's warm breath on her neck as he leaned to point. Other coaches followed and he gave her a running commentary of the family members and visiting dignitaries they held. He seemed very well versed in matters of the court, though she was conscious that he could have told her anything at all for she would not have been able to refute it. Nor did she care to—for the moment she was living in a dream, almost part of the glittering festivities—royalty was so close, only down below on the street!

The coaches moved by in a seeming endless procession as more bands played and horses pranced. Celia felt feverish with the bustle and ferment of it all.

Gregory Houghton gazed at the full high curves of her

youthful breasts outlined under the tight grey dress. She had pulled off the bonnet, revealing a mass of blonde curls that danced on her pale neck, brushing his hand. She was not a tart from the streets, that much was obvious, but he was still hesitant about her because she looked shy and innocent even though she had not opposed him when he dared to whisk her inside and carry her up the stairs.

She must be innocent. There was no other explanation. She was obviously not well born or she would not have been in the company of commoners trying to catch sight of the procession from the street. Yet she had some breeding, and above all she had the fragile beauty of one who had never worked for her keep. She was young and sheltered—perhaps only come into London for the ceremonies. London was filled with people from other cities and villages today. Doubtless she had been telling the truth about becoming separated from her party.

He knew something else—having come this far, he wanted more than a casual flirtation. They were alone in the house except for some of the lower floor servants who would not dare to venture to this level, even with the Duke gone to the Service to take his place in the bank of peers in the Chapel. The house would be vacant for hours, perhaps even late into the night as His Lordship attended gatherings in honor of the Queen.

It had crossed Houghton's mind that the twisted ankle might have been a ploy to catch his attention, to get her inside the house. It was possible that she *knew* the Duke was absent. But the more he looked at her the more he was sure she was as innocent as she seemed. She was dressed modestly, in a manner that accentuated her youthfulness, but there was no hiding the full rich heaviness of her breasts as she leaned, so unconscious of her beauty, to view the scene below.

"Have you been in London long?" he asked with no inflection at all.

She shook her head and the blonde curls danced. "Less than a year." She turned and her smile was dazzling. "I've been at school."

"Ahhh ..." He nodded, saying no more. She was a student! He hadn't thought of that. Her father was probably a wealthy tradesman who'd sent her to a very fashion-

39

able school—there were several in the neighborhood—in hopes of snaring a husband. His Lordship had entertained many such young women himself in the secluded study rooms.

This girl was doubtless after the same thing, a rich husband. Not an underpaid equerry like himself.

Houghton slid his hand along her shoulder, leaning very close to speak softly in her ear. "The last of the coaches is rounding the corner. I fear the procession is over for the time being." He could smell the warm scent of her flesh, and a tendril of hair fluttered at his breath . . . he felt the power within him growing.

Celia had forgotten the hurt ankle and was floating in a daze. The full glory of the pageant on the street below left her trembling with awe. She had managed to push all doubts about her presence on the balcony from conscious thought. She had seen the Queen—wouldn't the others be green with envy!?

She bit her lip, momentarily recalling Miss Claredon. But Celia told herself she'd been powerless in the mob until it was too late to get back to the carriages. And she'd managed quite well.

But now she must get on. She turned to thank the generous young man and found him so close it startled her, and she pulled back.

"Let me get you something," he said quickly, rising and brushing his fingertips along the neckline of her dress. It made her shiver.

"I must go back. My friends will be concerned." She smiled and tried to stand but he slid an arm about her shoulders and gently pushed her back into the chair.

"The streets are still thronged." He indicated the avenue below with a movement of his chin. "It's impossible to get through, and have you forgotten your ankle? I can't let you go out to injure it again."

She turned the ankle this way and that. It hurt but the sharpness of the pain had diminished. "It feels much better." She'd forgotten it completely, so absorbed had she been in the spectacle. Holding the arms of the chair, she tested the foot gingerly. It twinged when she put weight on it.

His arm went about her, helping her to her feet; the

arm slipped almost casually to her waist as he drew her from the chair. His closeness was intoxicating ... dangerous. Celia tried to pull away but he held her. Her pulse raced with fear and with a strange emotion she could not identify. She had never felt this way when Joseph helped her from the carriage or when he'd kissed her hand. She had never felt like this before—

They were back in the cool bedroom; he closed the double doors, shutting off the noise. Then his arm at her waist was no longer casual. He was demanding, pulling her body to him, covering her lips with his mouth.

Too late she realized his intent. She was dizzy with panic and struggled to escape his grip, but he was too strong. When he released her mouth, she twisted her face away. "How dare you!" She beat at him with feeble fists.

"Come now, you have no objection to a small payment for the pleasure of seeing the royal procession from such a vantage point ..." He held her close, feeling his own need grow as she tried to fight him off. She was a wild one, and it would make his prize all the more rewarding.

At first his words confused her, but there was no mistaking the way he looked at her. She felt undressed in his gaze.

"Let me go!"

"Here now—what about that poor ankle?" He thrust her back all at once and she tripped over a small table that went crashing to the floor. Celia gasped, stumbling as the man advanced on her, his eyes mocking. How could she have thought him kind!? Her eyes were drawn to the obvious swelling of his flesh under the tight breeches, and she looked away quickly.

He saw her glance and laughed. "For all your pretense you're more than eager, my sweet. And you shall be pleased, mark my words. Never a woman has left my bed unhappy, I'll tell you." He was pulling off his shirt, exposing thickly matted dark hair on his chest. The muscles of his chest and arms rippled with every motion.

Celia moved back, then found herself boxed in a corner. He laughed cruelly. "So the mouse is trapped ..." He undid his breeches and yanked them down, kicking to free his feet of boots so he could pull the clothing off.

Celia muffled a cry of despair and terror, closing her

41

eyes and covering her face with her hands. She had never glimpsed a naked man before, and the first shock almost made her swoon. He was upon her then, his strong hands gripping her, holding her as he worked at the fastenings of her dress. She was trapped in his embrace, unable to do anything more than cry. His fingers were surprisingly quick; moments later she felt the dress yanked free of her shoulders and down her body.

"No—please—"

He had no answer except the heavy sound of his breathing. His hands were on her again, tearing off the chemise, then caressing her bare flesh. She was paralyzed with fear, shivering under his touch, and hot tears stung her eyes. His hands were rough as he cupped her breasts and let his fingers linger momentarily at the nipples.

"Dear God—" The words of the prayer would not form. She was swirling, sinking into a black void. Her body tingled and felt very warm, not part of her at all—something over which she had no control. She wanted to scream, to plead, to flee, but she was helpless in the huge waves of sensuous pleasure that filled her.

He felt the tension in her body change subtly. It was no longer fear but desire. She had cast aside the game she'd been playing and now she was being a woman. A very desirable and promising woman. He pushed himself to her, backing her until her legs encountered the bed, then lowering her onto it and coming down atop her. He pulled her hands away from her face. Her flesh was hot and pulsating under him as he covered her mouth, his tongue probing.

Celia felt the heat and his firmness against her naked breasts and belly. He was kissing her again—differently. His tongue was hot and wet, forcing between her lips and rolling and stabbing inside her mouth. She whimpered and prayed silently that she might die and be removed from such shame. Her body was betraying her, unable to resist the passion he was stirring in her. She was caught in a rush of physical feeling that was completely foreign to her as he forced a knee between her thighs and touched her intimately. Her breath caught and escaped as a soft moan as he forced her legs apart and moved onto her. Then he was urgent, pushing upward and searching for entry.

Celia opened her eyes, terrified now with new realization of what was happening. His face was distorted and hard, and she knew he would have his way and nothing she could do would stop him. She cried out and tried to squirm from under his weight but he was already entering her, the first hesitant push yielding to a rush of pain as her movement drove him to frenzy. She collapsed against the satin spread, eyes closed as the tears overflowed and coursed down her face.

It was over in a few moments and Celia was numb with shock and pain. Above the sound of his labored breathing, she heard her own sobs. He lay atop her panting, his breath hot at her neck as he buried his face in her shoulder. Then without warning he climbed off and a rush of cool air washed over her. She gulped her sobs and peered at him from under heavy lashes. He was leaning against the bedpost, his body relaxed now and his face drained of all emotion. When he glanced at her, she shut her eyes quickly and lay without moving.

"Payment in full, m'lady, and good it was. I had no idea I was to be the first with such a beauty as you." He laughed and bent over her, forcing her face toward him. She screwed her eyes tight as though she might make him vanish, and he laughed again. "No matter. The only wonder is that you stayed a virgin this long. Now that you know how to please a man, you'll have no trouble catching yourself the husband you're after."

Celia's eyes opened as though she'd been struck. He was laughing at her as though the whole matter could be treated as a jest. He had defiled her and now pretended he had done her a favor! Anger filled her and she lashed out. Her hand stung his cheek and caught him by surprise but did little harm. He threw back his head and roared with laughter.

"So, you would play the hellion again. I like that in a woman." He grasped her hands, pinning them to the bed above her head as he began to fondle her with his free hand.

Celia tried to scream but his mouth smothered the sound. The more she fought him, the wilder he became, until at last he was taking her again in a new surge of heat and the strange undeniable reaction it caused in her body. Not pain this time . . . something far more disturbing.

When at last he was through with her she lay limp as she watched him pull on his clothes.

"Get yourself up and smooth the bed. If His Lordship finds out I've been dallying in his chambers, there'll be the devil to pay, that's certain."

He strode from the room, and she was alone. For a moment she lay quivering with fright that he might change his mind and return; she scrambled from the bed and grabbed up her chemise. She caught sight of herself in the long glass near the wardrobe and stared. Her eyes were red from weeping and her hair pulled from its pins; but her body was unmarked. Despite his roughness, she was not bruised—at least not visibly. She looked exactly as she always had, yet she knew everything about her was changed. It could never be the same again.

She had wanted to feel life. She had regretted that Joseph had not stirred her, not made her feel alive. Was *this* what she sought? The thought made her ill and she turned away from the image in the glass. The thin cotton chemise was torn at one shoulder but it would hold until she had time to repair it. She dressed hurriedly, with frequent glances at the door in fear he might return. With trembling hands she tugged at the coverlet, brushing it smooth and noting with shame the flecks of blood that stained it and would not rub away. How would he explain that to his master? She hoped it brought Gregory Houghton the trouble he deserved.

Finishing, she righted the table then searched the chest for a comb so she might smooth her hair. Would he let her go now? If he came after her again she made up her mind to scream and fight him till he backed off. No matter the crowds outside, she would not stay here a moment longer.

She listened at the door, opened it cautiously and peered along the hall. It was empty, the huge house cool and shut off from the world. Hurrying to the stairs, she limped down, pausing at the bottom to make sure she was alone. Her heart was hammering as she scurried across the hall.

Abruptly, the outside door opened. Celia gave a little squeak of alarm, but it was not Gregory Houghton who entered. It was a tall officer in full uniform, clanking saber and glittering accouterments, with a huge golden plume on his helmet. He looked at her in surprise as he closed the heavy door and pulled off his black gloves.

"Well, good morning." He advanced on her, smiling and looking her up and down with roguish eyes. "I didn't know His Lordship had a guest . . . such a pretty guest."

"I'm—I'm not a guest." Celia shook her head. How could she explain her presence here? Did this booted, red-coated officer live in the house? She backed away from him, biting her lip. He seemed eight feet tall, a tanned handsome man, slapping the gloves against his thigh. She had an impression of sparkling gold buttons, green facings sewn in intricate patterns, a huge lustrous gold epaulet on his shoulder. There was a sash of red across his front. She had never seen a uniform so magnificent.

"God's blood, you're not a guest?" He turned as quick footsteps came along a passageway. Celia looked to see Gregory Houghton approach. He had removed his coat and rolled up his wide sleeves, possibly to give the impression he'd been working. His face was surprised, brows arching.

"Captain Devy! I didn't expect you, sir."

"I see you have a friend, Houghton."

Houghton glanced at Celia and she felt her face flush. Surely her guilt was visible!

Houghton said, "The young lady felt faint in the mob outside, sir. I took the liberty of inviting her in to sit and refresh herself with a bit of water." His voice was not at all like it had been with her. He was speaking with the utmost deference, and she realized suddenly that he was but a servant in the presence of his betters. How easily he lied! But she felt a certain gratefulness for it, since the officer seemed to accept the story, smiling at her again.

"I trust you are better then?"

"Oh yes . . ." she said quickly.

The officer's voice snapped. "That'll be all, Houghton."

"Yes, sir." Houghton hurried out.

"The crowd is breaking up," the Captain said, the smile dazzling her again. "Do you live nearby?"

"I attend Miss Claredon's School on Marley Row." Her voice was barely a whisper.

"Ah—yes, I know the place."

"We were on our way to view the procession . . ." He was quite near, leaning to look at her; he could not be twenty-five, she thought. His eyes were brown, with flecks of black and tiny bits of green and they held her as if hypnotized. She could feel that her palms were damp and her knees weak, but she would not have traded places with the Queen herself. She had known this man only a few moments, but his presence made her giddy and she knew she was breathing hard though she did her best to control it.

"And did you see the procession?"

"Oh—yes—H-Houghton opened a window, sir."

He drew a finger along her cheek. "You mustn't call me sir. My name is Francis Devy."

Her cheek was afire. "I—I am Celia Skerritt." For a long moment what he'd said did not register.

"Let me escort you back to the school, Miss Skerritt, but first I have a chore to perform. Please give me a moment." He went into a room off the foyer and was gone less than five minutes. Celia was able to compose herself slightly. He had said his name was Francis Devy! Could it be the same Francis Devy who lived at Aylesford?!

He returned, shutting a door behind him. "I've had my horse taken around to the back and have ordered a coach, Miss Skerritt." He frowned thoughtfully. "There's a Reverend Skerritt in Renfield parish—"

"My father," she said, staring at him. So he was *the* Francis Devy!

"Your father!" He laughed and slapped his thigh with the gloves. "Fancy that. Then we're neighbors. I live at Aylesford, you know."

"Yes, I know."

He took her hand. "I can't imagine that we've never met, you and I. But of course I've been away for so long. I had no idea the parson had such a beautiful daughter!"

She felt her face flame. "You're making fun of me."

"No—I swear it by all that's holy!" He put his hand up and she almost laughed at his sudden serious expression. Then he took her hand again. "Come along, Miss Skerritt—neighbor Skerritt—we'll go out the back way if you don't mind." He led her along a hallway, chatting as though they'd been friends for ages. He said he had come back to the house to arrange last details of a dinner party, since His Lordship had been unable to get away. He hoped that Houghton or any of the servants had not been unkind to her; she said they had not, praying he would not pursue the matter in depth. He hustled her down the steps, and when he saw that she limped, he worried about the injury until she assured him it was nothing. They crossed a yard to the stables and into a great bronzed and silver coach with a heavy coat of arms emblazoned on the side. He signaled the coachman and they rattled off through a pair of gates swung open by a stable boy.

He gave her no time to reflect on her shame. Her attention was all on him—the magnetism of him—and by the time the carriage turned into Marley Row, she had pushed the terrible event into the back of her mind.

"I am most concerned about your health, Miss Skerritt," Francis said. "I do hope your ankle will be better soon . . ." Francis Devy frowned, looking at the girl again. She most certainly did look ill. Whatever had the mistress of the school been thinking to let her out without taking precautions that she would not be separated from the group? Such a fragile creature, and a beauty! The excitement had been too much for her. Fortunate he had come along before she ventured into the street again. That stupid lout Houghton would not have the sense to see that she was not strong enough to be on her way again.

She had almost forgotten her ankle. "It is much better, thank you." How could she worry about a trifling injury while she sat in a coach with Francis Devy!?

"But you look pale."

"I do? It must be the excitement—of the coronation, of course."

"Of course. Your hand is trembling." He took it in his.

She was about to assure him that she was fine, then stopped. It was such a delicious feeling that he was concerned about her.

"May I call you Celia?" He smiled. "What a lovely name. I believe one of my aunts was named Celia—a hundred years ago or so."

She nodded, surrendering her other hand when he reached for it. He had taken off the glittering helmet and laid it aside. His hair was a rich brown, tumbling over his forehead. How incredible that she should meet him this way! She had known Francis Devy existed, and someone in Renfield had mentioned in her hearing that he'd been away as a soldier several years—in India or some far place. But here he was before her, in the flesh.

She became conscious that a girlish voice had shouted her name, and she turned her head to look through the coach window. Several of the girls from the school were standing on the walk, craning their necks to see inside. Sight of them drew Celia back to the present. She realized the coach was halted before the school, that Francis was holding both her hands in his and talking earnestly to her.

"I must go—Miss Claredon—"

"Shall I come inside with you?"

"Oh no!" What would Miss Claredon say? But she knew the gossip would be all over the school in moments now that the young girls had seen her with the mysterious uniformed officer.

One of the coachmen opened the door at Francis's signal and tipped down the clanking metal steps. Celia took a deep breath and in the next instant Francis kissed her fingers and she rose, heart fluttering, and climbed out.

What a day it had been! She went inside to stand in the doorway watching the coach clatter away and turn at the next corner. Her heart was still pounding and she felt in a daze. A half dozen girls surrounded her, pestering her with questions, but she only smiled and pushed through them to go upstairs where she could be alone with her thoughts.

CHAPTER THREE

Miss Claredon was so relieved at finding Celia safe that she did not inquire deeply into the events of the day. She had seen Celia swept away the moment she stepped from the coach, and Celia reported that she'd been hustled along to the embankment but had been able to view the procession. Exactly how Celia had gained entrance to Lord Arbel's house was not clear—and Miss Claredon had every intention of reviewing with Celia that portion of the story but had not gotten around to it—but Celia *had* been brought back to the school by a certain Captain Devy whom Celia said was a neighbor in Renfield. Miss Claredon thought Celia had been very fortunate indeed.

Celia seemed withdrawn, a circumstance Miss Claredon had seen before and which did not worry her particularly. Obviously the girl was dwelling excessively on the fact that she must soon return to a small town in the country when she'd much rather stay in London. Celia *was* a delicate and sometimes high-strung girl, to be sure, but when Miss Claredon suggested calling a physician, Celia had reacted with hysterics and was put to bed.

Miss Claredon spent an hour reassuring her, patting her hand and soothing her, and above all asking no questions. Celia responded remarkably well to such personal treatment, Miss Claredon thought. Young ladies needed a bit of soothing from time to time. The high excitement of the coronation was not something that happened every day; indeed, several girls had been overcome; one fainted and two others ran fevers for a day or so. It was to be expected.

Celia was immensely grateful that Miss Claredon did not pursue the matter of her absence during the coronation. She was such a poor liar she feared the entire truth would come out—and then what would happen to her? She shuddered to think of it. And she was terrified at the prospect of a medical man examining her. She was sure he would know at a glance that she had lost that most precious of all treasures. She felt so branded she wondered that Miss Claredon didn't notice.

The morning after the coronation the girls crowded about her, wanting to know about the handsome officer who had brought her home and how she came to be in such a fine coach. Celia burst into tears, fought her way through them and ran. Miss Claredon cautioned the girls about upsetting Celia and gave Celia a strong dose of senna tea.

Celia was relieved of the necessity of attending classes during the last days of the school term. She had only to sit through morning prayers and meals and was permitted to spend the rest of the time by herself, mostly lying on her cot staring at the ceiling. She did her best to close her mind to the horror that had befallen her, and she was helped in this by her marvelous memories of Francis Devy. The other was over and done, and no one knew except herself and Gregory Houghton. She had longed for adventure—but she had found something beyond understanding. The burden was already heavy on her conscience and fraying her nerves. If anyone learned the truth, her life would be over. She would not be able to bear the disgrace. What would her parents do? It was too dreadful to consider.

Her chances for marriage would be gone. Joseph—she shivered and felt hot tears sting her eyes. She did not want him but now the thought of being dismissed from his life for such a reason left her filled with shame. She would be treated as an outcast, hidden away to live her disgrace in solitude. At best, she might be married off quietly to some local youth who would accept her in ignorance or who would not feel shame in taking a less-than-perfect wife.

Many of the girls in Renfield were less than pure, she

was certain. Her own brother had seen to that. Kevin was as roguish as he was charming, and each time he returned to Renfield village girls flocked around him like bees to honeysuckle. More than once Celia had heard whispers in shops or at church socials about her brother and his exploits among the young lasses. She'd blushed but the stories flamed her imagination of what it would be like to have a young man of her own. She sometimes regretted that she was unlike Kevin. He was so at ease among others, so skillful at meeting strangers and making friends, while she was reticent when confronted by the unknown. It was partly for this reason that her parents had decided to send her to school in London.

Each night when the sleeping room quieted, she lay in the darkness and thought about the physical surprises her body had held. She had not been a cold lump under Gregory Houghton ... his touch had excited her in a way Joseph's never had and despite the horror of the rape, his caresses had not been altogether unpleasant. She'd felt a warmth and need she'd never known before, never knew existed. Her body had come alive for those brief moments she had fought him off. She had been a woman, responding like a woman in spite of herself.

The knowledge troubled her as much as the guilt.

She left London midmorning by public coach without a backward glance at the school. She was closing the door on part of her life and the sooner she forgot it the better. She had been spared seeing Henrietta and Samuel again after the coronation, and for that she breathed a prayer of thanksgiving. Joseph called at the school to say goodbye her last evening, and she'd sat stiffly in the parlor with him, refusing to walk out into the garden. He knew of her traumatic experience, at least the few details she had brought herself to admit to others. He'd been properly shocked and willing to let her recover good spirits at her own pace. Yet she found him watching her covertly, and she imagined she saw accusation in his eyes. He did not speak again of visiting her at Renfield.

The day turned hot and sultry; Celia was uncomfortable in the crowded coach and turned resolutely away from her fellow travelers. She was fortunate to secure a seat near a window, next to a young mother with two squalling children, and she stared at the passing scenery doing her best to ignore the smells of the coach.

The outskirts of the city soon gave way to rolling countryside, green and bright with recent rain; the flowers seemed more brilliant, the sky more blue, and she could look out over the fields for miles as the heavy coach rolled and creaked, the driver occasionally shouting to others met along the road. The air was clean and fresh, and Celia found herself suddenly longing for the green hills and familiar surroundings of home.

The sun quickly baked the roadway dry and before long the iron tires of the coach stirred a continuing cloud of dust which filtered in and covered the passengers with a grey layer of grime. People disembarked at the various stops, hauling down their baggage amid shouts and chatter, then the coach was away again. The remaining passengers settled to fretful silence. By late afternoon the two children, cross and tired, napped fitfully while the mother leaned back wearily with her eyes closed, only to come alert each time one of her young ones whimpered.

Celia removed her bonnet and lounged against the window, searching the horizon for indications they were nearing Renfield. She felt dull and near exhaustion, drained and wearied by the long trip. It was only two days before the Sabbath. Her father would be working on his sermon and would not ride into the village to meet her. That duty would be delegated to Kevin who had recently returned from Portsmouth.

She recognized the acreage of the huge Devy estate that covered miles of countryside to the south of Renfield and felt her cheeks flush at the thought of Captain Devy. He'd seemed to accept Houghton's story of her momentary indisposition, but she wondered if in truth her own guilt and shame had been obvious. Surely not, or he would not have been so solicitous.

She let her thoughts drift, feeling again his gentle touch on her arm, his smiling concern. Would she ever see him again? If he returned to Renfield he might attend the Sabbath services; members of his family did as a rule. Celia's father was sometimes called to Aylesford to minister to cottagers, but the parson's family was far removed in so-

52

cial class from the Devys. At home Captain Devy would choose more suitable companions than a poor parson's daughter.

In the distance she saw the shapes of the town buildings, and she pressed against the window frame, trying to pick out the church steeple. Yes, there it was! She was home.

All at once a terrible emptiness overcame her. Her one chance at another kind of life was finished and behind her. She was doomed to this little country town forever.

Dully she was aware of the coach drawing up in the post yard as handlers ran to grab the bridles. Dust rose and drifted along the walls of the building as the brakes were applied and the coach shuddered to a halt, the harness chains jingling. Passengers chattered and moved about in a sudden bustle. The coach door opened and all at once Kevin was there, holding out his arms and swinging her down as soon as she stepped out.

"Celia, my beautiful sister!" He was exuberant, swinging her in a circle, her skirts flying. "Welcome back to Renfield."

"Oh, Kevin—" She almost sobbed. "I am glad to be home."

"Of course you are ... let me look at you! My goodness, you've grown into a woman. Is this what one year has done?"

He was gazing at her in a way that made her blush, despite her weariness. "Stop it, Kevin—get my luggage."

"Oh yes, madam. In an instant, madam." He pulled her bags off the coach, grinning like an urchin, and hauled them to the small chaise her father kept. It looked the same, a little more battered perhaps, but the horse was different, a patient chestnut. Kevin helped her into the chaise, secured the portmanteau to the back and jumped over the wheel, gathering up the reins, slapping them briskly. He shouted to a few people in the yard; a knot of boys stared as they wheeled by.

"You look ten years prettier, love, but you'd best rub off the cosmetics before Father sees you."

"I'm not wearing cosmetics!"

He pretended vast surprise. "You mean those roses in your cheeks are real? What *has* London done to you!

53

You've left a trail of broken hearts behind, I'll venture." He winked and leaned to kiss her cheek. "Will we be having a daily set of callers from now on?"

She smiled, accustomed to Kevin's teasing; it had always pleased her to have him call her pretty. His good humor was infectious, and he had her laughing and relaxed before they were halfway home. Kevin looked only on the bright side and when he was around one could not be gloomy. It was easy to forget her weariness and dark mood.

The post inn was at the eastern edge of the village, a mile distant from the London highway that continued north to Cambridge. Ascension Chapel and the rectory were at the west end, set below the gentle hills of the village cemetery. Renfield was little more than a hamlet, with a few shops clustered around the village common, a small pond where ducks paddled lazily in the summer sun, whitewashed cottages with thatched roofs and doorways opening to small neat gardens where summer flowers blossomed in profusion. Several people looked up from their labors to wave and Celia waved back, thinking how different it was from the city. A young girl, face eager and flushed, ran from a doorway and hung over the gate, calling something to Kevin who blew her a kiss from his fingertips. The girl pretended to catch it and press it to her lips.

"Oh, that Katie," he said, winking at her again. "A good thing she knows you're my sister."

Celia laughed, glancing back at the girl. How easily Kevin met life, how uncluttered his world seemed. She sighed and glanced at her quickly.

"Did you catch yourself a man in London, love?"

"Kevin!"

He turned a guileless eye upon her. "Good lord, girl, that's what you went there for, what? No need to play games with old Kevin. Did you find a man? Tell me about him. Is he rich and handsome, dumpy and fat? Dashing and poor ... tell me the worst, but I hope you made no promises to a pauper. I want the best for my only sister."

Celia sighed again and shook her head slightly. Her parents would be more discreet, she knew, but they would ask the very same questions—at least her mother would and relate the sad news to her father. But Kevin was one person with whom she could be honest.

"There was someone . . ."

Kevin peered at her. "Oh? You don't sound ecstatic. What happened to him?"

How astute he was. She chose her words. "He's a wonderful person and he's asked permission to visit Renfield this summer."

"Ah . . . and speak to Father about you?"

She nodded numbly, recalling Aunt Henrietta's prediction. "I suppose so."

"A wonderful person," Kevin repeated slowly, studying his sister's face. He saw again the hint of sadness in her eyes that he'd noticed at first sight of her. She was not in love with the "wonderful" young man, of that much he was sure. "Tell me more."

Celia described Joseph, being scrupulously fair, telling his admirable qualities as though preparing a list.

Her voice told Kevin more than words. She felt no excitement at all toward Joseph. How dull the man must be, he thought, another parson under the heavy thumb of morality and tradition. There'd be little laughter in that match. It was a shame that a woman like Celia had to settle for so little. Not that a young parson didn't have a potential, but she'd work herself to death as a helpmate just as their mother was doing. True, the young parson was probably a damned sight better than any youth Celia might catch around Renfield, but Kevin had hoped for better for her in London . . . a little adventure and romance. God knew she'd had little of either. The right man might bring her out of the shell and make her blossom. She was too often a moody one, needing to be urged into more pleasant paths by others.

Celia was changed by the year away—he couldn't quite put his finger on it but something was there. A polish to her way of speaking perhaps, a touch of poise. The men in London must be blind. Sister or no sister, she was easily the most beautiful girl in Renfield—in all this part of England!

He let her recite Joseph Cole's good points without interruption and glanced at her as she sat staring ahead. Then he touched her arm. "You don't love him," he said.

He saw her instant confusion, the way she bit her lip. "I don't know . . ."

"Of course you don't. It shows in every word you speak. I was hoping you might—" He broke off, realizing he was making matters worse, making her suffer more. What really had he hoped? That she would be swept into some rogue's bed and taught the delights of passion? He thought about the girls he had bedded, their eager lips and bodies. But he'd never consciously imagined his sister in that role with a man. Maybe she'd be the better for it—how could one be sure? A girl like Celia needed a strong man and a sensual one; and Joseph didn't fit the part. He knew it without even seeing the fellow.

He put the serious thoughts behind him and smiled gaily. "No matter. You're home now and I'm happy to see you—and so will everyone else be. Time enough to fret about Joseph's visit when he arrives. Maybe I can take him aside and tell him a few ways to make a lass happy."

"Kevin—you're impossible!" She almost laughed at the idea of Joseph being romantic.

"Well, any girl could do with a bit of love and passion in her life, d'you think? Who's the exception?"

Her lips pressed more tightly together as she looked away across the fields, but she didn't deny it. He glimpsed a momentary fire in her eyes and the thought crossed his mind that maybe there had been someone else who had sparked a flame in her more than Joseph. He knew also he was wasting his time trying to drag it out of her.

They reached the end of the village and passed between green hedges to a gritty road between rolling farmlands. The church tower rose against a blue sky, a fluffy cloud lingering over it as though caught on the steeple. Celia felt her heart beat faster when her mother emerged from the rectory as the chaise came along the drive and pulled up in front of the stable.

"Mother!" Celia jumped down, embracing her.

"It's good to have you back, dear."

Celia felt a rush of love as the older woman hugged and kissed her, not wanting to let her go.

"You look well, Celia. I do think you've grown."

"She's filled out, hasn't she?" Kevin called.

"Pay attention to the baggage," her mother said, and

56

Celia smiled as they walked arm in arm to the house, slightly surprised to see that she was taller than her mother. Had that happened in one year?

"I've asked cook to prepare your favorite supper, child, and the water's heating for a bath. You look as if you can use one."

"Thank you, Mama, I *am* tired." She glanced back to see Kevin struggling under the heavy portmanteau but whistling nevertheless.

The rectory was an almost square two-storey building with no ornamentation to ease the hard lines. The lower floor contained a large parlor, a smaller sitting room, a library which the Reverend Skerritt also used as his study, and a dining room beside the kitchen with a morning room at the corner. Upstairs the five bedrooms had been designed for the usual large parish family; Mrs. Skerritt, with only two children, had converted one of the extra rooms to a sewing room and the other was used for guests.

Kevin panted upstairs with the trunk and dropped it at the end of the bed, flopping over it like a fish and pretending to be half dead. "I suppose you saw the coronation and all . . ."

"Yes, it was a perfectly marvelous parade. I saw the Queen and the—"

"You actually saw the Queen!?"

"Yes, in the carriage waving to the crowds." Celia turned as a maid came in with a large copper tub. Kevin took it and slapped the girl's rump playfully as she skittered out the door. He set the tub in the center of the room and bowed to his sister. "Your bath, love. I'll help Daisy fetch the water or she'll be all night about it. Back in a moment." He hurried downstairs.

Celia hung her bonnet in the alcove and gazed about the room. Nothing had changed in her absence. The walls were freshly scrubbed and the window glistened against the sky burnished by the setting sun beyond the blue hills. The room was filled with a golden glow of light that made the dark wood of the fourposter gleam and danced bright images over the counterpane. There was little other furniture, a small commode with a blue-flowered pitcher and basin atop it, a writing table with chair, and an oak chest that had been her mother's as a girl. The white curtains at the window fluttered in a vagrant breeze as Celia gazed out. She stood for a dreamy bit staring at the green and gold expanse of hill crowded with grey and white wooden crosses and small stone grave markers. She'd grown up with the view of the graveyard and saw nothing disquieting about it now. The sight soothed her far more than the tiny garden below the window of the sleeping room at Miss Claredon's school.

Kevin returned staggering under a huge kettle of steaming water. "Out of the way—avast there—" He poured it into the copper tub, holding his head aside out of the cascade of white steam. The girl brought another pitcher and Kevin dumped it in. "Off you go for more, gal."

Celia laid out soap and sponge on a small stool and took a clean change of clothing, placing it on the bed. She waited till Kevin and Daisy filled the tub and departed. Alone, she unhooked her dress and let the brown muslin fall in a heap about her feet as she stared at herself in the long glass beside the commode. In the fading light, the reflection seemed quite apart from her, as though she were viewing someone who resembled her. The thin cotton chemise strained across her breasts, forming dark shadows at the peaks. She had grown, as her mother had said. Not in height but in womanliness. Her body had filled out where youthful curves had been. She sat to take off her shoes and cotton stockings, then slid the straps of the chemise from her shoulders and let it fall free. She had never judged her own body this way before, and as she studied it in the glass, she realized her figure was one men might find very attractive.

The thought brought a rush of memory of how that callous groom had found her more than that, how he had forced himself on her. It had been seven days now . . . and she had survived. Already the painful memory was dimming. She would be able to forget in time . . .

She lowered herself into the tub and sank to her chin in the steaming water. She lay her head back against the edge, enjoying the heat as it eased away her weariness and revitalized her. She was home and she was safe.

Celia was drawn quickly into the routine of parish life and home, her days filled with small tasks that occupied her time but not her mind. It was almost as if she had never gone away—except for the dreams and the memories. She accompanied her mother on visits to the sick, greeting people she had known all her life and who now asked perfunctory questions about her year at school. She found herself less and less willing to talk about it as she realized the villagers had no knowledge of the city nor did they particularly care. A few expressed interest in the recent coronation and were impressed that she had seen the procession.

The Reverend Skerritt greeted his daughter warmly upon her return, but he was deeply involved in his upcoming sermon, pondering his words in the privacy of the study, speaking them aloud so that his voice rumbled through the parsonage as though communicating with the Almighty. Celia knew it would be difficult to talk with him until that part of his work was done for the week. Even then he would quickly be caught up in his other parish duties and spend little time with his children. It had always been that way, and she expected nothing different. William Skerritt was a good man, devoted to his work—often at the cost of sacrificing his own needs or those of his family. He was dedicated to helping the poor of Renfield, and tending their spiritual and physical needs whenever possible. He maintained a Sunday School for the children as well as teaching them their letters and numbers for an hour each morning during the week. He listened to complaints and often interceded as mediator between workers and farmers when problems arose. He was generally well liked and certainly overworked.

On Sunday morning, Celia walked to the church between her mother and brother. The day was clear and bright; the sun shimmered over the village pond and a careless breeze toyed with small clouds of dust along the road as the village flocked to the Sabbath service. Celia and Kevin were left alone to sit in the family pew while their mother hurried to the music loft to welcome parishioners with music from the barrel organ. Celia felt eyes upon her and stared nervously at her hands in her lap.

A small flurry of motion made heads turn. Squire Devy and his wife and daughter were taking their places in the Aylesford pew. Celia felt her breath tighten in her throat, turning to steal a sidelong glance and noting with disappointment that Francis was not with them.

Charles Devy was a handsome man, tall with dark hair touched with grey along the temples and brow. She knew him to be about fifty although he appeared older. It was said that he indulged himself, and he carried perhaps a stone extra weight on his large frame. He had the same good bone structure and even features as Francis—the same good looks.

Mrs. Devy was a stout woman with carefully curled hair and a pale complexion that gave her the look of a Dresden doll. She was wearing a green dress that slimmed her heavy figure and a matching bonnet with silk ribbons tied beneath her plump chin. A large diamond pendant at her throat caught shafts of light from the high gothic-arched window and broke it into dancing rainbows. As she took her seat, she spread a green silk fan on slender bamboo strips and waved it before her face with impatient motions.

The girl was pretty. Celia frowned and tried to recall her name. Theodora . . . that was it—and her brothers were Anthony and Francis. All at once remembered bits of gossip took shape in Celia's mind. Anthony was the eldest and would become Squire at his father's death; he'd married a few years ago but his wife died in childbirth and he had not remarried. Francis had purchased a commission in the Royal Army.

Celia stole another glance at Theodora. The girl, no older than Celia herself, was poised and at ease, her oval face composed despite the stares of the townspeople. She had the Devy features and good looks on a delicate scale, and she was blessedly free of her mother's plumpness. Her eyes seemed to sparkle even in the muted light of the church and her dark hair was braided in loose loops over her ears to hang below the pale yellow straw bonnet. She wore a tight-fitting dress of delicate cambric that was embroidered with yellow rosebuds over the skirt. Celia had not seen a finer dress in London. Theodora seemed to glance in Celia's direction and quickly lowered her gaze. Celia turned back to the pulpit, embarrassed at being caught staring.

But she could not devote her attention to the service. Her

mind was too filled with thoughts of the Devys—especially Francis. Was he at Aylesford or still in London? Was it possible that she might see him again? She sighed and Kevin glanced at her questioningly.

She found herself slipping into daydreams of Aylesford as she often had as a child. The big house seemed even farther from reality now. Had she ever believed such a dream?

She realized that the music had ceased and her father was in the pulpit. She tried to focus her attention on his sermon but it wandered again and again until at last she gave up and allowed her thoughts to escape. What was to become of her now? A life of spinsterhood, living at the parsonage and spending her days with the problems and concerns of others? Marriage? To a local lad who would expect her to breed like a farm animal, producing him a large family and herself growing old and worn before she passed her thirtieth year?

She stifled another sigh and glanced sidelong at her brother. He was staring straight ahead, seemingly absorbed in the sermon, but she knew that he was hearing not a word. Kevin often jested that he heard enough preaching from his father at home so he had no need of additional sermons on Sunday.

At long last the organ signaled the close of the service and the congregation rose. Celia wanted to hurry outside in order that she might see the Devys depart but she was detained by people who paused to chat and welcome her. By the time she got outside, the Devy carriage was gone, with only a dust cloud to mark its trail. Celia felt a moment of disappointment although she couldn't say why. What were the Devys to her? Even if Francis came home to Aylesford, he would not remember the incident in London. To him it had been nothing more than a chance meeting and his gallantry a matter of course. He would have done as much for any young lady in distress.

Someone spoke her name and she turned, finding a sandy-haired youth at her side. Terrence Whitaker smiled.

"You look a hundred miles off. What puts such dreams in a girl's eyes?"

Celia felt her cheeks flush. "I didn't hear you come up." She tried to smile. She'd known Terrence as long as she'd

61

lived in Renfield. Older by several years, he was one of Kevin's friends and had been about the rectory often as a child. He'd always been kind to Celia, almost brotherly. Son of the village carpenter, Terrence was apprenticed in his father's trade. He was a pleasant lad, smiling and patient, with heavy features and a stocky, muscular body that showed his fitness for the labor he did.

"May I walk with you as far as the parsonage?" he said. He was gazing at her, his eyes more intent than she had ever seen them.

Celia looked about to her mother and saw her deep in conversation with two women. She would be involved for a time. There was no reason for Celia to refuse Terrence. She rarely lingered about the churchyard while her mother and father greeted people and chatted endlessly of church and village affairs. Many times she and Kevin had rushed off with Terrence or others, out of earshot of the adults, to whisper over their own matters of interest. Terrence lived beyond the church, almost at the limits of Renfield, and had to pass the parsonage directly. Still, she had not been alone with him recently. . . . Celia smiled to herself at his changed attitude. He was treating her as he might Theodora Devy.

He fell in step beside her as they went through the gate, strolling slowly. The noonday brightness made Celia squint and dip her head so her hat brim shaded her eyes. The day was hot and although she wore her lightest muslin, she was already quite warm.

"I don't understand how anyone can enjoy London to live in," he said.

Surprised, she turned to find him scowling as though he had considered the matter at great length. "It's a grand place—and most exciting," she exclaimed.

"Crowded from all I hear tell. And dirty streets and foul air to breathe—"

"It's not like that at all! It's—it's really quite lovely." She was surprised at her own emotions, not sure why she felt called upon to defend a way of life Terrence had no knowledge of.

He was watching her, his expression serious and his gaze probing. "Did you miss Renfield?"

She looked up. "Yes, very much at times."

He smiled for the first time and the lines on his brow vanished and his eyes came alive. "Then you're not all sorry to be back?"

"Of course not." She was curious why he asked his questions.

"You've grown to a beautiful woman, Celia." His voice was low and she was not sure she heard him right. She had not expected such a comment from him. When his glance met hers, he looked away. "Would you be agreeable to walking with me one evening?" He stared straight ahead, his neck red above the stiff white collar of his Sunday shirt.

Celia was so taken with surprise she did not answer at once. She felt nothing for Terrence ... but she had known him a long time.

He looked at her, the frown etching his tanned brow again. The look was softer, almost pleading. "There's a fair at Wells Row Saturday a week. Would you like to go? There's many from Renfield goin'. There's to be a balloon ascent, a tightrope walker, bands ..."

"I think that would be very nice," she said softly, ending his embarrassment and her own indecision.

He looked about quickly, smiling as though pleased with his good fortune. She returned the smile and they walked in silence until they reached the parsonage gate.

"If you've no objection, I'll come by on Wednesday soon's work's done at home."

Celia paused to pluck a rose from the bush overflowing the fence. She twirled it in her fingers, watching the pale pink petals flutter as though to fly free of the restraining stem. There was no easy way to refuse. "Yes," she said finally.

Terrence smiled broadly and shuffled his feet about. "Near dusk it will be. If the evening's warm we might sit by the pond awhile."

She felt no anticipation or joy at the prospect but she forced another smile. "Until Wednesday then," she said and turned to the house. She felt his gaze on her until she was inside. Behind the shelter of the window, she watched him walk away. His step was light and she thought she heard him whistling.

She stood a long time at the window, shielded by the

curtain that hung limp in the still room. Why did she not feel anything? Even the thought of the fair did not stir her as it would have once. Sighing, she went upstairs to her room.

The Reverend Skerritt was very much aware of his daughter's homecoming. It troubled him that she was so restless and that she returned without commitment for her future. The girl was almost out of her teens, of marrying age certainly. Hadn't he seen the way young lads of the parish looked at her? Most girls her age were settled to motherhood and glad of it. Celia should be too, but she'd always been a dreamer, wanting what she couldn't have and what she shouldn't desire. She'd grown comely these past years, much like her mother at a young age.

Emma had been a year younger when he took her as his wife. He had been twenty and five, the chaplain of Dunswaithe and with the prospect of transfer to a large London church because of his family's influence—a prospect that had not become a reality because of a rift between him and his brother Henry, Squire of Dunswaithe. From the beginning of his church life, William felt a dedication to bettering the lives of the poor in every measure. A noble aspiration, but one that soon brought him at odds with his own family. Henry found more pleasure in wild conduct and unrestrained license than he did in ministering to the needy. As Squire, he had none to give him pause about his conduct; he kept a pack of foxhounds, a racing establishment and a game preserve. He scattered his money freely for his own pleasure but refused to improve the lot of those who made his fortune possible. William found it impossible to remain silent or even to influence his brother in subtle ways. He attacked like a pack of hungry wolves, denouncing his own family for their wanton ways and uncharitable hearts. Instead of a fine London parish, he found himself in the remote district of Renfield, with a stipend of four hundred pounds per annum and a parsonage that made no pretense at elegance. Aylesford was the only large estate and although Reverend Skerritt enjoyed the patronage of the Devy family, he had refused all invitations to ride with the hunt. Any such sport recalled too vividly his brother's sinful ways, and William had no heart for it. Unlike Henry, Squire Devy was benevolent and kind to his people. He ruled the estate well and profitably and was generally well liked, and he usually attended both morning and evening services at Ascension Chapel.

Emma had insisted on the year in London for Celia. Emma had so rarely been insistent on anything that William had been taken aback by her refusal to drop the subject. She wrote to her sister in London to locate a good school within the Skerritt means. Several months later Celia had gone off to Miss Claredon's.

Not that he wasn't pleased to see the girl have every opportunity. It would please him greatly if she made a good marriage, but she'd returned with no prospects, despite Henrietta Bridgeman's letters telling of a young parson calling on Celia. To have his only daughter marry a man of the church would please him, but Celia had not yet mentioned the young man.

On the Tuesday after her return, Celia responded to her father's invitation to chat with him in his study.

"Your mother tells me you enjoyed your school year greatly but that you were unsuccessful in the matter of marriage prospects."

She flushed and lowered her eyes. Her father was not one to choose his words carefully.

"No shame in that, girl. Look at me when I speak to you." She raised her gaze dutifully. "Now, we accept the Lord's will in these matters, hey? And we will be practical. First, what of the young parson your aunt writes of?"

Her cheeks flamed again, though Celia had considered the possibility that Aunt Henrietta would write of Joseph. "He—he's a very nice person, Father, but he did not speak of personal ties . . ." That much was true. Joseph had not indicated anything more than a desire to see her again; even that had been vague.

"Very well then, we'll consider the matter finished. The question remains, what are you to do now, hey?" He leaned and picked up his spectacles to place them on his nose and peer at her. "Many fine young men about. A tradesman's wife is well situated these days."

Celia felt her anger rise. He was discussing her fate like a parcel to be handed out to a faithful parishioner, with no regard for her feelings or objections. She tightened her hands in her lap. She would *not* marry a butcher—or an apprentice carpenter like Terrence! She wouldn't! She was alarmed by her thoughts and cowed by her father's directness. "There are several eligible youths . . ." He seemed to be making a mental list, scowling and drumming his fingertips on the table top, then looking at her intently. "Terrence Whitaker asked if he might call on you. I gave him my blessing. Terrence is a good worker and the way the village is growing, he and his father are hard pressed to stay ahead in their work."

Celia listened to her father's words with a cold heart. It had not occurred to her that Terrence had already spoken to him. But he would be that proper, getting the parson's permission before asking her out. She felt a numbness and was sorry she had accepted Terrence's invitation.

Her father continued. "You'll not have much in the way of a dowry with the costs of this past year." He did not mention her sojourn in London but they both knew it was uppermost in his mind. The thoughts that Celia had avoided were being laid out for careful examination: she had failed to catch a husband during the past year; there was little sense in dreaming that she would marry beyond the limits of Renfield; and she'd best choose from the lot. She wondered if he would give her hand without her consent. She was afraid to ask, afraid to even think about it. When her father made up his mind, he was a very determined man. And he seemed determined to marry her off.

She pleated her skirt between nervous fingers, not daring to look away lest she be called to task again.

"A woman's life is not complete until she has a husband and children of her own," he said. "You'll want some time getting to know him, I think, but he is a good lad."

Celia's rage grew, her heart hammering beneath her breasts as she fought answering angrily. If only she dared! Why couldn't she be left alone, allowed to settle her thoughts about Terrence in her own way? It would be impossible now to act naturally with Terrence. She would feel trapped by every word she uttered.

Her father gathered his papers to indicate the talk was over. She rose and swept from the room, only to be halted in the doorway by his adding, "Terrence has asked if he might take you to the fair at Wells Row mid-month. We'll all be going and your mother has a good many boxes of handiwork done by the women to take along. It would be convenient if you rode with Terrence."

In her room Celia threw herself across the bed and buried her face in the coverlet, raging muted cries of anguish for no one to hear.

CHAPTER FOUR

The day of the fair dawned with a blush of crimson across the eastern sky and mauve-tipped clouds low on the horizon. Celia was awake with the sun, rolling over and staring out the window. Her father said nothing more about Terrence, only nodding approval on the two evenings the youth had stopped by to call on Celia. They'd walked across the meadow and sat at the far side of the pond, silent as they searched for topics of conversation. Celia felt awkward, answering Terrence's questions but barely able to conceal her boredom when he rambled on of family and his work. The evenings passed slowly and Celia was relieved when she was once more alone.

Today she was obliged to spend the entire day with him! Whatever would they talk about? Of course, there would be others about who might lighten the burden of conversation and perhaps make the day pleasant. She rose and dressed in a light, flowered pink calico. The day promised to be hot, and clouds that gathered along the horizon threatened rain.

At breakfast Kevin was full of talk of the fair and Celia felt her excitement begin to stir. He made it sound lively and gay. Her mother was flushed and fluttering about, seeing to last minute details and supervising the packing of the picnic hamper with baked goods to be sold for the church. Reverend Skerritt said little but Celia saw him watching her as though to read her thoughts.

Kevin vanished as soon as the meal was finished, slinging

his jacket over his shoulder as he strode down the lane. He'd confided to Celia that he was taking a cottager's daughter from the Aylesford estate to the fair. Kevin laughed aside her protest that their father would not take kindly to his being seen with a girl who ranked lower than a servant. "Then we shan't tell him who my girl is, shall we?" He'd petted Celia's head and winked.

Terrence arrived in a cart, the back piled high with small articles of furniture he had made and was to exhibit for sale at the fair. He'd arranged the stools and tables carefully so they would not become dislodged in transport and there was barely room left for the two of them to sit close.

As soon as they approached the meadow where the fair was set up, Celia's eagerness swelled. As Terrence tied the sorrel to a sapling, she looked about, taking in the colorful booths and stands. The crowds were already gathering and people strolled along the dusty lanes between bright stalls, pausing and blocking the way as they examined the articles set out for sale.

She was impatient to be part of it but said nothing to hurry Terrence as he unloaded the cart. He lifted each piece down carefully, rubbing his sleeve across the wood to dust it. He arranged them, nestling them carefully to make a single load. With furrowed brow, he squatted to lift the unwieldy pile to his broad shoulders, bowing his head under it. He grunted and straightened up, squinting at her as he took a breath.

"I'll take these to the stall and set them out, then we can be about to see the sights."

She nodded, walking beside him. Music played by an unseen band blared, echoes tossed about by the hanging signs and the walls of the booths. The crowds were laughing and chattering, dogs barked and children ran screaming about. The furor reminded her of the coronation celebration. The crowd was smaller of course, and the occasion somewhat less, but the hustle and bustle fanned excitement, and she felt anticipation and hope for the day. She'd had little to laugh about since her return from London, save for Kevin's jokes.

The weather stayed bright until noon, when the clouds spread and began to blot out the sun at intervals, bringing some relief from the heat and humidity. A cool breeze stirred the heavy air and Celia sighed in relief. She and Terrence had walked miles, she was sure, watching men on stilts, tightrope walkers, clowns and jugglers. They sat on hard wooden benches to listen to the bands. They made the rounds of stalls, looking at everything and sampling the delicacies and baked goods; Terrence bought her a small porcelain figure of the Queen in coronation robes which an enterprising peddler had brought from London to sell.

They lunched under the shade of a huge oak, chatting with several others from Renfield who asked her about London while Terrence sat patiently, smiling the while.

The balloon ascent was scheduled to take place in a meadow beyond the oak and when the breeze freshened, the large striped bag was brought forth and readied. It was yellow and blue, with a square wicker basket underneath heavy with sandbags in brown sacks. Hundreds of people ringed the spot, sitting on the grass while the men fired a gas flame and heated the air in the balloon so it swelled to a great shape and began to tug on the guy ropes.

When at last it rose smoothly in the air, the crowd cheered and the two figures in the basket waved small British flags briskly. The balloon rose up till it seemed half its size, then gradually drifted to the south as the wind took it. When it disappeared, the crowd broke up and tramped back to the fair.

Late in the afternoon the sky began to darken and people glanced upward, worrying about the rain. At the stall, Terrence's father had sold all the furniture and packed up his wagon. Terrence hurried Celia to the cart and hitched the horse. Celia's heart was light; she was tired, but it had been a wonderful day with much to see and do. She'd gotten over her initial shyness with Terrence and they'd been as companionable as they had been as children.

Dozens of riders, carts and wagons were leaving the fairgrounds and their progress was slow for a time. It was almost dark by the time they were well away and along the road to Renfield. Terrence urged the horse along, but they should have left an hour earlier, he thought, glancing at the gathering storm. He hated to spoil the day with a drenching. He watched Celia covertly, and when she smiled, his heart lifted. He'd seen the way others had looked at her, and he knew he was the envy of every lad there. Celia seemed unaware of her beauty and its effect on men, and he loved her the more for it. When she'd gone to London, he'd been sure she would meet and marry some fine gentleman—but she hadn't. Her return had given him the courage to speak to her father. And it was as good as done; they'd be married by harvest time and she would be his forever. He had already asked his father about adding a room at the rear of the cottage where he and Celia could live while he built them a home of their own.

Thunder rumbled ominously and Terrence shook the reins to coax more speed from the sorrel. Celia shivered and pulled her wrap tightly about her, folding her arms under the firm swell of her breasts, pushing them upward so they strained against the thin cloth. Terrence swallowed hard, ashamed of his quickened desire. She was an innocent, completely unaware that she had done anything to excite him.

The wrap was hardly enough; the day had started so warm she'd brought only a light shawl, and she was shivering now in the cold air. Lightning crackled again and she pressed closer to Terrence, gazing about and wishing she were safe at home. It was really her fault they were on the road so late. She had stopped to watch a Punch and Judy show, even though Terrence had warned her they might encounter rain.

A thunderous clap sounded close by and she clutched Terrence's arm. The first big drops of rain splashed down and he said, "We're not going to make it. We'll get wet."

Celia moaned to herself. The parsonage was more than two miles distant. She grabbed for her bonnet as a gust of wind tried to tear it from her head. She was shivering with the cold and the rain began to come down in earnest.

Terrence shouted, "There's a rental cottage along here . . ." He craned his neck, looking ahead. "Father and I are making repairs so I have a key. The Devys won't mind if we take shelter there, d'you think?"

"No, of course not." She recalled the cottage, one of

71

several in the area rented out to small farmers. It was a heaven-sent idea.

"There it is," Terrence yelled, his voice shrill above the wind. "We'll be inside in a minute." His strong arm encircled her shoulders and tried to shield her from the rain that was being flung like bullets by the wind and from lashing branches of bent trees. He turned the cart from the road. Then he was jumping down, pulling at her. "Come along. Here, let me carry you, it's all muddy." He swept her from the cart and deposited her in the doorway as he fished in his pocket for the key. He got the door open and hurried her inside. "It's a tiny place but there's a good roof and a stove."

She felt frozen, her hands like ice; she leaned against the wall, desperately tired and sodden—almost enough to cry. Dully she watched him rattle in the woodbox for kindling, then stuff wood into a black, spider-legged stove. Glancing anxiously at her, he produced a flint and steel and struck sparks into a bit of charred linen. In another moment orange flames licked at the dry wood and sent out the pungent odor of burning pine.

He led her to the fire, massaging her hands. "You're cold as a cod, girl." He looked around. "We left some candles, I think ..." He left her and returned with a candle on a bit of tin. He lit it with a twig from the fire and placed it on the table. "There, that'll take off some of the gloom."

The rain drummed on the roof and streamed across the windows, but the warmth was beginning to steal outward from the stove. Terrence went outside and led the horse and cart to a shed and returned, slamming the door quickly, wringing his wet hands and grinning at her. "It'll rain the night from the looks of it. Maybe I should ride for help ..."

"Please don't leave me here alone!"

"Your father will be worried. I promised to see you home safely."

"And you shall. As soon as I'm warmed." She was still shuddering with the damp chill and could not face setting out so soon again.

"All right." He put more wood in the fire and soon the stove was a cherry red and the room was warm. Jagged

72

streaks of lightning illuminated the room from time to time, making Celia jump in alarm. Terrence patted her shoulder, trying to calm her. "There now . . ."

She tried to relax—they were safe in the cottage after all. The flickering light softened Terrence's features and made his smile more pleasant. He *was* kind, and worried about her, wanting to put her at ease.

"You're safe, no need to be frightened." His voice was soothing and low. Celia let herself be drawn to a narrow cot. The room was small, barely space for the stove, table, chairs and cot. Her clothes were nearly dry now, and she sat close to him, glad of his strength when she felt so weak and tired.

She did not protest when he rubbed her arms, saying she needed to bring back her circulation. Her flesh began to tingle under his ministrations and she closed her eyes wearily. The warmth of the room relaxed her, the tensions of the day had taken their toll. Celia closed her eyes and let herself drift off. Terrence drew her closer to him, still rubbing her arms and shoulders more slowly, laying her head against his chest. He was so good and kind, so concerned about her welfare . . .

For a while he sat very still, afraid that any movement might waken her. She was warm and soft against him, his body heat heightened by hers. He held her close without purpose or plan except to comfort her, but his body was suddenly responding in a way that was difficult for him to control. He could feel the delicious pressure of her breast against his arm with each breath she took, and his pulse raced with desire. He bit his lip hard to control his emotions.

She was asleep, completely relaxed against him, her hand sliding down his chest and coming to rest in his lap. Stroking her hair gently, he murmured in his distress. She had no idea what she was doing to him! She turned her face as she slept. Her skin was satiny in the candlelight, her hair like spun gold, lashes sooty at her cheeks. She was so incredibly beautiful Terrence thought he would burst with pride that she would soon be his wife. To spend his lifetime with such an exquisite creature was more than he deserved and he would see that she never lacked for anything his willing hands were able to provide. And he would give himself to her totally.

Her hand on his flesh was too much. God, she was lovely, and he wanted her more than anything. He tried to choke back the need that set his teeth on edge. Her innocent touch was a flame consuming him. He stroked her hair, letting his hand slip to her shoulder, then to the full curve of her breast. The touch suffused him with awful fire and he moaned softly; she stirred.

Celia came awake as another burst of thunder shook the cottage. Terrence's arms tightened about her as thunder rolled and crashed. She pressed against him, her hand clutching at him. She felt his body jerk.

With a strangled cry she came awake instantly and pulled from him. His arm seemed to entrap her, and she pushed at him in desperation. Terrence made a harsh sound and pinned her with his weight, forcing her back against the cot.

"Celia . . . Celia . . . I won't hurt you—"

"Leave me alone!" She beat at him until he pulled back, startled as though from a dream. She kicked and hit at him until he rose from the cot and backed toward the fire, his face shocked and his eyes wide.

"I didn't mean—"

There was no mistaking the outline of his desire under the tight fitting breeches, and Celia gasped in horror. He had meant to take her! He was an animal—like the unspeakable groom who'd stolen her maidenhood in London!

"Don't touch me!" she cried. "Don't touch me!"

He stood dumbfounded, unable to deny his want and unable to declare his innocence. He would not have taken her by force; he had too much respect for her not to wait until after their marriage vows. She was not some tart to be had for quick pleasure and then left. He took a step toward her and she screamed again.

"No!"

She was on her feet, stumbling past him and pulling open the door of the cottage.

"Celia—wait—I swear—"

She was outside, her fear of the storm forgotten in the terror of his lust. The rain slashed like needles against her face. Her bonnet had come loose and now the wind caught it and ripped it away. Her feet tangled in the wet skirts and she stumbled into the darkness. Her heart pounded wildly beneath the clinging wet dress and her breath was a band of fire. She was crying but the tears vanished in the torrent of rain. She glanced back at the cottage and saw Terrence outlined in the doorway a moment before he plunged after her. Sobbing, she raced mindless of the slippery mud that threatened to pitch her headlong at any moment. She had to escape him at any cost! She prayed the growing darkness would hide her and cover her tracks.

After a long time she was forced to halt and gasp for breath. Shivering and wet, she peered at the gloom behind her. She could no longer see the lights of the cottage and there was no sign of Terrence in pursuit. She had lost him ... she sobbed with relief. Her whole body was trembling with the cold which had seeped to her bones. She felt as if she might never be warm again. She had no notion which direction would lead her to safety or take her to the road. She was more frightened than she had ever been—but nothing would induce her to go back to the cottage.

Lightning rent the sky, sending a jagged bolt earthward to strike perilously close. A huge tree was hit and she heard it splinter and crash as thunder rose to a crescendo above her. In a momentary glare of light she saw the rutted tracks of the road and tried to run again but she was trembling so her legs would not move. Her shoes were sodden, her skirts and petticoat a wet mass about her legs. She grabbed out to catch a bush and pull herself to the road, but its nettles stung her palm viciously and brought new tears to her eyes. She gained the road and almost pitched headlong, stumbling on as the road sloped downhill.

She became vaguely aware of the sound before she recognized its threat. A horse—

She glanced about quickly but the road offered no shelter. She rushed into the weeds, praying he would pass. A flare of lightning lit the meadow and outlined her clearly for an instant. Terrified, she threw herself into the grass—but not before she realized it was not Terrence's horse and cart coming toward her. It was a single rider, buried in a heavy cloak that was drawn up to his hat. Had he seen her? She lay with hands pressed to her mouth to stifle the screams that rose in her throat. The rider *had* seen her and was reining in his mount, walking the animal until he was abreast of her.

The man uttered a curse and swung himself down. Celia buried her face in the wet grass and waited for the blow she was sure would come. She closed her eyes and began to pray. A rough hand grasped her and pulled her up, spinning her about.

"What in the name of—" The man's voice was low and muffled, as though he spoke through the protection of his cloak, but she dared not open her eyes.

"Who are you?" he demanded. "What are you doing here?"

She could not answer so uncontrollable was her shivering. She waited, eyes still closed, for what might come. Her entire body was numb with cold and fear, and her mind would no longer function. She felt herself pulled roughly, then a hand under her chin forced her head up.

"I'll be damned," Francis Devy peered at the bedraggled creature that had scurried off the road in his path. He had supposed her one of the cottagers somehow lost in the storm. The old road was little used these days since his father had opened the new one; he himself had taken it only because the storm broke when he was still some distance from Aylesford and the old path was shorter. He had not expected to find a girl—or anyone, for that matter. He stared at her in the fading light. It was the same girl he'd met in London! The parson's daughter! Celia, yes, Celia Skerritt. What in God's name was she doing here in this storm?

"Celia?" He shook her gently until she opened her eyes. Her hair was plastered about her face, her eyes wide with fear. The flowered calico dress she wore was soaked and muddy, clinging to her body so it outlined her full breasts. In spite of her complete disarray, she was incredibly beautiful.

Celia stared, not recognizing him as terror blotted out reason. He was shaking her, trying to coax an answer from her. He spoke her name again.

"Celia—what is it? How do you come to be here?"

Not Terrence ... a voice she recognized ... where had she seen him before?

76

His strong arm was about her, pulling her out of the soaking grass and to the road. "You'll catch your death standing about like this. Come along, let's get you warmed and dry."

He lifted her to the horse, holding her tightly about the waist as he swung up behind her. He wrapped his great cloak around her and spurred the animal into motion. She huddled to his chest seeking warmth, still shivering, teeth chattering.

Francis Devy. Recognition came all at once but she was too numb to speak. She was content to lie against him, her face burrowed in the cloak, pressed to the buttons of his uniform. It seemed natural and right that she was here and her fuzzy brain asked no questions. She was only dimly aware of the running horse and the wind and the rain.

Francis pulled up before the great front doors of the house, dropping the reins over the animal's head and lifting Celia down as he dismounted. She'd said nothing since he found her and he wondered if she was already too ill with fever to speak. She shuddered against him like a drowning kitten. He took the wide steps at a run and kicked at the door. A servant threw it open and Francis carried his pitiful burden in.

"See to a room quickly, Hobson—and ask my mother to come at once."

"Yes, sir—" The surprised servant was already hurrying up the marble stairs, glancing back as Francis shook off his cape and stared at the girl in his arms. She seemed in a faint, her shuddering stopped for the moment, her flesh icy. He bolted up after Hobson who swung open the door to one of the guest rooms in the east wing and pulled down the counterpane of a high-postered bed. Francis lay the girl on it, frowning impatiently as he waited for his mother.

She rushed in. "Whatever is it, Francis? My word! Who in the world is she—why have you brought her here?"

"The parson's daughter. I found her wandering about on the old road, though I'm damned if I know how she got there. But she's on her way to her death of chill unless we get her out of those wet things."

"Call Alice—and stay out of here then." His mother

77

glanced at him. "You look as if you could do with a bit of brandy yourself," she added as he went from the room. She turned her curious attention back to the girl on the bed. Moments later an elderly woman in grey merino with a white apron and cap hurried into the room. She frowned and clucked as she set to work over the girl, undressing her and rubbing her flesh to bring the blood back.

Celia felt a hand at her brow and it was as delightfully cool as a spring breeze. She tried to speak but her lips were stiff and caked and would not move. Hands rubbed her flesh, driving the icy chill from it and making it tingle with sudden warmth, as though a thousand pins were pricking her all at once. She tried to speak again but only a whimpering sound came.

"Sip this—" Her head was lifted as something pressed to her lips. She swallowed obediently and choked on the sharp brandy that trickled down her throat. The unseen hands were spooning hot broth between her lips, and the chill began to thaw. She fluttered her eyelids open for an instant, having a glimpse of creamy white walls and a high white canopy over her head. Two faces blurred and moved before her but she could not bring them into focus. Her eyelids were much too heavy to hold open. Drowsy warmth began to fill her, and she let herself drift into its welcome oblivion.

She was caught in the storm, buffeted by the winds and tossed about . . . floating, whirling. . . . Her body ached with fever that would not abate. She was frightened, racing from the hidden danger of the storm, her terror mounting because there was no escape.

The mists thinned and the wind died, yet she was unable to move. Strong arms held her down as she thrashed and beat at them.

"You are very beautiful, Celia . . ."

"I won't hurt you . . ."

She tried to scream and the hands reached for her again.

"A small price to pay . . ."

"You know how to please a man . . ."

Her body was afire, quivering and heavy. She was filled

78

with dread, yet there was an expectancy—of what? No! her mind cried again. Let me be—let me be—

The grey fog closed about her like a shroud.

When she opened her eyes again it was dark in the room, only a candle glowing from the far side. Celia saw a figure bent in a chair, head fallen forward in sleep, white cap shadowed in the pale light from the window. Where was she . . . and how had she come here? She stared about, sure that she had never seen the room before. She felt weak and tired . . . perhaps she was ill . . . was the woman a nurse? The effort of concentrating tired her and she gave it up, closing her eyes and drifting back into slumber.

It was full day when she woke again, and the room was bright with sunshine. The moment her eyes opened, she heard a rustle of sound and the woman in the white cap rose from the chair and came toward her.

"Ah, that's better now," the woman said. She was old, her face wrinkled and leathery. Celia saw that she wore the cap and apron of a servant.

Celia turned to look about the unfamiliar room. "What place is this?"

"Aylesford, miss. And lucky the young master came along to find you when he did or you might be out there yet."

Celia frowned, trying to put fragments of memory together, the fair . . . the storm . . . and her flight from Terrence. A shudder passed through her and the old woman touched her brow.

"Here now, no more chills. I've told the mistress you're almost well and I'll have you up soon."

"I'm all right." Celia was instantly sorry to cause anyone concern. "I—I don't remember."

"Wandering about in the storm, you were, and Mister Francis found you and brought you here." She sat on the edge of the bed and dipped a cloth in a basin and began to sponge Celia's face. "Fevered and tossing and rambling—but that's done now. I'll fetch you some broth and tea to put some strength in you, then we'll talk again." She clamped her lips, the conversation finished, and Celia sank back, surprised at her own exhaustion. She was content to be still and let Alice brush her hair and tie it back with a ribbon. She felt as though she'd made a long journey and was safe at last.

The old woman left, drawing the door shut behind her, but not before Celia glimpsed a wide hall and polished stair rail. Aylesford ... and Francis Devy had brought her here.

The door opened and a young girl came in. "I'm Theo," she said all in a rush. "How ghastly to be lost in a storm and wandering about all cold and wet. But Alice has nursed many of us through all manner of illness, and if she says you are going to be all right then you will be." She stopped abruptly and giggled. "I talk too much. You look confused and no wonder. Waking up in a strange place with people you don't know rushing in on you this way. But I'm so happy you're well and that you're here. No need to worry about your family—Father sent someone to tell them you were all right."

Celia felt a guilty start. She had not even thought of her parents and that they might be worried. Concern filled her now. "How long have I been here?"

Theo said, "Four days, but Alice says you'll be up and about, good as new very soon." She smiled and her face was radiant. "I've told Papa that I shan't let you run off home at once. You shall stay and talk with me and rest."

Alice returned and shooed Theo from the room impatiently, as she set down a tray and propped pillows behind Celia. She spread a napkin and began to feed her a thick broth. Celia protested that she could manage by herself but Alice ignored her and continued to spoon the rich liquid into her mouth. It was good, and Celia felt better when she'd finished it. Alice allowed her to hold the teacup and sip while she set the tray aside.

"Now if you've a mind to, you might sit a bit in a chair by the window. The sun is warm and you can do with some of it." She settled a small easy chair in the path of sunlight, spreading a quilt over it and a footstool before it.

Celia was reminded of a wren readying a nest. How wonderful to be pampered so! Judging from the way Alice spoke to Theo, the servant had been with the family a long time and was well loved. Celia sipped the tea, wondering what it was like to have such care all one's life.

The door opened again and a young girl in uniform entered, bobbing at Celia and clearing away the tray. Alice turned back to the bed and drew the covers. Celia was amazed to see her own body clad in a silk gown with a lace bodice and small ribboned bows down the front over her high breasts. It was smooth against her skin, and rich feeling, rustling softly as Alice lifted her to sit on the edge of the bed. The woman appeared fragile but had amazing strength. She brought Celia to her feet, slipping an arm about her to hold her, then led her to the readied chair. She fussed to make sure Celia was covered by the quilt.

"There now, only for a little while, mind you. Then back to bed until your strength returns in better measure."

Celia nodded. The fever had taken its toll, and her legs felt tingly with the sudden rush of blood. She'd been glad of the woman's arm to help her in the short journey from bed to chair, and now she was content to sit quietly. Alice left her alone with her thoughts.

Celia gazed out the window at the rolling fields below. She could see little of the house but in the distance several low buildings that must be stables and carriage houses were grouped with fences containing them. There was a garden near the house—she glimpsed rows of planted borders and the brilliant colors of blossoms. Beyond, the sun glinted on a pond in a lower garden. How magnificent! She'd never seen anything to equal it. Her first real close-up view of Aylesford excited her so that she felt weak and dizzy and had to sit back.

As the door opened, she turned expecting Alice and was very surprised to see Francis Devy instead. He no longer wore the uniform but a white shirt, open at the throat, and dark breeches that met high boots. He smiled and came to her.

"You are determined to make a hero of me, Celia Skerritt, and I thank you . . ."

She looked away, unable to meet his steady gaze. He laughed softly. "Have you no word of thanks for my rescuing you a second time? Are you already accustomed to my coming along when you need me most?"

Her head came up abruptly. He thought her ungrateful. "Oh no—I am so filled with thanks I scarcely know how to express it," she said. "I'm afraid I don't recall what happened."

He lifted an eyebrow and looked at her quizzically. "I can shed little light on it, only that you became frightened in the storm and ran from the cottage where you'd taken refuge. The young lad—Terrence Whitaker?—was beside himself searching for you. One of the stableboys found him running around calling your name. He was much relieved to hear you were safe." He peered at her. "He demanded to see you and wanted to take you home right then and there, but of course that was impossible."

Celia bit her lip and looked away. She was shamed at the idea of Terrence making such demands and more than glad they had been refused. Did Francis Devy suspect what had transpired in the cottage? The very thought made her grow warm, and her pulse quickened.

"One of the servants rode to the parsonage to inform your mother and father you were safe and would remain at Aylesford until you were well."

She looked up. "Have I really been here four days?"

He nodded. "Your mother would have come to nurse you but your father had need of her services at home. Besides, you were well cared for—were you not? Is there anything you desire? I shall be happy—"

She shook her head quickly. "You've been more than kind. There's nothing." He was smiling again and she could not help smiling in return.

Francis found her a constant source of wonder. She seemed more fragile than before; the fever had left her pale and her eyes circled with dark shadows—yet she was more beautiful than ever. From the conduct of the lad who'd demanded her release, Francis wondered if the fellow had tried to force his attentions on her. She was in enough of a panic when he found her to show she'd had a genuine fright, much more than the storm could account for. But it would be wrong to question her and force her to relive her anguish. She needed cheering, not painful memories.

He saw that the quilt had fallen free of her shoulder and slid to reveal the lace bodice of a gown Theo had supplied. Her breast swelled with enticing loveliness and he was reminded of the womanly body he'd noticed on their first meeting. She seemed to sense his glance and pulled the quilt back into place quickly. When she looked at him, his face was composed and gave no indication of his thoughts.

"I shan't tire you—" He turned to leave.

"Oh, no—" The protest escaped her lips before she could stop it. She did not want him to go.

He shook his head. "Alice has given me strict orders. I am allowed several minutes, no more. She's nursed the three of us all our lives and I wouldn't dare disobey." His eyes were gay and Celia laughed at his pretense. "But I shall come again if you'll let me."

"Oh, yes, please do." She was being too eager but she was unable to hide her pleasure.

"My mother sends her good wishes and expresses the hope you will be better quickly."

"Thank her for me—and your father too. It's most kind of them to allow me—"

"The pleasure is ours, dear Miss Celia." He took her hand and patted it. "All ours, I assure you, and especially mine." His smile warmed her. "How often do I find such a flower in a stormy meadow?"

Celia bit her lip. Then he kissed her hand and bowed himself out. He was gone so quickly she sighed and looked at her hand, regarding it first one way and then the other. An ordinary hand, yet not ordinary at all now. She was actually a guest at Aylesford! One of her childhood dreams had really come true. How many others might follow? Dared she dream more . . . ?

She looked around the room with awed eyes. How much more elegant it was than the parsonage, or any of the rooms she'd seen in London—save one. She shook her head, unwilling to think of that time, least of all here.

How handsome Francis was! She sighed again as the comparison between Francis and Terrence gave her a certain feeling of annoyance. Was she to go through life being lusted after by servants and oafs who thought of nothing but her body? It was a disgusting idea. Terrence had seemed to act out of an animal passion he could not control. She had done nothing to arouse him. She hoped devoutly that he would not have the audacity to call again.

Alice returned and led her back to bed. Celia sank onto the smooth sheets in relief; she was tired and her limbs were trembling with weakness. She dozed through much of the day, and as the sky grew pink and lavender with evening, she sat up to eat the food Alice brought. Then she slept again, peacefully and deeply, with no troubled dreams to haunt her.

She felt much stronger in the morning after a breakfast of a small steak, poached egg, toast, marmalade and piping hot tea. Alice got her up to bathe in a huge copper tub two maids carried in and filled with warm water. Alice hovered like a mother bird, wringing the cloth and washing her back as though she were a child. Celia's hair was limp from the fever and the old servant lathered it and rinsed it until it squeaked between her fingers.

Dressed in a heavy silk robe, Celia sat in the chair by the window again enjoying the sun, thinking random thoughts—all of which centered about Aylesford. She looked about with a start when someone rapped lightly on the door and Squire Charles Devy entered.

He stood over her, looking at her as though she were a butterfly lighted on his favorite flower. "You appear much better, Miss Skerritt. When you were brought here you were a sorry sight and we feared for your recovery."

Celia was uncomfortable under his scrutiny. "I—I'm truly sorry to have imposed on your hospitality, sir."

"Nonsense, child." His stern look faded. "You've been no trouble. Alice dotes on having someone to tend, never happier. We are all much relieved that you are feeling better."

"Thank you, sir."

"Your father wishes you to return to the vicarage as soon as possible."

Celia felt a pang of disappointment. She did not want her brief stay at Aylesford to end but she knew that was a foolish dream. "Yes, of course," she said softly.

"If you're sure you're feeling well enough to go . . ." he hesitated.

She longed to beg to be allowed to stay but she said, "I'm really quite well. Everyone has been more than kind and I do appreciate it. I shall go immediately if it is convenient."

"Yes, of course. I will arrange for a carriage."

"Thank you."

"Alice will help you prepare." He turned and started

from the room, glancing back at her before closing the door.

For several moments, Celia sat feeling quite desolate. There was no reason to be uneasy at the thought of returning to the parsonage but she dreaded facing her father. Would he want to know how she came to be running away in the storm, fleeing from Terrence? The memory of Terrence's hard body against her made her shiver. She could not tell her father *that*! She would take refuge in her recent illness, pretend she could not recall . . .

Alice helped her dress in her own pink calico which had been carefully laundered so it showed no traces of mud and rain. The old woman shook her head, despairing that Celia was leaving so soon. Although Celia hoped she might see Theo and Francis again, neither came to bid her farewell. When she finally descended the marble stairs, she had only Alice for company and to hand her into the landau and watch her ride away. Celia stared back at the house as long as she could glimpse it from the window of the carriage, then sank against the velvet cushion and into melancholy.

Her mother fussed and exclaimed over her, insisting she go immediately to bed. Celia let herself be pampered; it kept her from having to talk. Kevin looked in at dusk, saying little and staring at her strangely as though he knew her secret. He smiled and told her to get well quickly, nothing more. Her father peered in after dinner, tugging at his cassock and frowning as he asked how she felt. He did not mention Terrence.

In several days' time, Celia was up and about with no traces of her ordeal other than the emotional scars that would be slow to heal. She resumed her duties around the parsonage without enthusiasm as she felt her life slipping back into the same dull pattern. Terrence came to call, apologizing profusely and begging her forgiveness; he whispered nervously that he had not intended to hurt her—he'd been carried away by a moment's excitement. She turned from him and asked him to please leave her alone.

85

CHAPTER FIVE

It was mid-August; hot and sultry days followed each other in slow procession as the summer wore on. The Devys, without Francis, appeared in church each Sunday, nodding pleasantly to Celia but making no overtures to resume the more intimate relationship she hoped might ensue. Several times Celia found Theo Devy staring at the Skerritt pew and when their eyes met, the girl smiled warmly. But each time Celia reached the church door, the Devy carriage was already vanishing down the road.

So it was more than a surprise when her father announced one afternoon that the family had received an invitation to Aylesford for a fete honoring Francis Devy who was on leave from the Army.

Celia could scarcely contain herself. "When—oh, please, Father, may we go?"

Reverend Skerritt frowned, turning over the stiff parchment invitation in his hands as though it might give him some clue to its own existence. He had been at Aylesford often, but always in his capacity as vicar. But an unexpected invitation to a party was a total surprise and source of wonder.

He looked at his daughter's animated face. She had not shown such interest in anything since the day of the fair at Wells Row and the illness that followed. It might do her good to be more among people. The invitation specifically mentioned both Celia and Kevin. He glanced at his wife, seeing the sudden gleam in her eyes. Could it be that she too might enjoy such an outing?

"May we go, Father?" Celia asked again.

He nodded slowly. "If Squire Devy requests our presence we should do him the honor of accepting."

Celia rushed to him, flinging her arms about him and hugging him, something she had not done since she was a small child. It took him by surprise and left him speechless for the moment.

Celia's joy bubbled inside her, welling up and overflowing. A party at Aylesford! She would see Francis and Theo again. Her cheeks flushed and her eyes were bright. She longed to spin about the room, dance with glee ... but she knew her father would disapprove.

The days that followed were filled with daily sewing to ready a dress Celia considered fit for the occasion. Her mother was patient, fitting and stitching by the hour, refitting and scolding Celia to stand still when she began to fidget under the delays. The dress was delicate white muslin from a bolt of cloth that had been a gift from the village dressmaker, whom Mrs. Skerritt had nursed through a near-fatal bout with fever the past winter. Emma Skerritt had protested the gift but the woman would not hear otherwise, and Emma had saved the bolt for a suitable occasion since it was much too fine for everyday wear.

The dress she fashioned for Celia had a tight bodice that accented Celia's good bosom and small waist. The full skirt fell in soft folds over a stiffly starched petticoat; the bodice had an underbodice of pink silk and was accented with rose-colored ribbon that trailed to a matching pink silk waist-belt; the sleeves were tight at the top, wider below but tightening again at the wrists—the very latest fashion Celia had admired in London.

They worked a fortnight on the dress, sewing with tiny stitches until the light faded and forced them to halt. At last Celia was pleased with her reflection in the mottled mirror. The dress was more magnificent than anything she had ever owned, still she worried that it would not compare with the fine silks and satins others would wear to the party. When she voiced her concern aloud, her mother chided her for being vain and her father frowned over his book as though to add words of caution, and Celia quickly retired to her room. She was not vain—it was just that she wanted everything to be perfect. It was as though she were being given another chance to touch upon the life she dreamed of for so long. Had Francis Devy asked that she be invited? The idea made her shiver with anticipation. Francis . . . she would see him again.

She'd heard talk in the village that he was home only for a short time then would return to his regiment in India. How very far away that seemed. To think that a man had such choices, that he could control his own life and decide his own fate, while women . . . she . . . had to be content with whatever came her way and accept without complaint. If only she could choose—she would choose a life similar to Theo Devy's!

She lay awake a long time, staring at the stars in the black sky and listening to the crickets sing in the meadow. She thought vaguely of London but it seemed far in the past now and very far away.

The party at Aylesford was only three days off . . .

She leaned forward and peered out the window of the rattling carriage. Excitement made her temples throb. The familiar green hills took on a new hue and the rows of arching oaks flanking the drive cast blue shadows across the road. How different everything looked now that she was driving to Aylesford.

She stared at her hands folded demurely in her lap and forced herself to sit still lest her father glance impatiently at her again. She listened to the steady clip-clopping of the horses and felt herself sway with the rocking of the carriage. She seemed suspended in time and place, not part of the physical world around her but viewing it from afar and seeing herself move in it.

She knew the party would be grander than anything she had ever attended. How few there had been! The church fetes or small garden parties where her father more often than not took up collections for the poor hardly counted. Nor did the few affairs Miss Claredon had arranged for the girls of the school.

A worried frown appeared between her brows and she

plucked at her skirt nervously as she wondered again if Francis Devy would dance with her.

"Stop fussing, Celia." Mrs. Skerritt touched her daughter's arm and smiled gently.

"Mama, I'm so excited!" Celia's cheeks flushed and she opened the small ivory and silk fan that had come from the depths of her mother's trunk, buried from a long-ago day when the vicar and his wife had entertained fellow churchmen who had been missionaries in the East. She fanned herself and rearranged the ribbons at her bodice.

"You look lovely, child. Just be yourself and mind your manners."

Across from Celia, her father frowned again and she quickly folded the fan and clasped her hands. They didn't understand—how could they when they had come to Renfield of their own choosing. The parish was their whole life. Neither of them knew what it was like to be young and bored with the tiny village. They didn't understand the longing that was stirred by an invitation to Aylesford.

She leaned to the window, staring out at the distant cottages were laborers lived, the fields of crops—grain swaying in the gentle hot breeze. Then she glimpsed the manor house that stood like a castle against the trees and sky, surrounded by tall and noble trees and the clipped hedges of gardens. How much sharper and brighter it looked than when she'd ridden away in the carriage Squire Devy had summoned for her.

All at once her heart began to race as the carriage pulled onto the circular drive leading to the portico. People were moving about on the walks, in the garden, and beyond the huge carved doors of the entry. Strains of music drifted to her and she bit her lip to smother a cry of delight. She could not sit still as the carriage drew up before the entrance and a liveried footman quickly opened the door. Bowing slightly, the man helped her mother, then held out a gloved hand to Celia. Her father motioned impatiently and she stepped down.

She tried to look straight ahead but her eyes were everywhere. It was as if she were seeing the house for the first time—each individual brick, the metal casements, the fretted features and the carvings of the great front doors. The thick shrubbery bordering the house gleamed as though it had been polished for the occasion. The air was perfumed with the smell of flowers.

The horses snorted as the driver shook the reins and the heavy carriage moved off around the drive, metal tires gritting on gravel. A half dozen people were gathered on the stone steps in front of the great door, smiling and chatting, gentlemen in frock coats and tall hats, women in silks with skirts sweeping the ground. Celia smoothed the dress nervously and climbed the wide steps beside her parents. She was conscious of eyes turned toward them; she felt on display and she fought back a fit of nerves. The cool muslin was heavy about her ankles and she raised it with one hand just enough so her dainty pointed leather slipper would not catch and send her sprawling.

At the door, they paused while her father waited to be properly received. A servant bowed and took his hat, then Squire Devy stepped toward them, smiling as he greeted them.

"Ah, Reverend Skerritt and Mrs. Skerritt." He took Emma Skerritt's hand and pressed it to his lips briefly. He looked at the vicar and then at Celia. "And your charming daughter. How are you, my dear? You look well. I trust you had no ill effects from the fever?"

She murmured an answer as he took her hand and bowed over it. She wondered that she had ever thought him stern and cold, so warmly did he greet her now. She was impressed by his rich broadcloth coat with high collar, dark cravat and spreading lapels that showed a pearl satin waistcoat beneath. His trousers were grey striped, adding to his height and helping diminish his bulk. A large gold ring set with black onyx and a crest adorned his finger.

Squire Devy looked about. "And your son? Is he not with you?"

"He is coming," the vicar assured him, almost as though afraid to be found lacking.

Celia was impatient to be inside, to glimpse the magnificent house once more and to meet people, to see everything, to hear the music. And to dance! She had been practicing alone in her room, humming softly to herself and moving about with eyes half closed as she pretended it was a great ballroom.

Charles Devy led them to a small group inside the

foyer. Mrs. Devy, in blue satin trimmed with lace around her plump neck and arms, looked at each in turn. Her smile was fixed and without warmth, her small eyes seemed to stare through Celia. She gave no indication that she had ever seen Celia before, much less had her as a guest—albeit uninvited. The Squire was making formal introductions which Celia scarcely heard.

All at once Theodora Devy rushed to them, taking Celia's hand. "Celia!"

"And my daughter, Theodora," Devy added, frowning as Theo murmured quick greetings then pulled Celia away from the group. She was flushed with excitement, her dark eyes shining, as she smiled at her father and drew Celia toward the ballroom. She was wearing a dress of pale green silk, tight at the waist, the full skirt whispering as she moved. Her dark hair was pulled up and plaited at her crown, with tiny pink rosebuds caught in it at intervals. Celia thought she had never seen her lovelier.

"I'm so glad you came!" Theo led her to the edge of the grand ballroom which opened off the foyer to the right. Celia had seen the ornate doors on her earlier visit but had no idea of the magnificent room behind them—gold papered walls, gilt columns, and huge crystal chandeliers set with hundreds of tiny tapers. Dozens of people milled about, and the sound of music filtered through their laughter and chatter. The Devys had obviously reached far beyond the parish boundaries with invitations. Celia spotted a few familiar faces—people from the village, the more affluent tradesmen, landowners of other estates. But mostly they were strangers, people who moved in a world foreign to Celia, a world made of dreams . . . the kind of dreams she'd had about London that had never materialized.

Theo was chattering again. "There are so few girls our age in Renfield, I insisted that Papa invite you."

"That was very kind of you, Miss Devy." Celia felt a moment of disappointment as the illusion that Francis had been the instigator of the invitation crumbled.

"You promised to call me Theo—please?"

Celia smiled. "Yes . . . Theo." It seemed strange to be on such intimate terms with her.

Theo squeezed her arm and giggled. "I'm glad we can be friends." She glanced toward the foyer where Reverend and Mrs. Skerritt had paused to chat with a small group. Theo's dark gaze swept the crowd. "Where is your brother—Kevin? Is that his name?" Her eyes grew even brighter and the bloom at her cheeks deepened.

Celia understood then. Theo had not really cared about her. The invitation had been a means of getting Kevin here. It was Kevin who earned the glances in church each Sunday, not herself. Theo wanted to meet him and the rest of the Skerritt family was camouflage.

She felt nervous and awkward all at once, and it was difficult to keep her voice steady. "Kevin had to tend some matters in town but he'll be along shortly. He is most anxious to come." That much was true. Kevin had been more impressed, if that was possible, with the invitation to Aylesford than Celia. He'd seemed slightly amused and had asked his sister numerous questions about the Devys. She'd been so wrapped in her own delight that she did not realize he'd been prying out the little she knew about the lovely Theo.

Celia glanced at the smiling girl. "And your brother?" she dared to ask.

"Anthony is in London but Francis is about somewhere. After all, the party is in his honor. He looks ever so dashing in his uniform—there he is. Come, he'll want to greet you." Theo was pulling Celia through the crowded room, pushing past people who smiled at her and stared at Celia.

Francis was standing at a long table near the musicians' alcove where a punchbowl had been set up. Theo tapped his arm and he turned. Celia felt herself drowning in the dark pools of his eyes.

"Francis, this is Celia Skerritt—the girl you rescued from the storm. Doesn't she look lovely?" Theo thrust Celia toward Francis, smiling and quickly making her way back to the entrance—to watch for Kevin, no doubt.

A wave of confusion swept Celia and her palms grew damp. She felt alone with Francis, although the room was crowded. He regarded her quizzically, as though seeing her for the first time, his eyes holding hers until she looked away in embarrassment. He laughed gently.

"You have destroyed my vision of you as a damsel in distress, Miss Skerritt. Not unhappily, I might add. It is good to see you so well and so lovely." He tilted his head and smiled warmly.

Celia felt a flood of relief as she marveled at how wonderfully at ease he was. Her fingers twisted absently as she tried to recall the lessons in decorum Miss Claredon had taught. Francis Devy looked very handsome indeed in his uniform; it was the same as he'd worn the day of the coronation except lacking the helmet and gloves. Celia was again reminded of the strong family resemblance, a younger, stronger version of the Squire, with thick chestnut hair and eyes that seemed almost black in light from the tall window.

Celia curtsied slightly. "How do you do, Mr. Devy."

His brows went up and a small frown appeared between them. "It is against all manner of heroes to be addressed so formally. You must call me Francis."

He found himself both amused and pleased at her shyness. She was very different from most of the women he knew—the bold, flirting ones who were so obvious in their ploys. Celia Skerritt was a rare and exotic flower in a wild meadow. He'd been furious that his father had let her get away before they'd had a chance to become better acquainted. He'd returned from riding to find her gone, and much as he wanted to see her again, he'd been unwilling to attend church services or seek her out in her own domain. When Theo confided her interest in Kevin Skerritt, Francis suggested she push their father into inviting the parson's family to the party.

And now Celia was staring at him with eyes that held something he could not define. He smiled and took her hand, slipping it to his arm and holding it tightly. "Come along. The party is just beginning but already I find the ballroom stifling."

He led her toward double doors that stood open to a terrace bordered with rows of very red and lovely roses in full bloom. Beyond she could see dozens of flowerbeds, each limited to a particular color, ranging from the deepest shades to delicate pastels. The fragrance drifted through the warm afternoon. Celia glanced at Francis and became aware that he'd been watching her. She said, "Do you cultivate roses, Captain Devy?"

"You promised to call me Francis."

She smiled bewitchingly. "Francis . . ."

"That's much better." He fingered one of the bushes, turning the face of a rose to catch the sunlight. "No, it was only an excuse to bring you here."

Her cheeks grew pink and she became flustered. She had never chatted with a young man in this manner, especially one she'd fancied in her dreams so often of late.

He laughed at her expression. "The party is in my honor and surely that entitles me to choose my companions. Besides, most of the guests are friends of my father and they're his age or beyond. Except you."

"There must be others . . ."

"Perhaps I exaggerate but then, you are by far the prettiest." He studied her leisurely as her heart raced. "I had hoped to see you again during your convalescence but you vanished too quickly. I trust you have recovered fully from your ordeal?"

She nodded, not wanting the conversation to turn to that horrible incident. Except that it had given her an opportunity to meet Francis Devy again, she would wish that it never happened. "I have never felt better," she said, and it seemed so at the moment.

"Would you care to see the garden?"

"More roses?"

He smiled. "Father's had tables and pavilions set up to take advantage of the weather. Come along, see for yourself."

As he led her to the end of the terrace, Celia observed her father talking volubly with a group of people. She prayed he would temper his opinions. Other carriages had arrived and guests were alighting; people moved toward the house.

Francis led her down four wide stone steps. A path followed the border of roses, winding under a trellis. The formal garden was a vast level area of closely cropped grass interspersed with elm trees. At one side the high hedges of a puzzle maze walled off the lawn where three blue and white striped awnings had been set up. Under two of them, long tables covered with gleaming white linen clothes were laden with punch and pastries; servants prepared trays and arranged cups; in the center pavilion, another group of musicians were playing. Guests had begun to make their way from the ballroom, strolling over the green grass.

A large woman in a mauve gown and sparkling rings on plump fingers spotted Francis and hurried toward them. "It's so nice to see you again, Francis. Are you staying or must you go back? You simply must come to tea and tell me all about your adventures—I want to hear everything!" She bit into a tiny sugared cake she held.

"Of course, Mrs. Courtney."

"Promise?"

"I promise."

Francis extricated himself deftly and led Celia to a table where a servant filled two cups. Francis handed one to Celia. "It seems I must chatter with everyone but the one I would like most to talk with." His glance held hers until she was forced to look away. She was so lovely. He still marveled at the fragile beauty that reminded him of a flower more delicate than any in his father's gardens. From time to time he stole a glance at her high bosom and tiny waist and felt a deep stirring within him. What was it about her that drew him like a magnet, compelled his interest each time he saw her? Someone called to him from a distance and he looked around. Lord Hyatt. Damn!

Celia recognized the tall thin man who came to claim Francis. After perfunctory introductions, His Lordship bowed to her. "You will let me steal the guest of honor for a few minutes, my dear? Major Thornby is interested in news from Calcutta, Francis. Is it true that Auckland is going into Kabul?" Francis gazed over his shoulder as Lord Hyatt steered him across the garden. His look plainly said, "Don't go away—I'll be back."

Celia sipped the punch, following Francis with her eyes. He was deep in conversation with a group of men but found time now and then to steal a glance in her direction. She smiled shyly each time he did. He was terribly handsome, even more so than she'd found him at first. His proud bearing, his ability to be comfortable with anyone fascinated her. He was so different from the young men she knew—like Terrence.

She had heard that Francis spent more than a year in India. Imagine traveling so far! She'd seen a few newspaper stories of the trouble there—horrible things that made her ill to read about. She knew no one in the Army and she'd managed to banish all thoughts of the distant skirmishes from her mind.

Until now. She tried to imagine Francis in battle and visualized him smiling back at her, a promise to return.

She brought herself from the daydreams as Theo came across the lawn, face aglow. "Celia, do introduce me to your brother. He's just arrived, there—by the path—" She took Celia's arm and turned her about.

Kevin was chatting with two women with matching silk gowns and identical faces. They were listening breathlessly to him, smiling and giggling behind their fans like two school girls.

He turned as Celia and Theo approached, and his eyes were merry as he let his gaze sweep over the daughter of the manor. Theo's quick blush of pleasure was not lost on Celia. Theo's hand tightened on her arm.

"Kevin, this is—" Celia hesitated a moment, then went on boldly, "my friend, Theo Devy."

"Ah, my hostess," Kevin said, beaming. "What a charming party."

"Have you seen the maze, Kevin?" No pretense of formality. Theo fluttered her lashes and gave him her hand.

"I would be delighted to have you show it to me, Miss Devy," Kevin said, turning to excuse himself to the two women in blue. He took Theo's arm and tucked it under his own, and they turned and walked across the lawn. Theo's laughter drifted over the chatter of the crowd as they disappeared behind a sculptured hedge.

The twins in matching gowns were obviously annoyed and barely glanced at Celia as they moved off. Celia accepted another cup of punch from a passing servant and felt envy at how quickly Theo had been at ease with Kevin and he with her.

She glanced about in search of Francis but could not find him in the crowd. How long was he going to be in Renfield? India was so far off, the other end of the world. Would she have a chance to become better acquainted with him before he left? She hoped so ... and he had voiced regret at her leaving Aylesford so soon on her earlier stay.

Thoughts of Francis Devy stirred her, as it did to be with him, to have him look at her the way he did. Did he mean the things he said about wanting to be with her above all? Or was he merely passing the time, flirting as Theo was doing with Kevin?

Her ordeals with Joseph and Terrence had left her very inexperienced in matters of the heart. Neither of them had made her feel as she did now after only a brief talk with Francis. Suppose he was planning a career of foreign service? He might be away for a very long time—or forever!

She finished the punch and set the cup aside, then strolled along the outer rim of the garden, gazing at the huge, ivy-crinkled structure of Aylesford against a rippled sky fluffy with clouds. What would it be like to live in this kind of grandeur?

She was dreaming again, set off by the casual remark of a handsome young man who had twice plucked her from most dangerous situations. She tried to convince herself that Francis was just being polite but her daydreams refused to fade.

She wandered down a flower-bordered path, pulling at a leaf occasionally and inhaling the sweet aroma of the gardens about her. Not roses here, but a profusion of lilies, irises and primroses in rainbow colors. The flower-beds ended and a row of yews formed the edges of a small clearing, the center of which was an ornamental pond. Three majestic black swans glided on the smooth surface. Celia sat on a stone bench watching them. She'd never seen black swans before and marveled at their magnificent plumage and stately bearing. She smelled the damp moss and freshly spaded earth and felt the warm sun on her head. The noise of the party was muted. She stared at the ripples fanning out behind the silently moving birds.

She tried to imagine what it would be like being married to Francis Devy. The thought made her flesh tingle so it was difficult to catch her breath. A swan came near and seemed to stare at her. She sighed again as she watched the sun weave a pattern on the dark water.

"Why so sad?"

97

She turned in a rush and found Francis Devy staring at her, his face solemn.

"I didn't hear you."

"No wonder. You were sitting here looking like the last cat in the bag watching the others drown." He put out his hand and pulled her to her feet. "Surely you have a smile for a favorite hero?"

She smiled. "Did I really look like that?"

"Worse. You will ruin the reputation of Devy parties if it's known that you sit here alone talking to swans."

"But I'm enjoying the party immensely—really I am!" She laughed at his serious expression.

"That's better," he said, smiling. "I thought I had lost you. When I finished defending the Governor's move to Kabul for the Major, you had disappeared. I decided I couldn't face another cousin or uncle. I've already jabbered with far too many of them. A bunch of quacking geese." He put his hand to his mouth and flapped it up and down as a goose bill, and she laughed. He made a face and took her arm. "Let's walk—unless you're tired, of course?" He looked concerned. "You are fully recovered?"

"Yes, I am." Again she marveled at how readily he lightened her spirits.

They circled the pond and stopped facing the swans which had swum across to the other side. He said, "Have you ever seen black swans before?"

"No, I didn't even know there were such creatures."

"Nor I. Odd looking beggars, aren't they? Dressed up for a funeral. One wonders if you could cross them with white ones."

Celia giggled at the thought of speckled swans. Francis's hand tightened on hers and swung her about. "My father brought them from Australia a few years ago. He says they're the only black swans in England. He's rather proud of the whole thing."

She felt a rush of warmth to her cheeks as he continued to stare at her and she saw her reflection mirrored in his dark eyes. Her breath caught in a tiny gasp but he seemed not to notice.

They walked along another path bordered with olive green, flowerless plants to a sunken garden laid out with gravel paths around patches of grass in geometric designs.

It must require a band of gardeners to keep the grounds so pristine. The gardens at Aylesford were more magnificent than any she'd seen, even in London. She knew her father would think them extravagant.

She summoned her courage to ask, "Are you going back to India?"

He looked surprised that she knew so much of him. "Yes. I expect I'll reach my station about a month before Christmas, give or take a week. I leave late in September."

"It seems a very long journey."

"It's on the far side of the world, you know. Takes forever on shipboard. Have you sailed much?" When she shook her head, he went on. "I got seasick coming home. Sick as a monkey the first few days out. Didn't care if I lived or died—and would have preferred the latter. Lost pounds, even my boots were loose."

"Do you like it there?"

He wrinkled his forehead. "India is everything you hear about it and more. It's huge and teeming with people, half of them smiling at you and the other half brandishing knives. We're sending troops to the Afghanistan border. There have been stories about the Shah in the newspapers—"

"The one they put on the throne in Kabul?" Celia recalled talk of current events by Miss Claredon, who claimed that a well-educated young lady had to keep up with the world around her.

He looked at her admiringly. "The very same! Name of Shuja. The politicians are running about having a time for themselves trying to make the government stick."

"Is there going to be more trouble?" She felt a cold dread at the thought of his going into danger.

He patted her hand. "Not in this garden today. Let's put aside the settling of foreign office business in favor of more pleasant things. I'd rather talk about you. Do you ride?"

"You mean a horse?"

"Of course, a horse." He laughed at his rhyme and she laughed with him. That seemed to please him and he stroked her hand which he was still holding.

She was embarrassed but did not pull away. "No, I've never been on a horse."

"No matter. We've an open carriage, we shall use that if the weather is not too hot."

"A carriage?"

"Yes, for our picnic tomorrow. I want—"

"Picnic?" Celia was caught in a whirlpool.

"—to get to know you better, and we don't have much time. I don't intend to let you slip away again."

He was smiling, and he took her breath away. He was saying things she'd been afraid to dream. Her heart beat so loudly she was sure he must hear it.

He stopped to face her, brows knitted intently. "You will go, won't you?" He lifted her chin and gazed into her eyes, seeing the clear blue pools of innocent delight. She was like a child, a beautiful, incredible child—but nevertheless a very desirable woman. He looked away, afraid she might read his thoughts that were very masculine at the moment. "Say you will?"

More than anything he wanted her to accept so that he could rest in the thought she wouldn't slide out of his life again. He had been unable to forget her since the first time he laid eyes on her, although he had told himself it was foolishness. There was a haunting quality about her beauty, one that stayed with him long after her physical presence was gone. His two brief encounters with her had left him strangely disturbed.

She seemed hesitant but finally said, "Yes, I would love to go on a picnic." Her smile was tremulous.

He felt much relieved. "Then it's done."

"If Father will let me."

He brushed aside the idea. "I'll speak to him." Vicar Skerritt was not close to the Devy family but the man was not fool enough to defy them. Besides, what reasonable objection could he raise to his daughter's attending a picnic? "We'll go over to the lake—" He snapped his fingers. "What do they call it?"

"Mononoc."

"Yes, miserable name ... never could remember it. We'll spend the day. Would you like that?" He went on without an answer. "Will mid-morning be all right? I'll come by with the rig—and Theo too, as chaperone, I suppose."

"You mean tomorrow?"

"Yes, is that all right?" He saw the tiny frown wrinkle her forehead.

"It's Sunday."

Damn! He'd forgotten that small detail. Her father would not hear of her skipping church service, he supposed. "After church," he amended.

"That'll be past noon—and my father will expect me back for evening services." The frown deepened and seemed terribly misplaced on her lovely face.

Francis touched her cheek. "I'll speak to him. Perhaps in so worthy a cause he will permit you to absent yourself this once." At her glance of astonishment, he added, "How can he refuse the request of a soldier and hero who must soon ride again into battle?"

His mock seriousness was comical and Celia's tension eased as a laugh escaped her lips. His fingers were cool on her cheek, yet her flesh burned as though touched by fire; she felt a tremor of pleasure course through her. Would Father allow her to go? To spend an entire afternoon with Francis?

"I'll do better than that," he declared abruptly. "I shall attend church so I can be near you."

Celia glanced about afraid someone might overhear such a scandalous remark. Her face glowed pink. It was so sudden, his words rushing at her and putting her emotions in a turmoil. He lifted her hand and brushed his lips to her fingers, sending a tingle through her that astonished her by its intensity. He was being quite proper, yet very daring. She'd never had a man say such things, she'd never felt such an overwhelming response to a man before. Her gaze fell nervously.

"You may be sure I'll behave quite properly," he said, studying her. She was a strange moody creature, with peaks and valleys of emotion that showed clearly in her face. "I shall sit in the Aylesford pew and watch you from afar."

She looked about again but they were quite alone in the lower garden. The music was a murmur on the summer breeze. They might be alone in the world for all the notice Francis took. He was looking at her with frank interest— no, something more. She tried to smile and her lips trembled.

"Perhaps we should go back to the party," she whispered.

He stared another moment, then sighed. "Perhaps we should. For now . . ."

He turned her to the path and they walked in silence, Francis frowning at his own mixed emotions. Being with her gave him an exhilaration no other woman had ever done. His breath was tight in his chest and his body tense with the closeness of her. He smelled the fresh fragrance of her hair, the delicate odor of rosewater. She made him feel like a schoolboy, inexperienced and innocent, awkward and unsure of himself. What was it about her that affected him thus? Lord, he'd known women aplenty, bedded many without guilt. Yet this delicate creature made him feel a cad for his desirous thoughts. His insides were tied in knots, and he knew that he *did* want her.

She was different from the willing partners he'd had—that was her appeal. She was not one to pursue him like Gwenn Katon or others he'd had affairs with. Celia was not a woman to be taken for physical delight, then left without further thought. She was a virgin, beyond doubt, someone to be cherished and treated with delicate care.

Good God! He pulled his thoughts up abruptly as he realized he was considering courting her. A parson's daughter! His father would be livid. A casual dalliance with a village girl was one thing, but courting!

He glanced sidelong at her profile, the lovely face that masked whatever innocent thoughts she entertained. And he knew that he would never succeed in driving her from his mind.

They returned to the party and Francis was quickly claimed by others. Several people paused to chat with Celia and she was able to converse without difficulty. It was as though Francis had instilled her with courage to face others, as though she had somehow become part of this world instead of merely an observer. All the lessons Miss Claredon had taught served Celia in good stead, and she found herself laughing and smiling, far more relaxed than she'd believed possible.

Theo, face flushed and eyes shining, emerged from the maze with Kevin, pulling him into the ballroom to dance, unmindful of the stares and whispered remarks behind fans. Reverend Skerritt frowned at his son and glanced about to make sure Celia was not making such a fool of herself.

When Francis asked Celia to join him in a quadrille, she accepted joyously and let him lead her to the floor. She prayed fervently that she would not lose time with the music and stumble. She danced on a cloud of pure joy, returning Francis's smile and delighting at the touch of his hand and his arm about her waist.

When at long last the party was over and she sat in the carriage, she sighed inwardly. Her life would never be the same; she thought she might burst with happiness. True to his word, Francis had spoken to her father and gained his consent for the picnic. Francis would call at the vicarage in the early afternoon. Kevin had been included in the invitation since Theo was to accompany them. The Reverend Skerritt had not conceded Celia's missing evening services, however, and she was expected to be home in time.

She slept restlessly, her mind awhirl with thoughts of the party past and the upcoming outing. To believe that Francis was interested in her in more than a casual manner set her dreams soaring. Hadn't he rescued her gallantly twice? And hadn't he spent as much time—even more—as propriety would allow with her at the party? Surely it indicated his intent.

Doubts assailed her, and she tossed sleeplessly. Francis Devy could not seriously care for her—they were from different worlds. He was bored with his leave ... nothing more.

She sighed heavily and at last fell into fitful slumber, to dream of standing beyond Aylesford, reaching and begging to be allowed in ... and of Francis Devy's smiling face.

The entire Devy family sat in the pew at Ascension Chapel for the morning service. Celia heard the murmurs of gossip and the rustle of surprise of the villagers at seeing young Devy, who chose not to wear his uniform but a dark frock coat and trousers instead. Celia risked a glance and found him staring at her, a twinkling smile in his eyes. When she blushed, he pretended to turn his attention to the pulpit.

She heard only a drone of the service, moving mechanically when the congregation rose or knelt. Beside her, Kevin glanced wonderingly at her several times as she fidgeted. Finally, after what seemed hours, her father was intoning the benediction like a mournful church bell. She gathered her skirts and followed Kevin down the aisle. Miraculously, the Devys paused in their pew, and Celia felt Francis's eyes follow her. Standing in the noon sun near the church door, she saw the villagers make room for the Devys to pass, and a murmur of greetings and comments followed in their wake. Reverend Skerrit hurried from the vestry to impart last words to his flock. Celia was intent on Francis, who was looking directly at her, the smile still in his eyes. The parson extended a greeting, smiling and nodding to the Squire who barely glanced at him until Theo drew him up short.

"A fine sermon, Reverend Skerritt," she said warmly; her glance was already on Kevin, her eyes aglow.

"Thank you, Miss Devy. I trust you enjoyed it also, Squire Devy?"

The Squire nodded and extricated his arm from Theo's that he might continue to the landau, and the pair pulled up at the gate. The footman jumped down and opened the door, folding down the steps then standing stiffly. Mrs. Devy barely glanced at the Skerritts as she passed, her head held high and gaze unwavering.

Francis stood beside his sister with his hand extended to the parson in greeting. "A fine sermon, Reverend. It makes a man think he ought be more faithful in his worship." He said it with a solemn look that belied the twinkle in his eyes.

Reverend Skerritt accepted the compliment gravely. "Thank you, Captain Devy. Our church is honored by your presence. I sincerely hope we shall see more of you while you are at home."

"You may be sure of that," Francis said, his glance sliding to Celia mischievously.

Once again she was struck by the vehemence of the feelings his glance evoked. She did her best to appear unconcerned but she could not stop the wild beating of her heart or the flush that came to her cheeks as he bowed to her. He said in a very matter-of-fact voice, "Will you be ready in an hour, Miss Skerritt?"

"Oh yes . . . an hour will be fine." The words came as a quavering whisper, causing him to smile again.

"The weather is excellent, isn't it?" he went on earnestly as though it were the most important thing in the world. "I had rather expected rain and fog when I returned from abroad. This is such a wonderful surprise."

Celia felt helpless in his piercing gaze. He was talking about the weather but he made it sound as if he meant her. She wondered if people were staring but she could not break away from his gaze. He bowed again. "An hour will seem a long time." She could hardly be sure she heard the words, so softly had he spoken.

She took a deep breath as he followed his parents, dragging Theo from her animated conversation with Kevin. Francis handed his sister into the carriage and climbed up beside her. The footman latched the door and in a moment the heavy coach rumbled off along the dusty road. Francis turned and stared out the window until the carriage rounded a curve and was out of sight.

She fled lest her father detain her, almost running from the church and down the lane to the parsonage. What should she wear? She had so few clothes, and she had never been on a proper picnic in her life. A proper picnic she defined as one with others her own age, with baskets of food, perhaps even light wine, strolling on a greensward beneath oaks, with no chores to do afterward and no hurrying to please critical adults.

She went over her dresses a dozen times, selecting and discarding, judging and sighing. She should wear something simple, not her best muslin, not the flowered calico—perhaps the striped gingham. Theo would doubtless be resplendent in silk or Italian linen and would know to the penny what Celia's dress cost—and worse, that it was not new. Celia shook her head in frustration, remembering the feel of the fine gown of Theo's she'd worn during her brief stay at Aylesford.

She slipped out of the green taffeta and donned the gingham, spreading a blue and white Norwich shawl on her shoulders and catching it in a wide cumberbund of

105

blue satin. She was breathless and her cheeks were highlighted with bright spots of color as she peered in the glass trying to see her full image and glimpsing only bits and pieces that had to be put together like a puzzle.

Downstairs, her mother was fussing about the parlor, plumping the goosedown pillows on the sofa, straightening the already perfect books on a shelf near the big stone fireplace.

"Do I look all right, Mama?" Celia posed for a moment. "Will he approve, do you think?"

"Turn around ... yes, yes, you look lovely, dear." She pulled a thread from Celia's skirt. "You must say to yourself—I'm the prettiest girl in Renfield."

"But I'm not!"

"If you convince yourself, then it will be true. It's an old secret. There's no royal blood in your veins but 'tis blue enough for a Devy." Emma Skerritt looked away, embarrassed by her own volubility.

Kevin lounged in the doorway, watching them. He said, "Mama's right, Celia. Believe it. Francis Devy's a fool if he doesn't get you in a haystack today."

"Kevin!" his mother said. "What if your father should hear!"

Celia's face flamed and she felt a moment of panic at the idea of Francis trying such a thing.

"She's a grown girl, it's about time she realizes men find her attractive, God knows, and if she thinks to get herself a husband, she'd better use it to her advantage." He glanced at Celia with a frown. "Terrance is only a country lad, girl, but he's a man. So is Francis Devy." He turned and went upstairs, his steps heavy on the treads.

For a moment the room was silent. Celia's pulse was rapid and uneven. Why had Kevin mentioned Terrence? What had he to do with her now? She felt her mother's eyes on her, probing.

Celia regained her composure, pushing aside all thoughts of Terrence and the incident in the cottage. Francis Devy was different—no matter what Kevin said. Francis would not treat her in such a manner; he would be a gentleman.

Her mother's face was worried as she fussed with the shawl, drawing it up, patting the fringe in place, a look of

106

concentration on her face. Celia felt both love and pity as she watched her. At forty-three, her mother had already gained the lines of age; her skin was sallow and dry, with a scrubbed-clean look that had been a bloom in her youth but now gave her a washed out appearance. Her hands were leathery and swollen in the joints. She complained of the swelling which seemed to grow worse year by year, though sometimes she soaked them for hours.

Was this what she would become in a dozen years or two, Celia wondered? The thought filled her with guilt and she quickly brushed aside her mother's hands and hugged her.

"My goodness, girl, you'll muss yourself."

"I love you, Mama."

The frown vanished from Emma's face and her eyes were gentle. She busied herself with the shawl for another moment. "There, that'll do."

Kevin appeared in the doorway in dark breeches and a light shirt, open at the throat to reveal tanned flesh and tightly curled dark hair. When he moved, his muscles rippled beneath the snug sleeves and seemed to strain the cloth. It was no wonder Theo found him attractive, Celia thought.

"See if the carriage is coming," his mother said.

He lounged toward the front door, stepping outside.

Celia fussed and fluttered, more unsure of herself than ever. Her mother touched her arm. "It's only a picnic, girl," she said gently. "This evening it will be over."

Celia laughed nervously. "It's a dream, a wonderful dream."

"Dreams sometimes vanish very quickly, Celia. Don't expect too much of them."

Celia gazed soberly at her. "But he does like me, I know it. Didn't he choose me from all the rest at the party?"

"Of course he did."

Kevin opened the door. "They're coming."

Celia ran to the window, pushing back the curtains. It was a two-horse, undercut carriage painted dark blue. The body had black and silver accents and the Aylesford crest on the panel. The horses were blacks, prancing as the driver reined in and looked around. Francis and Theo sat

107

in the open coach and as it halted, Francis leaped down and strode toward the house.

Celia's breath quickened as her mother settled a bonnet on her curls and tied the ribbons. She pulled on white gloves as Kevin and Francis entered the room.

Francis was elegant in white buckskin trousers and a grey frock coat over a silky white shirt and grey cravat. He bowed and smiled gaily.

"It's a pleasure to see you again, Mrs. Skerritt." He took Emma's hand and kissed it. She drew it away quickly when he released it, burying it in the folds of her skirt. He took Celia's hand and let his lips linger on it momentarily. "You look marvelous, Celia. As beautiful as the day that awaits us." Quite calmly he slipped her arm through his and held her hand. "I shall have her back in time for evening services as I promised, Mrs. Skerritt." He gazed at Celia, already regretting the promise.

They were out of doors, approaching the carriage and Theo was calling to her. The doubts of the day vanished and Celia was caught in a tide of delight. Kevin was already seated beside Theo, his arm carelessly touching hers. Francis handed Celia into the coach and she was most conscious of his strong hands guiding her as she slid onto the leather seat and he took his place beside her. The coach was roomy but he sat close, almost touching her, as the driver snapped the reins and the carriage clattered down the drive. Celia glimpsed her mother at the window, her hand raised to her face as she watched them depart.

Theo said, "How lucky we are. Was there ever such a wonderful day for a picnic?" She smiled at Kevin who took her hand as though it were the most natural thing in the world.

Francis reached for Celia's hand. "I had not believed I could be so delighted to see you again. I found it difficult to concentrate on your father's sermon with you so near."

Her face warmed and her gaze fell. She was dizzy with excitement to hear him say such things. Sensing her confusion, he drew her into conversation about the countryside they passed, pointing out things he knew, asking her about others he did not. She began to relax and feel herself drawn into a spirit of camaraderie.

By the time the lake came into view, all four were

laughing and chattering as intimates. Kevin told humorous stories of happenings in the village; Francis spoke lightly of his adventures in the Army, avoiding all talk of the war and the more serious side of his life. He drew responses from Celia when he began to chat about London and the things he had seen there—things she too had seen and places she had visited. Thankfully he did not mention meeting her at the Duke of Arbel's townhouse.

Lake Mononoc nestled in a valley of green hills, with tall stands of ash and poplar skirting the shoreline and gathering in deep woods in the lowlands where a stream gurgled over rocks and sand. The driver looked around and Francis signaled him to turn in to the meadow following a faint trail left by previous travelers. The horses' hooves made only a deep thudding on the coarse grass and the tires were muted. The breeze was fresh and huge shadows rushed across the land as fluffy billows of clouds passed overhead.

Another carriage stood in the shade of a coppice, the horses tethered to a willow that hung over the water. Two servants were carrying picnic hampers to a cloth spread on the low rise of a hill overlooking the water. Four places were set with fine china, heavy silver and tall wine glasses.

The food, prepared by the Aylesford cooks, was a feast—roast pheasant, a joint of cold beef, fresh melon ... Yet Celia tasted nothing as she stared at Francis and listened raptly to everything he said. He was most attentive, pouring wine to keep her glass filled, chatting with her about herself and the village. From time to time Kevin questioned Francis about the war, but Theo pouted prettily and reclaimed his attention.

The servants cleared the dishes and brought trays of tiny cakes and fresh fruit. Francis pulled off a large bunch of grapes and rose, holding out a hand to Celia. "A stroll will aid the digestion." He drew off his coat and hung it on a low branch.

She let him pull her to her feet, and arm in arm they walked to the placid lake, following a narrow path around it. Francis pulled single grapes from the cluster and held them to her lips. She took each, savoring the juicy flavor and he laughed. Joy filled her and she was giddy with it, moving in a haze where Francis's smile was the most important thing in the world.

They came to a stream where water splashed and disappeared into the woods. Francis took her hand and helped her over low stones to a large flat rock which overhung the tiny gossamer falls. He drew a linen handkerchief from his sleeve and spread it for her to sit on. The dappled light was cool and welcome after the glare of the sun on the meadow. Francis took her hand.

"Why did I never meet you before?"

"But you did."

He smiled, shaking his head. "We have lived in the same village all our lives, each not knowing the other existed."

She felt awkward, reminded again of the gulf that separated them.

"Had I known, we should have had many picnics like this," he said.

"You must have been away at school much of the time."

He nodded. "And other meaningless places." He fondled her hand, looking at each finger individually as though he had never seen such a mechanism before. "I've been on leave two months, the time wasted because I hadn't met you."

The beat of her heart pounded in her ears and her hand felt very warm in his. He didn't seem to notice.

"How marvelously we could have spent the days," he went on, glancing up at her. "I cannot count your recent illness a tragedy because it brought us together again," he said softly. "Am I very selfish?"

She shook her head, struck dumb by his words.

"May I see you often during the remainder of my leave?"

She nodded, still afraid to speak and break the spell.

"Good, that pleases me greatly. I want to know you much better and to make up for the time we've lost—if that's possible."

Her voice trembled. "When must you go back?"

"In three weeks and five days . . . much too soon."

"Will you have another leave?"

110

"I don't know. In another year, perhaps longer. It depends on many things."

"So long—" The words were wrenched from her before she could stop them.

He smiled. "Do you mind so much?"

Her face warmed. "Yes," she said carefully. "You might be wounded—or worse!" She would mind very much indeed.

"And that would bother you?"

"Of course!" He was teasing her, searching her face for reactions and moved by her emotion. She tried to steady her voice. "I would not like any tragedy to befall you. Think of your poor mama and your family."

He snatched up a twig and broke it in his fingers, throwing the pieces into the flowing stream where they twisted and turned as the current caught them.

"And you? You must have some thought of how I feel. I cannot take my eyes from your loveliness. I tossed about the night long thinking of you."

She was caught in a whirlpool of heady emotion. He was saying words she'd never dreamed of hearing . . . saying his interest was more than casual. She could not meet his gaze, and she stared at the rushing water below them.

He got to his feet abruptly, breaking the spell. "We'd best return. I would not wish to break my promise to your father and the hour is growing late." He drew her to her feet and stood very close for a moment, looking down at her. He dared not stay alone in this secluded place or he could not be responsible for his actions. She was much too desirable.

CHAPTER SIX

Francis came to call three days after the picnic, apologizing that family obligations had kept him away so long. He was being so open in his attentions, Celia felt she would not be able to bear the humiliation if it were a passing fancy. She dwelled on thoughts of his touch, the excitement she felt when he was near, and the incredible longing she felt when they were not together.

Francis began coming by every day the second week, chatting with her father a bit, then walking in the garden with Celia while Emma Skerritt watched from the window. He asked her to ride and came for her in a small open carriage. He took her to Aylesford, driving through the entire estate and pointing out fields, cottages, and the woods where hunts were held. They returned to the house and had tea with Theo in a small sitting room off the garden. Squire and Mrs. Devy were away for the day and both Francis and Theo seemed in exceptionally good spirits. Theo asked dozens of questions about Kevin, as if trying to learn all she could. Celia was surprised at how little she knew of her own brother's routine and daily habits—his friends and pleasures. Francis ended the conversation by asking Celia to walk in the garden.

Celia commented on Theo's interest in Kevin, and Francis stared at her. At her look of innocence, he shook his head. "She's mad about him, you silly little goose. She'd like to have him attend her every whim and be about whenever she fancies him."

Celia was startled, though it had occurred to her that Theo found Kevin charming. "Has she seen him since the party?"

"She does not confide in me but from the gleam in her eye and the way she's been managing to slip out many evenings and comes back all flustered, I'd say yes. I suspect they meet at the vacant rental cottage."

Kevin taking Theo to the cottage where Terrence had—She felt stricken.

"Damn! I'm sorry, I didn't mean to upset you. Let's talk of more pleasant things." He quickly diverted her attention with the story of a ball he'd attended in Calcutta. She was such a delicate creature he found himself wanting to spare her any grief he could. More and more the past days, he'd thought of her in a protective way . . . as well as caring for her more than he believed possible. Their times together were becoming more and more precious to him. Was he in love? He'd never loved a woman before; women were a comfortable commodity to have about, a most satisfactory answer to a man's needs and inner passions. But love . . . no, he had never loved before.

Why couldn't he pull Celia into the woods and romp with her on a moss-covered knoll? Why did he fight the passion that increased each time they were together and deny his flesh the pleasure of her? It was not from lack of desire, to be sure. It was all he could do to keep his emotions in check and his manliness in harness. She was so damned desirable, he could think of little else.

Still, he had not even kissed her. Instead he talked of inconsequential things and ogled her to feast his eyes. Alone, he tossed and twisted at night, wanting her, cursing himself for ten kinds of fool for his thoughts.

Each night with her head on the pillow, Celia stared blankly into the darkness, reliving the moments she'd spent with Francis and bemoaning the fact that the days were getting fewer. He had said nothing to indicate his intentions. She had to face the idea of his returning to India and her staying behind without him . . . forever.

In the third week, Francis asked Celia to dine with his family. Her joy knew no bounds; even Emma Skerritt began to hope the young Captain's attentions were serious. A

113

young man in his position did not invite a girl into the family bosom unless his thoughts were on marriage.

Celia was so nervous she knew she would not be able to swallow a mouthful; when Francis came for her, he acted as though nothing were amiss. In truth he'd had a devil of a row with his mother over the invitation and about his continued interest in Celia.

"Really, Francis, you can't be serious. The girl is the parson's daughter. What in the world would we talk about?"

"She's well educated, Mother, I'm sure you'll be able to find a common ground for conversation."

Mrs. Devy sniffed, showing her disapproval openly, but Francis was adamant and at last she gave in. The formal invitation was written and Francis delivered it by hand.

Riding to Aylesford, Celia had even more misgivings than she'd had at first. "Oh, Francis, I'm so nervous. Will Theo be there?"

He patted her hand. "Of course she will be. Besides, I'll be there and I plan to occupy your time as much as possible. You shall talk to me and the rest of them be damned!"

"Francis—" She protested automatically in spite of the knowledge he was teasing her again. She had grown more and more comfortable with him, finding it easy to relax in his presence and be herself. She still had many qualms about her own inadequacies but Francis's strong personality overshadowed them.

Mrs. Devy received them in the drawing room, turning to bestow a glance on Celia as Francis spoke.

"Mother, Celia is here."

"Miss Skerritt, how good of you to join us."

Celia curtsied, feeling the pressure of Francis's hand on her arm. He ushered her to a small sofa and when she had seated herself, sat beside her. Celia did not miss the quick glance of disapproval from Mrs. Devy.

"Thank you for inviting me," Celia said softly.

The older woman's scrutiny seemed cold. She was dressed in pale violet, a flowing gossamer material that Celia could not identify but which looked cool. Her eyes met Celia's and turned away immediately. Celia felt rebuffed and looked to Francis.

114

He smiled. "Did you know that in India the hot climate makes it impossible for any activity immediately after dining? The custom is to rest during the heat of the day."

"How very odd," Mrs. Devy said. "Barbaric people. I don't know why you insist on staying in the Army, Francis."

He glanced at her impatiently. Obviously the argument was not new. Francis said, "The *jana* say that only mad dogs and Englishmen venture out in the noonday sun. It's quite a joke with them."

"The *jana?*" Celia asked.

"The people. Millions of them. You can't begin to imagine how populated the country is. They breed like flies."

"Really, Francis, that's hardly proper conversation. It's a wonder that you have returned safely to us this time and I do wish you would not go back again to that dreadful place. I'm sure if you spoke with Edward—"

"No, Mother." He cut her off imperiously. He would not speak to the Duke about any such favor; he had no wish to cut short his duty with the regiment or to stay at home idly passing time. He had done so long enough to be sure it was not to his liking. He was a man of action and the adventure of India appealed to him. He was, however, distressed to think of leaving Celia. His desire for her had grown stronger these recent weeks, and now with only days before his departure, he found the thought of leaving her enormously upsetting. Of late he'd entertained thoughts of asking for additional time but that would be difficult.

Squire Devy appeared in the doorway, smiling politely as he came forward to take Celia's hand. "How delightful to see you again, my dear. You are looking marvelous."

"Thank you, sir."

He strode about the room, pausing to glance out the window and frown at something he saw, then turning his attention to Celia. "Francis tells me you spent a year in London."

She nodded, glancing at Francis and wondering if he'd mentioned their first meeting there. His smile assured her that he had not. "I was at school," she said.

"Yes . . ." He seemed to be measuring her with his eyes,

and she was suddenly uneasy. Had the Devys been discussing her before her arrival?

Mrs. Devy said, "Were you at the Dreyfus Academy?"

Celia recognized the name of the most exclusive and costly school in London. "No, I attended Miss Claredon's." She spoke with a calmness she did not feel. From the look on the woman's face it was obvious she'd never heard of Miss Claredon's or if she had it did not merit her approval. Mrs. Devy settled back, fixing her gaze on her son, shutting Celia from her mind.

Even Squire Devy seemed at a loss for further topics of conversation. He paced the length of the long room, pausing to study the music set upon a stand near a piano and music cabinet.

Francis touched her shoulder with his fingertips. He sensed her discomfort and wanted to put her at ease. His parents were behaving badly and he wondered if he'd made a mistake in insisting on the invitation. Still, he had to adhere to the proprieties. He knew he could not leave Aylesford without stating his intentions and asking Celia to wait for his return. He wasn't sure when the decision had been made, but there was no turning from it now. He would wed her and have her as his own forever. He smiled and wished he could erase the look of doom from her face. She felt on exhibit, he knew, and neither his mother nor father was doing much to relieve her.

There was a flurry of motion at the door and Theo rushed in, hurrying to her father and kissing him on the cheek, then smiling at her mother and Celia. "I'm sorry I'm late—I was in the lower garden and lost track of time. Do forgive me?" The question was directed at Celia, though she turned to include her parents as an afterthought. Mrs. Devy scowled and rose from her chair as a servant appeared to announce dinner.

"Tardiness is becoming a habit with you, Theodora. It is not fitting for a young lady to make such a spectacle of herself." Head high, Mrs. Devy came forward and claimed Francis to escort her to the dining room. Francis hesitated until his stare caused his father to bow to Celia and present his arm. Theo walked beside them, chattering rapidly.

"I'm so glad you could come, Celia. I do tire of stodgy

116

meals with nothing to talk about but crops and prices of grain—"

"That will be quite enough!" her father said with a warning glance. He drew out Celia's chair. Theo made a face and took her place across the table while Francis seated his mother.

"It's quite true, Papa," Theo added defiantly. Squire Devy scowled but said nothing.

The dining room was opulent, with a huge crystal chandelier over the table, a carved sideboard laden with a silver tea set and serving dishes, and panelled walls of rich, dark wood. The table was set with a fine damask cloth and napkins held in silver rings engraved with the Aylesford crest. Heavy silver service, delicate bone china, cut glass wine goblets.

Three servants entered, moving about silently, serving each of them deftly. The meal began with thick turtle soup presented in warm bowls, followed by a delicate white fish. The removes, a haunch of mutton and broiled capons *à l'Ecarlate*, were served up on large dishes placed at the top and bottom of the table; the *flancs*, stewed veal in a mildly spiced sauce and curried fowl, were set at the four corners of the table.

Celia was thankful for the food which lessened conversation. She took very small portions since her appetite had vanished completely. She ate slowly and deliberately, consciously bringing to mind the etiquette she had been taught. She would have been glad to dine in silence but her hostess would not allow such a luxury. Francis and his father chatted about estate matters, glancing from time to time at the women to include them in the conversation. Theo giggled and smiled at Celia as if to say she had predicted just such a happening. Mrs. Devy silenced her with a glance, then directed herself to Celia.

"I find London quite charming in the spring. We spent several weeks there before going on to Paris this year."

Celia could think of no comment.

"Do you know the Mortimers?" Mrs. Devy asked.

"No, at least I don't think so."

"Everyone in London attends their parties during the season—"

"Oh, Mother, the Mortimers are *ancient!* Why in the

world would Celia want to go to one of their parties?"
Theo shook her dark curls and rattled on. "Have you been
to Vauxhall Gardens? I adore them—such gaiety and
color—and the music!"

"Oh yes." Celia recalled the excursion to the pleasure
garden, a tour for the students but thrilling nonetheless.
They had gone early and left at dusk when the crowd became more high spirited. Miss Claredon had hinted at
dark tragedies that might befall young ladies who ventured
alone in such a place, but Celia heard only the music and
the laughter and longed to be part of the dancing and to
view the fireworks that were advertised.

"There was a circus and strange animals," Theo said,
"and a most delightful puppet show at the theatre north of
the long lawn." She glanced at Francis and her father who
had paused to listen. "And of course the maze. Far more
complicated than ours, Papa. It took *hours* to find our way
out!"

Theo was describing London the way Celia had envisioned it—the way she had longed for it to be. She envied Theo's high spirits and was sorry she'd never known
similar delights.

Mrs. Devy said, "The gardens have become roisterous
and common, hardly a fit place for young ladies of proper
breeding. I should think your escort would know better
than to take you there."

"But Mama, it's a lovely place! Far more exciting than
sitting about staring at *dull* people."

"Theo—!" Her father almost growled the word.

The girl sighed and said nothing more, but Celia was
confused by the interchange. Somehow she had thought of
Theo as leading a wonderful, carefree existence, without
restraints. She glanced at the pouting girl in surprise.

Mrs. Devy supervised the serving of the entrees, and
when she had sampled her plate and nodded her approval,
she looked at Celia. "Miss Claredon's? I don't believe I recall the school. Is it very new?"

Francis quickly said, "I am quite familiar with it,
Mother. It's on Marley Row, is it not?"

"Yes, it is," Celia said softly.

"An elegant building and quite a fashionable school, I
assure you, Mother."

He was saving her embarrassment, and Celia was grateful. She was relieved when Mrs. Devy reluctantly let the matter drop. Celia tasted the fillet of beef on her plate. It was deliciously spiced and very tender but she had difficulty swallowing each morsel. Mrs. Devy was openly hostile, and Celia sensed that she did not consider her a suitable companion for her son. It was impossible not to feel anger but at the same time, Celia was humiliated. She risked a glance at Francis and though he smiled encouragingly, his eyes betrayed his annoyance.

Mrs. Devy said, "I'm sure you attended the races, my dear?"

"No, we did not," Celia murmured.

"And the regatta? The receptions afterward at the St. George are the talk of London. Did you meet—"

"Mother!" Francis said. "Is this necessary?"

"Whatever do you mean?"

Francis glanced at his father who sat with his gaze on his plate or flicking to the window. "Would it not be better if we discussed something other than the royal regatta?"

Mrs. Devy smiled—like a leopardess, Celia thought. "I only wondered if . . . dear Celia—"

Francis pushed back his chair and stood abruptly. His fork clattered on the plate and there was a spot of color in each cheek. Celia started at the unexpected movement, watching him with round eyes. She realized he was very angry and her heart began to hammer so that it was difficult to breathe. Her hand went to her throat as she saw him come around the table to her and grasp her chair.

Mrs. Devy sat stiffly. "Whatever are you doing, Francis?"

"Come, Celia," he said in a low tone. "It's time for us to go."

Obediently Celia allowed him to pull out the chair and she rose, trying not to look at Mrs. Devy.

"I say, Francis—" his father began.

"Please excuse us," Francis said firmly, managing a tight smile. He led her from the room.

Celia leaned against him, feeling faint. She was unaccustomed to family arguments—her father would never allow such a thing—but Francis had been magnificent. He had faced them down for her! Whatever the future

119

brought, she would have that memory. She felt his lips on her cheek, heard him murmur soothing words. The world seemed to come around again and straighten itself out. He led her across the hall and through the side door. They were in a garden with the cool breeze whispering about them. The sun had gone, leaving the western sky a deep violet in the growing dusk. The air was heavy with the scent of flowers and crickets were everywhere.

Francis paused at the end of a box hedge, turning to her and slipping his hands to her shoulders. "I'm dreadfully sorry about all that, Celia. It was rude and cruel—I don't know what gets into Mother sometimes."

Celia blinked rapidly, trying to hold back the tears. Everything was finished ... his mother would forbid his seeing her again.

He drew her into his arms. "You must know how I feel, Celia."

She did not understand at first, thinking he referred to the exchange in the dining room. "She is your mother, Francis."

He shook his head impatiently. "I mean how I feel about you. What I mean is—damn it, I love you!" He pulled her close and she felt herself sway against him as he bent his lips to hers. His kiss was tender at first but quickly grew to something far more exciting. She trembled in his arms and felt the stirring pleasure of his hard, lean body against her.

He loved her! How she had longed to hear him utter those words! She gave herself to the kiss, her lips yielding to the pressure of his. "Francis ... Francis ..."

His emotions ran rampant and his body stirred with wanting her. She was so desirable, so completely feminine and warm. He could feel the full curve of her breasts beneath the thin summer gown, feel the beating of her heart against his. His pulse was wild and erratic as he strained to fight off the need that filled him. He'd waited so long to hold her, to declare his love, the fire within him burned more brightly for it.

Celia moved to the urgency of the kiss; it roused her to giddy heights and her being seemed to tingle and come alive as he held her, kissing her cheeks and hair, burying his face at her neck and murmuring her name over and

120

over. She was suddenly aware of the new pressure of his body and the pleasure it brought her. He was not like the others, not pulling her down roughly and forcing himself on her. Francis ... She sighed as he touched her throat and she felt his warm breath. His hands moved over her breasts and down the length of her body. He moaned aloud and covered her mouth again. The kiss was fiery and demanding, all gentleness gone.

Celia gave a strangled, muted cry and pushed at him, knowing she had let him go too far. He was expecting more than she was willing to give. "Don't—oh, please—"

He broke away. What had he been thinking?! He dropped his hands and stepped back, grateful for the darkness that hid his guilt. "Forgive me—I didn't mean—" He could find no words to form an apology he had never used before.

Celia put her hand to her flaming face and looked away. He had given in so readily it surprised her and left her breathless. She wanted him to take her in his arms again and satisfy the terrible longing that burned in her. She felt desolate without him, yet she was frightened of her own emotions and the knowledge that she had driven him to lust. She felt the terrible frustration of desire and fear, and she could not speak.

"I'm sorry, Celia. Can you forgive me? A man has needs that sometimes are difficult to control." He touched her cheek and turned her face about so she had to look at him. "You are very precious to me. Hard as it will be, I shall wait until you are my wife to have you as a man needs a woman." He bent and brushed his lips to hers for a fraction of a breath.

Had she heard him right? She gaped, eyes wide, lips parted until he laughed softly.

"There—I've been stupid again. Why is it I am tongue-tied near you? What I'm trying to say is I love you and want you to be my wife." He let his fingers trace the soft curve of her chin, touch her lips. "Say you will marry me."

Celia's breath was a tight pain beneath her ribs. Marry him!

"Have I shocked you speechless? May I take your

silence for acceptance?" He studied her face in the shadows, trying to read her expression.

"Yes ... oh, yes, Francis!" At long last the words came. He pulled her into his arms into a passionate kiss. She could scarcely breathe, but it was no matter. Mrs. Francis Devy!

If he had wanted to take her again, she would have welcomed his embrace! But he had gained control, and he parted from her reluctantly.

"I shall speak to your father tomorrow," he said. "And then to my parents."

She nodded. She had no desire to face the Devys again tonight if she could avoid it. She could not bear exposing her happiness to Mrs. Devy's cold scrutiny and lashing tongue. "I think it would be proper," she said.

"Are you always so proper, my darling?"

"No." She was alarmed at the thought. She wanted nothing more than to be able to discard the cloak of restraint that had held her all her life, to be mad and impetuous, enjoying each moment as it came without regard for the consequences.

He kissed her again. "I'm very glad to hear that. I do not think I should be able to live up to the expectations of a very proper wife."

"You're teasing me," she said, pretending hurt.

"Yes, I am, my love. But only because I adore you so madly. I have been driven out of my mind with loving you these past weeks—ever since I first met you at the Duke's house in London."

She sobered at the memory of Gregory Houghton, looking away momentarily so Francis would not read her expression. She would never speak of that terrible thing that had befallen her in London, and she would not think of it again. She turned back with a smile. "And I you. I was afraid to hope you might love me in return."

"My darling." They embraced again, kissing until Celia gasped for breath and he forced himself away from her. "Will you marry me before I leave for India?" he whispered.

"So soon—the banns—" She was astonished.

"Must we observe such dictates? I want you now."

"My father would never consent to a wedding outside

122

the church. The banns must be posted three consecutive Sabbaths—"

He smothered a curse. "What a fool I've been to let the time slip away." He tilted her face, gazing into her eyes. "Then you must come to India and we'll be wed there. I cannot live without you."

"India!" It was too startling.

"Yes, there is a substantial English settlement in Calcutta and we can be wed by the Bishop," he said matter-of-factly. "Surely your father cannot object to that."

"But how will I reach India?"

"I shall arrange passage for you on the next available ship. I have friends in London who will see to it. You will come to me as soon as possible and we will be married the instant you land. Say you will do it, love."

Travel all the way to India! It was too much to comprehend. She had envisioned the far-off place, but only as one where Francis must return and carry on his duties.

"Say you will do it," he urged.

"Yes, oh yes!" She would sail to the ends of the earth to be with him!

He sighed. "Then it is settled. I'll make arrangements and Theo will keep you informed." He knew he could count on his sister regardless of any objections his parents raised. He had plenty of money in his own right. He gazed lovingly at her. "I'll find us a house near the Fort. You shall have servants and every comfort, I promise you—and most of all I will love you madly."

Faintly she said, "I could not ask more." It sounded too wonderful to be true. "The ship—" She had no money for passage.

"Never worry your pretty head about it. I will arrange every detail with my solicitor. He will inform you of the sailing date and even see that you are safely conducted to the ship."

"Francis, I'm frightened. I've never been so far."

"My darling ..." He brushed the hair from her cheeks. "It is the only way we can be together. I shan't have another leave for a year, maybe longer. I can't wait that long." He held her close.

She nodded, her cheek against his. He was right; it was

the only way; when he said it, the objections dissolved and the long journey seemed very possible.

Francis slid a gold-crested ring from his finger and put it on hers. "Wear it and think of me. Very soon you shall have a proper wedding band to take its place."

She turned the ring, clasping her hand over it.

"And what will you give me of you?" he asked.

She raised her hands to her neck and unfastened the tiny gold chain she wore. "My locket—it's all I have." She dropped it into his palm.

"I shall keep it close to my heart until death." He slipped it into his waistcoat pocket and pressed his hand over it.

"Don't speak of death—not now when I'm so happy."

He laughed. "You are a serious little thing. You must learn not to look on the dark side of every remark I make."

She smiled, wanting to please him and wanting nothing to mar their bliss. She was going to be Mrs. Francis Devy . . . nothing could ever match that wonder and joy.

Francis appeared at the parsonage the following morning and was closeted with the vicar for a long time. Celia retired to her room, waiting nervously until her mother came for her. She had worked herself into a state of anxiety and was scarcely able to talk. But her mother was smiling and quickly came to her to hug her.

The vicar had consented! Celia laughed and cried and stammered in joy until her mother shushed her and told her to dry her eyes and come downstairs.

They toasted the engagement with small glasses of sherry, and Francis stared at Celia hungrily the whole time. He was impatient to be alone with her but he guarded his expression and listened politely as the vicar rambled.

The Devys were far less exuberant when the news was broken to them. Francis spoke of the engagement and wedding plans at dinner that evening; Mrs. Devy burst into tears and cried about what people would say when her son married a parson's daughter. Squire Devy looked solemn and rubbed his hands together, shaking his head and preparing arguments against the marriage: Celia had no dowry to speak of; had Francis considered how they would be received on his return from India when he presented his wife to the people in the Devy social circles?

Francis would not listen, and he left the dining room without finishing his meal.

Only Theo was happy for him, although a little shocked. Her own affair with Kevin was something to while away summer evenings, and she had no thoughts of a permanent liaison. That Francis wanted to marry Celia was confusing, but if it made him happy she would do what he asked.

Celia and Francis spent as much time as possible together in the days that followed. Francis was hampered by family obligations, and Celia was content not to have to face the Devys again. When she and Francis returned from India, she would make her peace with them. But that was a blessedly long way off; she would not worry about it now. Her mind and heart were too full of Francis for anything else.

The days passed quickly and suddenly Francis's leave was over. They spent the last evening walking in the meadow below the parsonage, planning their future, clinging together in last embraces at every opportunity. Francis had been in touch with his solicitor; there was a ship sailing for India in four weeks. "You will be on it, my love."

Four weeks was not nearly enough time to prepare for a new life in a strange place, to gather a trousseau and pack the things she must take. But it was eternity away from Francis, and Celia feared she might not endure it.

He kissed her and brushed her hair with his fingertips. "It will pass, and we will be together forever," he said. "Now I must go." He kissed her again, then released her slowly.

"Francis . . ."

"Be brave and hurry to me. I shall spend the rest of my life making up to you the emptiness of the days that lie ahead. And we shall be happy." He smiled radiantly and she clung to him. "We will always be happy."

"I know we will."

He kissed her one last time then ran to his horse, jumped in the saddle and dug in his heels as the animal skittered. He turned to wave farewell, then rode across the fields to vanish amid the trees.

Celia stood in the darkness by the open gate until the last echoes of hoofbeats faded, until the last sight of him could never be erased from her being.

"I know we will," she whispered to the night sky. "I know we will."

CHAPTER SEVEN

September came and went, a succession of busy days in which Celia stood patiently while her mother and two servants fitted, pinned and refitted, sewing a trousseau of garments for her new life. Celia was by turns ecstatic and depressed, both excited and worried about the endless journey she was about to make to a strange land.

She had no real word from Francis, the time being too short for anything but a quickly scrawled note from London, delivered by his solicitor, telling her of the passage he'd arranged. She was to sail on the Aramack on the 14th of October and would be with Francis before Christmas. She was surprised to learn she would travel by a route through the Mediterranean, overland across Egypt, thence by ship again down the Red Sea and Indian Ocean. A second ship from Suez would touch at Madras before going on to Calcutta—where Francis would be waiting. There was also a thick packet of banknotes enclosed, and when she counted them she sat down abruptly to stare at the money. It was more than her father earned in a year!

She saw Theo several times when the other came to the parsonage or paused to speak to the vicar after church, but Celia was not invited again to Aylesford.

She felt a stab of fear when a messenger appeared with a letter for her father that turned out to be a brief request for him to present himself at Aylesford. The summons came three days after Francis had left to rejoin his regiment. Parson Skerritt suspected the nature of the request but kept his own counsel. Squire Devy would probably consider a marriage between his son and Celia to be an unsuitable match.

When he was admitted to Devy's study, a square, darkly paneled room with heavy draperies and gloomy portraits, his surmise proved correct. Squire Devy paced the room and provided arguments why Skerritt should forbid his daughter to marry Francis. The parson was quickly aware that Devy had already tried and failed to dissuade Francis in the matter and was now taking the only other option open to him.

"I will not play a part in such a scheme," he said. Though he had his own reservations, he would not destroy Celia's happiness because of Devy's threats, though the man had influential friends in high places and the parson might easily find himself shunted off to a remote parish. But he had given his blessing to the marriage; Francis was of age and did not have to account for his actions other than to himself and to the Almighty. When William Skerritt gave his word it would be kept.

Kevin heard from Theo how her parents raged and quarrelled. Her mother was furious, Theo said, had taken to her bed with palpitations, and would never forgive Celia for stealing away her precious son while breath stirred within her. Kevin and Theo met in the empty cottage in the shadowy woods. Theo had been forbidden to see him but she defied her father's wishes, though he never knew. Kevin had been stunned by Francis and Celia's sudden betrothal, and he worried that Celia would be hurt. Francis's reputation among women was far from unblemished ... still Celia was so incredibly happy he could only wish her well. Devy was at least rich and she would never want for anything.

To Kevin fell the duty of taking Celia to Southampton when the sailing date neared. They left the parsonage at dawn on the eleventh amid tears and promises and a hundred reassuring words from both parents. Keyed high, Celia talked and laughed for half the journey and slept the rest, having worn herself out.

They were two days on the road, then Southampton was before them at last, buried in an avalanche of cold mist through which a few spires thrust. The sea was a booming surf as Kevin inquired the way and learned that the Aramack lay a gunshot from shore. He took the chaise to the pier, pulling his hat down tightly because of the nippy sea breeze.

Celia was enthralled by the bustle of activity. Several ships were anchored, tall masts and rigging dark against the grey cloudy sky. Men in thick sweaters and dark trousers hurried about, hoisting cargo into boats to ferry it to the waiting ships. The noise and shouts rang loud. The smell of garbage blended with the heavy odor of burning wood from a fire a group of street urchins stood about, hands held out to ward off the damp chill.

Kevin brought the chaise into the sheltered lee of a building, and several ragged boys scampered up as though spilled from a sack. As Kevin swung himself down, he tossed one of them a coin.

"Mind the carriage well or I'll have my farthing back and ten pennies worth from your hide!"

The child bobbed his head. "Yes, guv'ner." He grabbed the reins, lashing out with them at the companions who had lost the scramble so that they moved back toward the fire.

A chill wind caught Celia's skirts, whipping them about her ankles as she stepped from the chaise and looked out over the foggy water. A number of boats were ferrying passengers and baggage to the ship, and Kevin quickly struck up a bargain with one of the boatmen, carried her bags to the edge of the pier and saw them safely stowed in the wide-beamed boat. He took her arm and hurried her down a steep stairway to a platform on the cold water. She clutched at her bonnet lest it be ripped off in a sudden gust of wind and stepped into a small bobbing craft as Kevin guided her. He caught her and lowered her into a seat, seating himself beside her with a grin. They were underway in a moment, four men pulling hard on oars that seemed to bend with their efforts. The cold salt spray dashed into her face but Celia scarcely noticed. She was actually on her way at last!

The ship seemed huge as Kevin helped her up the narrow teetering stairs, up the ship's side to the deck, and it was thronged with passengers and hurrying sailors who tugged and moved cargo and baggage. Trunks, pieces of

129

furniture and other personal articles were piled helter-skelter wherever space afforded. Atop a trunk, a parrot in a wire cage squawked stridently as the breeze ruffled its feathers and caused it to hunch its head into its wings. Kevin led her to a sheltered space opposite the ladder and promised to return in a moment. Celia stood staring about in wonder.

She turned suddenly, aware of someone's gaze upon her and thinking Kevin had returned but finding instead a tall, handsome man with piercing eyes under thick brown brows watching her. He was several yards away, leaning casually on the rail and ignoring the hustle about him. Celia felt her face warm and turned away quickly, relieved to see Kevin pushing toward her.

"You're in cabin 4A," he said, taking her arm again. "It's this way." He led her through a door, out of the wind, and she sighed in relief and folded her collar back. Kevin made inquiries as they walked and came to the door of 4A triumphantly. "You're opposite the captain's cabin, love! Francis has done himself proud by you!"

Celia entered the cabin, looking about with wide eyes. It was large, about the size of her own room at home, but compact and arranged to utilize space to best advantage. A bed built into one corner was covered with a rich satin spread and hangings the color of ruby wine. Beneath it, several cabinets and drawers were built into the framework of the bed, their brass knobs gleaming in the golden light. A wardrobe of dark mahogany stood at the opposite side of two small windows draped in red. There was also a writing desk, a high lamp, and two yellow cushioned chairs. Celia exclaimed in delight. The lustrous paneling gave the room a warm, comfortable feeling though the square iron stove was cold.

A man in white uniform came to the door, with a cart piled high with baggage. Kevin helped the man bring in a trunk and set it against the wall. The larger trunk would be placed in the hold out of the way. "If you've need of anything from it, ma'am," the steward said, "you've only to ring."

"Thank you," she said, and he closed the door.

Kevin took her hands. "Francis has seen to everything,

love. I've one last packet from him to give you—I promised to give it to you when you came on board."

"A packet?"

He produced a small box coated with velvet. She gasped, opening it. Inside was a glittering jewel, silvery and sparkling, a diamond on an intricate gold chain, with a small plate that bore a script. Even Kevin's mouth dropped, seeing it.

"A necklace!" she said lifting it, holding it to the light, her voice awed. It must cost a fortune! She lifted the plate and read: "To my only love, FD."

She sat down to catch her breath. It was a magnificent gift—a real diamond! She felt giddy and Kevin caught up her hand, patting it sharply. "Celia—are you all right?"

"I—I'm all right," she said weakly.

"There's more." He continued patting her hand. "You'll have a maid to clean the cabin and bring you meals if you're not of a mind to go to the dining room."

"A maid! Oh, Kevin, was ever a girl so fortunate! Francis is—" She broke off, blushing at her own words and he laughed softly.

"You're a dear child—no, you're a woman about to be married." He dragged the second chair over and sat. "Life is not all laughter, Celia, and each of us has to take our share of tears. Don't expect so much of life that it can't measure up, or of Francis ..." How could he warn her that Devy's ways might not change because he had a wife? "Francis is the one who's fortunate and you can tell him so for me. If he doesn't keep you as happy as you are this moment, I shall journey to India and thrash him proper."

His fierce scowl made her smile. "I do hope we'll come back to England soon."

"Hush, none of that, girl. A wife's place is with her husband. You'll visit often and play the grand lady and Father will look at you and scowl and have to use his most impressive words."

They both laughed at his picture of their father. Kevin put hands in his pockets. "I'm off to America, you know—but if it's not to my liking I shall come on to India and you will grow tired of having me underfoot and order your dozens of servants to toss me into the streets to beg for alms."

She laughed again at his foolishness. She would certainly miss him. She was conscious of the new and exciting sounds, distant shouts, the rumble of cargo beneath her feet. The floor beneath her seemed to move now and then—they were afloat, after all.

Kevin came close and took her hands. He cocked his head at the bells ringing in the passageway. "I must be off or the captain will sign me on as cabin boy."

"I'm frightened, Kevin."

"No you aren't. You'll have a happy and safe voyage and arrive to find Francis waiting." He kissed her. "Take care, dear sister, and write to Mama. She will send me your address."

Celia sighed and clung to him for a moment.

He lifted her chin. "A smile . . ." She smiled and he nodded. "That's better." He went to the door and opened it. "You're going to be very happy—think about nothing else."

"I will . . ."

As he closed the door, he collided with a young woman.

"Oh—oh my—" The woman grabbed for the green velvet bonnet perched atop a mass of red curls.

"I beg your pardon!" Kevin caught her in his arms to keep her from tumbling. "What a clumsy oaf I am! Have I hurt you?"

"No—no—" The woman shook her head, trying to right the hat that had slipped askew, finally pulling it off in irritation. "No, not at all." She looked at him sharply, then smiled, gleaming teeth against red lips, and her hand fluttered to the deep neckline of the gown beneath the green coat.

Kevin did not release her at once, and his eyes dropped to the full breasts that swelled upward under the tight bodice. "No, I see you are not."

"I—I'm delighted to meet one of my fellow passengers so early in the voyage," she said, "even in such uncommon manner."

Kevin released her reluctantly and bowed, stepping back a trifle, still smiling. "Alas, I am not a passenger. Had I known what charming company I would encounter I certainly would have rushed to book passage."

The woman smiled and brushed at a curl that had fallen

over her cheek. The motion made her breasts strain at the edge of the neckline and Kevin sighed and moved closer again.

"Are you journeying to India?"

She nodded, "To Calcutta."

"Ah," he brightened. "Then you'll be traveling the entire way with Celia." He turned, rapping at the cabin door, opening it. Celia dabbed at her eyes and looked at him inquiringly. He said, "May I introduce my sister, Celia Skerritt . . . Miss . . .?"

The woman's green eyes turned to Celia in a pert glance. Her features were plain except for the large and wide-set eyes, but her face was carefully made up to give an illusion of beauty. Her cheeks were flushed, her lips crimson against pale skin. The amber curls piled atop her head were in slight disarray, falling carelessly across her forehead and along her neck. She seemed to study Celia for several moments, appraising her dress and the cabin behind her.

"Iris Beddington," she said at last and smiled. Turning back to Kevin, she added, "Mrs. Beddington."

Kevin paid no notice to the amendment. "Celia has never been at sea before. I hope that you two will become friends." He stepped aside, taking Iris's arm casually and leading her into the cabin. Iris looked along the passageway but did not resist. Her glance at Celia was friendly.

"What takes you to India, Mrs. Beddington?" Kevin said brightly.

"I join my husband in Calcutta."

"Your first sea voyage?"

She shook her head and the red curls danced like fingers caressing her pale neck and the dark fur of the coat. "James and I spent a year in North Africa before he signed on with the East India Company."

"Ah, I hear there are fortunes to be made in spices and silks."

"My husband is but a junior merchant." She looked at Kevin with a hint of smile, then turned to Celia. "And you? Surely you do not travel to Calcutta for a holiday. Your husband—?"

Celia felt compelled to explain in a rush of words. "I'm

133

to be married. Francis will meet me when the ship docks and we shall be wed at once."

"I wish you happiness." Iris's smile was warm. "Is Francis with the Company?"

"No, he's a captain in the Army. He was recently on leave but had to go back." She sighed. "It seems ever so long ago."

"You will live near the Fort then?"

Celia nodded, "Yes, I imagine."

Kevin said, "Will you live in Calcutta or one of the Company's other posts, Iris?"

"James has leased a house in Calcutta. I shall remain there, I think, even though he occasionally must visit other places. I dare say I shall be content to stay at home if all I hear of the miserable climate is true."

Kevin frowned as a bell clanged. He turned to Celia and lifted her chin in his hand. "I must go." Seeing Celia's tears threaten again, he took his leave quickly, kissing her cheeks and bowing to Iris once. "If I don't see to that boy he will steal my horse for certain. I've trusted him too long as it is. Goodbye, Celia. Iris, may I see you to your cabin? Are you close by?"

"Immediately next door," she said and let him take her arm. In the doorway, Kevin paused to blow a kiss back into the room before pulling the door shut.

Celia dropped into the cushioned chair and sighed tremulously. She would not cry—not now, when she had so much to be happy about!

The Aramack sailed on the morning tide. Celia wakened with the heavy creaking of the ship and the rattling of the chains of the helm wheel. She was at first startled by the scurrying of running feet on the deck above, then realized it was the sailors about their duties.

She had slept remarkably well, far better than she had hoped. The bed was as comfortable as her own at home, and the gentle motion of the ship had lulled her. The sea air was brisk and she felt quite invigorated as she slid out of bed and crossed to the small windows. The deck was cold beneath her feet and the chill made her hurry back to the bed for robe and slippers. The sky beyond the glass

134

was grey except for a slash of crimson along the eastern sky where the sun rose sluggishly behind thick clouds.

She had dined alone in the cabin the night before, unable to bring herself to face a crowd of strangers. The girl Francis's solicitor had hired was a quiet child, no more than fourteen, with large blue eyes that seemed to take in everything and a thin body that was little more than skin and bones. Her name was Mary Lyle and she spoke softly when addressed but was otherwise shy and silent. Mary's quarters were on the lower deck amidships near the engine room, and she shared the cabin with half a dozen others, she'd said. Celia had dismissed her when the supper tray was cleared, preferring to tend to her own undressing. It would take time to become accustomed to the idea of having servants at her call, yet she knew Francis would expect her to learn. She would be a Devy, and she must learn to live as one.

She stared out the misted glass watching the dark waters of the bay. The masts of anchored ships became threads against the grey sky; the towers and arches of a church were dark on the horizon, the spire standing like the pointing needle of a compass. A few low buildings were outlined along the waterfront where lights winked softly. The sea was growing choppy and Celia wondered if a storm was gathering. The clouds along the horizon seemed to roll into menacing shapes even as she watched, and she shivered and pulled her robe tight about her, realizing she was becoming chilled.

She scurried back to bed and slipped beneath the comforter, rubbing her flesh to warm herself. She lay turning over in her mind the dreams of her future. India would be warm, of course. Francis had jested of the heat—something the natives said. Only he had called them—what was it? *Jana*—people, yes. She would have to learn some of the language. She tried to recall everything Francis had told her of Calcutta. A large city, teeming with people. The Fort was located in the center of the city, surrounded by a high wall to discourage attacks—although he had assured her that the Army was powerful and respected. Married officers generally took houses close to the Fort, and they might have dozens of native servants to care for them and the needs of the family. Dark-skinned nurses, cooks and houseboys were commonplace, Francis said.

She sighed and turned at the sound of the door. She had given Mary a key so she might enter without disturbing her if she were asleep. The child slipped into the room soundlessly, glancing quickly to the bed and seeming surprised that her mistress was awake.

"Good morning, Mary," Celia said with a smile.

The girl bobbed and murmured softly as she moved to the stove to light a fire. When the flames danced over the coals she looked to Celia questioningly.

"I think I shall dine in the saloon. It's time I meet my fellow passengers if I'm to be with them for so many weeks."

"Yes'm." Mary went to the chest and opened a drawer to take out one of the linen chemises Celia and her mother had sewn so carefully. She laid it on the bed before opening the wardrobe and standing aside. It took Celia a moment to realize the girl expected her to select a gown. Trying to hide her confusion, Celia sat up. "The brown one, I think. The day seems damp and cold."

Without a word, Mary removed the dress from its peg and brought it to her. She spread the soft wool with a loving touch, as though enjoying the fine cloth. Celia felt compassion for the child and a terrible sense of her own inadequacy. She recognized the longing she saw in Mary's face . . . the wanting to reach for beauty beyond her grasp . . . the dream of a life she had never known.

With eyes averted, Celia slipped from her gown and drew the chemise over her head. She felt quick hands tug it in place, and she rewarded the child with a smile. The soft wool of the brown dress was tight at the waist then fell into pleats that whispered as Celia moved. Mary's fingers lingered, arranging a fold, smoothing the skirt. Then she ran across the room to bring shoes as Celia drew on long cotton stockings.

Celia had not the heart to refuse the child who snatched up the hairbrush and waited for Celia to seat herself. She had never known the luxury of having someone do her hair. Mary wielded the brush in long, gentle strokes, unsnarling the night's tangles diligently, then carefully plaiting it and catching the ends of the braids over Celia's ears

136

to form soft loops. It was a style quite fashionable, similar to the way Theo Devy had worn her hair when Celia first met her. Celia was pleased when Mary handed her the small bone-handled glass to view the results.

"That's very nice, Mary. You do well with hair. You must have had a lot of experience."

The compliment took the child by surprise and she bobbed her head quickly, smiling shyly. "Yes'm. I was in service to Lady Whittington."

Celia was not familiar with the name. "And why did you leave Her Ladyship?" The question was innocent of malice. Celia wanted to put the girl at ease, and she was unprepared for the instant fear that came to the child's eyes.

"I was not let out, ma'am—truly not. When Lord Skeffington said his friend needed a girl, m'mum said it was proper for me to go. And the five shillings was more than I was worth, she said."

Celia felt her cheeks grow pink. The girl had no say in her life—she had been sold from one job to another without concern for her wishes or probably even her well being. That she had been hired to serve Celia was a stroke of fortune; the child might easily have gone to a hard taskmaster.

"And I'm glad to have you, truly I am," Celia said with a smile. "It is a long voyage to India and I will be glad of your company and help."

Mary tried another tremulous smile.

"Now then," Celia said, rising. "Have you inquired the way to the dining saloon?"

"Yes'm, I'll take you."

The dining saloon was a long room furnished with rectangular tables to seat eight. White cloths covered each, set with heavy silver and linen that might have been used at a fine London table. Only the dishes gave evidence to the more rugged life aboard ship—heavy china that would not be likely to shatter easily. Each passenger on the first class deck had been assigned a table, and Mary led Celia to one set slightly apart from the others.

"The capt'n's table, mum," she whispered almost reverently, then hurried away.

There were three people already seated, two men and a

137

woman. The woman and the man next to her were grey-haired, he tanned and leathery looking except for a white patch atop his bald head where he normally wore a hat; her plump face was powdered to chalky whiteness to cover age spots, and her thick white fingers were like pale sausages caught in heavy rings. She was wearing a dress of green and lilac shot taffeta, and a cream-colored fichu covered her heavy bosom and disappeared into her lap. She stared at Celia openly. The thin man beside her unfolded himself from the chair and rose to his feet with a murmur.

The other man also rose, smiling warmly. It was the tall, sandy-haired man Celia had seen on deck. Those seated at the captain's table were not without rank, she knew that much about such things. Francis had seen that she was given the best accommodations available and every comfort the ship afforded.

The sandy-haired man drew out a chair and said, "Miss Skerritt . . ."

It surprised her that he knew her name. "Thank you."

He resumed his seat, leaning forward slightly as he made introductions. His gaze seemed to penetrate and she felt her pulse flutter nervously. "Miss Skerritt, may I introduce Mr. and Mrs. Emory Gladstone. Mr. Gladstone is with the governor-general's office in Calcutta."

"Delighted, my dear." Emory Gladstone bobbed his head as though it were caught on a string. His wife's expression flickered and her lips moved silently. He said, "Mr. Chadwick tells us you'll be living in Calcutta."

She turned to the man at her side, wondering how he knew so much about her, and once more feeling his gaze so deep that she was forced to lower her eyes.

"Oliver Chadwick," he said. "I am an agent with the East India Company. Captain Zapatha tenders his regrets that our departure keeps him too busy to join us this morning. Since I make this voyage often, he is kind enough to seat me at his table and provide me with a list of my fellow diners." He smiled and his expression softened. "The passage is far more pleasant when one knows others, don't you think?"

"Yes . . ." She felt immense relief. He had not singled her out but was performing a courtesy for all of them. She

138

relaxed visibly, sitting back in her chair and smiling around at the three.

"I trust you slept well," Emory Gladstone said. "The first night on board is generally quiet."

"I thought I would be restless but was amazed to discover I slept the night through," Celia said, finding her self-assurance growing. She felt none of the constraint that usually plagued her at such times. It was as though leaving England had somehow released her from the fetters of her own insecurity. She was a woman—about to be married—her dream of adventure to be fulfilled.

"Sea air is most bracing," Gladstone said. His wife glanced at him, then at Celia. Was it Celia's imagination or did the woman's gaze sweep over the brown wool dress and the diamond pendant at her throat?

Iris Beddington entered the dining room and came toward them, her eyes bright and her lips smiling. Her gaze swept the table. The two men rose and Oliver Chadwick came around to seat her.

"Good morning," she said brightly, her smile including all of them but settling on Oliver. She was wearing a rust-colored dress of heavy silk, one Celia thought improper for morning wear. The bodice was fastened with tiny covered buttons that seemed strained to the bursting point over her full heavy breasts. Emory Gladstone gazed at her until he realized his wife was glaring at him, then he looked away quickly. Oliver Chadwick was less self-conscious in his frank appraisal. None of the scrutiny seemed to bother Iris in the least.

She looked about, waiting for introductions, which Oliver made. Iris spared the Gladstones a glance, then attached her interest on Oliver. "Your name is familiar to me. I believe my husband works with you."

The remark seemed to amuse Chadwick but he nodded. "Yes, James is with the factory."

Iris frowned slightly and did not pursue it. She turned to Celia. "Your brother got off all right?"

"Yes—" Celia had not given a thought to Kevin since last night, so caught was she in her new adventure. She smiled as a steward leaned in to her with a tray of eggs and sausage. She hadn't realized how hungry she was but the smell of the food made her stomach rumble in a most unladylike manner.

"Will there be others dining with us?" she asked.

Oliver Chadwick nodded. "The Aramack is filled to capacity this voyage. The Company is expanding its holdings in Bengal and more than a hundred new families are coming over."

"So many!"

He laughed softly. "India is a very large country, Miss Skerritt."

Emory Gladstone said, "Lord Auckland is applying himself to bettering the Indian populace as well as England's interests. You may be astounded at the number of schools in operation. The heathen show a reluctance to learn but some education can be beaten into them." He looked about the table and smiled as though to show he was jesting.

"Ah, our other guests," Oliver said, glancing at a couple who approached the table. "Mr. and Mrs. Hare," Oliver said, standing until Mrs. Hare, a thin woman with a tired face and frightened eyes, took her place across from him. He continued the introductions, going around the table until each name had been spoken. As he sat, he signalled the waiter who hurried forward with hot food.

The Hares were also with the Company, she discovered. Benton Hare operated a trading post more than a hundred miles from Calcutta in the small province of Jharpur. Celia listened to the conversation and tried to absorb as much as she could. From time to time, the men tried to include her and Iris in the talk; each time Oliver Chadwick's gaze fell on her, Celia felt her face warm and had to look away. He seemed to see beneath the surface of her smile and probe her innermost thoughts, and the feeling made her distinctly uneasy. She was glad when the meal was finally over and she could escape to the deck for air.

She stood at the railing in a brisk wind that whipped at her skirts. She was glad of the wool cloak and warm bonnet Mary brought. The sky was still leaden and the breeze damp with spray. The dark waters were more roiled now that the ship had passed beyond the protection of the harbor. Waves rolled under frothy whitecaps, pitching the ship so the deck slanted. The food sat heavily in her stomach and Celia wondered at the wisdom of having come outside. She breathed deeply and found if she did not watch the churning water she felt better. She turned and came face to face with Oliver Chadwick.

"Enjoying the sea air, Miss Skerritt?"

She smiled. Once again she had the feeling he was looking inside her, yet he had been the soul of kindness and she could not fault his manners. "Yes, but it is chillier than I supposed."

"October is often treacherous—sun, then blowing, can't depend on it."

She bit her lip anxiously. "Are we in for a storm?" She glanced at the misty horizon; to think of the ship tossing and pitching made her stomach queasy once more.

He followed her glance to the northern sky where murky clouds skimmed the surface of the water. "I think not, at least for the present. The barometer is holding steady and that's a good sign." He offered his arm. "Will you do me the pleasure of walking around the deck?"

She hesitated, afraid of seeming rude if she refused, yet not sure she wanted to be alone with him any longer. What was it about him that disturbed her so? Before she could bring herself to answer, Oliver lifted her hand and slipped it under his arm, turning her about so the wind was at their backs, and began to stroll. "I understand from Captain Zapatha that you are traveling to meet Francis Devy in Calcutta."

He was a man of constant surprises. "Yes." What else did he know about her?

"Forgive me if it seems I've been prying. I assure you such was not my intent."

She nodded. "Francis and I are to be wed, as you undoubtedly know."

"Yes, and I know that Captain Devy is attached to the Queen's 49th Regiment, that he has spent two years in India and has recently returned from several months' leave at home." He looked at her with frank approval. "As a guess I would say that he met you during that leave, else he would have married you long ago and not left you behind."

Her cheeks flamed and she pretended to look out over

the waves. "You are quite right on all counts, Mr. Chadwick. I had no idea you were so well informed."

"It is not difficult when your betrothed is a man of such reputation." When she looked at him quickly, he smiled. "There is hardly a person in London who has not heard of him. The Devy family draws attention readily." He did not say that Francis Devy's escapades with women were the gossip of every elegant club in the city. "When Captain Devy asked Lord Skeffington to arrange the fastest and best passage for you, the Aramack was the logical choice, so I have the pleasure of walking with you now."

"Lord Skeffington?" It was the same name Mary had used.

"The Duke of Arbel. He's a close friend of the Devy family and holds a large interest in the East India Company.

"I see." She looked away that he might not notice the rush of color to her cheeks. The Duke of Arbel! Mention of him brought memories she would rather forget, though she had never met the man, but had the mischance to venture into his townhouse on the day of the Queen's coronation! "Is the Duke a friend of yours?"

He scowled for a moment but it was quickly replaced with a half-smile. "I have met him but I do not socialize with men of the Duke's standing. I am quite an ordinary businessman. I was fortunate enough to realize the opportunities that abound in the East and sign on with the Company. But I am acquainted with your husband-to-be."

She turned, wide-eyed. "Francis?"

He laughed. "Of course. Is there another?"

He was teasing her and she blushed prettily. "No, it is only that you surprise me."

"I've been in India so long as to be acquainted with many of the officers stationed in Calcutta. Francis Devy is a popular figure in social circles of Calcutta." He saw a warm glow of pride in her eyes, and he wondered again how Devy had managed to capture such an innocent prize. Devy's wealth kept his reputation from being blackened publicly but it was well known that he bedded women as easily as he sat his horse. He was known from the Dignity Balls of Cossitollah, where wenches had to content themselves with the few rupees tossed their way after a night's

142

entertaining, to the very finest homes along the Maidan where women of breeding were no less passionate in their dreams of marriage to the handsome young rogue. But Devy was not the type to settle down and be true to one woman—at least until now. Would this sweet beauty tame him at last?

Celia was pleased to hear that Francis was so well liked. How different her life would be with him! There would be parties, teas—all the things she had always envied for others and never shared. Belatedly she remembered her manners and turned the conversation back to her escort. "Have you been with the Company long?"

"Eight years. I started as a writer, counting bales and adding up invoices."

"Have you been in India the whole time?"

"My time is now divided between London and Calcutta."

"And your family?"

His dark eyes met hers once more and glinted in the grey light. "I am quite alone, with nothing to tie me to one place if I've a fancy for another."

His gaze seemed quite personal and probing all at once and Celia was relieved to see that they were once again at the passageway. She refused a second turn and went to her cabin. He was still staring after her as she closed the cabin door behind her.

CHAPTER EIGHT

The sea calmed as the shoreline of England faded from sight. To her surprise, Celia felt no lessening of the queasiness that had struck her after breakfast, and she remained in her cabin the rest of the day, refusing the meals Mary brought. The steady rolling motion of the ship seemed to unsettle her and by dusk she was violently ill, retching into a basin, too miserable to do more than moan as the girl wrung cold cloths and placed them on her brow. Mary undid the buttons of the brown dress and managed to slip the garment off, then removed Celia's shoes and stockings, leaving her in her chemise and covering her with a blanket.

Celia lay motionless as she tried to ease the dreadful nausea which had no end, in spite of the fact her stomach was empty. Mary hovered, her thin face pinched and drawn with worry. The cabin dimmed as the day faded and the sky outside the window became dark. Mary lighted the lantern, keeping it at the far side of the room so it would not disturb Celia but give enough light for her vigil.

Ceila dozed, only to come awake and retch again. The infernal motion of the ship was ceaseless and she was sure she would die. Francis ... Francis had said he too had suffered the malady of seasickness ... days, he'd said. The very thought made her shudder and set her stomach heaving again.

The next day was no better. Celia lay almost comatose,

rousing herself with effort when Mary held a cup to her lips and tried to coax her to sip water. She pushed the cup away, sure that it would make her violently ill again, and heard it crash to the floor. Mary looked stricken and Celia had not the strength to apologize for her unthinking act. The child was trying to help, she knew, but Celia wanted only to be left alone . . . to die, if she might.

Minutes or hours passed, she could no longer judge time. She heard a low murmur of voices and tried to open her eyes but the room was blurred and dim, with a wavering light at the opposite side that accented the motion of the ship. She moaned and closed her eyes.

The room quieted except for the creaking of the ship. A cool hand touched her brow and someone spoke her name.

"Celia . . . you must take this."

Not Mary . . . a man's voice. She stirred and licked her thick tongue over dry lips as she opened her eyes.

"I will hold you so you can sip." Hands raised her from the pillow, holding her steady as a cup was pressed to her lips. She tried to turn away from the pungent odor but the hands restrained her.

"It will make you feel better. There now, be a good girl and swallow."

The warm liquid was forced between her lips and trickled down her throat. When she thought she would gag, a hand lifted her chin and she swallowed miraculously.

"Again." More soothing liquid, slightly sweet but somehow calming. She swallowed more easily.

For several moments she lay back, still unable to rouse herself to full consciousness. The cabin was silent except for an occasional creak or the clank of a chain. Finally she opened her eyes.

Oliver Chadwick was sitting on the edge of the bed watching her with a concerned frown. When he saw her glance, he smiled. "The medicine will put your stomach to rights shortly. It would not be wise to try to get up just yet."

She nodded numbly, laying her head back and sighing deeply. She was beginning to feel better. How did he come to be here? She was grateful for his presence, though, and for the potion he had given her that calmed the unruly seething in her.

"Seasickness is a common malady," he said, talking softly as though to comfort her with the steady sound of his voice. "Many people suffer from it to some degree. You will be happy to know it usually doesn't last long."

She fluttered her lashes wearily. It seemed as if she had been ill for a very long time. Turning her head, she glanced at the window and was surprised to see the sky black beyond it.

"Mary was about to collapse with fatigue." At her quick look of alarm, he smiled. "She has fallen asleep in the chair." He pointed behind him. "Best let her sleep. You will have need of her services in the morning. Mark my words, you will be up and about."

Celia felt calmer and suddenly sleepy. Her eyelids were heavy and she found it difficult to keep them open. "Thank you," she murmured.

Oliver smiled and brushed the damp hair away from her face with gentle motions. His hand was cool, and a fluttering sigh escaped Celia's lips. She was beginning to feel better, some of the terrible anguish relieved. Even the motion of the ship seemed to lessen.

She slipped into a comforting sleep that soothed her body and mind. From time to time she drifted back to consciousness to see Oliver sitting at the side of the bed, watching her. How fortunate he had come along, but then a man who made many sea voyages would know the best remedy for sickness. She slept again.

The cabin was in deep shadows when she woke, the lantern wick turned down so it issued only a feeble glow. Celia was momentarily confused; she turned her head on the pillow and looked about. Oliver Chadwick was at the writing desk, his head fallen forward as he dozed. She remembered the medicine he'd given her and a rush of gratitude filled her. She felt completely over the sickness and ravenously hungry. Her mouth was dry and she longed for water. Lifting herself to one elbow she tried to reach the tumbler standing on the table near the bed. Her hand struck the table edge and the glass clattered. The sound brought Oliver awake instantly.

He crossed to her, reaching for the water tumbler. "You're feeling better?"

"Yes—" He slipped an arm under her head and lifted the glass to her lips. She drank greedily until he pulled the glass away.

"Not too much. It's better to take only a bit in your stomach at a time." He replaced the glass and lowered her to the pillow. In the shadowed room, his gaze seemed intent and his hand lingered at her shoulder. It was several moments before Celia realized that his hand was touching her flesh. With a gasp, she saw that she was clad in only a thin chemise. Oliver's gaze lingered on the high rise of her breasts and his fingers pressed into her shoulder.

"I—I am feeling much better," she said quickly, trying to draw back.

The pressure of his fingers eased but his hand did not pull away. Instead it moved to her throat and brushed the tangled hair with caressing motions.

"Please—" She did not want to seem ungrateful but she could not let him take such liberties. His closeness made her dizzy and frightened her. She clutched the cover which had slipped away and tried to draw it over her.

His gaze was piercing and his eyes darkened; then, quite suddenly, he withdrew his hand, pausing to tuck the cover about her chin as though she were a child.

"Have you sat here all night?" she asked. "I am most grateful."

"In some instances a stubborn case of mal-de-mer requires a second dose of medication. Besides, Mary is sound asleep. It would be a shame to wake her to keep vigil."

"But I am well, truly I am. There is no need—"

His smile lingered. "No need perhaps, but desire." His voice was deep and low and seemed full of hidden meaning. She felt her pulse race nervously. She was glad of the dim light in the cabin which hid her confusion.

"You must sleep again," he said in a very different tone, rising as he spoke and refilling the water glass from a pitcher. "I shall leave the glass close by. Drink only small amounts each time you wake." He stood a moment looking down at her and she watched him with wide eyes. His manner had changed so abruptly, she did not understand his shifting mood.

She nodded mutely, not trusting her voice. He crossed to the cabin door, and a moment later was gone.

By morning Celia felt completely well and ate a good breakfast which Mary brought on a tray. As soon as she had eaten, Celia bathed and let Mary brush her hair and arrange it in soft curls. After being in the cabin for two days, Celia was anxious for air, and Mary told her that the weather was wet and she'd best dress warmly.

On deck, Celia discovered that the sea was rough; she walked slowly in the lee of the cabins, pausing from time to time as the wind whipped the dark wool skirt about her feet. Still the brisk air was invigorating, and she filled her lungs gladly.

Oliver Chadwick emerged from a passageway and touched the wool cap that covered his head. "Mary told me you were up and about," he said, taking her arm without asking and leading her around the promenade in a slow circle, shielding her from the worst of the wind with his own body.

"I have not thanked you properly for your kindness," Celia said, raising her voice to carry over the wind.

"I am rewarded by your being well so quickly. I only regret that I did not know of your illness sooner so I could have spared you so much suffering."

"Are we in for a storm?" she asked.

"Yes. The waters of the Bay of Biscay are turbulent and storms are common here, but the Aramack is a sturdy vessel and there is no cause for alarm."

She was suddenly aware that she was not frightened at the increasing violence of the weather. She wondered aloud how it was possible to feel so well now when the lesser motion of the ship in calm weather had been enough to indispose her so wretchedly.

Oliver said it was often the case, and now that she had gotten her sea legs he doubted she would be ill again. They stood at the afterdeck and watched the dark clouds gather along the horizon as though resting on the distant waves. The sea was dotted with frothy whitecaps which rode high one moment and were sucked into deep troughs

148

the next. The wind took on a bite that made Celia shiver and draw her cloak close. Huge waves thrashed against the ship, sending up misty spray that stung her cheeks.

"You would be more comfortable in the saloon," Oliver said. "The Captain has ordered music to take minds off the storm."

She nodded, unable to speak in the face of the wind, and let him lead her inside. The ship was rolling hard and it was difficult to keep her footing. Oliver steadied her.

The saloon was crowded and everyone was chattering and laughing to dispel the gloom. Celia shook back her cloak and felt the warmth at her cheeks as Iris hurried toward them.

"You're well! And looking none the worse for your ordeal," she said, smiling at Celia and taking her arm as Oliver removed the cloak and hung it near the door. The three sat and were joined by several other passengers whom Celia did not know. Iris seemed to have lost no time in becoming acquainted, and several young men asked her to dance and she swept out to the floor without hesitation. Oliver ordered tea and they sipped it as they watched the dancers.

"Would you care to dance?"

Celia was tempted—the sound of the lively music had set her feet tapping, but she was still a little weak. She encouraged Oliver to seek another partner.

"I would prefer talking with you," he said, dismissing the matter. "Tell me about yourself. You are not from London."

"No, a village called Renfield," she said. She began to tell of her life there and of her year at school in the city. He listened, smiling now and then at her animated description and thinking how lovely she was. Francis Devy was a lucky man to have found himself a woman like Celia. Oliver knew enough about the Devy family to recognize that a parson's daughter was a step down, even when she was as lovely as this creature. He suspected that young Devy pushed for marriage only when he could get her no other way. He watched Celia's expressive face and her sparkling eyes. She was innocent, to be sure, and it set a man's heart and body afire knowing it. She seemed totally unaware of her effect on him. He thought again of the smooth silk-

iness of her skin as he'd lifted her to sip the medicine ...
and how his fingers had lingered. She deserved better than
young Devy.

When she finished her recital, her cheeks glowed and
she looked lovelier than before, if that was possible. Oliver
saw Iris Beddington watching covertly as she danced by.
There was quite a different woman, one who had learned
the delights of passion well, he'd wager. And one who fancied herself above her station because of her husband's rising position. He'd been amused at her question as to
whether or not he knew James Beddington. The man was
a mere clerk at the factory. Yet Iris had supposed he
might work at Oliver's side. At least she had wished to
impress others that he might. No harm in her little deception, he'd let her play it without exposing her.

Still, he had been surprised to meet Iris in first class.
Beddington's salary would not seem to warrant such luxury. Perhaps the man had other income. Service with the
East India Company was attracting people of caliber these
days, and many middle class men found respectable
careers for themselves in the east. Hadn't he left an un-
promising clerk's job to do that very thing himself? He
rarely thought of his wretched beginnings or his life in a
London slum anymore. Even now, he pushed the thought
from his mind impatiently. He was on his way to becoming a rich man and he did not have to look back.

The rest of the day passed pleasantly. Celia remained in
the saloon, listening to the music and chatting with various
people who stopped at the table to be introduced by Oliver. They lunched in the dining room, then ventured to
the deck again to find the storm had broken and the deck
awash with rain and spray and completely unsafe for
walking. They returned to the saloon and joined a group
gathered to watch an impromptu playlet put on by some
of the young children. Celia was delighted, clapping her
hands and laughing merrily, completely enjoying herself.
When she found Oliver staring at her, her cheeks warmed.

Celia retired to her cabin immediately after dinner, tired
from the day's activities. The rain streamed the windows,
blurring the darkness outside. The sounds of the storm
were loud; she sighed as she sat at the writing desk to pen
a letter to her parents. The Aramack would be touching

port at Gibraltar in two days, and she would be able to post it there. How far away Renfield seemed!

The fifth day out they sighted the Spanish mountains and Cape St. Vincent, then Cadiz and Trafalgar Bay. Through the hazy, lingering light of the setting sun, they saw the massive outlines of Gibraltar, like a crouching lion in the midst of the sea. A strong current from the west favored them, and the Aramack drove forward rapidly in order to gain the bay before gun-fire. The brilliant light of Europa Point appeared in the growing darkness.

"The Rock ahead!" thundered the gruff, husky voice of the watch at the bow. The ship's pace slackened at once. The steam fumed and screeched; the chain cable rattled and shook the vessel, then fell for the night. The officer of *pratique* appeared in a boat, came on board, and after his inspection of the ship's papers, gave permission for the passengers and crew to visit the city between the hours of sunrise and sunset the following day. Celia arranged to go ashore with Oliver and Iris, then retired early so she might be rested and fresh for the exciting day ahead.

Gibraltar was so unlike the English countryside she was accustomed to that it took Celia's breath away. The city sloped rapidly upward from the water's edge to the ridge of the mountain rock, some 1300 feet high. The town and a line of military works skirted the base of the rock along the western side; fortifications and batteries formed tiers, one above the other to the very summit, and numerous holes from interior galleries showed the mouths of cannons pointing toward the sea. Celia felt awed by such a display of military power, yet was comforted by the knowledge that the power was England's.

They toured the city by carriage, and Celia was as excited as on her first visit to London. Much smaller, Gibraltar had an exotic air. Spanish peasants, swarthy, stalwart figures clad in velvet breeches and tight embroidered jackets, with slouched, conical black hats and crimson sashes—oftener than not with long gleaming knives tucked in them—rode large powerful mules showily arrayed in crimson and yellow trappings. The animals were burdened with bundles of grain, fruits, and various hidden provisions that filled the air with mingled spicy aromas. The Moors from the Barbary coast were resplendent in loose flowing

151

blue robes and crimson and yellow upturned pointed slippers, their ebony faces overshadowed by huge white turbans. Dark men with flowing beards and greasy clothing ... coarsely clad Spanish peasants laden with baskets atop their heads ... Spanish ladies in graceful mantillas of black lace and closely drawn veils ... and English soldiers in bright scarlet uniforms, English women dressed as though to ride in Hyde Park, rosy children tended by uniformed nurses as they played in small parks ...

The hillsides were covered with cactus, aloe and geraniums flowering in profusion wherever they could find footing on the steep and rugged rock. The market place overflowed with people and bright wares; above the noise, a military band played "God Save the Queen" and "Rule, Britannia."

Celia felt caught in the wonder of it all. How exciting to be outside her native land, seeing such color and excitement at first hand. Would India be similar? To think she would be part of it!

When they returned to the ship, Celia was exhausted and sure that the wonderful day was a portent of her new life. She had seen things she never dreamed of, and thanks to Oliver Chadwick's knowledgeable commentary, she had learned a great deal about Gibraltar. She could hardly wait to write her family or to tell Francis the wonders of the day. The Aramack sailed at gun-fire. The passengers lined the rails to watch the coast of Barbary pass in the fading light. Celia, like many others, retired to her cabin early and fell into exhausted sleep as the ship moved into the Mediterranean.

The days grew steadily warmer as the ship passed the Spanish coast, with the high Sierras visible for the entire first day, then into the blue waters off Africa. Celia drifted into the easy shipboard life, one so idyllic as to seem unreal, and she had to continually remind herself it was all true. She was thousands of miles from Renfield, and she felt somehow older than the few intervening days would account for. Life at the parsonage and the school, and her indecisions were all behind her. She was learning about Algiers, Tunis, Carthage, not from pages of a book but from interesting accounts given by Oliver Chadwick as the

Aramack followed its course through clear blue water where huge fishes sported and darted.

The second port of call was the island of Malta, which they reached on the tenth day. Celia accepted Oliver's invitation to show her the city of Valetta, and they joined dozens of others in the picturesque boats that put off from the quay and vied to ferry passengers ashore. From antique, canoelike skiffs, tawny men and boys, dark skinned and all but naked, exhibited extraordinary feats of diving after coins people threw.

On shore, Celia and Oliver climbed successive streets of "cursed stairs," pushing their way through hosts of touters and beggars who grasped and pleaded in soft sibilant tones. Celia would have paused to fish coins from her reticule, but Oliver warned her that to do so would cause them to be harassed endlessly. They visited an ancient church and wandered along twisting streets, past quaint shops and whitewashed houses. The day passed quickly and most enjoyably. When Oliver led her along a shadowy side street and into the dim dining room of a small hotel, Celia was glad to relax over a glass of wine while Oliver talked. It seemed he had been everywhere; she listened in fascination as he told of Egypt, India and the Orient. She caught herself staring and was suddenly aware of his bold handsomeness. When his eyes met hers, she dropped her gaze.

She asked dozens of questions about India and what her life might be like there. He answered carefully, not wanting to tell her the many hardships she would face. She was like a child eager for adventure. It worried him that she was so fragile, and he wondered if she would withstand the rigors of eastern climate and disease. When she laughed, it stirred his blood, renewing his desire for her. He had watched her with longing since his first glimpse of her, his blood running hot each time she was close. He'd said nothing, biding his time until he was sure she would accept him. What matter if her soldier waited at voyage's end? Likely enough young Devy was not wasting time pining for his betrothed, not with the ready availability of wenches in Calcutta. He'd stay away from the unattached English females, at least for the time. There'd been enough of a scandal last year when the daughter of one of the Company subalterns killed herself when Devy broke off their affair. She'd fancied herself as Mrs. Devy, but the young Captain had no such intentions, and the girl couldn't face the gossip when she discovered she was with child. The matter had been hushed up quickly—Devy's money had seen to that—and soon afterwards Devy had taken leave to return to England.

And now he had a bride joining him, and he'd be very proper and respectable.

Oliver poured wine again and spoke to the waiter in Maltese to order a light dinner for both of them and ask the man to arrange a room. Celia was gazing about, her face animated and her eyes shining. He had never seen her lovelier.

Celia felt giddy and lightheaded, but she accepted another glass of wine as he poured. The dinner was superb, delicate shrimp in a tasty sauce, seafood bisque, thinly sliced fowl baked en casserole, and tiny fresh vegetables. She was surprised at her appetite; Oliver smiled and attributed it to the clear air and delicious wine. When she protested she'd had enough, he frowned and said the maitre d' would be insulted if the wine bottle was not emptied. They laughed and drank again.

Celia let him hold her arm as they left the dining room. She was quite dizzy and glad of his support, and she frowned in puzzlement as they went along a dim corridor and upstairs. Then all at once they were in a clean, neat, small room. She looked about and tried to clear her thoughts.

"The Aramack does not sail until morning," Oliver said. "I think you will be comfortable here."

"We should go back." But the effort seemed too much, and she let him take her bonnet and shawl. From somewhere, he brought another bottle of wine and two glasses.

"No more, really!"

"To toast your loveliness," he said, standing very close and holding the glass to her lips.

She sipped and turned away, dizzy as the room spun about her. "Francis—"

"Francis would want you to enjoy yourself."

She sighed, remembering Francis's smile and the delight

he took in her laughter. She closed her eyes and would have swayed but was caught in Oliver's strong arms. Then he was holding her close, murmuring her name over and over, pressing his lips to her throat so that she felt his warm breath.

"Francis—"

Oliver stifled his anger and impatience at the innocence of her longing. Francis Devy be damned—India was a far distance. They were here and now. He raised his eyes from the sweet-smelling hair and gazed at her upturned face. Her eyes were closed, a dreamy smile played upon her full red lips, inviting him, taunting him. He kissed her, crushing her mouth under his and feeling his pulse race.

Celia felt a moment of panic and tried to pull away but Oliver's arms held her too tightly; his lips sought hers again, urging, promising, setting her aflame. His hands caressed her, making her flesh tingle and stirring a deep need within her. She sighed tremulously.

She was almost limp in his arms. Oliver felt the subtle yielding of her body to his caresses. She would forget Francis Devy. He would bring her passion to flowering and give life to the woman in her.

He lifted her and carried her to the bed. Celia tried to speak, but she was caught in a maelstrom, drawn deeper and deeper by rioting passions. His hands were deft and gentle at her dress, undoing it and drawing it off. She shivered, though the air was warm and his touch gentle. She wanted to cry out, to send him away, but her mouth was dry and her tongue thick.

Then it was too late. His body was hot against hers and his voice entreating.

"Celia—Celia—"

He was upon her, pinning her as she tried to writhe free. Her eyes opened in terror but his face was a blur ... so close.

"No—"

"Don't deny me—"

She struggled but every move seemed only to aid him. His surging weight was heavy on her. She could not stop the quivering of her body as he thrust, entering her in a warm rush and sending her into a paroxysm of passion. Thrashing her head from side to side, she bit her lip until she tasted blood and her fingers raked his flesh. A cry escaped her as her body joined his and seemed to explode.

She fell back, panting and unable to control her shivering. Oliver roused himself to stare at her in wonder. His own pleasure had been intense yet he was sure she had given herself to him completely, despite her early protests. He touched her cheek and wiped away the tears that trickled there, soothing her as she whimpered. He drew her into his arms and caressed her silky skin, whispering soft, tender endearments to gentle her.

Celia lay satiated of body and wretched of mind, filled with revulsion at what she had done. How could her body torment and trap her so? She felt tears burn at her eyelids, and felt Oliver's gentle touch brush them away as they overflowed. She tried to turn from him but his hand cupped her cheek and she was powerless to move. A thought of Francis blurred her mind and she shuddered in humiliation. How could such a thing happen when she loved him so? She sobbed and turned her face to the wall.

"It's all right," Oliver said softly, still brushing at her cheek with his fingertips.

"I'm so ashamed—" The words came with a sob and she caught her lip between her teeth.

"You are a woman. It is nothing to be ashamed of."

She opened her eyes and stared at him, pushing at his body as though it suddenly burned her. He gaped in surprise, so abrupt was the change in her mood.

"I am betrothed! You had no right—"

He sat back, an amused smile playing at his lips. "You seemed willing enough a few moments ago."

The truth of his words stung her like a whip. She scrambled from the bed, snatching at her clothing and pressing as far from him as possible while she struggled into the chemise. Her cheeks burned and her hands trembled; the fine linen seemed to tangle in her fingers as she pulled the garment in place, not daring to look at Oliver's nakedness and not trusting herself to speak again. When he moved, she looked up in alarm, but he did not come near her; instead he dressed in silence and strode from the room. She completed her dressing, wanting nothing more than to flee before he might return. She had no idea how to get back to the quay, but she would manage. She could never face Oliver Chadwick again!

But he was waiting in the hall when she emerged from the room, his face dark and his eyes guarded. He took her arm and she pulled away from him in fury.

His voice was impatient. "I have a carriage waiting downstairs. It is not safe for you to be on the streets alone." He gripped her hand so she could not free herself. Arm in arm they descended the stairs and went through the small lobby of the hotel. There was only a sleepy-eyed clerk who roused himself to stare at them. Celia felt that her shame must be exposed for public view, and she walked with eyes downcast.

Oliver helped her into the small open carriage, sitting beside her and signaling the driver curtly. The horse stepped into motion, its hoofs echoing on the cobblestoned street.

They rode in silence to the waterfront; Celia stood numbly while Oliver paid off the cab and arranged for a boat to ferry them across to the Aramack. Now and then she felt Oliver's gaze but she did not look at him. She was strangely subdued, yet much unsettled, and she longed for the privacy of her cabin.

She was glad to see most of the ship's lights dimmed and the deck empty of passengers. She could not bear to face anyone now! Oliver left her at the door of the cabin and she rushed inside, leaning against the door and fighting back the hot tears that threatened. Mary, who had been dozing in the chair near the foot of the bed, jumped up at the sound of the door. The lantern was turned low, and Celia cried out when Mary moved to raise it.

"No—" The shadows afforded a measure of security. "I—you may go to your cabin now, Mary, I shan't need you." Bobbing her head, the girl went out, glancing back in wonder but saying nothing.

Celia sank to the bed, covering her face with her hands and allowing the tears to come. What had she done? Oh God, what had she done! She sobbed uncontrollably until at last she was drained of tears; she rose to blow out the lantern, undressed in the dark and slid into bed. She tried to think of Francis, but her mind rejected such relief; she shivered and pressed her face to the pillow, moaning.

Iris strolled the deck, watching the shore lights blink and waver. Oliver and Celia had not returned to the ship with the others ... had still not returned, though it was close to midnight. When she saw the small boat approaching, a lantern at the bow, she slipped into the shadows of a companionway as Oliver and Celia came aboard. Curious, Iris made her way along the passage, staying far enough behind that she would not be seen if one of them should turn unexpectedly, and watched until Oliver bid Celia goodnight—quite properly—and departed to his own cabin.

She had hoped to see more of Oliver Chadwick during the voyage. He was in a position to be helpful in her husband's career, or in her own life if James's new-found prosperity vanished as suddenly as it had come. Or if his drinking habits brought him to grief. She gathered that many of the Company men in India drank to excess. There seemed little else to do in such a hot, heathen land.

What would her life be like there? It was hard to visualize. James assured her that she would be accepted as any proper Englishwoman, and there was a sizable English colony in Calcutta. She would have servants—that idea amused her. Long ago, she had run away from home and sold herself into service with a fine family, one whose master found special pleasure in having a young girl to warm his bed whenever he took a fancy for her. She had early learned that the surest place for a man to ignore a girl's background was in bed, and she'd used the knowledge to get herself the things she wanted in life. Except a husband. None of the fine men who found her body so delightful had any ideas of marrying her. James was cut of the same cloth as herself. He knew what he wanted and he was determined to get it, though sometimes she had misgivings about his schemes. The South Africa diamond affair had almost cost him his life—and hers—and they were lucky to get out of it alive. They had to start over but she had the feeling that this time it would work. Hadn't James already sent enough money for the fine new clothes and first-class passage to join him? She was traveling with the very best, and none doubted her right to do so.

She frowned, thinking of Oliver Chadwick again. No matter what his position with the Company, he was not the fine gentleman he pretended. His background paralleled her own, she was sure. Market Court left scars on a child that could not be disguised by fancy clothing or a polished manner of speech. Oliver had the same smouldering anger in his eyes that confronted her each time she studied her reflection in the glass ... a hatred and determination to climb out of the squalor that was their heritage, to escape the physical bonds of the slum and never look back.

She sighed and made her way to her cabin, thinking about Oliver and Celia being ashore until so late an hour. Was the future Mrs. Devy as innocent as she appeared?

CHAPTER NINE

Celia woke feeling sluggish in the morning, her head still throbbing from the unaccustomed wine. She'd slept poorly, and dreamed troubled dreams that did not fade with the light. She dreaded facing Oliver, yet she worried about remaining in the cabin lest he should come in search of her. She knew she could not isolate herself forever. Reluctantly, she resumed shipboard life, keeping Mary close at her side during the day and bidding her sleep in the big chair at the foot of the bed at night.

The journey from Malta to Alexandria was short, taking less than three days before the Aramack came into sight of the harbor and an Arab pilot came on board to conduct them between the outlying sunken rocks. Oliver had made no reference to the events in Malta, and Celia put the episode out of her mind.

The last night on board was one of festivity, with laughter and music that even Celia found irresistible. She let herself be drawn into the dancing, although she avoided Oliver, and she felt more lighthearted than she had for many days. The sun set gloriously, flooding the ship with vermilion and gold, while opposite, the moon rose as from a furnace of molten metal. Celia slept soundly and was up early the next morning, as Mary scurried about tending to the last packing and readying the bags for unloading. When the Aramack neared the city, several barge-like boats approached from both sides; Arabs, Egyptians and Nubians, some scarcely clothed, others in all variety of garments, clambered up the sides and crowded the deck. One of the ship's officers shouted instructions and they set to work in unbelievable confusion and hurry. Trunks tumbled over the ship in all directions as the Arabs screamed and gesticulated frantically, running about and unloading the baggage onto the tender that was to take the passengers ashore.

The harbor was crowded with ships flying flags of many nations. As soon as the tender landed, eager children, dark-skinned and ragged looking, rushed to vie for porter duties, and surly, bearded dragomen called out, trying to sell their services as interpreters and guides. Celia was overcome by the bustle and confusion. She stood at the dock's edge staring about and not knowing what to do.

"Allow me once again to serve as escort . . ." Oliver Chadwick touched her elbow. His dark eyes held hers for a moment and she felt a moment of rage. Still she could not refuse—she would never manage to find her way alone. The din was deafening and Celia thought she might retch with the odor of dead fish and live Arabs.

Oliver snapped his fingers and a dark, melancholy dragoman scurried to them, bobbing and nodding as Oliver gave him instructions for the baggage. Seeing Iris nearby, Oliver asked her to join them and instructed the man about her baggage as well. Celia recovered from her first dismay at the strangeness and stared in wonder. It was so vastly different from anyplace she had seen thus far on the journey. Despite the heat and the dirt, it had a certain fascination and she felt a distinct sense of relief at Oliver's taking charge.

Oliver led the two women, with Mary following at Celia's heels, across the crumbling quay piled with bales of merchandise and the newly arrived cargo from the Aramack. A sea of white-turbaned heads followed their progress; beyond, Celia saw ugly long-necked camels that kicked out viciously with their hind legs, spitting, grunting and groaning angrily. She was glad when only the baggage was piled on the beasts. Oliver led them to the mouth of a narrow, irregular street where an open carriage, pulled by a handsome white horse, waited. Oliver spoke to the driver as he helped the women in. Celia quickly beckoned Mary to sit beside her, thus forcing Oliver to seat himself next to Iris, who didn't seem to mind at all.

The edges of the city were encrusted with the wretched hovels of Arab poor; immense mounds and tracts of rubbish filled the wide space between the city and its walls. Flies droned ceaselessly and the heat seemed to wrap the incredible stench about them. Celia pressed a handkerchief to her nose and forced herself not to retch. She tried to fill her mind with the beauty of the Oriental, mud-colored buildings with terraced roofs, fat mosques and soaring minarets. Their emergence into the European sector of the city was akin to coming from a nightmare to a soothing dream. The filthy lanes gave way to wide, clean streets, flanked by spotless square white houses over which flags of every nation in Europe fluttered in the warm breeze. Oliver explained that they were in the Frank quarter and the flags denoted the residences of the various consuls. An endless variety of costumes were to be seen. A drove of camels knelt as jet black slaves in crimson caps arranged the burdens. Women whispered by in shroudlike veils that left only their gleaming ebon eyes uncovered.

Iris exclaimed over each new sight and listened intently as Oliver spoke of native customs and pointed out landmarks of the city. Celia was silent; she still found it difficult to believe that she was so far from home, and she was content to avoid any conversation that might lead Oliver to believe he could resume their intimacy.

They stayed the night in the Orient Hotel, and Celia declined Oliver's offer of a ride to view the city. He accepted her refusal in the same unperturbed manner that he had evidenced toward her ever since the incident at Malta. She was delighted to learn that Francis had arranged a room for her, one with the marvelous luxury of a huge tiled tub in a small alcove near the windows! She had not had a comfortable bath since leaving home, and she watched impatiently while two maids in flowing white robes caught tight at their waists filled the tub with tepid water. From Celia's traveling case, Mary brought out soap and a soft sponge while Celia undressed and lowered herself into the tub. Mary would have scrubbed her back, but Celia waved the girl away and laid back to soak for a long time before she stirred enough to use the soap. The water was delightful. Celia squeezed the sponge and let streams trickle over her body, then scrubbed at her flesh until it gleamed pink under the frothy bubbles of foam. It was as though she were scrubbing away all memories of Oliver's lovemaking—no, she could not use the term love for what he had done—his degradation of her body, erasing the slate clean if she could, so she might go to Francis unblemished.

The journey began again shortly after sunup. They were taken to another waterway that connected the port of Alexandria with the Rosetta branch of the Nile, from thence to travel down the canal on a barge towed by a small steamer. On their arrival in Atféh, they transferred to another steamer to take them to Cairo. Celia had a comfortable cabin and was pleased at the privacy it afforded. The ship was smaller and less pretentious than the Aramack, but she was able to shield herself from the ugly sights along the shore. Egypt was depressing, and she longed for the journey to be over. She retired early and slept a troubled sleep, fraught with disturbing dreams. The air was heavy with the insistent buzzing of flies at the netting. She tossed and tangled in the bedclothes, coming awake from dreams of Oliver Chadwick with her heart pounding and limbs trembling.

She rose red-eyed and weary in the morning and bathed before dressing in a light muslin gown. She instructed Mary to bring her tea and biscuits; she had no appetite for the fruits or strange-tasting cakes that had become staple in their diet since arriving in Egypt but longed for the simple fare she'd known all her life. Though the heat of the cabin was oppressive, she would not go on deck where she would surely meet Oliver. She could not sort her feelings about him. Alone with her conscience, she despised his boldness and arrogance, yet in his presence her resolve seemed to waver and threaten to vanish.

The passengers traveling on to Suez spent one night at a hotel in Cairo before proceeding by coach across the desert. Celia had been warned that the desert travel was arduous, but it was worse than she imagined anything could be. Many times during the sixty hours she thought she would not survive, so hot was the carriage, so dusty the air. The travelers were divided into several conveyances drawn by gleaming black teams; the cargo was piled upon camels to cover the miles from Cairo to Suez. The carriages raced as though through the flames of hell with the devil himself chasing. Conversation was impossible and the women were too unnerved to do more than cling to the sides of the coach. Nights were passed in crude tents which offered few comforts or conveniences. By the time they reached Suez and the steamer that was to take them down the Red Sea and across India, Celia was exhausted beyond belief. She could scarcely walk and was unable to protest when Oliver assisted her aboard and saw her to her cabin. She collapsed upon the bunk for a few moments, then managed to rouse herself. "Where is Mary?"

"I will send her to you immediately," he said softly.

She nodded and closed her eyes. She ached over every inch of her body; her eyes and throat were raw and dry from the constant buffeting of wind and sand. She heard Mary and struggled to open her eyes. The girl's pinched face was pale but she smiled bravely.

"Mr. Chadwick gave me a letter for you," she said.

Celia could not muster the effort to answer.

"It's from India, from Captain Devy, mum . . ."

Francis? Celia tried to sit up but fell back against the pillow. She wet her lips with a thick tongue and whispered, "Read it—"

The child shook her head. "I don't know my letters, mum."

Celia wept as Mary placed the letter in her outstretched hand so she might clasp it, trying to feel Francis's presence through the words written within. She was numb and only dimly aware of Mary coaxing her to undress, the cool cloth laid upon her brow. She felt the motion of the boat and knew that they were underway but she could not raise her head from the pillow.

She tossed with fever throughout the night, still clutching Francis's letter. Mary grew more and more worried, and when she heard the stirring of other passengers, went in search of Mr. Chadwick. Her mistress seemed not to know her, and was far too ill to be cured by a bit of rest.

Oliver went to Celia's cabin at once and after a quick glance, summoned the physician who had joined them in

Cairo. The doctor could not put a name to the illness but there was no doubt that Celia required constant nursing—sponge baths to hold down the fever, cool compresses to shield her eyes from the light. He dosed her liberally with a prescription of calomel and julep in case she had somehow come in contact with the plague, though the season was well over. He promised to visit her daily; there was not much else to be done, though Oliver pressed him.

Mary refused to leave Celia's side even when she was ready to drop with exhaustion. Iris came on the third day and took charge, putting Mary to bed, then tending Celia with a brisk efficiency that surprised Oliver. He had not thought Iris the kind to look after anyone but herself. Still, he supposed there was a touch of compassion in every woman.

The steamer journeyed through the Red Sea, putting in at Aden to refuel, then setting across the last leg of the voyage. Though Oliver fretted over Celia, there was nothing more he could do. She was being tended and doctored in every manner possible, though he would have given anything to ease her suffering. He called at her cabin daily, often being refused admittance by Iris but glimpsing Celia lying pale and feverish on the bed. Her face was drawn, with dark circles beneath the blue eyes that had enchanted him so. Iris watched him with a curious stare, but said nothing other than a few words concerning Celia when he asked about her condition.

On the fifth day past Aden, Iris slipped out into the passageway to talk with Oliver. Mary had appeared, rested from a nap, to take over the nursing duties; Iris sighed and told Oliver there was no change. "She's delirious and speaks constantly of Francis."

Oliver felt a twinge of irritation but quickly hid it, though not quickly enough to escape Iris's notice. She was right then—there was, or at least had been, something between them. Strangely, the knowledge did not upset her, although she had to admit a fondness for Celia's naive, almost childlike wonder at the world. During the past days, Celia babbled often of Francis and her love for him to Iris's constant amazement. She had never felt anything akin to such emotion for James.

Oliver walked her to her cabin, and she invited him in

for a glass of brandy. She had secured a bottle from the steward to ease her weary muscles and mind these past days. Oliver seemed preoccupied with Celia's condition, asking questions as Iris took the brandy bottle from the cupboard and set out two glasses. Oliver poured, and she lifted her glass. "It's poor hospitality but the best I can offer."

He recalled his manners tardily. "Forgive me, you are exhausted and I continue to babble on. To your very good health and your kindness."

They drank, Iris quaffing the brandy in only a few swallows as she sank into the chair and sighed. "The doctor thinks the fever must break soon. Perhaps seeing Francis will cure her."

A shadow crossed his eyes and she suppressed a smile of jealous satisfaction. She was sorry she was not wearing something that showed her figure to better advantage. She'd taken to wearing plain cottons and muslins while tending Celia; now she was mussed and tired, hardly at her best. Still, the yellow dress was provocatively tight across her bosom and showed a deep shadow of cleavage at the neckline. His gaze was drawn to it and she smiled inwardly. She held out her glass and allowed him to fill it once more, drinking slowly this time and feeling her tired muscles relax.

"How long have you been away from India, Oliver?"

"Five months. I handled some Company affairs in London."

"Will you be glad to be back in Calcutta?"

"Yes. I find the factory a challenge."

"And does a woman wait for you?"

"I have no one. As you know I am unmarried."

"But not unattracted, surely."

His eyes caressed her and she saw a glow of interest. He read her meaning well. She had been away from James more than a year, and although not without satisfying partners in the interim, she was weary of the young soldier who had occupied her time since leaving England.

"A man is attracted by all lovely women. It is only a question of reciprocal feelings."

She lowered her gaze and watched him covertly. "James and I have been separated much during our marriage."

166

She sipped the brandy and felt its heady glow. "It is sometimes difficult for a man to get ahead in his career."

"A hard-working man succeeds." He watched her over the rim of the goblet. She was without Celia Skerritt's loveliness but he could read the willingness in her words and expression. Iris Beddington was a woman who knew what she wanted from life and was not timid about getting it. He felt a quickened pulse of physical desire as he watched her breasts rise and fall with each breath. The dark line of shadow between the creamy-fleshed mounds enticed his eyes. She leaned to place the glass on the table, and he made no effort to avoid the glimpse of additional loveliness it gave him. She looked up, a slight smile at the corners of her mouth.

"James is very hard working, I assure you, Oliver. But then you said you knew him?"

"I know all the men who work under me. It aids the operation of the factory to be aware of each man's capabilities."

"And the men's wives?" She smiled invitingly. "Does it help to know them as well?"

He finished the brandy in a swallow and set aside the glass. He rose and moved to her, taking her hand and drawing her from the chair, holding her close so that her breath was hot against his face. "Most assuredly." He bent his lips to her eager mouth and felt the instant response of her body. He blotted out thoughts of Celia and gave himself to the moment, moving with Iris to the bed and watching with open interest as she removed her dress and chemise, then lay upon the bed to watch him undress.

Her body was responsive and eager, meeting his in a rush of passion that surprised and delighted him. For the time, all other thoughts were driven from his mind. There was no pretense of love with Iris, only release in the physical act which she enjoyed as much as he. She was a wanton, writhing and twisting under him until she gained her own erotic peaks and brought him to his. When it was over, they lay immersed in silent thoughts as if they had never been intimate at all.

Celia showed the first signs of throwing off the illness when the mail packet was well across the Indian Ocean.

167

The greatest part of the journey was behind them, the ship having rounded Cape Cormorin and touched briefly at Ceylon before proceeding up the Coromandel Coast. When they reached Madras, Celia was well enough to sit in a chair on deck, wrapped about with a light blanket to ward off sudden chills. The doctor pronounced her out of danger, and she was dazed to think that so much of the journey had passed unbeknownst to her.

At long last, she opened and read the letter Mary had brought her at Suez, and she lingered lovingly over each word that Francis had written. He loved her ... they would be together soon ... he was waiting ...

Nothing else mattered.

CHAPTER TEN

December 1838, Calcutta

The Aramack steamed up the Hooghly, nearing Calcutta. Celia's excitement grew as she viewed the richly wooded river banks, splendidly green and studded with handsome buildings one moment and picturesque native villages with thatch-roofed huts the next. Occasionally a native woman clad in white and carrying a water urn on her head paused to stare at the passing ship. Celia sat on deck with Mary at her side, exclaiming over each new sight as if it had been placed there for her enjoyment alone. A touch of color had returned to her cheeks, kept bright by thoughts of Francis. She was in high spirits and eager with anticipation. When Iris stopped to chat, Celia was filled with gratitude and a deep affection for the woman who had nursed her through the long illness. She was even kindly disposed toward Oliver when he paused and studied her with a concerned gaze. She had not forgotten the incident in Malta, nor would she forgive his conduct, but the edges of the memory had already begun to blur.

About five miles out of the city, the first palatial buildings could be seen along the Garden Reach. A succession of white houses, gleaming in the brilliant sun, was surrounded by lawns and plantations like so many English country estates. On one shore, a huge botanical garden showed splashes of riotous colors. The bold winding of the river, masts of ships in the harbor and a broad expanse of public buildings in the distance gave an air of grandeur that took Celia's breath away. She had not expected anything so wonderful, and her anticipation seemed to increase by the moment. She could barely sit still while the ship approached the harbor and dozens of small boats put out from shore to meet it.

Her baggage had been brought up and was arranged neatly along the rail, where it could be removed quickly. Mary stared wide eyed at the naked natives who propelled skiffs and dinghies toward the ship, yelling and crying out as they competed for attention.

Standing at the rail, Celia watched the boats approach. This was Calcutta, the end of her long journey! Her heart thudded in her breast and her pulse was racing. Only a brief span of water separated her now from Francis! He would be waiting for her and they would— She gasped, holding the rail with both hands, leaning out. That man— in the leading boat! It looked like—it *was!*

"Francis! Francis!" She screamed his name, almost fainting with joy at sight of him. Francis was in uniform, the scarlet coat the brightest sun she had ever seen. His tall figure was poised and straight. As he saw her, he tore off his cap, waved it, calling her name then urging the dinghy-wallah to more speed.

Celia ran along the rail, heedless of the other passengers as she shoved to gain a place near the head of the ladder flung over the side. In the next moment Francis was rushing up the steps, vaulting the rail, driving like a wedge into the crowd to take her in his arms.

"Celia—Celia—my dearest love!"

She turned her face to his kisses, feeling faint in the warm circle of his arms. The uncertainties of the past months vanished and suddenly she was marvelously alive. It was as if she had come through a long, dark tunnel to emerge into the sunlight of Francis's smile.

He drew her aside, out of the press. "Darling, let me look at you! It's been a blasted eternity!" He drew back for an instant then, laughing, pulled her close again, kissing her. She had an impression of other people smiling at Francis's ardor, but she didn't care. Her body quivered against his and she felt a rush of emotion that startled her.

Abruptly he pulled free again, his eyes pools of desire. He took her arm. "Come, I've got a boat waiting." He led her to the ladder.

"My trunks—Francis! And Mary—"

He laughed. "I completely forgot. I've eyes for nothing but you, love." He turned and spoke to two natives, indicating the luggage Celia pointed out. They seized it and began to load it into the boat.

She looked around to find Mary at her elbow, biting her lips anxiously. Francis said, "Ah, this must be Mary—take the hand baggage, girl."

He took Celia's arm again, sliding his own about her waist, holding her close as he guided her down the rocking steps. The boatmen stowed the trunks and helped Mary aboard; Francis saw to it that Celia was seated in the stern, then gave the signal to pull away.

Celia closed her eyes and leaned toward him, almost unaware of the pitching of the small boat and the splashing water. She was with Francis again! His strong arms were about her; nothing else mattered. She sighed in happiness. The boatmen pulled at the oars with great strokes, sending the craft out into the sparkling waters.

"I have longed for you so," Francis whispered, kissing her temple. "I am happy you are here at last." When he kissed her a shiver raced along her spine. They might be alone in the world for all the mind he paid the boatmen and Mary.

"Was it a difficult trip?" he asked.

"Not when I knew you'd be at the end of it."

He laughed, hugging her. "Each day I marked off one square on the calendar—but that's all past now. You're here safe and sound and that's all that matters. And I shall never let you out of my sight again." He stroked her hair, holding her close; how wonderful to be with him, to be at this far place at last! He pointed out the sights of the harbor, the frowning fort she could barely see beyond the trees, then they were heading for a pier, passing other native boats. She was startled to note the total lack of clothing exhibited and turned her face away determined not to show shock. In front of them Mary sat with hunched shoulders and downcast eyes.

The boatmen skillfully evaded other craft, pulling up to

171

the long quay and a float beside it where steps led up. Francis chattered of the climate, and how she must not overdo.

She grimaced. "The climate! I have heard nothing but the dreadful climate of India since I set out. I am much surprised in fact. I think it a lovely day, not the oppressive heat I was led to expect."

"I ordered it especially for your arrival. December is the kindest month in India, with balmy days and cool nights. Time enough to worry about the heat when summer comes." He took her hand and pressed it to his lips.

He helped her from the boat and led her to a carriage. She scarcely had eyes for the crowded dockside, the magnificent elephants, some saddled with swaying baskets set upon glittering cloths with gold embroidery and in which turbaned natives rode, and the strange coffin-like *palanquins* borne by running natives. Francis would have whisked her off at once except Celia caught sight of Mary's frightened expression as she was left to ride with the trunks in an open cart pulled by a huge ox.

"Let her come with us," she begged Francis.

Surprised, he turned and beckoned to the girl who scampered into the carriage and squeezed into a corner. Francis dismissed her with a glance but Celia smiled encouragingly. The child was obviously alarmed by the strangeness and clamour that surrounded them. Had it not been for Francis, Celia would share the terror, and her heart went out to Mary.

"I have arranged a house," Francis said. "It is close to the Fort so I can spend as much time with you as possible. There is to be a party at Government House in a week's time and you shall meet everyone although your arrival has been the talk of every tea for weeks, I dare say."

She flushed at the thought. She smiled at him. "And what of our wedding?"

He looked startled, then laughed. "This very day, of course. Did I not tell you? The Bishop will perform the ceremony this evening in the Anglican chapel."

She smiled, feeling warm and safe at last. All the horrors of the past were just that—past, never to be considered again. She would build a new life with Francis.

She listened as he identified the places they passed: the

172

Fort, with its battlements and towers and the British flag flying against the clear blue sky; rows of substantial Georgian houses that contrasted sharply with the thatched Indian huts and larger bungalows that belonged to the East India Company; large public buildings in a mixture of European and Eastern styles. Celia was pleasantly surprised by the number of carriages she saw on the streets, with English women in hats and gowns that had come from Regent Street. Several women turned and waggled fingers at Francis, smiling and staring at Celia as the phaeton passed. Obviously Francis had spoken widely of her coming, and people were curious to have a glimpse of her.

The carriage drew into the fenced yard of a two-story house set well back from Chowringhee-road. The house was large, with a green verandah that spread across the entire front, and jalousied windows of the same color, bright against the dazzling whiteness of the house itself. The style was English rather than Indian, and Celia felt at home almost instantly.

"It's quite grand," she said, putting out her arms to let Francis lift her down from the carriage.

He laughed. "Hardly elegant, but passable by India's standards." He swung her in a circle and set her upon her feet, bending to kiss her before he let her loose, then standing with his arm about her waist.

She smiled inwardly, thinking that she had to become accustomed to elegance. She was no longer a poor parson's daughter but the wife—or soon to be—of a rich, handsome man. She gazed about, admiring the greensward on the opposite side of the street and the view overlooking the water.

A native in turban and white robe hurried toward them from a hut near the gate bowing low and smiling an expanse of teeth stained with red betel juice.

"*Sahib . . . memsahib . . .*"

The man grabbed the reins, shouting to a boy who scampered to take the animal to the stable behind the house. Mary watched with round eyes, looking about when several servants emerged to stand along the verandah as Francis and Celia approached.

Francis had hired a reliable *khansamah,* a combination steward-butler-housekeeper, who in turn supervised all that

173

needed being done. The man stood stiffly by the door, smiling when Francis paused to introduce him.

"This is Ram Coomar. If you require anything, he will see to it, you need only ask."

"I'm sure we'll get on," Celia said. She smiled as the man bowed and Francis led her inside. The interior of the house was a delightful surprise. Not as grand as the parlor at Aylesford, it was tastefully furnished with pieces that had surely come from one of the best furniture makers in London. She was not sure what she had expected, but she felt immense relief at seeing the brocaded sofa, cushioned chairs, tables, draperies, lamps and pictures. She would feel quite at home with a little time.

"Oh, Francis—it's marvelous!" She turned to him with eyes sparkling. "I've never been so happy!"

He smiled, pleased at her ecstasy. He touched her cheek, wanting to carry her upstairs and claim her that very moment. By tonight, they would be wed. God—how beautiful she was! He quickly banished such thoughts from his mind, lest he display his desire too openly.

He led her through the house, showing the rooms as if offering gifts for her approval. The dining room was complete with elegant china and crystal, silverware and linens over which Celia ran her hand in awe. He did not take her to the kitchen, only indicated that it existed behind as a separate portion of the house and would be tended by the *babachee* and his assistant. Celia need not worry about it other than to instruct the *khansamah* if she desired special dishes. Ram Coomar would relay her instructions.

They went upstairs and stood in the doorway of the bedroom, while she exclaimed in delight over the four-postered bed draped with mosquito netting that had been pulled back to show a satin spread in rich shades of red and gold. Like all the rooms, it had a broad flat board suspended vertically from the ceiling; Francis explained that the *punkah* moved back and forth to stir the air and cool the room when the outside rope was pulled.

"I had not expected anything so lovely!" she said, turning to him and clapping her hands together as she stared about at the spacious wardrobe, the commode and chest, the curtained windows. "It—it's like London, or Aylesford."

He laughed. "Did you think I would bring you to a native hut somewhere in the jungle?"

Celia flushed. "I would love you as much if you had."

He smiled again, touched by her naivete. "You shall have the best as I promised you. I had considerable time to prepare for your arrival, you see. If there's anything missing—?" He looked about the room, frowning in concentration.

"Nothing." She gazed at the wide double bed, thinking that she would not lie alone tonight. Her heart quickened and she felt warm all at once.

"You will want to rest and freshen up—you seem tired."

She had not told him of her illness and she did not wish to distress him now. "I am fine."

"The wedding is planned for six, if that's suitable to you?"

"Of course."

"I shall leave you for a bit then. The bearers will bring up your things, and I will send the *ayah* to you at once." At her curious gaze, he explained. "Maid—nurse—she will do whatever you need." Smiling, he kissed her lingeringly, his hands caressing her shoulders and neck until he pulled away quite abruptly once more and left her.

When Francis helped her down from the barouche before the Cathedral, Celia was shivering with excitement. She wore white satin, a dress fashioned with tight bodice and waist and full skirt. Several rows of delicate lace trimmed the high neckline and wrist-length sleeves, and tiny seed pearls formed an intricate front panel and sleeve bands. Over it a white lace shawl whispered like a breeze, covering her hair and falling loosely to her shoulders like a Spanish mantilla; about her throat hung the diamond pendant Francis had given her.

She was a vision of loveliness and Francis could scarcely keep his eyes from her or from taking her in his arms and crushing her to his breast. He knew that she would be envied by every woman at the service and he by every man. Celia's color was high, with pink spots at her cheeks that had not been touched with cosmetics. Her delicate oval face was serene, though her eyes were bright and dancing. She looked about her, taking in sights and sounds and letting them add to her excitement.

The Cathedral was not unlike many in England, and Celia was comforted by the familiarity. Inside it was a swirl of color, every uniform in Calcutta must be there! The women's gowns were shimmery with jewels and she found her arm taken by a tall, gray-haired man in a gorgeous scarlet and gold uniform.

Francis said, "Allow me to present Miss Celia Skerritt, sir. Celia, this is Colonel Collingworth, my commanding officer."

"Charmed, my dear," Collingworth said. "Get along, Devy, take your place."

With a wink, Francis was gone. Celia was dizzy with excitement. Colonel Collingworth smiled and she had an impression of white teeth behind a luxurious moustache, a red face and an immense expanse of scarlet coat blazoned with gold, with glittering decorations and buttons. Somewhere an organ was playing a tune she did not recognize and hundreds of faces were turning toward her from the pews.

Collingworth patted her hand and led her around banks of fragrant flowers to the church aisle. "Are you ready?"

She nodded, unable to speak at all. The aisle stretched away before her a thousand miles—could she ever get down it to the distant altar? Collingworth urged her forward, softly speaking words she could not comprehend, so mixed were her thoughts. She wished her mother were there, and Papa, with Kevin beside her with some bright quip on his lips. Tears started and she bit her lip to hold them back. Francis was waiting ... there just a little bit farther on, at the altar. She could see his smile and her heart was bursting. The music faded and then she was standing beside Francis who was gazing at her with longing and squeezing her hand.

A round-faced Bishop in a gleaming mitre came forward. When he began to speak, Francis's arm pressed hers and she looked at him; her heart was pounding and she thought, "I must concentrate on the ceremony," but the words washed over her, rolling out into the hushed cathedral, like waves on a distant beach. She was aware of Francis's smile, the silence about her, and she was consumed with love. She was warm, then almost shivering with an icy spine as she came to full realization at last that the day she had waited for so long had arrived. She was pronouncing the vows, speaking softly as though she and Francis were alone in the vast cavern of the church. Then Francis was kissing her. The music swelled and they were walking rapidly back along the aisle. The next moments were a riot of impressions, laughter and chattering, people pressing good wishes upon her. They halted in the dim narthex as Francis greeted friends and presented her as his wife. She clung to him, smiling, murmuring greetings and listening to names that were only a blur in her mind. Colonel and Mrs. Chapman, Major and Mrs. Watson, Captain and Mrs. Pierce, Captain and Mrs. Harrington—Celia was in a daze. It was difficult to think beyond the fact that she was Mrs. Francis Devy. The day she had awaited and hoped for so long was finally a reality, and Francis's arm was about her as he introduced the long line of waiting guests. A young officer and his wife moved on and quite suddenly Francis's smile vanished and a scowl creased his forehead. He recovered quickly and said, "Darling, may I present Claude Ashmore, Councillor with the East India Company, his wife Glenda, and their houseguest, Gwenn Katon."

Mr. Ashmore bowed and touched his lips to Celia's hand. Mrs. Ashmore, a faded mousy woman in beige linen, congratulated Celia then moved on nervously. Gwenn Katon stared, the smile on her face as carefully arranged as the dark curls that poked from under her pink bonnet. She was an attractive woman who displayed her good figure boldly. She studied Celia frankly, her gaze sweeping over each detail of her face and gown. Her eyes smouldered with some hidden fire and a faint flush rose to her cheeks as though she had suddenly become too warm.

"You are to be congratulated, Mrs. Devy. You have tamed and captured the most unpredictable of the male beasts."

"Gwenn!" Claude Ashmore's face darkened and he put his arm through Gwenn's as though to draw her away. "We are looking forward to the Christmas Ball at Government House. Will we have the pleasure of seeing you there, Mrs. Devy?"

"Yes, of course," Francis answered for her. The frown was gone but a hint of anger lingered in his eyes as he regarded Gwenn Katon. Celia was puzzled by the interchange but there was no time to consider it as Claude Ashmore turned with a gesture.

"Oliver Chadwick has just returned on the same ship with your bride. I took the liberty of inviting him along, Francis."

The moment was passed and Francis was smiling again. "The devil! Oliver, good to see you again. And you already know Celia?"

Celia found herself caught in Oliver's gaze and felt her cheeks warm and her breath tighten. Of all people, why did he have to be here to spoil her complete happiness?!

"My very best wishes to both of you," Oliver said softly.

"Thank you . . ." She could scarcely whisper and the smile felt stiff on her face. She glanced past Oliver, hoping that someone else would come along and force him to move on, but the crowd had thinned and scattered to the street where many were already climbing into carriages and driving off. She looked to Francis for salvation.

Stunned she heard him say, "I'll count on you then, Oliver, to help Celia feel at home here in Calcutta. A few familiar faces make life more pleasant. We'll expect you to dinner soon, but only after I've had my bride to myself for a few days!" He grinned and squeezed Celia to him possessively.

"You're a man to be envied, Devy. I'd consider it a pleasure to do whatever I can to make Celia's stay in Calcutta pleasant." His dark eyes lingered on Celia so that she was forced to look away.

Was she never to be free of his watchful gaze, of the memory of the passion she'd been unable to control when he'd roused her? She wanted nothing more than to flee and be alone with Francis, but she knew that she would be forced to face Oliver frequently as long as they were in Calcutta. She had to push the disturbing thoughts from her mind. She would not be cowed by him! Determinedly, she met his gaze.

"It's a pleasure to see you again so soon, Oliver." Turning to Francis, she said, "Oliver was most courteous in showing me Gibraltar and Malta."

178

"And nothing of Egypt?" Claude Ashmore asked, relieved to have the conversation move to neutral topics. "I find Egypt most fascinating." He still gripped Gwenn's arm and she stood silent at his side.

Oliver shrugged and there was a flicker of amusement in his eyes before he looked away from Celia. "Women often retreat from its filth and squalor."

The barouche drew up and Francis drew Celia toward the doors. "I'm sure you gentlemen will excuse us."

The two men smiled knowingly and Gwenn Katon yanked her arm free of her host's and walked rapidly to the far end of the narthex. Francis led Celia down the steps and into the carriage. She felt Oliver's gaze on her until the barouche was away from the Cathedral and once more on the way to Chowringhee-road.

They dined alone, sitting close at one end of the long table and barely tasting the food that was set before them. When the meal was over, they went arm in arm upstairs to the bedroom. Francis spoke sharply to the bearer who would have entered the bedchamber to assist them in preparing for the night, finally shoving the man out the door and closing it firmly behind him. Turning to Celia, he came to her with arms open.

Then he was kissing her, pulling her body to his until she was weak in his embrace and helpless against him. His kiss was fiery and hard, burning at her lips. She swayed against him, letting her body mold to his and feeling his hands hot on her flesh through the material of her gown. She gasped for breath, so intense was his ardor. Her heart was beating like a caged bird struggling for escape. When his fingers touched her breast, excitement shivered through her. After a very long time, when he released her lips, his breath was heavy and warm on her upturned face.

"Celia . . ." It was almost a moan. Then his hands were at the fastenings of the dress, his eyes dark and wild. For a moment she was frightened, and she pulled away.

"No—"

He looked at her with a startled expression and his face darkened. She was immediately contrite and tried to smile. "Let me do it—" Her voice quavered.

Francis grinned and stepped back, unbuttoning his tunic

and dropping it carelessly to a chair. Shadows fell across his face from the low-burning lamp as he bent to remove his boots. Celia's fingers faltered at the buttons but she undid them quickly. She hung the dress carefully in the wardrobe, sliding her hand over the satin as though to reassure herself the wedding had actually taken place. She was a married woman now, and the rights of the marriage bed belonged to Francis. Without looking at him, she removed her slippers and petticoats. She heard Francis's sharp intake of breath as she drew down the straps of the chemise and slid it off. She was reaching for a blue silk dressing robe when she heard his quick footstep behind her and then his arms were pinning her. He turned her about, pressing her naked flesh to his hard lean body, erasing her fear and filling her with sudden desire.

His mouth found hers and there was no hesitation in their kiss. He lifted her from her feet, carrying her to the bed and pulling back the spread in a single motion before laying her down. His face was immediately above her, with deep shadows playing at his probing eyes and smiling lips.

"You are a wondrous creation ..." His hands caressed her flesh, sending fiery tingles through her body so that she shivered and stared at him wide-eyed. The blood pounded in her temples as his touch lingered first here, then there. Her breath came in broken gasps as he moved toward her and she had a quick glimpse of his desire. Then all at once she was caught in a whirlpool of dizzy excitement as he was atop her, the heat of his body covering her, his weight heavy on her. She felt a moment of panic and bit her lip to keep from crying out. His eyes burned with fires of passion; he stroked her body as he kissed the hollow of her throat, breathing her name over and over and tracing a path with his lips to her breasts. She quivered and held her breath as the waves of delight shook her and left her panting. Her entire body seemed alive and expectant, ready for whatever embrace he offered. When at last his hardness searched for her, she welcomed him. She could no longer lie still; her body was aflame with need and longing. She whimpered softly and closed her eyes so that he would not see the knowledge they held.

She felt a moment of confusion, unsure of how a new

bride should react but unable to hide the wildness that grew steadily inside her. Her body arched and her hands caught at his naked flesh to hold him close. She felt him pause momentarily and look at her, but she did not open her eyes. Then his own desire became a storm that would not relent and his thrusts were no longer gentle but demanding.

Francis felt the soft curves of her body under him. The vision of her loveliness had made him tremble with desire, and now she was no longer a distant temptation but warm pulsing flesh under his own. He felt the urgency in his loins and knew he should be gentle but could not. His need was too great. He thrust deep into her and gave himself to the hungry passion.

Celia felt the fire rage through her. She was unprepared for the surging demand she felt or for the complete abandon with which she gave herself to him. It was as though she had lived her life for this moment, in wait for the complete satisfaction her body found.

When it was over, she lay trembling under his gentle caresses and tears of joy filled her eyes. He had brought her to a peak of pleasure that had been dormant within her for so long. She let her breath out in a tremulous sigh. When at last his hand went limp on her breast and his breathing fell into a soft, regular pattern, she reached for the sheet and pulled it over them gently without waking him.

CHAPTER ELEVEN

Celia discovered that as Francis's wife she had little to
do save please him and amuse herself in his absence. The
house overflowed with servants who cooked, cleaned and
tended every personal duty that Celia had once done for
herself. She was waited on from morning till night, so
much so that she sometimes shooed the *ayah* away impatiently when she longed to sit quietly and consider her
good fortune.

Francis had not had to report to duty for three days following the wedding, and they spent every moment of the
time together. Francis told her bits and pieces of life in
Calcutta, whom she would meet and be expected to entertain and the places they would visit. When he spoke of
Claude Ashmore, Celia mustered the courage to ask about
Gwenn Katon. She had not seen the girl since the day of
the wedding but she had not been able to forget the
smouldering anger in those dark eyes.

Francis dismissed the subject airily. "Like many of the
women here, Gwenn spends too much time in idle specula-
tion and gossip."

"But she called you an unpredictable beast."

Francis pulled her into his arms and smothered her
words with a searing kiss that drove all thoughts of out-
siders from her mind. Laughing, he looked at her. "And
would you have me any other way, my sweet loving
wife?" His hands were at her flesh, his smile teasing. In
moments, all her questions were swept away by his ardent

182

kisses, and none seemed important enough to raise again.

Francis took her riding through the city and surrounding countryside. They visited native bazaars and shops that filled narrow side streets, and he bought anything that took her fancy so that they always returned home laden with parcels of all sizes and shapes. Celia learned to guard her tongue lest the carriage overflow with bolts of cloth, brass urns, pottery. They retired early each night and found mutual pleasure in their lovemaking; Francis was considerate and gentle, yet passionate and demanding, so that Celia found herself caught in a whirl of sensuous pleasure that she had dreamed of since the first faint stirring of her womanhood.

After the first few days, during which Francis had let it be known that he wanted to be alone with his bride, people began to call. The first was Colonel Collingworth's wife, a thin pale woman with a birdlike expression and small eyes that darted as though in search of prey. She arrived shortly after Francis left for the Fort and was shown into the parlor by one of the *syces*.

"You're looking well, Celia. I thought you a bit pale when you first arrived. Marriage agrees with you." The dark eyes flitted about the room, evaluating, approving.

Celia felt a flush of embarrassment at the intimate suggestion. "How nice of you to call, Mrs. Collingworth," she said. "Would you like some tea?" She had never entertained so early in the day and wasn't sure what was expected of her. She made a mental note to ask Francis to outline proper procedures.

"You must call me Amanda. I hope we can be friends." The older woman sighed heavily and sank into one of the upholstered chairs. "Perhaps a glass of toast-and-water. I suffer frequent spells of indigestion, though the doctor assures me it is nothing serious. The cooler weather helps but I long to return to England." She let her gaze settle on Celia. "Francis tells us you are from Renfield. You've known him many years then?"

"Not nearly long enough," she said evasively. The question seemed edged with more than casual curiosity. Celia was relieved when a servant appeared and she could turn aside to give instructions. She was composed and smiling when she looked back to Mrs. Collingworth.

183

Amanda's head pecked forward. "Francis's duties will resume on full scale now, and you'll have oceans of time on your hands. You'll want to meet everyone. You'll be glad of friends to help pass the days. Is there anything I can do to help you get settled?"

"That's most kind of you, Mrs. Collin—" At the other woman's quick frown, she amended, "Amanda."

"You need only send a *chuprassie*."

Francis had explained the duties of the messenger, and Celia nodded. The servant returned with the toast-and-water which Amanda accepted and sipped absently.

"The ball at Government House opens the Christmas festivities, though the natives do not hold with Christian holidays. It will be a *burrakhana*, of course. Guests will be coming from the far reaches of the presidency. The young Rajah will be there. Since the military settled the dispute in his province, he has been most friendly."

Celia said, "I'm honored to be included in the invitation."

Amanda's gaze flitted over her. "Francis has always been considered the most eligible bachelor in Calcutta and has never lacked for invitations. It's only natural that his wife will be included from now on." Her words seemed to probe. "We were all very pleased to hear that he was bringing over a bride, although there was considerable lament among the single ladies and widows, to be sure." Her smile added to the malice of the words.

Celia felt her face heat and steeled herself against the questions that rushed to mind. To inquire into Francis's past romantic interests would give Amanda food for gossip—and besides, whatever Francis had done before meeting her was in the past and had no bearing on their life together. Celia deliberately returned to the subject of the ball.

"When is the party to be?"

"The twenty-third." Sipping at the toast-and-water again, Amanda said, "But do come to tea tomorrow. I've invited several women who want to know you. Government House balls are such huge affairs that one can easily feel lost without a few familiar faces around." She set aside the glass and got up, extending a hand which Celia rose to clasp briefly.

"Thank you, Amanda."

"At three then?"

Celia stood at the window watching the phaeton vanish beyond the trees that bordered the gate. She had passed the first critical inspection. Amanda was without a doubt the leader of the English colony of Calcutta. Her opinion would make the difference between acceptance or rejection by the good ladies of the city.

The Collingworths lived in a large Georgian house a quarter of a mile distant. Celia dressed with care, changing her selection of gowns several times before she was satisfied that she would pass the scrutiny of the women at tea. She was nervous and fussed as Mary brushed and curled her hair to perfection. When at last she could find no fault, Celia descended to the light buggy Francis had acquired for her personal use.

The others were already gathered in the Collingworth parlor, and all eyes turned as Celia entered the room. Amanda motioned to a place beside her on the sofa, smiling as Celia sat, then introducing the four other women around the tea table. Celia vaguely recalled some of the faces from the wedding. Amanda offered introductions, nodding to each.

"Sybil Watson ... Harriet Evans ... Elena Harrington ... and Jenny Pierce."

Celia murmured greetings as she tried to fix the names and faces in her memory. Sybil Watson was a heavy woman, with grey hair that was carefully arranged in small curls about a puffy face with deep-set eyes that were almost lost in the fleshy cheeks. Despite the coolness of the room, her upper lip had a sheen of perspiration and she fanned herself every few moments with a plump hand. Celia recalled she had been with the stocky Major who tugged at his moustache with each sentence.

Harriet Evans's husband had not been in uniform but if anyone had mentioned what he did, Celia could not recall. Harriet was stern faced, with an angular jaw and lips that seemed to have trouble smiling and eyes that looked right through Celia.

Elena Harrington smiled warmly. Wasn't her husband a captain? Elena brushed back a strand of brown hair that

185

had escaped the bun at the nape of her neck. She was the only woman in the room who looked as if she had been out-of-doors. Tanned, with tiny lines at the corners of her eyes, she looked athletic and fit. Her brown eyes were wide spaced and clear, her hair touched with grey that she did not try to disguise.

Jenny Pierce was the youngest of the group, although several years older than Celia herself. She was pretty but her looks were beginning to fade, her face drawn and tired, her blonde hair drab. Her hands fluttered at the skirt of the pink linen dress, pleating and unpleating a bit of cloth, smoothing it quickly when Celia glanced at her. There had been a Captain Pierce at the wedding . . . alone.

"I was just saying how well you look, Celia," Amanda commented, her gaze sliding over the yellow muslin Celia had chosen.

"It's always easy to tell the new arrivals by the bloom of health they display, " Sybil Watson said, her voice almost pouting. "This dreadful climate will be the death of me. Two years—" She sighed heavily and fanned herself again.

"You should get outside and exercise more," Elena Harrington said, not unkindly. "The natives—"

"Their systems are different," Harriet insisted. "The English constitution was not designed for rigorous activity in such heat." She fastened her gaze on Celia. "You will find it beneficial to carry a parasol whenever you go out. Your fair complexion will not take to the sun."

"Yes . . ." Celia felt caught between the two in an argument not of her making. She smiled at Elena to show she meant no personal disagreement.

"I'm sorry I was unable to attend your wedding, Celia. Will you forgive me? I—" Jenny Pierce looked to her hostess, then at her hands in her lap. "I was not feeling well."

Celia said, "I trust you are better now?" Jenny did not look well at all but it seemed the proper thing to say.

A servant brought a tray and Amanda lifted the heavy silver pot and poured into each of the delicate bone china cups, passing them around the circle. Tiny sandwiches and cakes followed, and the women settled into easy gossip about social engagements, clothes and people—mainly women who were not present. Although she knew none of the names, Celia quickly recognized that the levels of Calcutta society were well drawn. Few Indian women were mentioned except for a certain princess whose name was mentioned with that of Oliver Chadwick.

"It's quite obvious that Princess Narain came to Calcutta to be on hand for his arrival," Sybil Watson said waspishly. "We've not seen her in the city since Oliver departed last spring!"

"Her father often has business here, she might have decided to accompany him on one of his visits," Elena Harrington ventured.

Sybil snorted. "Conveniently timed to coincide with the arrival of the handsome young man she's been seeing for more than a year. Don't be naïve, Elena."

Elena shrugged as though it were of no consequence. Amanda took up the morsel. "It's said that she was quite desolate without him. The troops have made several patrols in the upper provinces. Roger was invited to the palace, of course, and the young Princess refused to come from her apartment, even for the special musical entertainment the Rajah arranged for his guests. Simply pining away, I'd say."

"I saw them yesterday lunching at the Spence," Harriet Evans offered.

"In public! Good heavens, you don't suppose he's planning on marrying her?" Sybil looked aghast.

Celia listened with mixed feelings as the women chattered about Oliver and the Princess. She should feel relieved to know that his attentions were so well occupied elsewhere, but instead she felt a strange irritation she did not understand. She hoped Oliver did marry this Princess, whoever she was. It would give her a distinct sense of relief to have him belong to another so she could put him from her mind completely, though there seemed to be no way she would be able to avoid seeing him. From the conversation, she gathered that the affairs of the military and those of the East India Company were closely related, if not the same.

Celia perked at the mention of another familiar name. "I can't understand why Gwenn Katon refuses to go home to England," Jenny Pierce was saying. "I'd jump at the chance instantly, yet she stays on—" She broke off at

Elena's quick scowl and gesture toward Celia. Celia pretended not to notice as she bit into a small honey cake. Jenny was flustered and the teacup rattled in her hands.

Remembering her meeting with Gwenn at the wedding, Celia understood the woman's remarks now. She had been involved with Francis, perhaps even hoped to win him as a husband. She was angry and jealous because Celia had become Mrs. Francis Devy instead. Surely the woman would leave the city as soon as possible if Francis had been her only reason for staying! But Francis had been here some months already—why hadn't he made his marriage plans clear to Gwenn? Had Francis been seeing her right up until Celia's arrival? The thought made her anger flare, but she forced a smile and looked about the circle of faces.

"I realize I have only been here a short time," she said slowly, "but I find India captivating. A change from the countryside of England, yet fascinating."

Amanda picked up the cue and went immediately into a discussion of the less desirable aspects of Eastern climate that Celia would meet eventually, repeating Francis's statement that December was the pleasantest time of the year. Then the talk turned to clothing and a dressmaker on Randwai-road who seemed able to copy the latest fashions from sketches in newspapers or periodicals from London.

Celia was relieved when the tea was over and she stood on the wide steps of the verandah waiting for the carriage to come around the drive. The *syce* leaped down from his cramped perch under the hood and began whisking insects away from the chestnut horse's flanks. The *chuprassie*, who accompanied Celia on the brief ride to the Collingworth house and presented her card, bowed so low his head almost touched the dusty ground as Celia climbed in. The carriage moved off with the *syce* running alongside and managing to keep pace with the horse.

For the ball at Government House, Celia selected a satin gown the color of an unbleached English sky on a bright, cloudless day. It was close fitting at her tiny waist and high bosom, and except for several rows of small pleats in the bodice inset and the layered skirt, it was unadorned. The dressmaker in Renfield had assured her the simplicity of style was all the rage in London and abroad for women with the perfect figures to wear it. The *ayah* fastened the gold chain and diamond that Francis had given Celia about her throat as Celia studied herself in the glass approvingly. Marriage *did* agree with her! Despite the weeks of illness aboard ship, she had regained her color and her skin was taut and glowing. Her eyes gleamed darkly in contrast with the dress.

She saw Mary standing near the door and turned. The girl was holding several small blossoms, pale blue delicate orchids that looked unreal in their perfection. At Celia's glance, Mary came forward, casting a sidelong glance at the *ayah*.

"What have you there?" Celia asked gently. Mary had been unhappy these past days with little to do since the Indian servants seemed to be everywhere, rushing to do for Celia and Francis so that no task was left to chance.

"They match your gown."

Celia took the flowers. "I shall wear them in my hair. That will be all, *ayah*." She waited until the woman left the bedroom, then seated herself before the glass and held the flowers out to Mary. "The *ayah* did not arrange the curls right, do you think? Fix them for me, Mary, and tuck the blossoms in so I can enjoy their fragrance all evening."

Smiling shyly, Mary fussed with Celia's hair, loosening curls so they fell softly, fastening the tiny flowers to highlight the golden crown.

Francis entered as she finished and smiled. "You are the most beautiful woman in all of Calcutta, my love."

Celia came into his arms and he kissed her tenderly, unmindful of Mary. She felt his muscles tense and knew that he was sharing a quickening of passion. He drew away from her embrace slowly, unspoken words promising they would recapture the moment later.

"We'd best be off if you're ready. These affairs never begin on time but we are already late."

She picked up a handkerchief and took the delicate midnight blue shawl Mary held out to her. Smiling, she took Francis's arm and they descended to the carriage.

The ballroom at Government House glittered with lights reflected from the huge chandeliers and wall lanterns. It was crowded, with hundreds of people overflowing into adjoining rooms, standing about in groups chattering and watching newcomers, sipping punch from crystal cups served from huge trays carried by turbaned servants. A reception line was formed at the entrance, and Celia stared about as she and Francis waited to be introduced to the Governor-General and his staff.

She had never seen so many people in one place! Despite Francis's tales and the remarks by Amanda and the others, Celia was unprepared for the elegance of Government House or the people in attendance. Costumes ranged from English ballgowns such as her own to rich, oriental silks and native Indian saris edged with gold and silver. The proportion of Europeans to easterners was well divided, and Celia wondered who the visiting dignitaries were.

"Celia, may I introduce the Governor-General, Lord Auckland . . ."

"Delighted . . ." The grey-haired gentleman in formal attire and with a crimson sash across his middle took her hand and pressed it to his lips. "I am told you have only recently come to Calcutta. May I welcome you?" He bowed low.

"Thank you." She had never dreamed that the highest official in the country even knew she existed! Was there no end of surprises regarding Francis's connections? She was introduced to several others, including Mr. and Mrs. Gladstone whom she'd met aboard the Aramack. She was delighted to see them again, and Mrs. Gladstone seemed far more friendly.

The ball was festive; considerable attempt had been made to capture the Christmas spirit. Garlands of native leaves festooned the walls and doorways and bright bows held sprigs of scarlet flowering bush that substituted for mistletoe. The *punkahs,* ribboned in bright red and green, were in steady motion to keep the air of the huge rooms stirring. Even so, the ballroom bordered on being uncomfortably warm.

The band of the Queen's 49th Regiment and that of the Governor-General played alternately, and the main ballroom was given over to dancing. Francis was drawn into conversation from time to time with people he knew and to whom he presented Celia. She smiled, but said little,

190

content to listen and watch the people about her, excited by the variety of costumes and faces. There was an Oriental, his round face smooth and his hair plaited in a pigtail that hung past his waist, and dressed in an ornate black robe decorated with metallic stitching in intricate patterns. Envoys from outlying districts of Bengal were resplendent in loose-legged trousers of layered white gauze-like material, vests that glittered with jewels that caught the light and winked like stars, high turbans with huge stones set in the front center like the eyes of idols.

Francis led her to the ballroom and they danced as the band struck up a quadrille. Flushed and smiling, Celia felt many eyes upon her as she glided about, touching Francis's hand when they met and glowing with pride. Numerous English women seemed to prefer sitting and chatting to dancing, and Celia was struck with the unhealthy pallor of many. Amanda Collingworth claimed Celia when the musicians paused and Francis drifted into conversation with several men in uniform.

"You look more radiant each time I see you."

Celia blushed. "Thank you, Amanda."

"I was just speaking to a friend only to learn that you two are acquainted—there, Oliver!"

Oliver Chadwick turned from the elderly woman with whom he was talking, and Celia felt a pang of confusion at his quick smile. She had not seen him since the wedding, and his dark, piercing gaze unsettled her.

"How nice to see you again," she managed.

He bowed over her hand, the pressure of his fingers warm and lingering. "It's always a joy to see old friends," he said. Was he mocking her? She could not meet his look. "Are you happy in Calcutta?"

"Yes. It's lovely." Why did she feel so awkward and tongue-tied in his presence? She glanced about for Francis and saw him chatting, but as the music started again, he turned to a woman at his side and escorted her to the dance floor. Celia realized that Oliver was watching her and her gaze fell nervously.

"May I have the honor of this dance, Mrs. Devy?"

She wanted to refuse but Oliver had already slipped his hand to her arm and was guiding her to the floor. The music was a waltz and he held her much too tightly.

"I'm happy to see you so fully recovered," he said.

"I'm afraid I've never thanked you properly for your help and concern. Mary tells me it was you who summoned the doctor." His gaze was so intent she was forced to look away once more. The pressure of his hand at her waist seemed intimate and she wished fervently that she had refused him the dance. Around them, music and chatter swelled and faded. His silence became uncomfortable and Celia felt her pulse quicken. In desperation she tried another avenue of conversation. "Have you seen Iris? I have tried to find her address but cannot. Didn't she say her husband worked with you?"

He looked amused. "The Beddingtons live at the other side of the Maidan. I'm sure we have the number in our records. I will be happy to get it for you."

"I'll send a *chuprassie*—"

His smile did not change. "That won't be necessary. Surely you would not deny an old friend the pleasure of calling on you with such a small favor."

Her cheeks flamed and she felt trapped. He *was* a friend of Francis's, there was no way she could deny him the right to call. She didn't trust her voice again and inwardly breathed a sigh of relief when the waltz ended and he escorted her to the sidelines. She thanked him and quickly moved to where Jenny Pierce sat on a small velvet-cushioned gilt chair near the wall. She seemed more fragile than when Celia had first seen her, and her face was pale and clammy. She waved a bamboo and silk fan nervously. "Celia—how nice."

Captain Pierce, who had been sitting at his wife's side, rose and bowed to Celia and insisted she take his chair. He drifted into conversation with Oliver and the two men moved off.

Jenny wore a silk gown of dull rose that did nothing to brighten the sallowness of her face. She had applied spots of rouge that stood out like bloodstains on her cheeks. Her hands plucked at her skirt or moved the fan endlessly.

"I've been hoping to see you again."

Celia smiled. "I am slowly becoming accustomed to my new life and think I'm ready to entertain. Will you come to tea one day soon?"

Jenny smiled. "I'd be delighted. The days are so interminable. Oh, I do wish we could go back to England. I hate it here!" She looked about quickly as though afraid someone had heard.

Surprised, Celia tried to make light of it. "I have not been here long but I find India charming."

"It's filthy, and before long the hot season will be upon us again. I don't know if I can stand another year. Thomas says it will be that long before we can go home." She looked ready to cry.

Celia was relieved to see Francis approaching.

"Good evening, Jenny. You're looking well."

Jenny smiled and sighed. Celia rose to take the hand her husband held out to her. Francis said, "The *burra-khana* is being called. It is time we went into the dining room. Is Thomas about? Ah, yes, hullo there, Tom."

The men shook hands and Francis led Celia to the huge dining room where dozens of long tables had been set for the guests. The room was as large as the ballroom, glittering with lights and the gleaming cloths and silver. Hundreds of white-clad servants stood along the walls waiting for the guests to be seated. Celia had never seen a fete so large, and her mind whirled at the thought of the cost of feeding so many people.

Although she felt lost in the confusion, Francis seemed to know where they were to sit and he led her to a table. To her dismay, Oliver Chadwick took the seat directly across from her, smiling and greeting Francis. Beside him, a young Indian woman stared at Celia with dark, almond-shaped eyes. She was incredibly beautiful, with flawless skin and even white teeth that showed behind crimson lips when she smiled. Oliver introduced her as the Princess Narain of the province of Daktu. The girl acknowledged the introduction with a lowering of lashes and head.

There was another flurry of activity as the Evanses and the Watsons took their places at the table. Then as the conversation around the table picked up once more, the Ashmores and Gwenn Katon came to take the last vacant chairs directly across from Francis. For a moment, a wave of dizziness assailed Celia. How could she sit with the woman who had been—still was—in love with Francis? She was grateful for the buzz of conversation that made it unnecessary for her to do more than nod to the newcomers. She stole a sidelong glance at Francis and he seemed completely unperturbed by Gwenn's presence. Gwenn smiled and chatted with everyone but her eyes lingered on Celia more often than coincidence might account for. She seemed cold and calculating, like a sleek cat waiting her chance to pounce. Celia deliberately fastened her attention on the conversation of the men.

"The Hindus have grown opium for centuries," Claude Ashmore was saying. "Nothing we say or do will change their habits."

"Growing it is one thing but selling it in illicit trade is another. There's talk the Chinese government is clamping down on the importation of the stuff," George Evans replied.

Major Watson looked at the man speculatively. "Perhaps the Company should clamp down at this end."

Evans stiffened and his wife tightened her lips and frowned. Evans said, "The Company is engaged in legal trade."

Major Watson shrugged. "That trade and the profits to be made from it entice too many to steal and smuggle the flowers. The Company is moving such a large amount of opium these days it's no wonder every unprincipled ruffian sees his chance to get rich."

George Evans's face was red and his glance darted about the table for a sympathetic face. "The Army must take responsibility for the up-country troubles as much as the Company."

Celia felt the tension and she looked at Francis. His face was dark, his brow furrowed. "We do our best. Only a few weeks ago we quelled a disturbance in Sabathoo only to find we were fighting some of our own people." When faces turned to him, he continued. "Fighting broke out among some bearers while they were bringing out opium. It spread to the local villagers until the Prince had a full-scale revolt on his hands and called for help. By the time we had it settled, whoever had organized the train was long gone with the opium and none of the *syces* knew anything, of course."

"Damned rotten business," Major Watson said.

"You have no proof it was Company men," George Evans said.

"None at all," Harriet offered to support him.

"The bearers swore that the camel train had been hired by the John Company."

Oliver cast a glance about the table. "It's a popular excuse to blame anything that goes wrong on the Company."

"Quite so. Besides," Claude Ashmore said, "any Englishman can claim he's with the Company and the natives wouldn't question it. It could have been a private operation."

Major Watson started to say something but stopped, looking at Francis who smiled and said, "Let's hope that's the end of it. The trouble is settled for now—and we've a party to get on with. Shall we drink to the good health of the ladies?"

They raised the wine goblets, murmuring toasts. Francis looked at her, smiling. "To my wife."

She drank and saw Oliver staring at her over the rim of his glass. She looked away quickly, only to find Gwenn Katon also staring. Quite deliberately, Gwenn let her gaze move slowly to Francis until he looked in her direction. Then she gave him a knowing smile, and Francis returned it without embarrassment. Celia's hand shook as she set down her glass.

The meal took hours, with separate courses being brought on huge silver trays and served in individual portions which Celia could only pick at—clear soup, delicate fish and sweet baby shrimp nestled in beds of ice, tiny fresh vegetables arranged on platters like so many colorful flowers in a garden, meats heavily spiced and covered with creamy sauces, delicious fruits and small pastries and cakes. When it was at last over, the guests dispersed to the ballroom where chairs had been set about so they might view the entertainment that had been planned. Celia felt almost drowsy from the heat and the food, and she scarcely watched the jugglers, native dancers, and assortment of English and Indian singers. Many of the men stepped out to the wide verandahs that overlooked the gardens to smoke and escape the stuffy air, but the ladies were trapped by politeness and their own ennui. When Francis excused himself and left, Celia smiled and longed to escape with him. Bored, she studied those around her covertly. The Princess and Oliver Chadwick had disappeared immediately after dinner, and Celia wondered if they were at this moment in bed together. The thought shocked her and she pushed it from her mind. What Oliver Chadwick did was no concern of hers!

A musical selection by a thin English woman with a reedy voice ended and a smattering of applause eddied in the room. Conversations erupted and buzzed and on some unseen signal, the musicale broke up and groups began to mill. Celia moved toward the tall open windows to look for Francis. Outside, the air was cool and refreshing, and she pulled the thin shawl about her shoulders gratefully. The gardens were dimly lit with torches spaced along the paths. She heard Amanda Collingworth's shrill laugh close by and realized she would be trapped into conversation if she stayed where she was. She moved out of the light and down the broad steps of the verandah. Walking slowly along one of the paths, she hummed softly and breathed the heavy scent of the blooming flowers that grew in profusion. By daylight, the garden would be a riot of color. She plucked a leaf and rolled it between her fingers; how fortunate she was, and how happy. She must write to Mama and to Theo also.

The sound of low voices reached her and she stopped abruptly. She had no wish to intrude on anyone, but as she reversed her direction, she stopped again as she recognized Francis's voice.

"I'll not have you giving me orders nor telling me what I must or shall not do!" He sounded angry, yet there was a softness to his tone.

A woman's voice answered, "Darling, can you deny that you still want me? Am I not as desirable to you as I always have been?"

Gwenn Katon!

Celia's heart stopped beating for the span of a breath. Then her pulse roared in her ears so that she thought surely she would faint with the suddenness of it. She wanted to flee and blot out the words she was hearing but she could not move.

"You forget that I am married. Whatever there was between us is over."

"You lie!" There was a hushed sound of quick indrawn

breath and a soft moan as Gwenn pulled herself into Francis's arms and raised her lips against his.

"Damn you!" Very gently.

Gwenn laughed. "You see, the fire is still there. Oh God, Francis. I've been sick with hatred and jealousy of the woman you've brought to your bed. She is a mouse. She cannot please you the way I have done and will do again if you'll only give me the chance! Tell me that you will come to me—soon!"

"You vixen!" There were sounds of eager embrace.

Celia's head spun and nausea threatened. She pressed her hand to her mouth to smother the sob that rose in her throat.

"This very night," Francis said. "I shall slip away."

"I'll be waiting."

Celia stumbled along the path, heedless of anything but her own misery. When she came into the light of the windows, she collapsed onto a stone bench and sat with her heart pounding and face flaming until she could breathe normally again. All the innuendos, the chance remarks cut off so abruptly . . . She understood now. Francis had been having a flagrant affair with Gwenn—right up to the time of her arrival! And now, the two were making plans to resume it! She heard the sound of footsteps along the path behind her and fled the bench, crossing the verandah and returning to the ballroom. She spied a knot of people which included Elena Harrington and Oliver Chadwick, and she joined it quickly. Oliver stared at her when she laughed too readily, talked too fast, but by the time Francis entered from the garden alone, Celia had regained her composure. And when they returned home, she lay staring into the hazy darkness of the bedroom as she listened to Francis ride off.

CHAPTER TWELVE

Celia had neither the heart nor the courage to speak of that night to Francis. She feigned sleep when he returned near dawn, and when he went about as though nothing had happened, she hid her pain and wept silently when she was alone. Once when Francis came upon her unexpectedly and saw her tears, she told him she was homesick for her family because it was Christmas.

They spent a quiet Christmas at home except for an invitation to the Collingworth's for dinner. Francis gave her a lovely emerald ring that dazzled her beyond words. He also presented her with her very own horse, a sleek chestnut mare that was broken for riding. When she protested that she'd never ridden, he laughed and said he was preparing her for the hunt when they returned to Aylesford.

True to his word, Oliver secured Iris's address for Celia and brought it around four days after Christmas. He also bore a beribboned package which he presented to Celia, smiling at Francis, and saying, "A wedding gift as a token of my wishes for your happiness."

"Not necessary, old chap, but many thanks." Francis watched while Celia undid the package. The ivory carving was the most beautiful and intricate work Celia had ever seen. It was a figure of a woman, bent in exotic dance, arms upraised and face serene. The detail of gossamer gown and perfect body were exquisite, each feature of the face flawless in beauty. Celia held it aloft, exclaiming with pleasure.

"It's gorgeous!" The delight shone in her eyes as Oliver met her gaze.

Francis took the statue and turned it over in his hands, examining it approvingly. "A masterpiece."

"It is said to represent eternal love," Oliver said; his eyes held Celia's for a moment before she looked away.

"Well, thanks again. Very thoughtful of you." Francis set aside the statue and clapped his hands for the *syce*. "Brandy—not too early in the day for you?"

"Fine." Oliver seated himself and Francis engaged him in conversation about the Company and a recent incident at the Bengal Club. Celia was relieved to simply listen, with only a comment from time to time when it seemed necessary. When Oliver rose to take his leave, he spoke of Iris.

"Convey my best wishes to Mrs. Beddington when you see her, please."

"Of course."

"Seems uncalled for to hunt the woman up with all the new friends you've made," Francis said.

"But she is a dear friend and she nursed me through my illness!" Celia was shocked at his callous attitude.

Francis shrugged. "Do as you please. I'll walk out with you, Oliver. Tell me, is it true that Claude is entering that gelding in the races next week?"

The next morning Celia had the phaeton brought about immediately after breakfast and her morning bath. Beyond the Maidan, the houses had a less pretentious air, Georgian structures on a small scale, mixed with bungalows with thatched roofs and wide compounds around them, yet the section was quite pleasant and orderly. The Beddington house was small and set far back from the road amid clumps of dark green shrubbery.

The *chuprassie* ran to the door to hand Celia's card to the servant who answered his summons. Moments later, Celia was ushered into a small parlor crowded with heavy pieces of worn furniture. Iris came toward her, smiling.

"Iris! How wonderful to see you at last! I've looked everywhere for you—I should have gotten your address before I left the ship!" Celia hugged the other woman in a burst of enthusiasm.

"You were quite busy with Francis." Iris studied her. "You look the picture of health. You seem to have completely recovered from the fever." When Iris looked at her slyly, Celia felt her cheeks glow but she did not look away. Iris led her to a sofa. "Something cool—lemonade?"

Celia nodded. "I should have sent a chit but I couldn't wait another moment. Can you forgive me for popping in this way?"

"Of course. How did you find me?"

"Oliver Chadwick was kind enough to secure your address for me. I—I met him quite unexpectedly at a party last week."

Iris waited until the servant brought a tray and passed tall glasses of lemonade. "I'm delighted to see you, Celia."

"And I you. I'm sorry I was so thoughtless not to invite you to the wedding. Can you forgive me?"

"Of course." Iris had not expected such an invitation any more than she had this visit. Once the voyage from England was over, she had not counted on rubbing elbows with Mrs. Francis Devy. Celia was an innocent to believe otherwise, but Iris said nothing to disillusion her. Interesting that she had seen Oliver, but then they would travel in the same circles. She'd had no idea Oliver was as high in the Company or she would not have dared to approach him so boldly, not that she was sorry the way things had worked out.

"Tell me about yourself," Celia said, relaxing and trying to recapture some of the camaraderie they had shared en route from England.

"There's not much to tell," Iris said. "I've not had time to do anything but get settled. James is busy at the factory every day and he'll soon be going upcountry again."

"You'll be alone?"

Iris shrugged. It had not occurred to her that she would miss James.

"Then we can spend the days together!" Celia caught herself quickly. "Unless you have other plans?"

"No. I'm not even sure when James is leaving."

"We can see the city. I haven't seen the Botanical Gardens yet, have you?"

"The Gardens? No." She had never thought of looking at plants, even as a diversion, though she found Calcutta boring. So far it had been an endless procession of dull people and dull days. God, how she longed for London again. Maybe it would be fun to spend time with Celia. At least she'd see another segment of society—the upper crust. James had been impressed when she'd related the names of her traveling companions, especially Oliver Chadwick. When James told her Oliver's position with the Company, she knew she'd made a valuable ally. And now Celia was offering her a chance to move back into that charmed circle.

A tremendous crash came from the back of the house and James's voice rose. "You blasted fool!" There was a sound of something slamming hard against the floor. "Move out of my way, damn you! Can't you do the simplest thing right!" A door banged.

Iris hid her irritation and ignored the outburst. What the devil was James doing home at this time of day? To Celia she said, "Perhaps Francis would prefer to show you the city himself."

Celia shook her head, happy to ignore the disturbance without comment. "He spends more and more time at the Fort, and I hate being alone."

"Surely you have made many friends."

Celia made a face. "They are dull women who sit around and gossip endlessly." And who know about Francis's affair with Gwenn Katon, she thought. Through bits of gossip, she had learned that Gwenn was married to an elderly but very wealthy man who remained in England while she traveled abroad at whim. "Besides, you are a dear friend."

Iris turned at the sound of footsteps and a tall, stocky man entered the room. He stopped short on seeing Celia and his scowl was instantly replaced by a smile.

"I'm sorry," he said to Iris. "I didn't know you had a guest."

"James, this is Celia Sker—Devy. You remember, I told you we came out from England together."

"What a delightful surprise, Mrs. Devy." James's eyes widened and his expression altered as he made her a polite bow. "I've heard so many lovely things about you."

201

"Thank you." Celia thought him quite charming and found it hard to associate him with the angry shouting she had heard a few moments ago. He had dark hair and a heavy, angular face that was somewhat softened by a short beard and moustache. His eyes were coal black and set in deep sockets under bushy brows that almost met. He was a striking figure of a man but intense and quick in manner.

He sat beside Iris, smiling and staring at Celia until she lowered her eyes. He said, "Iris has talked of you so often I almost feel I know you. Does Calcutta meet your expectations?"

She forced herself to look up. "I really didn't know what to expect but I find it quite pleasant. I was just suggesting to Iris that we see some of the sights together."

He inclined his head slightly. "How nice. Iris would enjoy that, wouldn't you, dear?"

"Of course. What brings you home so early, James?"

"I'm being sent out sooner than I thought. I came home to pack. I must be on my way by early afternoon." He turned to Celia. "We're bringing in a new shipment of silk—but then you're not interested in Company business."

"Oh, but I am. I must admit, though, that I know little about it. It seems the topic of conversation everywhere I go."

He laughed softly. "Yes, I dare say the women tire of endless Company talk. I understand you live near the Fort?" He switched the subject deftly.

Celia told them of the house Francis had let and of her own difficulties in getting accustomed to the servants and the strange Indian customs. "I miss the familiar surroundings of home but I suppose I shall get over that. I'm already looking forward to spending time with Iris."

He looked at his wife. "I'm sure Iris is looking forward to it, too." Iris looked as though she might say something but merely nodded.

"It's settled then?" Celia exclaimed. "Tomorrow? We can have lunch at Spence's Hotel—I hear it's very pleasant."

James got to his feet. "I must see to my packing. Don't let me interrupt your visit." He bowed over Celia's hand and pressed it to his lips briefly. "Do come again, Mrs. Devy, you are always welcome here." With that he left.

"I should go," Celia said, feeling she was intruding. Iris would certainly want to spend a few last moments alone with her husband. Iris walked with her to the door.

"I'll come by for you mid-morning?" Celia said.

"Fine."

Celia went out to the carriage, turned to wave and stepped up. A strange man, James Beddington. And quite a temper. No wonder Iris never talked about him.

In the weeks that followed, Celia saw Iris often. They rode about the city, strolled the greensward of the Maidan and had lunch or tea at several of the fine restaurants frequented by the English. Iris asked innumerable questions about Francis and his work, which Celia answered to the best of her ability, though she knew few details. One afternoon, Celia invited several of the women to tea when Iris came, but she quickly realized her mistake. Iris was outside the perimeter of acceptability for officers' wives, and though Amanda and the others were polite, the afternoon was strained and awkward. Iris said little, but the next time Celia sent a *chuprassie* with a chit asking Iris to ride with her, Iris sent regrets that she was engaged. Their excursions dwindled to occasional calls, with Celia going to Iris rather than the other way around.

Francis's duties kept him away from the house more and more, and when he absented himself some evenings, Celia wondered if he was with Gwenn Katon. Celia filled the days with riding lessons under the watchful eye of a *syce*. When she had mastered the technique, she found it exhilarating, and insisted that Francis find a pony for Mary so that the child could ride with her. Mary was frightened but Celia encouraged her until she gained confidence.

The fourth week in January, Francis came home to find Celia and Mary returning from a brief jaunt along the river. She was alarmed at seeing him and she swung down from the mare and ran to him.

"What is it?"

"Unexpected orders. Here now, nothing to make you frown." He rubbed at the deep lines across her brow. "That's what soldiering is all about, you know."

"Must you go to fight? Oh, Francis—"

203

"Hush. No fighting, at least I hope not. Another skirmish that can be settled by showing the flag more than likely."

"How long will you be gone?"

"A few days at most. Come, I've time for a brandy and water before I leave." He took her hand and led her indoors, chatting about inconsequentials to keep her mind off the impending patrol.

She appreciated his trying to put her at ease, but she could not help worrying. It was the first time they had been separated for more than a few hours since their marriage, and she disliked the thought. She asked if wives ever went along with their soldier husbands, and Francis laughed.

"If things are quiet in the country, and the march is a long one. But this is nothing of the sort, and I shall be back before you would have time to ready yourself for such a trip. Besides, I don't think you would enjoy the tent life. Few women can tolerate the discomforts." He took her in his arms and kissed her. She clung to him until the *syce* appeared in the doorway and informed him all was ready. Then she stood on the verandah, waving until his horse was out of sight.

On the fifth day of his absence, she could no longer stand the empty house nor endure the company of other military wives. She sent a note to Iris asking her to come for the day, but the *chuprassie* reported that *memsahib* Beddington was not at home. Celia paced about and finally told Mary to prepare for a ride. Perhaps the air would clear her mind of worrisome thoughts which imagined Francis wounded or ill.

Celia had instructed the tailors to fashion a riding dress for Mary to match her own. Beige linen, the short, close-fitting coat was trimmed with black buttons and a small velvet bow at the throat; the full skirt was gathered at the left hip and pulled up into a puff that lifted it several inches to expose lace petticoats. The tall black velvet hat had a wide band and a long train of gossamer beige voile; soft black leather gloves and a short riding crop completed the outfit. Except for the unmistakable differences in their coloring, Celia thought they might seem to be sisters—or mother and child. No, she was too young to have a daughter that age ... but not too young to be a mother. Would she and Francis have a child soon? The thought both frightened and pleased her.

They rode north along the river bank, on a trail that occasionally wended a short distance into the cool, shadowed jungle. The landscape was totally different but put Celia in mind of Renfield because of the greenness and freshness of the warm day. The *syce* rode in front, turning frequently to make sure *memsahib* was close behind, pointing out any small depressions in the trail that might make the horses stumble. Mostly they rode in silence except for a cry of delight from Celia when they came upon a particularly huge banyan tree or some low, stunted growth that appeared like an ugly dwarf. They crossed a small stream that widened below and seemed almost a lake in the distance. When the path became rougher the *syce* turned back toward the river.

From time to time Celia engaged Mary in small talk but the child had not yet overcome her shyness nor stepped out of her role as servant, despite Celia's friendliness. Mary had a perpetual frightened look and her eyes darted about as though the unexpected might come upon her at any moment. She had learned to ride passably well, though she often clung to the pommel even when the pony was walking.

The sun was high and the day growing warm. They recrossed the stream and turned back in order to reach the city before the peak heat of the day. Celia had just instructed the *syce* to stop and rest the horses and was being helped from the saddle when she heard the sound of hoofbeats. To her amazement, Oliver Chadwick came riding along the trail, reining in when he saw them. He sat looking down at her, his dark riding coat and fawn-colored breeches adding to his stature so that he looked like a giant towering over her.

"I did not know you were in the habit of riding along this trail, Celia. A most pleasant surprise, I assure you." His eyes held her as though daring her to look away.

She met his look boldly. "This is the first time I have come this far, but one tires of the view along the Maidan as a daily diet."

"Quite so." He swung easily from the huge black he was

riding. "The forest is cool and pleasant this time of year."

"Do you ride here often?"

"Whenever I can escape my duties." He was staring at her again and she felt the tingling sensation his look elicited.

She turned and began to stroll along the path. When the *syce*, rifle slung over his shoulder, made to fall in step behind her, Oliver motioned him back. "Stay with the young *memsahib*," he commanded. With two long strides he was beside Celia. She nervously inspected tiny wild flowers, plucking a few blossoms to form a small bouquet. Was it accident that Oliver should come along at this moment, or had he known she was here?

Oliver watched her with smouldering passion. She was so determined not to look at him, busying herself with the flowers she held. She was beautiful and he was consumed with envy of Francis, who didn't deserve her. He wondered if Celia knew that Francis had resumed his affair with Gwenn Katon, who at this very moment was visiting acquaintances in the province of Jharpur, where Devy's unit was on patrol.

"You located Iris without trouble?"

Celia nodded without looking up. "Yes, we've spent many enjoyable days together."

He reached for her arm and turned her about. Her eyes went wide but there was no fear in them. "And what about me?" he asked softly. "Have you no compassion for my loneliness?" He pulled her into his arms.

She struggled for a moment but was no match for his strength. Her heart raced as he bent to her. "No—" His lips crushed against hers and blotted out her protest. She was swept in a tide of desire beyond her control. As she had in Malta, she felt herself responding against her will. Her mind balked and she tore her lips from his. She was a married woman—no matter that her husband was away or that he had broken their marriage vows.

"Don't!"

"Why not? Can you deny you want me as I want you?"

"No—I mean yes—let me go!"

"Come with me now. We can be alone for a few hours and I swear you'll lose any doubts." He kissed her again until she was breathless and shaking.

"Please!" It was almost a whimper. "I cannot ... you mustn't." She was shivering with tormented desire which might easily consume her.

"Celia, I have thought of you and wanted you since I first set eyes on you. Come with me. We can return to England."

Abruptly she tore herself away from him. "Do you think that I am some wanton that can be had at a whim? Let me go, or I shall scream!" She was frightened now, of what he might do and of the raging emotions within her own body and mind. She turned from him and buried her face in her hands while her shoulders heaved. She could not allow him to touch her!

Oliver's face flamed. Any other woman he would have taken against her will, but he could not bring himself to do so with Celia. Nor could he put her out of his mind and pretend he did not want her as he had never wanted any other woman. He'd been haunted by the memory of her, and his need had grown despite the comforting presence of other women in his bed. They were substitutes, nothing more. It was Celia he wanted. Damn! He cursed himself for a fool for not carrying her off before she married Devy. What kind of a miracle was he hoping for? That she'd tire of Francis and realize her mistake? Come to him of her own accord?

A piercing shriek wheeled him about, and Celia looked up with terror-stricken eyes.

"Mary!"

Oliver was already moving, his long legs biting off huge strides as he ran back toward the spot where they'd left Mary and the horses. A rifle shot cracked as new screaming erupted.

Celia picked up her skirts and ran behind, her heart hammering beneath her ribs and icy sweat trickling between her shoulder blades. Oliver was lost around a bend in the trail. Celia did not realize they had come so far. Then all at once she heard the dreadful commotion of Mary's screams and the frightened whinnying of the horses. The *syce* was shrieking wildly, and above it all Oliver's command, "Stand aside, you fool!"

She came around the bend to see Mary lying on the ground, an immense tiger standing over her with one huge paw on her shoulder, its head turned toward the gesticulating *syce*. The animal made a low throaty sound that caused shivers along Celia's spine and rooted her with fear. The animal's gleaming eyes flicked to her for an instant, then went back warily to the *syce* and Oliver who had drawn his pistol and was taking aim. The animal sensed the motion and released Mary from the weight of its paw as it hunched forward. Mary whimpered, her face white, her mouth open and gasping. A smear of red ran across the beige coat where the claws had ripped cloth and flesh.

The huge beast crouched, ready to spring. Oliver's shot exploded through the silent jungle, the tiger roared with rage as the ball struck it. In almost the same instant, the animal leaped, but Oliver was already springing sideways to grab up the *syce*'s rifle which lay on the ground between them. He gripped it by the muzzle and brandished it like a club, striking the tiger a blow at the side of the skull as it landed on the spot where Oliver had stood a moment before. It hesitated, eyes wide, fangs bared, and a steady low snarl came from its throat. Oliver swung the rifle again and again, poking at the beast until quite suddenly it retreated, turning about and running into the jungle.

Celia gasped for breath and willed herself not to faint. She stumbled forward as Oliver rushed to lift Mary and examine the wound at her shoulder. Celia fell to her knees, tears flooding down her cheeks.

"Mary—oh, God! Mary—"

"She's all right," Oliver said as he tore the slashed jacket away from the wound and pressed a white handkerchief from his pocket to staunch the blood. "Clawed ... not too deep."

Mary's eyes fluttered and found Celia. Celia's relief was so great that she could not stop crying. "Oh Mary, Mary ..."

"We'd best get her home," Oliver said. He issued a sharp command to the *syce* who mounted his horse, and accepted Mary's huddled form when Oliver handed it up to him. Oliver helped Celia mount, then swung to his own horse, grabbing the reins of Mary's pony to lead behind. He reached over to touch Celia's hands reassuringly. "She'll be all right, don't be frightened."

208

Celia nodded mutely. The horse shied, restless and frightened with the scent of the tiger still in its nostrils. Oliver patted its neck and spoke softly. Ahead, the *syce* rode at a steady pace, Mary cradled in his arms, her eyes closed, her breathing settled to a fine rasping.

"I shall never forgive myself," Celia moaned.

"No one is to blame. The *syce* saw the animal as soon as it emerged from the jungle but his shot missed. He had the courage to distract the animal with his screams or it might have been much worse."

"I never should have stopped. I never should have left her there. She's always been frightened of the jungle." Fresh tears sprang to Celia's eyes.

Oliver reached across to pull at the reins to stop her horse. He leaned from the saddle and caught her face in his hand, turning it toward him and bending to touch his lips lightly to hers. "Don't blame yourself—not ever. This is a wild dangerous country. No man should bring a woman here!"

"Please, don't—" She was too miserable for such thoughts. Oliver released her and they set out once more. Try as she would, Celia could not erase his words. India was a dreadful place, and she wished fervently that she had never set foot in it.

When they reached the house, Oliver sent immediately for the doctor from the Fort and remained with Celia until he came. After examining Mary, Major Walker agreed with Oliver's diagnosis that the wounds were not serious. He applied fresh dressings and gave Mary a draught to help her sleep.

"She seems in a daze," he told Celia when they emerged from the room. "The shock has taken its toll and she needs rest. I'll be glad to stop by again if it will ease your mind."

"Yes, please do."

When he left, she asked Oliver to go also saying she wanted to rest; instead she sat staring at the sleeping Mary and reliving her guilt.

By the time Francis returned from patrol four days later, Mary's wounds were healing but her mind was not. She sat on the verandah in the chair Celia had prepared, staring out across the yard and barely responding when spoken to. The doctor had pronounced her out of danger, but despite Celia's entreaties, there was nothing he could prescribe for Mary's depressed state of mind except time.

Francis was furious on hearing of the incident. "I shall have the *syce*'s hide for taking you into such danger!"

Celia grabbed at his arm as he would have left to attend to the thrashing himself that moment. "The fault was not his—please, Francis!"

"You might have been killed. Pure luck that Oliver happened to come along and had the presence of mind to act as he did." Celia had not emphasized the fact that she and Oliver had strolled off alone, though it weighed heavily on her conscience. When she thought of Oliver kissing her and trying to convince her to run off with him, she went into a cold sweat.

In the next months, Mary was up and about but lacking in spirit. She was silent and withdrawn, and nothing Celia did brought her from the lethargy. She refused to ride or go near the horses, and her terror was so real that Celia had not the heart to insist. Francis grew impatient with his wife's preoccupation with Mary and would have switched the child to bring her out of her temper. His attitude astonished Celia and when she begged him to be gentle with Mary, he reminded her impatiently that Mary was a servant, nothing more. Celia found it prudent to avoid the subject and to keep Mary out of sight when Francis was at home. On the infrequent occasions Celia could entice Mary to talk, Mary begged tearfully to go home to England. When Celia finally found the courage to broach the subject to Francis she was surprised at his ready agreement, and he made arrangements for Mary to accompany one of the officers' families that was going on leave in April.

Francis too seemed changed after his return from the up-country patrol. His duties took him away each day, and he no longer made the effort to steal an hour or two with Celia during slack periods. He also absented himself many evenings and spent his time at the Bengal Club, taverns and public houses where men whiled away hours over drinks and gaming tables. Celia knew too that he was seeing Gwenn Katon, and her heart burned with shame at the thought. More than once she had caught veiled remarks about Francis's conduct, though none of the women were rude enough to discuss Francis's infidelities openly.

By March the weather grew hot and Celia lost much of the enthusiasm that had marked her arrival in Calcutta. The cool evenings and pleasant days that had delighted her gave way to foggy mornings that turned bright and hot by noon. By month's end, an occasional storm dumped heavy rain that was swallowed up by the dry ground, a token of what was to come. The temperature climbed steadily as the hot season approached, and nights gave little respite. Coolies were assigned to keep the *punkahs* in motion, but the fans seemed to do little good. The heat was an endless thing, wrapping the house in its tight embrace.

At last Celia understood the lethargy the other women displayed. She forced herself to ride occasionally, staying close to home along the Maidan where she might catch some vagrant breeze from the river. She rode alone, except for the *syce* who remained at her side even in the safety of the city. She avoided the market places and bazaars where the heat thickened the fetid smells that hung in the air.

She received a letter from her mother, and to her surprise, learned that her father had been transferred to the northern London parish. Her mother wrote little of the new post except to say that the Reverend Skerritt was pleased to do the Lord's work wherever he was needed and he was meeting the challenge of establishing a school for the ragged children of factory workers. There was no news from Kevin.

Mary left on a hot day in mid-April when the temperature rose to 110° and the air was difficult to breathe. Celia rode with her to the quay; Mary sat silent in the carriage and looked very lost surrounded by boxes and a small trunk packed with the numerous dresses Celia had ordered sewn for her. Even the thought of going home had not put any spark in the child's eyes, and Celia wondered what would become of her. In the dinghy, Mary did not once turn to look back.

Celia watched until she could no longer see the small figure in the distant boat and fought back her own longing for England. When she turned, she found Oliver Chadwick watching her. She felt a tide of embarrassment and irritation. He had called at the house several times to inquire after Mary, and Celia invented excuses not to be alone with him for even a moment; when possible, she avoided seeing him altogether. She could not avoid him now since he was standing directly in her path, his hand resting lightly on the wheel of the carriage.

His dark eyes swept toward the packet anchored off shore. "I think it is wise you are sending her home. I only wish to God it were in my power to do the same for you."

Celia's cheeks flamed and she busied herself with her reticule so that he would not see her discomfort.

"Celia—" His hand touched hers and she drew back as if scorched. "Ride with me, I have a carriage there." He indicated a closed coach with the East India Company seal on its door. "I must speak with you."

"No, I cannot—"

"Dammit, do you want me to say my piece here where any passing sailor or citizen can hear?"

She looked about in alarm. She had never heard him so vehement, and the expression on his face was so terrifying she knew he meant every word. She nodded mutely, and he slipped his hand under her arm. He spoke quickly to Celia's driver, then he led her to his own coach and instructed the driver before climbing up. The carriage moved away from the waterfront along a road that skirted the central part of the city and bypassed the Fort and the Maidan.

"I really must not stay away too long," Celia started.

Oliver peered at her. "And what important task awaits you at home? A dress to be fitted? A letter to write? Or perhaps an exciting afternoon of tea with the good ladies of Calcutta?"

"Stop it—"

"Then stop inventing excuses to escape me." He turned abruptly and pulled her into his arms. "Can't you see that I am going mad without you?"

She pummeled his coat front and twisted from him. "I am a married—"

"For God's sake, stop repeating that inane fact! If I were able to change that don't you think I would do so— in an instant!? I'm talking about you and me. We belong together, Celia, I've known that from the first."

"No."

He glared at her, angry yet at the same time wanting her more than he had ever wanted anything. "Can you swear to me that you are happy with Francis?"

The question took her off guard. "I—of course I am—" her voice faltered, "—happy."

"Your husband sees fit to play you for the fool and you say you are happy?"

"I—I don't know what you're talking about."

He laughed harshly. "Francis boasts of his affair with Gwenn Katon and she is shameless in following him about. Every man in the Regiment knows that she invents visits upcountry whenever he goes on patrol and that he spends his nights with her instead of in the officers' tents. The gossip is on every tongue in Calcutta."

She was stunned. She had heard bits of gossip, of course, though most were quickly hushed when she entered a room. But Oliver was saying that Gwenn and Francis were together when he was away on patrol! Francis had made light of her inquiry if wives accompanied the men, and all along he was planning to be with *her!* Oliver's fierce gaze tore from her what little courage remained. She bit her lip and turned away to stare out the window.

"Celia, come with me. We can return to England. I can arrange a position in the Company offices. Life without you is torment."

Tears burned at her eyelids and she felt weak and helpless. She longed to let him embrace her, comfort her and drive the misery of reality from her mind. Why did life have to be so complicated? Oliver drew her to his bosom, his impatient hand knocking her bonnet askew as he bent and searched for her lips. His kiss was hungry and hot, and she clung to him breathlessly for a moment as tangled emotions swept through her. Her body tingled and desire was born, flaming too quickly and easily. All at once, reality flooded back like a tide of icy water. She tugged free and slid away as far as the carriage seat would allow.

"Stop—we must not—" Words seemed so terribly inadequate.

He stared at her, shaking his head. "How long can you

lie to yourself? You want me as much as I want you, why deny it? Say you'll come with me."

"No, it's impossible. I can't—I won't. What I mean is I don't want to. You have no right to treat me so." She was trembling and her mind whirled dizzily.

"Love is a right in itself."

"I will not betray Francis."

"Damn!" He slapped his palm against the leather cushion of the seat with a loud smacking sound that made her jump. "You speak of fidelity when that scoundrel beds another—"

"Stop it!" She clasped her hands over her ears and shook her head. "I won't listen. Tell the driver to take me home this instant!" She began to weep, and Oliver sighed heavily. He leaned back into the corner of the coach, not looking at her and giving her a chance to compose herself.

When he finally turned, his eyes were soft. "I'm sorry, Celia. It's only that Francis is such an ass that I find it difficult to be civil about him. I didn't mean to upset you, it's only that I think I shall go out of my mind needing you as I do."

"It's better that we don't see each other," she said lamely. She knew she should refute his statements of her feelings toward him, but she did not. She was angry at the liberties he took, and she was confused by her own emotions each time he touched her.

He said nothing more but rapped for the driver and instructed him to turn toward Chowringhee-road.

CHAPTER THIRTEEN

May settled into a blanket of pitiless heat that made the distant buildings shimmer and seem to flow into the dark river. Celia's energies waned. Francis arranged to purchase ice regularly from ships from America and instructed the *babaches* in making tall, frosted fruit drinks for the *memsahib*. She had little taste for the chilled wines or beer that he favored, and lately she had been suffering frequent bouts of indigestion upon waking.

When the monsoons came, most of the social life they'd known all winter ceased; the women retired to their houses and rarely stirred. Celia was glad to escape the wagging tongues, though she was sure the gossip about Francis continued. There had been a new rumor that he was tiring of Gwenn Katon and had taken up with some half-caste woman of easy virtue, but Celia ignored it as she did all the others. She spent her days lounging on the sofa under the slow-moving *punkah* and with two small, dark, nearly naked boys fanning her with broad palm leaves. She read or stitched on a sampler until her eyes bleared and her fingers cramped. She had not seen Iris lately, and she studiously avoided venturing into any places where she might accidentally meet Oliver. She had not forgotten their last encounter, and she did not trust herself to think about it often.

The house was marvelously endowed with a huge cistern in the rear yard near the carriage house, and Celia enjoyed the luxury of frequent baths to help cool her. A huge tin tub was kept in one of the extra bedrooms, and the *syces* had fashioned a bamboo pipeline to carry water from the cistern directly indoors. Most of the time the water was comfortably tepid.

One particularly unbearable day, Celia ordered a tub before lunch. She had little appetite and she wondered if more than the heat might be the cause. Her time was late and most mornings she felt decidedly queasy. Several times she had rushed from the bedchamber lest Francis see her retching. She lowered herself into the tub and sat with her chin barely above the water, eyes closed and mind wandering. Was she with child? It seemed more than likely, and she had mixed emotions at the prospect. India was hardly the place she would choose to bear and raise a child, but others were doing it. Harriet Evans's youngest was barely two—a dark solemn child who never seemed to laugh. Jenny Pierce had confided to Celia that she had borne a child a year before but that the baby had sickened and died in its first month. But Jenny was frail and sickly, while Celia was not. If she was with child, it would be a healthy child, she was sure. Except for the minor bouts of morning sickness, she had not been ill since the fever she'd suffered aboard ship.

Would Francis be happy? They had not talked of a family, but she supposed every man wanted a son. The Devys would look forward to male heirs.

She sighed and sat up, lifting the sponge and squeezing cool water over her shoulders and breasts. Perhaps a child would bind Francis to her more closely. And perhaps it would give Francis the desire to return to Aylesford as soon as possible. She rose from the tub, waving off the *ayah* who would rub her dry and rob her of the pleasant cool effects of the bath. She stood on a mat letting the water drip from her. She did not hear Francis until he was in the room, staring at her and ordering the *ayah* to leave them. He came to Celia, smiling and reaching to take the towel as she made to cover herself.

"A woman married so many months cannot be shy with her husband," he teased.

She let her hands fall to her sides. "Do you still find me beautiful?"

"More than words can describe." He came to her,

216

standing close enough to touch her damp flesh, first her shoulder and neck and brushing back a tendril of moist hair. His hands moved down her body and found the full curve of her breasts and held them, his fingers lingering over the rosy peaks. She shivered deliciously and he heard her breath escape. She was still the most beautiful creature he had ever seen. Her body was perfection, an alabaster statue of a goddess. He felt the hard, tight desire grow within him, and he drew her close and kissed her.

Celia came to him breathlessly, instantly excited by his touch, forgetting and forgiving the past. His hands were restless on her body, exploring and tasting, exciting both of them. When he released her mouth, she saw the desire in his eyes and felt the hard impression of it against her body. Without speaking, he drew her to the bed and lay her upon it, sitting beside her and stroking her. He bent and touched his lips to a breast, making her quiver with delight until she was moaning softly. He stood back then and undressed, and she watched him unashamedly. She found joy in the sight of his naked flesh ... the soft dark curled hairs at his chest, his narrow waist and hips ... the dark compelling triangle that held his promise.

He came to her, kissing her again and again and touching her in intimate places. He was gentle yet forceful, seeming to know when she had reached the point of need, then entering her and moving gently at first until they both built to a peak. She clung to him, her desire and love so complete that she could only cry his name over and over as the sudden rush of heat suffused them both. When it was over, he moved slowly from her and lay at her side, his arm across her belly and his hand resting lightly at her breast. She felt content and full of joy, and in a burst of love told him her suspicions.

He raised himself to one elbow and stared at her. "A child?!"

"I cannot be sure yet."

"Good God! I have never pictured myself as a father!"

She bit her lip. "Does it displease you?" The bubble of her happiness seemed threatened.

He looked at her, his dark eyes full of wonder. "Lord, no! A child!" He pulled her into his arms and kissed her with renewed ardor, then drew away abruptly and looked at her with serious eyes. "Have I hurt you—why didn't you tell me before I—"

She laughed softly and pulled his face down to kiss his mouth quickly. "I have never felt better—there is no harm."

He relaxed and smiled. "Of course ... but you must take care of yourself. I want nothing to befall my son."

"Nor I."

"You shall see the doctor at once," he said, sitting up and frowning as though already making plans.

"It is not time. There is nothing to be done."

"Still, I would feel better knowing you took every precaution. The right foods to keep you strong, perhaps a trip north until the hot season passes."

She laughed and shook her head. "I shall do everything at the proper time. But I will not be sent away when I want nothing but to be with you."

His face became somber and he sat up. She saw the quick change in his eyes. "What is it?"

He looked back to her. "I must be away a few days. I came home to tell you we are leaving this evening."

"Oh, Francis!" She wanted to cry but did not. The tales of Gwenn Katon joining him upcountry were like a knife wound. She also knew of the problems with the opium traffic, and she was frightened by the reports of shootings. He calmed her fears and said it would be over soon and he would be home quickly. "Less than a week, I think." He took her in his arms again and kissed her. "I forbid you to worry, darling. Think only of my return and of the child we must plan for. Will it be a boy, do you think?" He pressed his hand to her flat belly as though to determine an answer for himself.

"Yes ..."

"We'll name him Francis, of course."

He kissed her and she clung to the warm delight of his lean, hard body until they were both breathless and passionate again. Their lovemaking was gentle and prolonged and completely satisfying.

She spent the next five days much as all others but her heart was lighter. Sharing the hope for the child with Francis had strengthened her spirit and Celia knew tha*

she was entering a new phase of her life. When Francis returned, she would consult the post physician—to please her husband and to insure her peace of mind. And when there was no margin of doubt, she would write to her parents and to Francis's.

Ram Coomar came into the parlor, bowing as he announced that Colonel Collingworth wished to see her. Celia had been so lost in thought she had not heard the carriage, and she sat up quickly, telling the *khansamah* to show the Colonel in.

The Colonel entered, bowing and coming forward to take her hand. "Celia, my dear . . ."

"Good afternoon, Colonel. Please, won't you sit down? Will you take tea—or perhaps beer or wine?"

He sat across from her and shook his head. "Nothing, thank you."

"I'm delighted to see you again. It's been awhile. Amanda is well?"

"Quite, thank you." He cleared his throat, sitting stiffly, his kepi on his knees, his thin face solemn. "Celia—" He seemed terribly ill at ease and she felt a surge of panic.

"Francis—has something happened?" She came up from the sofa and the Colonel rose quickly, tossing aside the kepi and taking both her hands.

"He has been wounded—"

She stared at him, her eyes wide and frightened. "Where is he? I must go to him." She tried to tear herself loose but the Colonel gripped her more tightly.

"Everything is being done."

Tears flooded her eyes and she twisted from his grasp, turning to look about the room helplessly. A huge shuddering sob filled her and exploded, and she buried her face in her hands. She felt the Colonel's arms about her and she cried against the warm stiffness of his uniform. When some of the terrible anguish eased, she looked at him through tear-swollen eyes.

"Please . . . tell me everything."

Colonel Collingworth produced a handkerchief and handed it to her as he led her to the sofa. "There was a skirmish, really only a brief flurry of fighting but several of our men were wounded. Luckily, a field surgeon accompanied the patrol, so medical help was available at

219

once." He looked away as her gaze found him again. Lord, how could he tell her that her husband had come close enough to death to hear its whispering? Francis still wasn't out of danger by a long shot; wounds often festered in the stinking heat, causing complications that the doctors were powerless to halt.

"The—the wounds are not serious?" Even as she spoke she knew she was trying to reassure herself.

"The doctor has arranged to return him to Calcutta as soon as possible."

"May I go to him?"

"It's out of the question. The incident took place in a remote pass in the hills. Ambush—" His face suffused with anger and he cleared his throat. No point recounting the bloody horror of it. Devy was lucky to come out of it alive, more fortunate than two others. "My men will have him back within the week. Best that he come directly here. The doctor will look in regularly." He released her hands and rose to retrieve his kepi. "I'll bring you news the moment I hear anything." She looked so incredibly helpless and pathetic sitting with head bowed, that he felt a wave of pity. Damned ugly business for a woman, especially one so young and unaccustomed to brutality. How could he tell her that her husband was in grave condition and that the doctor despaired of total recovery?

"If there is anything we can do . . ."

She shook her head without looking up. She had covered her face with her hands once more and looked for all the world like a forlorn child.

"I can ask Amanda to come."

"No—thank you," Celia said, gulping the sobs and glancing at him. "I—I would prefer being alone. You will notify me as soon as—"

"Of course."

Celia lost track of time as she sat crying. Why? Why did it have to be *him?* And why now when they had such promise of happiness in store? She roused herself as the shadows in the room lengthened and found Ram Coomar staring at her from the doorway. "*Memsahib,* dinner . . . ?"

She shook her head and walked past. "No, nothing."

She went upstairs and lay across the bed to stare into

the gloom. She pressed her hands to her belly where Francis's child was.

Francis was brought home five days later, so pale and still on the stretcher that Celia's heart twisted at the sight. The bearers carried him upstairs to the big bedroom and laid him onto the fresh sheets, telling Celia that Major Walker, the post physician, would come by shortly. Alone with Francis, Celia sat at the side of the bed and tried to calm her throbbing heart. Her worst fears were realized at seeing him; he lay without moving, his breathing barely lifting the sheet that covered him, his face drawn and bloodless. She touched his hand, clasping it in her own as though to somehow transfer her strength to him. He could not die—she would not let him! She would nurse him back to health and he would be strong again. They would return to Aylesford, and their child would be born, their son, and they would watch him grow to manhood. Oh, Francis . . . Francis . . .

She did not realize she had spoken his name aloud until his eyelids fluttered and opened. He stared emptily and a small frown appeared between his brows. She rose and bent over him.

"Francis, darling . . . I'm here." She smiled and forced back the quick tears that threatened.

He looked confused for a moment then his gaze found her and he tried to smile. "Celia?"

"Yes, love. I'm here."

He sighed wearily and his eyes closed. Even such a small effort exhausted him, and he sank back into unconsciousness. Celia sat clasping his hand, willing her strength to him and making plans for their future. She would talk to the Colonel at once about their journey home so that as soon as Francis was strong enough, they could be on their way. When Major Walker and a nurse in a blue and white uniform arrived, Celia retired to the corner to watch as the doctor examined Francis and changed the dressings on his wounds. She had to bite a knuckle to keep from crying out at the sight of the bloodied bandages. When he was finished, Francis's pale face was bathed in sweat.

The doctor drew Celia from the room and tried to reassure her. "The wounds are serious, Mrs. Devy, but your husband has a strong constitution."

"He will—live?" It was scarcely a whisper.

"He has survived remarkably well, and the surgeon at Tokbahr did everything possible." He smiled and patted her arm. "Your strength will help him, you know, but you mustn't worry yourself into collapse. Do you have a woman friend who can come and stay with you?"

She shook her head impatiently. She didn't want anyone.

He sighed. "If there's any change, the nurse will notify me at once."

"Thank you, Major."

Francis developed a fever that raged for days; Celia and the nurse bathed him with cool cloths and coaxed small sips of water between his parched lips. The doctor left laudanum for the pain, but judging by Francis's thrashing and moaning, it seemed to have little effect.

Celia grew thin and drawn. The hot mugginess of the monsoon season lay heavily on Calcutta, and at times she felt barely able to drag herself about. She stayed at Francis's bedside every waking moment. She slept in the small spare bedroom where they had made love before his fateful journey, but came awake often during the night to tiptoe across the hall and stare down at him. People came to inquire, and though Celia met them briefly, she found no solace in their condolences. Oliver Chadwick came, and would not be turned away by the servants at Celia's message. She met him in the parlor, pulling away when he tried to take her hands. She had not been able to erase the memory that she'd been with him when Mary was almost killed; it was as though being with him again might cause some greater misfortune to befall Francis.

"I beg of you, leave me alone. My husband lies gravely ill and I have thoughts for no one but him." She left Oliver staring after her as she walked from the room.

Late that same day Gwenn Katon came. Celia had not expected the woman would dare, and she was shaking with rage as she faced her. "I would think you would have the decency not to show your face here," Celia said.

Gwenn's eyes were icy blue as she stared at Celia. She

had been weeping, and faint circles of redness still marked the puffiness of her eyes.

"I want to see Francis."

Celia glared at her. "Leave my house! Have I not suffered enough because of your wanton conduct with my husband?!"

"I love him—"

"You dare speak to me of love?! I am Francis's wife, you are nothing but a—strumpet! I pity your husband. Get out of this house. You will not see Francis—now or ever again!"

For a moment, Gwenn was ashen. Then she laughed, and the sound was ugly in the quiet room. "Francis does not love you! Have you been able to hold him in your marriage bed? He's glad enough to get away from you when he goes up-country—"

Celia's rage exploded and she struck Gwenn across the face with a furious slap. Gwenn staggered back, pressing her hand to her cheek where the stain of Celia's fingers was already rising.

"Go—now—or I shall call the servants and have you thrown out!" Celia's voice was shaking and her knees were weak but she held the other woman's eyes in a duel of hatred.

Gwenn started to say something, then stopped. She whirled and stalked from the room, and Celia sank weakly into a chair. She felt cold and empty ... and very much alone.

She refused supper and sank into bed to stare at the grey netting. The strain of Francis's illness and of facing Gwenn Katon had exhausted her beyond belief. She gave way to tears and wept until her stomach heaved with the turmoil and she lay sweating and miserable. She called the *ayah* at last and let herself be bathed and put to bed, even accepting the sleeping draught Major Walker had left for her. When she wakened in the night with severe cramps that doubled her over, she was terrified and cried out for the *ayah*. The doctor arrived a half-hour later but it was already too late to save the tiny forming life that would have been her firstborn.

When she was bathed and settled in a clean bed, the doctor stood over her frowning. "You should have told me that you were with child, Mrs. Devy." At the stricken look on her face, he dropped his chiding. She had enough to worry her. Life in this infernal country was devilishly hard on women. He smiled. "I looked in on Francis a moment ago. The fever's broken and the crisis has passed. I think your husband will improve steadily now." He mixed a mild tincture of laudanum and forced her to swallow it. "You'll be right as rain in a few days, and you'll be home in England before the leaves fall. . . ."

CHAPTER FOURTEEN

November 1839, Aylesford

The voyage was long and strenuous, but Celia could not suppress her joy at going home. They booked passage in September; Francis was still weak but the doctor had declared him able to endure the rigors of the trip. He walked with a crutch and his temper was often short, since he was unaccustomed to inactivity and dependence on others, and his wounds still pained. He drank more brandy than Celia thought wise but insisted it deadened the constant ache of his leg. He seemed changed since his illness, more self-centered and less inclined to worry about Celia's welfare and comfort but she laid it to the shock of the wound. Neither she nor Francis had seen Gwenn Katon since the day Celia ordered her from the house, though Celia had heard from Amanda that Gwenn had left for England early in the summer.

Francis hired a private coach to take them across the desert so that they could have frequent rest stops and he could walk to ease his cramped muscles. How very different from her first journey! Celia had written to the Devys early in Francis's convalescence, and there was a letter waiting for him at Gibraltar. After reading it, he dropped it into his writing case without sharing it except to tell her that an Aylesford coach would await them at Southampton.

They arrived at Aylesford on a blustery chill afternoon

in November. As the coach climbed the long driveway, Celia leaned to stare at the bare walls of the towering house. Leafless ivy webbed the grey stone, making it look grim and formidable, and Celia realized she was frightened. She dreaded facing the Devys, except Theo, though all the attention would be on Francis, of course.

There was a flurry of activity as the coach neared the portico, and the great doors were flung open and servants hurried down the steps. Mrs. Devy stood in the doorway with a tall man who must be Anthony—the resemblance to the Devys was unmistakable, tall, dark-haired and almost coal-black eyes under thick brows. He was handsome but already running to heaviness despite his youth. He stood with his arm about his mother's shoulder and restrained her when she would have run to embrace Francis.

Francis allowed two servants to assist him up the steps, where his brother clapped his shoulders heartily.

"Damned good to have you home, Francis."

"Oh, my poor darling—" Mrs. Devy burst into tears and flung herself at him so that he balanced awkwardly on the crutch.

Anthony tried to pull her away gently. "Better let him sit down, Mother. He's had a tiring trip." He motioned to the servants who flung open the doors of the drawing room. Mrs. Devy, still clinging to Francis, led him in. Anthony stared at Celia, his eyes taking in every aspect of her face and dress. Close up, he looked older than her first impression, and his face was suffused with color and his eyes too bright. When he smiled and leaned to her, she smelled the odor of whiskey on his breath. "Celia . . . here, let me take your wrap. We seem to have ignored you in the bustle." He slipped the dark green velvet cloak from her shoulders and handed it to a maid as Celia removed her bonnet and gloves. "I can see that it is my loss not to have met you sooner. Welcome home, Celia Devy." The smile reached his dark eyes.

"Thank you—Anthony?"

"Yes." He slid his hand under her arm and led her toward the drawing room. Running footsteps sounded behind them as Theo clattered down the stairs, skirts held out of the way of her racing feet.

"Celia!" She rushed to embrace her, chattering and weeping until Anthony drew her to one side impatiently.

"I'm sure Celia is weary and would appreciate not having to stand here in the draughty hall while you carry on."

"Forgive me!" Theo slipped her arm through Celia's and they followed Anthony into the drawing room. Francis was seated on a sofa, his feet propped on a petit-point footstool and covered with an afghan, though the room was comfortably warm. A fire in the grate blazed cheerily and in the far corner of the room the gas stove had been lighted. Mrs. Devy sat beside Francis, still holding his hand. Squire Devy was seated in a huge armchair, hunched under a blanket and one leg out before him on a cushioned ottoman. His swollen foot was swathed in bandages that disappeared under the edge of a silk dressing gown. Francis had apparently asked him about it and he was just answering. "Damned gout. Idiot doctor can't do a thing to relieve it—but what about yourself, my boy? Don't have to tell you we were shocked and damned worried to hear that you'd been wounded. How'd it happen?"

"Charles, do be reasonable," Mrs. Devy pouted. "Francis doesn't want to think about that dreadful time in India. Thank heaven you are out of the Army, love." She petted Francis's hand as though he were a child who had suffered a nasty experience that could be erased with a cup of hot milk and a sweet. "Now that you're home, you shall get strong and well and put all that from your mind."

Squire Devy glanced at Celia, recalling his manners tardily. "Welcome back, Celia. You're looking well."

"I am, thank you." She smiled and some of the chill she felt began to dissipate. She was at Aylesford at last, and her life would settle to the comfortable existence of a Devy. Mrs. Devy said nothing; she had eyes for no one but Francis. Theo was on her knees before Francis, smiling at him and babbling with joy at seeing him safe and sound.

"Or almost," Francis amended.

"You will get well?" Theo looked frightened.

He laughed. "Of course, you ninny. I am well now except for the dreadful pain and anguish." He made a terrible face and his mother suppressed a small cry. Anthony caught the joke and moved to the mahogany table near the window and lifted the brandy decanter, pouring three glasses and carrying one each to his father and Francis before lifting his own in a toast.

"To erase the pain and to having you home, Francis—and Celia, too, of course," he said, glancing at her with an easy smile.

"Mama's planned a party," Theo said. "Everyone is so anxious to see you again."

Francis looked pleased and drank the brandy down in a gulp. Watching him, Celia prayed fervently that being home would mend his body and spirit and they might recapture some of the joy they had known earlier in their marriage.

"When's it to be and who's coming?" he asked.

"Weekend after next, that is if you're up to it. I had all I could do to put off people that long."

"I'm sure I will be. Anthony, a refill—" He held the brandy glass out. "Then I shall retire until dinner time. Blasted leg is throbbing again."

"Oh, you poor dear."

Celia sat in the winged armchair and listened to the family conversation in which Anthony or Theo occasionally included her. She felt nothing when she realized Mrs. Devy had begun talking about the Duke of Arbel. Her accidental presence in his house seemed so very long ago that it was like part of another's life, not hers. Many names drifted into the conversation, some that Celia recognized as wealthy or even noble families. She wanted to ask after her own family, but she thought it better to wait until she might talk with Theo in private. When at last she and Francis were shown upstairs, he on the arms of his brother and mother, leaving her to trail behind with a maid, she was glad to be alone with Francis.

The apartment had been newly decorated, with wallpaper of an embossed pattern of gold leaves against a linen background and rich, dark woodwork that gleamed with polish. Gossamer curtains covered the windows and were overlaid with heavy velvet draperies of a deep amber, the coverlet on the bed in a matching satin. Several smaller chairs and a gilt chaise were padded with the finest pale gold velvet. The apartment consisted of four rooms, a sitting room and two dressing rooms opening off the huge bedroom; there was also a small windowless bath that contained a huge tub built into a wooden frame and an apparatus called a water closet discreetly screened behind a panelled door. Celia had read of such things but never seen one, and she marveled at the convenience. The bath also contained a stand which held a built-in basin and had water that ran in a sluggish stream from a tap. She washed her hands and face, reluctant to turn off the water in her fascination.

When at last she emerged, Francis had undressed and lay upon the bed, a thick comforter pulled over him. He had grown thin over the months of his illness, and the injury had debilitated him and drained him of sexual energy. Now he watched her as she removed the green woolen traveling dress and reached for a dressing gown.

"Come here—"

She turned to find him gazing at her with interest. She let the dressing gown fall to the chair and crossed to him. His hand touched her shoulder and slipped the strap of her chemise down.

"You are as lovely as the first time I saw you," he said. His fingers lingered at the warm curve of her breast.

Celia felt a shiver of pleasure. It had been so long since they'd shared any intimacy.

"Lie with me."

"Your wounds—?"

"They affect only my leg and belly, not my manhood." He was already pulling the chemise free and staring at her creamy flesh. His breath quickened, and Celia rose to divest herself of her garments and climb into the bed beside him. He pulled her close, stroking and kissing her with ardor.

She could feel his hardness and she welcomed him desperately. Her own buried desires flared at his touch. She felt the quick surge of his need and she could no longer control her emotions.

"Love me—"

She moved urgently beneath him as she found his lips and slid her tongue over them. The deep kiss ignited the fuse of his passion and he parted her thighs roughly. She met him in a sudden dizzy climb of desire, their bodies fusing in the white heat of long-dormant need. All the

229

misery and pain vanished in ecstasy as they found release in each other. And when it was over, Celia lay with her head nestled at his shoulder, her body warm against his. His breathing was labored but his satisfaction was as complete as her own. In moments he was fast asleep but she did not move. She felt safe and secure once more, home with Francis.

Francis gained strength rapidly during the next days, though his leg still troubled him and his limp did not improve. It was as if being at Aylesford renewed his spirits, and from the bits of conversation Celia heard between him and his father and brother, she realized that Francis was glad to be out of the Army. His lust for adventure dimmed by his mishap, he had no further desire for soldiering.

From Theo, Celia learned that Squire Devy had played a major part in having Reverend Skerritt transferred to the factory parish on the outskirts of London, and it made her blood boil. The Devys had not accepted a poor parson's daughter for their son easily; even now she was aware of the constraint with which the Squire treated her and of Mrs. Devy's coolness. No effort was made to include Celia in decision-making or planning. Francis was pampered and coddled, Celia tolerated. It angered her but she said nothing, and she was sure that in time the Devys would forget their grievances. After all, she was Francis's wife, and they had to accept that reality; she had done nothing to harm them except to love Francis. She wished Francis were more perceptive of her discomfort when Mrs. Devy pointedly steered conversations to topics foreign to Celia, but she suffered the irritation in silence. She spent some time speculating about Anthony. He had taken over management of the estate when the Squire became ill, but though he devoted hours each day talking with overseers and workers and going over books and ledgers, he seemed to have little natural bent for the duties. At times he contradicted his own orders so that chaos developed. Once when Celia chanced upon him in the library, he was pacing in agitation and berating the overseer that he'd been around long enough to solve problems without running for advice all the time. Celia tried to make a hurried exit but Anthony had already seen her. He dismissed the overseer and poured himself a liberal drink from the decanter of whiskey on the desk, though it was not yet noon.

"Damned peasants are too lazy to work out the simplest solutions. The man's stupid, can't follow orders ..." He downed the liquor in a rush and poured another. "When he brings me the books once each month, I'm expected to right his mistakes and figure out his markings." He sighed, then smiled and changed the subject, asking her about her riding and suggesting she try the sleek bay he had recently purchased.

Theo was occupied so that Celia saw little of her. She was engaged to marry a French nobleman, and she spent much of her time in London being fitted for a trousseau and making plans for the wedding which would be held in June.

Mrs. Devy had assigned the elderly nurse, Alice, and a rosy-cheeked, inexperienced young girl to Celia as personal maids. Celia knew that she was being subtly insulted, but she did not complain. She enjoyed the old woman's motherly fussing, though Francis often became impatient and banished her from the apartment in favor of his manservant, Clive. Alice seemed to sense Celia's role as outsider among the Devys and tried to compensate for it by keeping Celia informed on the comings and goings of the family and news of expected guests. The maid, Jennie, was eager to learn and to please, and Celia felt more relaxed with her than she would have with a more skilled servant. Jennie was a local girl and Celia recalled the family in her father's parish. She could see the curiosity and awe in Jennie's face at the knowledge that Celia had once been a country girl like herself and was now a grand lady, but she was careful not to put on airs.

With so little to do, Celia found herself looking forward to the party Mrs. Devy was planning. The house was astir for days and people began arriving early the afternoon of the party. Dozens were to be houseguests for the weekend, and the halls were a constant bustle of activity as maids and valets tended to last minute details of wardrobe. Celia insisted that Francis spend the day resting, and she steadfastly refused everyone admittance to the apartment.

She chose a gown of brown silk, embroidered with tiny yellow and white flowers, that highlighted her fair coloring. The décolletage showed the lush lines of her bosom and the fitted waist accented her slimness. Francis gazed approvingly as she turned from the glass.

"You do a man proud, my sweet." He kissed her and then set to tying a silk cravat. The black silk, tailed coat and close-fitting dark breeches had been altered to hide the ravages of his illness. Except for the crutch, he looked quite fit. It still seemed strange to see him out of uniform, but at the same time it was gratifying to know that he never had to go off to fight again.

As they descended the stairs, Francis on his crutch and gripping the bannister, Celia walking slowly beside him, the music and sound of a hundred voices swirled about them. Standing near the door of the ballroom, Anthony turned as they neared, his glance sweeping over Celia in such a manner that she knew the Devys would find no fault with her appearance. Her cheeks glowed and there was no hesitation in her step. How different from her first party at Aylesford—could it be only a bit over a year ago? She smiled with the confidence of belonging as guests came to greet them.

"Francis—welcome home!"

"Good to see you looking so fit, and something of a hero too, I dare say."

"How dreadful to be wounded. Is it still painful?"

A small knot of people surrounded them; Francis laughed and answered the questions lightly, greeting people and introducing Celia. The women studied her covertly and the men looked approvingly. When at last they entered the ballroom, Mrs. Devy motioned from the far side of the room where several chairs had been placed in a semicircle. Francis was accorded the place of honor so that people could come and chat with him. Anthony smiled and asked Celia to dance.

"It would be a shame if anyone so lovely did not receive the full attention she deserves," he said gallantly.

She blushed prettily. "It is Francis they have come to see."

He swung her in a slow circle to the waltz music. "Francis has been very selfish, hiding you in India so long. I regret my brother's wounds but not the fact that they forced him to bring you home at last."

He was quite charming, and Celia was pleased at his compliments. She smiled and cast a glance toward Francis who was surrounded by well-wishers. "I am glad to escape India's climate and feel the cool English autumn once more."

He asked about her impressions of India but she had the feeling he was only half listening to her responses. He glanced over her shoulder and about the room, watching people who danced by, nodding or murmuring greetings to the guests. When the waltz ended, he led her to the circle of chairs where Francis was deep in conversation with a couple. The woman, gowned in an exquisite creation of red silk that displayed the rich curves of her figure, had pulled her chair close to Francis, her head turned so that Celia saw only a mass of dark curls.

"Your wife is an excellent partner, Francis. Every man here will be thankful for your invalid state which leaves her free to dance with them," Anthony said teasingly. The couple turned, the man rising quickly and bending over Celia's hand. He was short and rotund, with a florid face and balding head; he was impeccably dressed in white buckskin trousers and a honey-colored cutaway coat that strained over his middle.

"My dear . . ."

"Celia, may I present His Lordship, Duke of Arbel . . ."

"M'Lord . . ."

"And his niece, Gwenn Katon—but then maybe you two have already met. Weren't you in Calcutta at the same time?" Anthony said.

Celia stared at the woman whose icy eyes mocked her. "Celia and I have met," Gwenn said with a malicious smile. Her hand lay on Francis's arm intimately and she did not move when Celia glanced toward it; rather the fingers tightened noticeably. "I was just telling Francis how you refused me visiting rights when he lay ill in Calcutta."

"I was following the doctor's orders," Celia said, her neck cording.

"Of course." Gwenn turned back to Francis. "As long as you are well and home, that's what matters. Tell me, have you arranged to see a physician here? Edward knows the most marvelous man from Vienna. I hear he has done wonders with injuries similar to yours. You must see him.

We'd be delighted to have you come and stay at the townhouse when you're in London." She turned and smiled at her uncle. "Wouldn't we, Uncle Edward?"

"Anytime, anytime. The house is open to you, and you too, of course, Celia," he said turning to her politely.

"Thank you." She returned Gwenn's stare. "Is your husband with you this evening, Mrs. Katon?"

Gwenn ignored the sarcasm. "I'm afraid the poor dear isn't up to partying anymore. He's been ailing for several years and no longer accepts social invitations. He prefers the quiet life of Windsor."

Celia had no answer and was relieved when the Duke bowed to her. "May I have the honor of this dance?"

They moved to the floor and Celia knew her cheeks were flaming. Gwenn Katon's presence had taken her completely by surprise. She had not known of her relationship to the Duke, nor had it occurred to her that she would ever see the woman again. Gwenn's easy air of possessiveness with Francis was infuriating, but Francis's manner annoyed her even more. Certainly he knew that the gossip in Calcutta had reached Celia, yet he flagrantly displayed his attraction to Gwenn! She forced her attention to the Duke.

"Damn foolishness for a man of Francis's standing to be off soldiering. About time he settled down." He smiled indulgently. "He's got a wife to think about now, a very pretty one at that."

She smiled and nodded as the Duke went on about several business ventures he had an interest in. Celia scarcely listened. Her mind was full of Gwenn Katon, but she resolutely resisted glancing in her direction.

"Railroads, no doubt about it," Lord Skeffington said. "The London and Birmingham is already building a line through Camden. Mark my words, in another ten years rail travel will push horses right off the roads!"

She hadn't the faintest notion what he was talking about but murmured agreement and let him go on uninterrupted.

"Anthony and I have been discussing it. A man would be wise to invest in a line while the boom is in its infancy." He missed a step and apologized profusely. "Sorry, these new dances should be left to the younger men, I dare say. Never quite get the hang of it."

The music ended and Celia was immediately claimed by a smooth-faced young man who said he had met her at Aylesford before her engagement to Francis. She didn't remember him but pretended politely and listened to his babble about London with only an occasional reply. She was relieved when the musicians put up their instruments and she could rejoin Francis. Gwenn was nowhere in sight and Celia managed to forget her as Francis introduced her to dozens of people. He had a steady supply of brandy in his glass, and she thought him over-animated, even a bit tipsy, but when she suggested that he might be tiring and should go upstairs he brushed the idea aside in annoyance.

"I feel fine, stop mothering me. Hullo there, David." He turned to grasp the hand of a portly man with a red face.

Celia smiled as she was introduced and barely listened to the conversation around her. Her glance searched for Gwenn Katon and found her dancing with a hawk-nosed young man in military uniform. Gwenn had returned to England because she'd known Francis was coming home. Celia felt anger stir again. Would Francis renew the affair with Gwenn? Celia glanced at her husband and felt her heart tighten. His moods were so unpredictable she had to choose her words with care these days, and she wouldn't dare broach the subject of Gwenn. Besides, she wasn't sure she was ready to face the answer he might give.

The party lasted well into the morning, and although some guests retired, others became boisterous so that it seemed impossible anyone in the house was able to sleep. Celia was drooping with fatigue when at last Francis elected to go upstairs. He had to be assisted and protested loudly about the infernal wound that weakened him so, when Celia knew full well it was the liquor he'd consumed.

Warming fires had been lighted in the apartment and the rooms were comfortable despite the late hour. The servants helped Francis undress and get into bed while Celia busied herself in her dressing room until they were gone. The dressing room was fitted with a long, mirrored table and two tall chests as well as a huge wardrobe that covered one entire wall. Celia changed into a dressing gown and sat brushing her hair, staring at her tired face in the mirror and listening to the sound of her husband's heavy breathing from the bedroom. She could not get Gwenn Katon out of her mind. Somehow her connection with the Duke seemed to make her a more formidable adversary. The Devys apparently were well acquainted with the Duke, which meant they would see him often. He'd spoken too of some business with Anthony. Celia gnawed at her lip and wondered if the affair between her husband and Gwenn dated back longer than she'd suspected. She had assumed that Francis had taken up with her in Calcutta out of loneliness, but if they'd known each other even longer . . . She sighed and put aside the brush and extinguished the lamps before entering the bedroom. In the dancing shadows of the firelight, Francis looked as handsome as she had always seen him. How desperately she wanted to go back to the happiness they had known! She crept into bed beside him, lying close to seek comfort from his presence.

When she woke in the morning, Francis was still sound asleep, and Celia slipped from bed without waking him. She had slept poorly, with disturbing dreams of Gwenn Katon laughing triumphantly while clinging to Francis. The house was quiet; in the dining room, the sideboard was laid with an assortment of foods: kippers, bacon, hot eggs and muffins in covered silver dishes, sliced cold meats on huge platters. The table was set so that guests could dine whenever they came down, and a maid popped in every few minutes to bring hot coffee. Celia fixed herself a plate and ate alone, then carried her coffee to the small drawing room that overlooked the back gardens. She stood at the window looking out to the hills beyond, thinking how long ago it seemed that she was a child here in Renfield. She longed to see her parents, and wondered how soon she might get away to visit them. The idea that Squire Devy had used his influence to have her father transferred rankled, as did the knowledge that the Devys still considered her unsuitable for their son. How would she be able to endure life here? The memory of her dream and Gwenn Katon's laughter filled her mind, and she turned from the window impatiently. She could not let herself think such thoughts; madness lay in that direction. She set aside the empty coffee cup and hurried upstairs to change into a riding habit of deep green velvet. Francis had not stirred, and she closed the door quietly as she slipped out again.

The sun was climbing over the hills to the east but it gave little warmth to the crisp clear air. Celia was restless for the freedom of the open meadows and hills, to escape the grey confines of the house. As she passed the carriage house she saw that it was crowded with the coaches of guests who had stayed the night. Idly she wondered when they would leave; some today perhaps. She stood in the doorway of the stable accustoming her eyes to the dimness and trying to recall the groom's name. Nearby a horse whinnied, and the pungent smell of animals and hay was heavy in the air.

"Samuel?" she called out as a rustle of movement caught her attention.

"He's not here, ma'am." A tall, slim figure emerged from the shadows and came toward her. He hesitated, then took another step, drawing in his breath sharply. "Well, I'll be damned!"

Celia frowned. "I'd like to ride. Please saddle a horse for me."

The man laughed softly and came into the sunlight to stare at her. "It *is* you! What the devil are you doing here?"

She was startled by his tone and words and peered at him. His face was vaguely familiar but she was sure she did not know him. "I beg your pardon! I am Mrs. Devy. It is I who should be asking questions of you."

"Mrs. Devy?" His mouth gaped open and then he bowed with a mocking smile. "Forgive me, I had no idea. I thought—" He shook his head and grinned. "Mrs. Devy, is it? Well, you've come a long way."

"Who are you?" she demanded, angry now and curious. He was obviously a servant; he wore dark breeches and a heavy dark sweater rolled up at the sleeves to show the cuffs of a white shirt beneath. He was hatless, and had dark glossy hair and cold grey eyes that studied her intently. He was tanned as though he spent much time out of doors. Her mind would not bring the fragment of memory into focus.

"We met in London a long time ago." When she said

237

nothing, he added, "We watched the coronation parade together."

A rush of memory flooded her, and she felt a hot flush of shame, then anger. He was still grinning as though he expected her to be delighted at seeing him again.

"Gregory Houghton at your service, ma'am."

Of course! He was the Duke's equerry and had accompanied the party to the country for the weekend! She was shaking with fury but he didn't seem to notice. His voice dropped to an intimate softness. "I hoped for a long time that I'd run across you again. I had no idea you'd escaped to Aylesford. How is it that I have not seen you here before?"

The blood was pounding in her ears so loudly she could scarcely think. "My husband and I have recently returned from India." She answered automatically, then was angry with herself for bothering. What right did he have to question her?

"Ah, but of course, you met him that day!" He looked slyly at her and winked. "I remember now."

"Where is Samuel?" she demanded. She would not stand here chatting with this unspeakable man a moment longer.

"He's taken horses around for some of the guests. But I'm delighted that you chose to come here, since it's given me the chance to see you again."

She drew herself up and was determined not to let him see her nervousness. "Saddle me a horse at once," she ordered.

"Are you to slip out of my life so quickly again?" he asked with an evil smile.

Her anger exploded. "How dare you speak to me in such a manner!? I shall report your conduct to the Squire and to the Duke and you shall be dealt with severely."

He tilted his head and looked at her. "I think not. You never reported our first adventure together and there was much more to report then, wasn't there? Unless of course you're looking for a bit of the same. I hear that young Devy got himself pretty well shot up over in India. Maybe you could use a good man in your bed."

She struck out at him but he caught her wrist easily and twisted her arm so that she winced with pain. He pulled her close and she could feel his breath on her face. "No, I

238

don't suppose *Mrs.* Devy would need solace from a servant, but let's have no more talk about you carrying tales to His Lordship, eh? That would make me angry and I'd tell a few stories of my own. What do you think the Devys would say if they knew—"

"I will deny anything you say. I want to forget I ever laid eyes on you!"

He released her hand with a cruel laugh. "That's better. Now then, I've a mare saddled you can have." He led a black from a nearby stall and handed her the reins. "Enjoy your ride, Mrs. Devy, and if there's anything I can do—"

She rushed from the stable, pulling the reins so that the horse pranced behind her. As she came out into the sunlight, she almost collided with Gwenn Katon who was standing just outside the door. She was wearing a black velvet riding habit with a saucy velvet hat perched atop her dark curls; behind her stood Samuel holding the reins of a grey stallion.

"Oh—I—excuse me." Celia was overcome with confusion. How long had Gwenn been there? How much had she heard?

Gwenn's sly smile answered the question. Her voice was venomous. "I'm the one who must apologize for interrupting your tête-à-tête."

"It wasn't—" Her face was flaming and the words stuck in her throat. Gwenn would read what she wanted into the exchange with Gregory Houghton, any attempts at explanation would make matters worse. "If you'll excuse me, I was just setting out for a ride." She was grateful when Samuel held the black's reins and assisted her to the mounting block. She rode from the yard without looking back.

The horse was anxious to run, and Celia felt its power beneath her as she let the animal have its head and gallop across the wide meadow at the foot of the hills. There were several bridle paths, and she chose one that would take her to the top of the crest as far distant from the stable as she could get. Her cheeks still burned at Gregory Houghton's insinuations and the dreadful memories they roused, and from the unexpected meeting with Gwenn. The horse slowed for the climb and by the time they

239

reached the top, Celia was calmer. The air was exhilarating, and she realized how much she had missed riding; it helped clear the cobwebs of thought from her mind. She looked down over the estate and beyond to the sleepy village. The distant sound of the churchbell reminded her it was Sunday, and she felt a pang of guilt that she had not been to church in a long time. Somehow it seemed important here in Renfield, and she vowed that she would go next Sabbath. She thought too of her parents and vowed that she would some day bring them back to Renfield where they belonged.

Sighing, she turned the horse and rode down the other side of the hill and along a path that wended through a wooded glen. How huge the estate was, but not as well kept as it might be; she noticed numerous portions of fence that had not been mended, and a tangled briar patch that had once been a small garden. When at last she turned back toward the stable, she glimpsed several other riders on a distant path but Gwenn Katon was not among them. It had been a mistake to be rude, Celia realized that. Gwenn would gossip about what had happened, and the gossip would find its way to Mrs. Devy's ears.

She went into the house through a side entrance and hesitated a moment at the open doors of the drawing room. The Duke's voice boomed. "A man would be a fool not to jump at a chance like this. I wouldn't have a part in the Marlton Company if I weren't sure every investor could double his money in a year's time."

"How can you be so positive?" Anthony asked. "There must be a dozen railroad companies already, with new ones forming every week."

"I've looked into it thoroughly, you can be sure. I've got a man scouting to buy up the right of way for several lines. Plans for laying the rails are being drawn."

"Without the right man to head such a venture you could get into serious problems," Francis said.

"I've got him. Chap named Oliver Chadwick who's been working with the East India Company. Made a reputation for himself and has a head for business. He was in Calcutta about the same time you were, Francis."

"Yes, good man. I didn't know he was back in England."

240

"He'd be a fool to turn down a chance like this. I've offered him full management—with my approval, of course. Railroading is new to him but then it is to everyone, and he'll learn fast."

Celia leaned against the wall and tried to control her breathing. Oliver back in London! All at once her past seemed to be closing in about her.

"Still . . ." Anthony sounded doubtful.

"It's your decision to make, of course, Tony," Francis said, "but I'm inclined to favour it. I've been hearing about railroads for some time, even in India. Predictions are they'll change the world. Imagine being able to cover the distance to London in under two hours."

"Right, and the whole damned world is going to be moving goods and people on rails before long. No difference to me one way or the other, Anthony, but I thought you might welcome a chance to clean up the gambling debts hanging over you."

"Good Lord, Tony, have you been a fool at the gaming tables again? How much have you lost?"

Anthony didn't answer immediately. Celia wanted to move away from the doorway but she couldn't. She caught her breath when Anthony answered.

"Forty thousand pounds."

A low whistle. "Does Father know?"

"Stories like that have no trouble finding willing tongues to carry them," Anthony said in irritation.

"And it's not the first time, I suppose," Francis said wryly. "We Devys have always had a weakness for cards."

Anthony murmured something that didn't carry to Celia. Forty thousand pounds was a fortune. Could the Devys sustain the loss? There was a shuffle of movement in the drawing room and Celia quickly fled up the stairs, not wishing to be caught eavesdropping.

The apartment had already undergone its morning cleaning. Celia changed from the riding habit to a dress of pale violet linen with rows of lace across the bodice and sleeves, then brushed out her hair and rearranged the wind-blown curls. She had no knowledge of business, but the Duke's proposition seemed to answer Anthony's problems. He would be foolish to pass up a business investment that would double his money. The thought that

241

Oliver had returned to England to run the company was an assurance that the investment was sound. Oliver was an excellent businessman who would not enter into something lightly. It surprised her that he had given up his post with the East India Company. Did his decision have anything to do with her? She pushed the thought aside restlessly. There was nothing between them, nor would there be despite his return. Still, she felt a fluttering of pulse as she wondered if she would see him again.

A tap at the door brought her from her thoughts, and in answer to her bidding, Theo entered.

"Am I intruding?"

"Not at all. Francis is about somewhere and I have just returned from a ride."

"You were up early. Most of the household is still asleep or so groggy they might as well be. Late parties are incredibly wearying the next day." Theo wandered about the room, touching a chair, a porcelain on the mantle. "Anthony's organized a hunt for the men after a bit. Did you enjoy your ride?"

"Yes. I learned in India, you know, so this was my first time at Aylesford. It's quite lovely."

"Mmm." Theo was not listening, and Celia wondered why she had come. Obviously there was something on her mind. Finally she turned and came to Celia and took her hand.

"Have you had a run-in with Gwenn?"

"A—why do you ask?" Celia forced herself to meet Theo's earnest stare.

The other sighed. "She has just told Mother a dreadful tale about you and some servant out in the stables. I told Mama it was ridiculous—" She stopped at seeing Celia's face redden. "Celia? Oh, dear—" She turned away and paced the room. "I wish you had been more discreet. Mama has never forgiven you for marrying Francis, you know. If you are having a clandestine—"

"Theo! You don't believe Gwenn's story?!"

Theo's eyes went wide. "I thought—oh, Celia, forgive me if I've misjudged you. It's only that you looked so guilty just then. I shall not say another word!"

"Tell me what Gwenn has said."

"Perhaps it's best not—"

242

"How can I defend myself against her lies if you won't tell me what they are?" Celia said.

"She says she saw you in the stable with one of the grooms and that you were embracing, and that the two of you spoke of having met before."

Celia chewed at her lip. So Gwenn had heard the entire exchange with Houghton! And she was doing her best to set the Devys against her with it. "I was at the stable, and I did talk to the Duke's groom since Samuel wasn't around. But I went there for a horse, nothing more, and a horse is all I got. The man mistook me for someone else at first and said things he should not, but I have no wish to cause him trouble. It was a mistake, nothing more."

"Oh, I'm relieved to hear it and you can be sure I'll tell Mama." Theo came to her and hugged her impulsively. "Gwenn Katon is a witch! I have always hated her but Mama had so hoped that she and Francis would—" She broke off and looked embarrassed.

"That she and Francis would marry?"

"Yes."

"But Gwenn is already married!"

Theo shrugged. "To a man three times her age who can scarcely move about under his own power. It's no secret that she maneuvered the marriage so that she will inherit his money and she's waiting out the time until he dies. She puts in an appearance at Glen Oaks—that's the Katon estate in Windsor—every once in a while but otherwise she does as she pleases." She shook her head impatiently. "Let's not talk about it. Gwenn will tire of her stupid games, you'll see, and Mama will soon learn what a devoted wife and wonderful person you are." But she didn't sound convincing or even convinced.

The door had opened quietly and neither of them heard Francis until he spoke. "What games are those, my pet?"

Theo whirled about, hands to her face. "Don't you know it's not polite to sneak up on people! You may hear something about yourself not meant to be heard." Theo laughed and bent to kiss Celia's cheek, then walked past her brother. "Girl talk, Francis, and I forbid you to ask questions of Celia. Promise?"

She pouted prettily until he laughed and said, "It's all too silly. Yes, I promise. Now run along. Several of the

243

young men have been asking about you: I suspect they are of two minds about joining the hunt if you are going to hold court downstairs."

Theo tossed her dark curls and her eyes glittered. "I am engaged to be married. What would André say if he heard you talk that way?"

Francis laughed heartily. "André will have enough to worry about when he learns what a she-devil he has acquired as his wife. Now run along."

She raced from the room and Francis limped to the bed and fell upon it. The crutch clattered to the floor and Celia bent to retrieve it. Francis was looking at her curiously when she set the crutch against the bedpost.

"Are you tired?" she asked him.

"Tired of being an invalid and not being able to do a damn thing except sit around. Edward's been telling me about a physician from Vienna who uses a new treatment to speed the healing of wounds like mine. I've decided to drive to London with him tomorrow and see the chap."

"We've only just come home—"

He closed his eyes and lay his head back on his raised arm. "I wouldn't expect you to come along, naturally. Not much fun for you if there's no one to escort you about and show you a good time." He opened his eyes and looked at her with a frown. "You want me to get well as soon as possible, don't you?"

"Of course. It's just—" She broke off quickly. She could not let herself dwell on such perilous thoughts. "I shall miss you. Darling, I've been thinking how much I would like to visit my parents. Do you think it would be possible for me to do this while you're away?"

"Good idea. I'll speak to Anthony about arranging a carriage before we leave."

"He's going too?"

"Yes, business to attend to." He drew her into his arms and kissed her gently. "Now, let me rest a bit while the others are off at the hunt, then we shall dine together and attend the dreary musicale Mama has planned."

She kissed him and pulled a light coverlet over him before retiring to the sitting room to read. She had no desire to go downstairs and chance meeting Mrs. Devy or Gwenn Katon.

CHAPTER FIFTEEN

Celia found her parents in poor health and circumstances, and the visit depressed her. Reverend Skerritt had developed a persistent cough and seemed so frail that Celia wept. Her mother had aged noticeably and was no longer able to hide the constant pain in her stiff hands and body. Her father refused to lay blame for his transfer, saying only that it was the will of God, and he would hear no word against the Devys.

"A man does what he believes is right, child, and if you're to live with them you must cleanse your heart of resentments."

She stayed four days and returned to Aylesford to find Francis and Anthony still absent. Theo had departed also and Celia felt uncomfortable in the big house. The Squire stayed to his rooms or sat in the solarium where the temperature was kept high for the dozens of tropical plants that had been imported and arranged as an indoor garden. He was never without a whiskey decanter and glass at his side, and both his gout and temper worsened steadily. Mrs. Devy went about her life as though Celia had not happened into it. With Francis gone, she rarely spoke to Celia or even bothered to sit with her except at mealtimes when the Squire also joined them. Then the talk was of inconsequentials—servants, the house, social affairs among their circle of friends and the like.

Celia developed the habit of taking lunch alone in the small morning room where the family breakfasted. She was surprised the day after her return when Mrs. Devy joined her, instructing the maid to bring soup and toast. She opened the conversation quite abruptly.

"Did you enjoy your visit to your parents?"

"Yes, though neither of them is well." Celia couldn't hide her feelings, though the older woman took no notice.

"I'm surprised you did not stay longer," Mrs. Devy said acidly.

"I found their circumstances so depressing that I was not the best of company. Spitelfields is hardly a cheery atmosphere this time of year—or any other. I plan to see them again soon, however." It was difficult to control her voice.

Mrs. Devy laid aside her spoon and looked up. "Naturally you want to see them often but I'm sure you realize how inappropriate it would be to ask them to visit here."

Such an invitation had not occurred to Celia, only because it would distress her parents, not out of any regard for the Devys. "Would I be forbidden such a visit?" she demanded stonily.

Agatha Devy made an impatient gesture. "Forbidden? A strong word. Of course if Francis and Anthony gave their permission I would have to consent, but I assure you it would not be pleasant for me. I have been forced to accept you into this household because of your connivance in getting my son to marry you—"

"Connivance!" Celia was outraged. "It was Francis who begged me to wed him! You would not dare speak this way if he were here."

"But he is not. There is no one to overhear what I say to you and you might keep that in mind if you consider running to Francis with a story. I have known my son much longer than you, and I understand him. He was taken in by your innocent charm that summer, and you played heavily upon his infatuation in order to gain a wealthy husband. So be it, I cannot change what has been done." Her tone clearly indicated she hoped that was a temporary defeat. "But as long as you are in this house, I think we are entitled to expect proper behavior in accordance with *our* standards."

246

"I was not aware that our standards differed." Celia could barely conceal her anger.

"To openly consort with a stablehand—"

"I did not *consort* with anyone!" Celia's hand trembled; she had to hide it beneath the table. Gwenn Katon had told her tale well—and Mrs. Devy had been eager to receive it!

Mrs. Devy fixed steely blue eyes on her. The round face was so filled with hatred that she resembled an ugly toad. "Do you deny that you were in the man's arms in the stable?"

"Yes—of course I do!" She panicked for a moment, trapped between the truth and a lie, and struggled to regain her composure. "The man mistook me for someone else and grabbed my arm. There was nothing more to it than that, and if Gwenn claimed there was, then she is lying."

Mrs. Devy glared but Celia refused to be cowed. To give in to the woman's insufferable attitude would seal her fate forever as an intruder in the household. Surely if it came down to it, Francis would take her side, but the thought unsettled her and she hoped it would not come to that.

She tried to mend the breach. "I'm sure Gwenn believed she saw something she did not and meant no harm."

Mrs. Devy did not pursue the subject but rose abruptly, leaving her lunch unfinished, and walked stiffly from the room. Celia pushed away her plate. Her stomach was knotted with a turmoil of emotion and she was trembling. She left the table, calling to the maid to have someone tell Samuel to bring around a horse for her. She would spend the afternoon in the hills where she could escape all thoughts of Agatha Devy.

Theo, Anthony and Francis returned three days later, and Celia was delighted to see them. Francis was in good spirits; the doctor had prescribed a program of light exercises to strengthen the muscles rather than the near-total inactivity Francis had been favoring, and predicted complete recovery in a few month's time. Anthony and his father were closeted for several hours in the study to discuss the business venture they had gone into with the Duke.

Francis spoke of it to Celia without elaborating; the Devys were investing heavily in a railroad company the Duke was backing.

At dinner his first night back, Mrs. Devy fawned and fussed over Francis endlessly. She worried that he was pale, had perhaps exhausted himself with the long trip.

"Nonsense, Mother, I'm fine. A man can't sit around doing nothing all his life."

"Of course not, dear, that's just the point. I want you to be well and strong so you can begin to enjoy yourself after all those dreary months in India with no social life."

"I'd hardly call Calcutta devoid of social life, Agatha," the Squire said. "From what I hear it's quite civilized—even a race course, didn't you say, Francis?"

"Yes, and more parties than we could decently manage."

"I suppose," his mother mused, "but still not quite the same. Such a mixture of people, not nearly as selective as you are used to." Her gaze slid past Celia. "It was most fortunate that Gwenn was able to join you there."

Francis frowned. "She didn't 'join me,' Mother, only happened to be traveling to visit friends at the time I went back."

Celia could not hide her surprise. "You made the voyage together?"

"Yes, hadn't I mentioned it?" he said as calmly as though such a thing were not out of the ordinary.

Celia felt her neck cord; the smile was carved on her lips as she shook her head and dropped her gaze. She wanted to escape the dining room but she was afraid that her trembling legs would not hold her. She conveyed the fork to her mouth and chewed without tasting.

"Will Gwenn return to Windsor or remain with her uncle in London?" Mrs. Devy asked.

Francis hesitated. "I think she plans to remain in London. Glen Oaks does not appeal to her in winter."

"Then we must be sure to include her at all our gatherings. London can be dreary and lonely. She does enjoy Aylesford so."

Theo's fork tapped against her dish. "Gwenn Katon has never spent a lonely moment in her life!"

"That's unladylike to say—"

"Bother! Is it ladylike to discuss that designing man-chaser in front of Celia? Really, Mother—"

"Theo!"

"Well, it's true. Celia is ten times the woman Gwenn Katon ever might hope to be and I say good riddance to her. Let her pursue her prey elsewhere."

"That will be enough, young lady!" Squire Devy lifted his claret and glared at her menacingly.

Theo sighed and was quiet. Anthony cleared his throat and an uncomfortable silence settled about the table. A serving girl brought platters of salmon and capon and everyone turned attention to the food. When at last the meal was over, Celia went directly upstairs to leave Francis over brandy with his father and brother. She could not bear the thought of trying to make polite small talk, so sure was she that Mrs. Devy would manage to turn the conversation to Gwenn Katon once more. When Francis came up hours later, she confronted him.

"Have you no decency about flaunting your affair with that woman? I bore the shame in silence in Calcutta but I will not be made a fool of again!" She was close to tears and blinked them back angrily.

He stared, eyes round with surprise, as his face darkened. "I am not accustomed to having a woman tell me what I can and cannot do, Celia."

"I am your wife!"

"But not my master!" He flung aside his coat and stormed about the room, glaring at her over his shoulder. "Dammit, have I not given you everything a woman could ask for? You have a home here at Aylesford, clothes, position—"

"And your love? Do I have that or is it something I must share with others?"

He advanced on her, his face clouded with fury. For a moment she thought he would strike her, but she faced him without flinching. "Do not try my patience, Celia, I warn you."

She could bear his anger but not the coldness in his voice and eyes. "Oh, Francis, what is happening to us? Why can't we be happy as we were in the beginning?" She longed to be taken in his arms and have her fears stilled, but he turned away and began undressing.

"Perhaps you expect too much, Celia. You are a romantic, a child with stars in your eyes. Do you think that I have not heard the gossip about you and the Duke's equerry? Can you think a man takes pride in knowing that his wife finds the attentions of a servant to her liking?"

She had never seen him angrier and his words stung. "That's not true!"

"Do you deny intimacy between you and Houghton? I've heard the whole sordid story from Gwenn who had it from Houghton himself."

For a moment she was too stunned to speak. The room seemed to spin around her and blackness pressed behind her eyes. Her lips were tight and dry, and she ran her tongue over them nervously. "It was not an incident of my choosing . . ." The words were barely a whisper.

"But you do not deny it?" He reached for her and his fingers dug cruelly into her shoulders.

"He forced me—I had no idea—oh, you must believe me, Francis, I was foolish to enter the house but he took me against my will, I swear—"

His hands dropped from her and the sound of his harsh breathing filled the room. His eyes were like glowing coals, searing into her soul and exposing its shame. "One must choose which story to believe, but neither lessens the disgust I feel for you. I believed you chaste and wed you so that I might have what it seems you give other men freely. There is nothing we can do to change what is done, but under the circumstances I think it inappropriate that you find fault with my conduct with Gwenn—or anyone else!"

He turned from her, crutch thumping the floor dully with each step as he left the bedroom and slammed the sitting room door behind him.

She stood a moment staring at the door and shaking with anger and hopelessness. Her heart ached and tears threatened, but she clenched her fingers into her palms until the nails dug her flesh. She would not cry again—not now or ever!

Winter wrapped the countryside in cold embrace; by Christmas there was a light covering of snow on the hills and the air was crisp. Count André Bouchard came to spend the holidays with Theo. He was tall and stout and much older than Celia expected. In a burst of confidence, Theo told her that the Count was really dull but very rich, and Papa felt it was a good match so she had accepted André's proposal. Celia knew that such marriages were frequently arranged, but she felt pity that it should be Theo's lot. She wondered if money was a problem with the Devys—had Anthony's debts hurt them?

Anthony was gone from the estate for long periods of time; when he was at home, he and his father were closeted in the study from which raised voices could be heard. Francis joined them from time to time, but when Celia questioned him about their conversations, he said little except that his father did not wholly approve of the railroad company that was forming.

Francis gained strength and discarded the crutch in favor of a cane shortly after the New Year. He did not speak of Gregory Houghton again, and Celia was too angry and hurt to open the subject of her own accord. Obviously Gwenn had bribed some sort of story from Houghton, one that laid the fault with Celia instead of himself, or Gwenn had eagerly embroidered a tale for Francis.

Their lives settled to a pattern that Celia would have found pleasant if it were not for the gulf between her and Francis and Mrs. Devy's obvious pleasure in baiting her. The older woman spoke of Gwenn every chance she had, and Celia was sure that she hadn't given up the hope that Francis might still somehow rid himself of Celia and marry Gwenn when her ailing husband died. Francis would sometimes draw Celia to him in bed and take her with need that bordered on lust, and though her body responded to him, she lay afterward wondering if he enjoyed similar passion with Gwenn Katon.

During the coldest months, there were numerous parties and scarcely a weekend without guests. True to Mrs. Devy's promise, Gwenn Katon was invited and came often, and the triumphant look in her eyes made it clear that she was aware of her victory. Alice went about scowling and clucking that neither Gwenn nor her uncle was to be trusted, the two born under black stars that boded ill for anyone around them. In March, Anthony, Francis and Celia were guests at the Duke's townhouse on Northumberland Avenue for several days while the men conferred on business. Celia was uncomfortable at being in the house, doubly so because Gwenn was acting as hostess for her uncle and seemed to find many opportunities to be alone with Francis on one pretext or another.

Celia took advantage of the sojourn in the city to visit a dressmaker and be fitted for a spring wardrobe. Francis was generous with funds and it allayed Celia's worries that the Devys might be in financial difficulties. She had never before known the luxury of selecting so many materials and patterns, and she had to return to the shop on three different occasions for fittings and consultations. The Duke provided a carriage and she used each outing as an excuse to see the sights of London, some that she had visited during her year at Miss Claredon's and others that she had only dreamed of seeing. She rode past Miss Claredon's school and at seeing the girls in grey calico, wondered if she'd ever been that young. She also rode to Spitelfields on the fourth day to see her parents.

When she returned to the house on Northumberland, a servant took her coat and told her tea was being served in the sitting room. Celia smoothed her russet skirt and arranged the bow at the high neck of her amber blouse. She'd been gone longer than expected and decided not to take time to go upstairs before joining the others. She glanced in the gilt-framed mirror and patted the golden curls gathered at her crown as she went along the hall to the sitting room. The door was open and a murmur of masculine voices and Gwenn's lilting laughter floated to her.

"Ah, here she is." Anthony was standing at the fireplace, an elbow on the marble mantel as he held a teacup. He set the cup aside and came to take Celia's hand. "Forgive us for starting without you but our guest has a later appointment." He drew her toward the group and she was aware of Gwenn's careless look as though to dismiss the necessity of apologies. Gwenn was seated on a small divan, with Francis beside her, their knees almost touching as he lounged comfortably, legs outstretched.

"You've met Oliver Chadwick, I believe." Anthony turned her toward a large winged chair that was partially in shadows.

Oliver rose and bowed. "I am delighted to see you again, Mrs. Devy, and looking so well. England agrees with you even more than India did." His lips brushed her hand.

For a moment she thought everyone in the room must hear the racing of her heart and the rush of her breath. Her hand tingled in Oliver's and she was powerless to draw it away. Even knowing he was in London and connected with the business of the railroad which was the purpose of this visit, she was unprepared for the shock of seeing him. His eyes found hers and locked their gaze. She forced her lips to move in greeting.

"Do sit, Celia, you must be famished after your outing," Gwenn said. She poured a cup of tea and Anthony handed it to Celia as she took a chair distant from the fire. The room seemed very warm and heat flushed her face. Oliver had resumed his seat and was watching her with a dark unsettling gaze. She busied herself with the tea, deliberating at length over the tray of sandwiches and biscuits Anthony brought from the low table.

The Duke eased his weight in the armchair. "How soon do you think we can begin laying track, Oliver?"

"Oh, Uncle Edward, you mustn't talk business anymore," Gwenn pouted.

"Would you bore us instead with chatter of gowns and recipes for tea cakes?" His voice was indulgent.

"You do me an injustice, Uncle. Have I ever bored you or your guests?"

"I would imagine that impossible," Francis said gallantly.

Gwenn laid her hand upon his where it rested on the cushion. "You are a gentleman, Francis." She smiled prettily, and Celia dared not look at Oliver; she knew the exchange was not lost on him.

"Since Francis and Anthony came all the way from Renfield to talk with Oliver, I dare say they want to cover every bit of business that can be settled," the Duke said dryly. He turned his gaze to Oliver. "When will the first tracks be laid?"

"By autumn—if there are no problems with land acquisition and assuming the money is there."

"More than two-thirds of the shares have already been

spoken for and the rest will go quickly," the Duke said with a touch of irritation. "We've had numerous inquiries about small parcels and I think we should offer them. Give the little man a chance to invest—think what it will mean to him. In a few years the railroad won't be a novelty but an everyday convenience for city and country man alike. Absolute boon."

"Uncle Edward says the railroad coaches can be every bit as comfortable as our finest road carriages," Gwenn said, looking at Oliver. "Is this so?"

"I am not yet experienced in the planning of passenger cars, Miss Katon, but I see no reason why they shouldn't be. Perhaps even more comfortable, considering the smoothness of rails as compared with some of our highways."

"Where will the first line be?"

"The northern districts seem the most likely candidates," Oliver said. "If we link the factory and mining areas to London as well as provide transportation for people, we increase the revenue opportunities tenfold."

Gwenn's eyes sparkled mischievously. "Will the Marlton Company line go through Renfield?"

Francis laughed. "I should hope so if the Devys are investing so extensively."

"How wonderful to be able to come to London from Renfield in so short a time." Gwenn glanced at Celia. Celia returned the smile with a forced display of good humor.

Oliver sensed her discomfort and drew attention away from her. "Of course we must acquire the land first. Without a solid right of way we can't lay the first rail."

"We'll have it," the Duke said.

"The section between Trowing and Bedford is critical."

The Duke waved aside Oliver's doubt. "I'm not without influence with Her Majesty's government. We'll have it before the month is out."

"Will the line be a long one?" Celia asked. She had been hearing bits and pieces of the railroad talk for months but few details.

Oliver smiled. "As far as Birmingham and eventually all the way to Liverpool, we hope."

That surprised her. She knew there were numerous

railroads, mostly in the northeastern counties, but none of that length. It would be a costly undertaking. Anthony moved restlessly about the room. "The Stockton-Darlington and Manchester-Liverpool are doing well with short lines."

"We've been over that ground," Francis said, frowning at his brother. "Oliver's right, we've got to bring the line into the heart of London. Now I propose that we drop the subject before we bore the ladies."

Oliver set aside his teacup. "I must be going."

"I'll expect those figures and proposals as soon as possible," the Duke said, rising to see his guest to the door.

Oliver bowed to Gwenn, then to Celia. "I hope we'll meet again very soon, Celia." He spoke her name so softly she could not be sure she heard it, and his gaze held her eyes until she felt her courage ebb and looked away. He shook hands with Francis and Anthony, then was gone.

Spring descended on Aylesford and claimed it with loving embrace. The raw days gave way all at once to warm breezes, blue skies with only puffy white clouds floating aimlessly. The grass greened and buds appeared on trees to proclaim a new season. Celia made another brief visit to London, staying at the Hyde Park Hotel, though Francis insisted the Duke would welcome her, in order to have the final fittings done on her wardrobe. It was glorious to be away—and alone. Somehow the dreariness of winter seemed directly related to the coldness of Agatha Devy, and Celia wondered if spring—or anything else—would warm her.

Madame Louvère clucked and fussed over the gowns she'd made, declaring that Celia had become plumper and the seams would have to be altered. "Perhaps Madame is with child?" the woman said slyly.

Celia flushed and did not answer. Could it be? She had not thought of a child since miscarrying the first she bore. How happy she had been then. Now her emotions were mixed, more because of her relationship with the Devys than any resentment about a child itself. A baby . . . Francis's son. They'd been so sure it would be a boy the first time, and she felt as sure now.

When she left the dress shop, she walked to the park three blocks away and sat for a long time on a bench gazing at the Serpentine. Memory painted a clear picture of the afternoon before Francis departed on the ill-fated patrol that left him wounded and ended their stay in India. They'd loved, so sweetly and eagerly, and she'd told him her suspicions about her condition. He'd been elated, as she was, and full of plans and hopes. But when he returned, he had forgotten it all. Even when the pain of his wounds was gone, he had never asked her about the child. She might have borne that too except for the knowledge that Gwenn Katon had been with him upcountry.

A small boat glided by with a young man at the oars and a pretty girl smiling shyly across from him. Love— was there really such a thing or was it an elusive fancy? When she finally started back for the hotel, she accepted the possibility that she was with child again. What would Agatha Devy's reaction be? Best not to tell anyone until she was sure; besides, she wanted to hug the secret to herself for awhile before any of her illusions were shattered.

By June, preparations for Theo's wedding had taken over the household so that everything was in a constant turmoil. When Francis announced that they were going to Ascot-Heath for Royal Ascot Week, Celia was thrilled. She'd never been to the races, though Francis had talked of taking her in Calcutta. But to be attending the Gold Cup Race, and to see the splendor of Ascot Week was something she had never dreamed possible. She was aware of the elegance of dress among the men and women attending, and she chose her wardrobe with care, pleased that she had acquired numerous new gowns that were most fashionable and suitable. It did not occur to her in her excitement to inquire where they would stay during the visit, and it wasn't until they were on their way to Windsor that Francis spoke of their destination.

"Bradford Katon has maintained his home in Windsor for nearly fifty years."

"Bradford Katon?"

"Yes, Gwenn's husband. Made his money with the John Company back in its early days. It's said that he could buy and sell the company ten times over now." He gazed from the window at the rolling green hills that marked their approach to the town.

Celia stared with unseeing eyes. So they were to be Gwenn Katon's guests. It was a deliberate slap in the face to be brought to the home of her husband's mistress, and she wasn't sure if her shame or anger was stronger. Had he so little regard for her feelings that he could do such a thing without caring how she would be hurt? She admitted to herself what she had suspected, even known, for a long time. Francis had been a spoiled child and he was now a self-indulgent adult—if that word could be used to apply to him in view of his actions. He did as he pleased and brooked no interference. She had thought him strong at first, but he was only willful.

The estate was called Glen Oaks, and it sprawled over a valley and hills like a vast empire. The house was weathered stone, built centuries ago but modernized and repaired so that it kept its charm while offering every amenity. Gwenn met them in the entrance hall, smiling and welcoming Celia as if they were old friends instead of rivals, and glancing at Francis with bold welcome. Celia pretended not to notice since she knew she was faced with four days of this flagrant display of their affection. She was thankful that there were other houseguests so that some of the pressures of conversation would be eased. To spend a week alone with Gwenn and Francis would be beyond endurance!

They were shown to a suite at the corner of the east wing, an elegant apartment that rivaled the very best rooms at Aylesford. The bedroom was decorated in tones of green, rich and plush, with Queen Anne furniture that was polished in perfect condition. The sitting room had alcoved windows overlooking the front lawns and a view of Windsor Castle to the east. Celia exclaimed over it with the delight of a child.

"It's magnificent!"

"You are much too impressionable, my sweet. I sometimes wonder if you will ever really accustom yourself to a proper lifestyle," Francis said.

She turned quickly to see if he was ridiculing her but he was smiling and his eyes were gentle. She blushed and thought of how delighted she had been with her first view of Aylesford and later of the house in Calcutta. Perhaps she was too impressionable, too easily pleased. Did it

257

make her less discerning than she might otherwise be? She walked about the room, trailing her fingers over the dark polished top of the small writing desk below the window, the curve of a chair back. It was a beautiful house and she might enjoy a stay here were it not for Gwenn Katon. Francis was slipping from his traveling coat and donning a fawn-colored shirt with a bright yellow cravat at his throat.

"Bradford never leaves his apartment these days so we must pay our respects to him there. Best we do it now and get it over with."

"Of course." She began to undo the rows of small buttons at the front of the coral jacket. A maid was already unpacking her bag, shaking out each garment before hanging it in the huge wardrobe. Celia indicated a pink silk and the girl laid it on the bed.

Half an hour later, a woman in blue calico and white apron admitted them to a huge sunny room that seemed gloomy in spite of the light. The walls were paneled in dark wood, the appointments of the bed and windows a somber, heavy maroon velvet, the carpet an intricate combination of muted colors in a Persian design. Near the window, a large wing chair was pulled into a path of the sunlight. In it sat a man so wizened he seemed lost in the black dressing gown and the maroon lap robe that covered him from the waist down. His face was cracked and wrinkled like old leather, and his rheumy eyes moved with slow deliberation.

"Bradford, good to see you again. You're looking well," Francis said. "Can't tell you how pleased we are with the invitation." Celia had never heard Francis's voice so fawning, and she hid her surprise. The old man stared at him, then shifted his gaze to her. "My wife, Celia . . ." Francis said.

On impulse, Celia smiled and touched the old man's shoulder gently. "I'm delighted to be here, Mr. Katon. Your house is the most beautiful I have ever seen."

The old man's eyes glinted as he dipped his head in acknowledgment. "Celia . . . never met before, have we?"

"No, sir. This is my first time at Windsor, and I'm told you don't travel anymore." She was aware of Francis's quick impatient look.

258

The robe stirred and Bradford Katon's bony hand emerged to clamp over Celia's hand at his shoulder. "I'm delighted to have you, Celia. You're a welcome guest to brighten an old man's day. Sit, sit—" The blue eyes found the nurse and she immediately brought a small chair which Francis belatedly took from her and placed for Celia, close to the old man's chair. Katon dismissed him with a glance and turned to Celia again. "Tell me about yourself."

She laughed, aware of and uncomfortable under her husband's scrutiny. "There is not much to tell." Her cheeks felt unaccountably warm and she realized that Francis's presence made her awkward, as though she must guard each word. She was glad when he excused himself and murmured that he would see her later in their rooms.

"So you have married that young hellion, eh?" the old man said the moment the door had closed behind Francis.

"Yes . . ." She was unsure of her own reaction to his description of Francis, yet she felt at ease. Katon's fingers still held hers, though their hands had slipped down to rest on the arm of the chair.

He cackled softly. "Gwenn's had her cap set for him, y'know." He nodded and his face folded into a comic expression. "But I won't give her the pleasure of seeing me die just yet."

What was she to say to a remark like that?

"He'd soon tire of her, I've no doubt." He peered at Celia and looked solemn. "You've had a few of your dreams tarnished already, I can see. Francis Devy is not a man to be satisfied no matter what he has. All the Devys the same . . . I've known three generations." The long speech seemed to tire him and he sighed and sank deeper into the chair. His hand fell to his lap and she gently covered it with the robe once more. The old man turned his face to the sun to seek its strength a few moments before going on. "Don't let them hurt you, child. Cyrus Devy was smart enough to invest his money in the colonies when there were fortunes to be made, but he was a ruthless man—and his son is no better. Charles had too much money to spend without worrying where it came from, and he's lived high and fancy all these years. His sons have learned nothing of the values of the world or of life itself." His gaze was incredibly sad as he studied her face. "Don't let them hurt you, child." He closed his eyes again and lay his head against the cushion. His breath fluttered softly, then settled to an even shallow pattern.

The nurse said, "He's asleep. He tires quickly."

Celia rose and left. How strange that the old man had detained her to talk of such matters. His awareness of his wife's infidelity seemed to trouble him less than his concern for Celia, whom he'd known only a few minutes. She found her way back to their rooms but Francis was not there. She sat for a long time on the window seat of the alcove, staring out across the valleys at the distant castle. It seemed incredible that she could listen to such condemnation of her husband and feel no anger. It was as though the part of her that had looked forward so expectantly to marriage and seen Francis as a dashing knight in her dull existence was gone. She was no longer a child but a woman who had to face the realities of life. And the best way to do it was to heed Bradford Katon's advice and not let herself be wounded.

Gwenn had selected her guests well, and the house-party was a lively and merry affair. There were games on the lawn, cool drinks under the spreading sycamores and oaks, riding along well-defined paths that wound through the estate and over hill and dale. Groups went to the races each day, riding in bannered coaches that had been decorated in the holiday spirit. Evenings were spent dancing in the huge ballroom of Glen Oaks or in the fountain court lit with Japanese lanterns and splashing moonlight.

Celia found the races more exciting than anything she had seen. The sleek horses, with jockeys in fancy silks, were incredibly swift and graceful; she watched every race with fascination, without thought of betting, though Francis and the others did. She was content to admire the beautiful animals and their performances. The crowds grew by the day, and it was predicted that on the day of the Gold Cup Race, more than ten thousand would attend. The talk at Glen Oaks was of the entries, which animal was favored, and the private wagers which were laid among friends and sealed with handshakes.

Each day, Celia found time to stop at Bradford Katon's rooms and visit with him for a few minutes. He was always delighted to see her, but he never again brought up the subject of Francis. Instead they talked of her childhood in Renfield, and of the old man's memories of a life past. He had been a country lad, son of a shopkeeper, but ambitious and willing to work hard. He'd traveled to London and found his first job in a carriagemaker's shop. He acquired the company some years later when the owner passed away and the man's wife was willing to sell the business. As the company expanded, Katon invested in others, building his holdings and reputation steadily until his name became a synonym for fine carriages. He'd had a wife, and two children who died before their teens; the wife died in middle age, and he remained alone for many years afterward. When he spoke of his marriage to Gwenn, it was with the recognition that he had been a foolish old man trying to recapture his youth. He had met the Duke in business, and the beautiful young niece had flattered him with her attentions so that he had not seen her for what she was.

The day of the Gold Cup Race dawned with a blood-red sunrise and high white clouds. Gwenn had arranged carriages to transport her guests the six miles to the track early in the day so that they could greet friends and visit before the races. The promenade was crowded, as women in elegant silks, satins and furs strolled on the arms of grey-coated men. Celia wore an afternoon dress of blue-green silk, the color of the sea, and a matching light-weight coat with embroidered satin facings and rows of small silk tassels to accent the pockets and layers of the skirts. Both coat and dress were cut becomingly low at front, and about her throat she wore the diamond necklace Francis had given her as an engagement gift. She was pleased with the dress—it was the loveliest she had ever owned, and the most becoming. She saw Francis's look of approval, though he said nothing, and Gwenn's envious glance. Celia always had the feeling that Gwenn hoped she would play the part of a dowdy parson's daughter even now.

Gwenn had a private box in the stands for her party, and the guests were milling about with last minute talk of races and favorites. Francis and two other men had gone to place bets and Celia noticed that Gwenn had vanished as well. During the four days they'd been at Glen Oaks, Celia had determined that she would not let the other woman upset her. The outrageous flirting with Francis— and every other man present—was as natural to Gwenn as breathing. It surprised Celia how calmly she accepted the fact that Francis and Gwenn were carrying on their affair almost publicly; perhaps Bradford Katon's advice had given her the courage she needed. She wondered at times if she still loved Francis. Certainly her feelings had altered greatly since their return to England.

A race was called and people rushed back to the stands to view the running. Celia was caught in the excitement and felt her heart quicken as the horse which Francis had bet took the lead. She pushed away all dark thoughts and gave herself to the enjoyment of the day. When Francis's horse won, she jumped from her seat and threw herself into his arms with an exclamation of delight.

"You've won! You've won!"

He laughed indulgently. "Pity I didn't have more than ten pounds on him. Come along and we'll collect my winnings." He took her hand and led her from the box and into the jostling, boisterous throng. The ticket windows were crowded and while Francis awaited his turn, Celia strolled the walkway, idly eying the people who passed. She felt a hand at her arm and turned to find Oliver Chadwick smiling at her. For a moment, confusion swept her and she looked about for Francis but he had been swallowed up in the crowd.

"I thought my eyes were deceiving me," Oliver said, "but you are flesh and blood." His hand was still on her arm and the pressure of his fingers caused her to shiver inwardly. Would she never get used to seeing him where she did not expect him? And would she always feel so unsettled when she did?

She tried to be casual. "All of England seems to be here."

"My entire world, now that I have found you."

She blushed and looked past him again to search for Francis. Her pulse was too fast; seeing Oliver was a pleasant agony.

"Are you betting this race?"

"No, I know nothing of horses save how to ride one, and even that not too well."

He leaned against the rail, still watching her. "You are a vision of beauty."

She was pleased with the compliment but felt compelled to offer some token resistance. "There are many beautiful women here today. I can scarcely compete."

"It is they who must compete. No man would deny you first place in any such contest."

She blushed and smiled.

"I was distressed at not being able to say goodbye to you in Calcutta. I came by the house several times but the *syce* said you were not receiving."

"I was busy tending Francis and readying things for the journey home."

"So busy that you could not spare me a few moments?" His brows furrowed and his dark gaze seemed to burn through her.

"There was nothing to be gained by our talking again." She had been too afraid to face him and her own emotions.

"Perhaps, but as you can see I am a very determined man. I have not given up." A smile played at the corners of his mouth and Celia's resolve almost weakened.

"Why did you come back to England?" She looked at him searchingly.

He raised his dark brows and stared at her a moment. "I was offered an excellent position."

"You had an excellent position in Calcutta."

"A man changes his goals as his life changes." He was watching her so intently that she was forced to look away. She pretended interest in the activity on the track.

"I would have thought you would elect to stay with the East India Company. Did you not tell me once that you could arrange to work in their offices here?"

His tone was amused. "Yes."

She was uncomfortable in the silence. He was a maddening man, silent when she wanted him to talk and questioning when she wished him to be silent. "I recall your telling me how hard you worked to gain your position."

"Celia, look at me." He took her arm and turned her

263

about. "I came back to England so I could be near you. Is that what you want me to say?"

"No! I—" She could not control the rush of pleasure his words gave her. The pressure of his fingers on her arm was warm through the thin material of the coat.

"When His Lordship wrote inquiring if I would be interested in managing a new company some of his friends were forming, I jumped at the chance because it meant I could be near you again. I have no particular liking for the Duke or his affairs, but he is a friend of the Devys. I had every reason to expect the Devys would be involved in the railroad company. If they hadn't been, I'd have found another way to see you."

She could scarcely believe her ears. He'd come because of her. The thought made her dizzy—and frightened. She was married to Francis; she had no right to think of Oliver in the way her thoughts wanted to go. The blare of trumpets from the reviewing stand gave her an opportunity to turn from him and escape comment.

"It's time for the Cup Race," he said. "Where are you staying?"

"At Glen Oaks—"

"Katon's?" He laughed harshly. "But of course, that would be most convenient for Francis."

She was about to answer sharply when a young woman hurried toward them to take Oliver's arm intimately. "Here you are! I thought I'd lost you, darling." She cast a questioning, jealous glance at Celia.

"I met an old friend ... Mrs. Devy ... Miss Elizabeth Cartwright." Oliver made the introductions casually.

"Charmed," the girl said but her look denied it. "Come or we'll miss the—" A shout went up from the crowds. "Oh dear!" The girl tugged Oliver along an aisle toward the boxes. He smiled over his shoulder at Celia, and she leaned weakly against the rail. On the track below, a group of royal carriages came rolling along the race course, and the crowd went wild with shouts of "The Queen! The Queen!"

She knew she should return to the box but she did not move. Above the heads of the throngs she searched for Oliver's tall figure, saw the girl still clinging to his arm as they stood in a box several sections distant from the Katon

party. The crowd fell silent in expectation as the Queen's coach approached and the beautiful young sovereign, escorted by her handsome uniformed husband, presented herself to the people. The cheering rose joyfully as the carriage passed slowly and the Queen waved. Celia's eyes took in the scene but her mind was still on Oliver, and when he turned and met her gaze, she trembled and gripped the railing, then forced herself to cross the promenade and return to the box where Francis and the others were already seated.

The party that night was boisterous. Gwenn's guests were caught in the holiday spirit and copious amounts of liquor added to their merriment. Celia endured it for several hours after dinner, then sought the quiet of their rooms. Francis would drink and dance until dawn, but she had no heart for such entertainment this night. She had been upset ever since meeting Oliver. She was restless and bored with Glen Oaks and longed to go home. They were scheduled to leave the following day, but there was little chance of an early start if Francis were going to be up all night.

In the upper hall, she met Bradford Katon's nurse who was carrying a tray of milk and crackers. On impulse, she accompanied the nurse to the bedroom.

Katon was delighted to see her. "Come in, come in! I thought you'd be downstairs dancing. A pretty girl like you should have no problem with partners. But I'm glad to see you. Sit, child, sit."

He was still in the huge armchair, wrapped in a woolen robe and heavy blanket.

"I shan't keep you from retiring," she said. "I only wanted to say goodnight and to thank you for the lovely visit we've had."

He snorted. "Sleep is something needed by the young to restore their energies. I do nothing all day and there is no escape in sleep for me when darkness comes. I welcome company, especially some as pleasant as yours." He waved aside the nurse. "Mrs. Daggett, why don't you go downstairs and have yourself a cup of tea or whatever while Celia and I chat?"

The nurse left quickly, glad to escape for whatever time

she could. Bradford Katon sighed when the door closed behind her. "Blasted woman acts as if I might get up and run off if she leaves me alone a moment." He shoved aside the tray Mrs. Daggett had set beside him. "Pap—garbage. Bad enough a man has to die without being reduced to infancy in his final years."

Celia smiled. "I imagine Mrs. Daggett is following your doctor's orders."

"Of course she is! And he's an idiot—some young pup Gwenn engaged so she could make moon eyes at him. What does he care that I long for a snifter of brandy and a good cigar? No suffering for him to deny me my pleasures." He shook his head and sighed. "It's a damned conspiracy and I'm helpless to do anything about it."

Celia bit her lip and jumped up. "Just a moment—"

"Where are you going?"

"I'll be right back." She ran out and along the hall to the rooms she and Francis shared, returning minutes later with her fleecy white shawl wrapped about an awkward bundle. Bradford Katon frowned and watched her slide the bolt on the door. She turned and swept away the shawl to reveal a half-full bottle of brandy and two long, thin cigars.

"My God! You're a miracle worker!" He took the cigars and held one beneath his nose, savoring the aroma. "A mighty fine tobacco, mighty fine indeed."

Celia took a taper from the box below the gas lamp and held it to the flame, then brought it to him. Bradford puffed clouds of smoke and sighed contentedly. She found a small glass on the medicine tray and filled it with brandy.

"May I ask where you got these treasures?" Bradford asked, sipping the vintage brandy.

"My husband will not miss them."

He grinned and petted her hand. "I shall enjoy them all the more knowing they were spirited away from a Devy. Now make yourself comfortable and we'll chat. Must you go tomorrow?"

"Yes, but I shall miss our visits."

"But you will not miss my dear wife's attentions to your husband. There—don't feel compelled to defend him. We both know what he is. I only wish that fate had been more

266

kind to you in matters of the heart, but then fate seems to have little control when one fancies oneself in love, eh? We both know how treacherous romance can be. But enough of that, I'd rather talk about you. Have you ever thought of doing anything other than being a wife?"

"What do you mean?"

"Nothing wrong with a woman occupying her mind in intellectual ways. Some damned good writers and poets among them."

"I've no talent for that."

"Business? You've got a good head and plenty of common sense. Attributes worth having." At her surprised look, he went on. "I'm not suggesting something meaningless like clerking in a shop or domestic service. Get into investments. Study a business and then put some capital into it and let it grow." He sipped at the brandy and smacked his lips.

"I've no capital either, I'm afraid, though I would enjoy knowing more about many things. I've heard so much talk about the railroad it intrigues me."

"A boom coming, it can't miss."

"Francis and Anthony have gone into it."

He paused with the brandy glass at his lips. "Not Skeffington's company?"

"Yes, how did you guess. But of course, the Duke is Gwenn's uncle, I'd forgotten."

He drank from the glass again, his face puckered in a frown. "I'm sorry to hear that, sorry indeed. Skeffington is not to be trusted. He'd sell off his friends for a quick turn of profit."

"You don't mean the company will fail—" She felt her heart skip a beat. Anthony and Francis were in debt heavily and were counting on the profit they'd make.

"Didn't say that. Depends on many things. Edward came to me with the proposition and I turned him down. I see that didn't stop him." He looked thoughtful and swirled the amber liquor in the glass, then drained it and held it out to Celia with a wink. "Another drop, eh?"

She refilled the glass and turned the conversation back to the railroad company. "Why did you turn down the Duke's offer?"

"Because I know him and I don't like him and I don't

trust him. I'm not saying he hasn't made fortunes ten times over, but he's lost as many or more. He makes promises he can't keep and he's been known to pull out at the first sign of financial trouble and leave others holding the bag. Besides, I don't need any more money. I'm not going to live long enough to spend what I've got and I've no one to leave it to but Gwenn who will enjoy dancing on my grave to have it." He puffed at the cigar and looked more relaxed and happy than she'd ever seen him. "I wish you were staying on. If you ever find yourself in the neighborhood of Windsor, you are always welcome here. Many times Gwenn is gone for months at a time, and I would be delighted to see you."

"Thank you. Now I'd better do something about this smoke. Mrs. Daggett will be back shortly and if she smells it, it'll be my neck." They giggled like two conspirators as she bundled him in his blanket then opened the window and fanned the smoke out into the June night. She rinsed the medicine glass at the basin and returned it to the tray, then hid the brandy bottle beside the chair cushions where he could get at it easily but where Mrs. Daggett's casual glance would not detect it. Finally she unbolted the door.

"You've brought me a great deal of happiness these past days, Celia. I never expected to smile so much again in my lifetime."

She bent and kissed his leathery cheek. "I shall come to say goodbye before we leave tomorrow, and I shall try to come this way again, if it is at all possible." She heard the door. "Now here's Mrs. Daggett, so I will say goodnight and leave you to rest. Sleep well tonight."

"Maybe I will," he said with a wink. "Goodnight, Celia."

CHAPTER SIXTEEN

Theo's wedding took place at Aylesford, with the Bishop of the county presiding. Celia was surprised when Theo told her that the Devys no longer afforded their patronage to the local clergyman or to Ascension Church, but she wisely said nothing and did not push the issue of her own attendance.

The wedding was held the last Saturday in June; the day dawned bright and warm, with only a gentle breeze fluttering the leaves. Before sunup, workmen were setting up the bridal arch and fastening thousands of blossoms to the latticework. Chairs were laid out in curving rows at either side of an aisle covered by a white runner and bordered with small potted roses and lilies in full bloom. The entire garden took on the air of an open cathedral, and the fragrance of the flowers carried into the house. Celia had been wakened early by the sounds of tapping and whispering as the house came alive for the eventful day. She and Francis breakfasted in their room, out of the way of bustling servants, workmen, and houseguests.

"How fondly I recall our wedding day," Francis said. "You were in the final hours of your journey and I was left to stew and worry alone."

She was pleased by the burst of intimacy. "It was the loveliest wedding that ever was. You arranged everything beautifully."

He laughed. "But not easily. Lord, Amanda Collingworth would have made it the social event of the year if given her head."

"Amanda arranged it?"

"With some help from the other good ladies of Calcutta." He rose from the small table set near the window and began dressing. "I'm going to ride before getting ready for the ceremony. I feel the need of air and to get away from the house a bit. Would you care to join me?"

She shook her head. "No, I've a dozen things to do and there's scarcely time—"

He smiled indulgently. "Why is it that women take hours to put on a few simple garments and a man only minutes?" He bent to kiss her lightly. "I shall return in plenty of time, no worry on that score. It's only ten and the wedding's not until two."

She lingered over her coffee, watching from the window as he crossed the yard and headed for the stables. He turned suddenly at a sound Celia did not hear, and Gwenn was racing across the grass to catch up with him. She was wearing a brown linen habit and carrying a short riding crop. Celia drew back, though neither of them glanced upward as they linked arms and continued toward the stable.

Plan or chance? She could not bring herself to believe that Gwenn just happened to be dressed for riding on this of all mornings! She turned from the window and steeled herself against the nagging irritation. How like Gwenn to be fully aware of Francis's plans; and Francis had dared to ask Celia to join him. If she had accepted, would he have found some excuse to retract the invitation or would Gwenn have made an awkward threesome? Ever since the week at Glen Oaks, Celia had come to grips with the matter of her husband's affair. She could not change him, and she no longer cared, but she would do everything in her power to impede the romance each chance she got. Like Bradford Katon, she would not give Gwenn the satisfaction of having the last laugh!

When Francis returned past noon, Celia was too busy to question him. Several of Theo's friends from the fashionable school she had gone to in London were to attend her at the wedding, and Celia had promised to supervise the final stages of their dressing. The six young ladies were giggly and nervous, fussing and primping, though each had a

270

personal maid to see to her needs. The girls wore identical dresses of pale blue embroidered satin, full-skirted and unadorned except for a single white tulle rose at the waist. Theo had chosen friends with fair complexions and light coloring to set off her own dark beauty. From the garden, organ music rose above the chatter of voices as the wedding guests took their places; one of the maids popped her head into the room to tell them it was time. Celia hurried to descend with Francis, and arm in arm they walked to their places beside Mrs. Devy and Anthony. Celia saw Gwenn sitting a row behind with the Duke and ignored Gwenn's curious smile. She glanced along the aisle which Theo would use, and her heart lurched. Oliver Chadwick was standing a few rows back, watching her and smiling gently when he caught her gaze. She averted her eyes but not before her cheeks flushed with warmth. She had not known he was invited!

The music paused, then began again and the crowd fell silent. The Bishop emerged from a small, screened shelter set up behind the altar, his gold mitre gleaming in the dappled sunlight filtering through the canopy of white roses. André walked slowly from the side door of the study and took his place before the altar, his eyes turned to the aisle. He wore a black cutaway and waistcoat over a starched collar and dark cravat. His trousers were dark grey with a pin stripe, proper for an afternoon wedding. A thin moustache shadowed his upper lip, and his eyes gleamed as Theo came down the aisle on Squire Devy's arm.

She was radiant in a white gown of heavy, luxurious satin, the skirt gathered in the tiniest of pleats to a long bodice that was covered with seed pearls in a patterned scrollwork. The high neck and long sleeves were unadorned except for narrow self-piping. The full skirt lay over voluminous petticoats that had been stiffly starched so that the dress swept about Theo's slippered feet like a cloud. Along the hemline, the skirt was caught up at intervals with tiny satin bows to give the effect of draped layers. Atop Theo's gleaming black curls, she wore a crown of pearls and a long white veil that fell to the train of the dress. She smiled nervously as she took her place at the altar; her father stepped back to join the family members in the front row of seats.

Celia only half listened to the words of the ceremony. She wondered what Theo's life would be like. Certainly she was not entering into marriage with the same starry-eyed expectations that Celia had had. It was more of a practical arrangement, a good financial one that had nothing to do with love. Celia thought about her own dreams when she'd been betrothed to Francis. She had been aware of the prestige and position that would be hers as a Devy, but she had been madly in love. She'd pinned all her hopes and dreams on Francis as a person, apart from the Devy family name. And he had fallen short of the dream and left her wounded and disillusioned. She hadn't been willing to heed any warnings that Francis might have flaws. She smothered a sigh as she thought of how Kevin had tried to prepare her for reality . . . and her father too, but she'd closed her ears and mind to such possibilities; the reality had come nevertheless.

The Bishop was concluding the ceremony, pronouncing André and Theo man and wife, and after an almost chaste kiss, the two were walking back the length of the aisle to the reception line. As Celia and Francis followed the Devys, she glimpsed Oliver Chadwick smiling but did not turn toward him. The Devys stood beneath a huge oak as people swarmed to offer congratulations and wishes for happiness to the newlyweds. After a bit, Celia moved away.

She took a cup of punch from a servant with a tray and carried it toward the lower garden to escape the chatter and merriment which left her strangely discontent. Was it too much for a woman to ask for lasting romance? She thought of her excitement when she'd first known Francis. She'd felt as a woman should, and when they wed she felt complete, but that had vanished so swiftly. Unbidden, her thoughts went to Oliver. She had felt a woman with him as well! The buried memory of the hours they spent together in Malta came to her and though she was alone, her cheeks flamed. Was there a difference between love and physical attraction? How did a woman tell where one ended and the other began? She couldn't deny she found Oliver attractive, though she wanted no part of him! He

272

had taken advantage of her inexperience to trap her in a situation of his choosing. And now, he admitted coming back to England to be near her. Did he expect that she could welcome his friendship?

As though in response to her thoughts, Oliver was suddenly beside her. She had not heard his approach, and she jumped as he spoke. "You look more lovely each time I see you."

She was determined not to let him fluster her. "Thank you, but it is Theo who is the attraction today."

"Perhaps, but that does not detract from the truth." He saw her empty punch cup and took it from her, turning to set it on a low stone wall that bordered the garden. When he looked back, his face was solemn, his eyes speculative. "It grieves me to see you unhappy."

"I am not unhappy," she protested.

"I see it in your face, your eyes. Where there should be love and laughter there is pain."

"You are mistaken. I am tired from the rush of wedding activities, nothing more." She dropped her gaze nervously.

He ignored her as if he had not heard. "I want to see you in London."

She looked across the garden, her heart pounding. "I—I'm not planning a trip just now. Besides—"

"Celia—look at me, dammit!" He spun her about roughly and took her in his arms. "What must I do to convince you that I love you?"

She stared, mouth agape, pulse racing. Her whole body seemed to tremble and grow weak as he caressed her hair and looked earnestly into her eyes.

"I want you in every way a man wants a woman. Come away with me."

"Away?" The word sounded alien and impossible.

"I have money put by. We can go wherever you like."

"What are you saying?" Her voice was barely a whisper and she shivered with a sudden chill. "I am married."

He sneered. "You speak of marriage as some holy estate when your husband mocks it constantly? His affair with Gwenn Katon is the talk of London."

"How dare you say that!"

"Because it is true. You can't be so naïve to think that

273

others do not see what you know to be true, or that Francis's frequent trips to the city are business."

His dark smouldering gaze tore from her the little courage that remained. "He sees the doctor . . ."

Oliver laughed. "He has not seen the doctor for several months. He is as fit as he ever will be, and his slight limp does not hamper his amusements with the ladies, I can assure you. Celia, don't be a fool. Let's take our happiness while we can." He held her tight when she would have pulled away.

Her pulse was a throbbing drumbeat in her temples. What he said was true, Francis would never change. Still, she could not give herself wantonly to another as long as she was wed or she would be no better than Gwenn whom she despised. "I cannot . . ."

Oliver smothered her protest with a searing kiss, his lips hard on hers and his tongue speaking his passion. Celia felt her body suffuse with the heat of desire such as she had not known for a long time. Trembling, she finally drew back. "You mustn't—we can't—" It was insane to let herself be swept into a torrent she could not control.

"Say you will see me."

"That's impossible."

"Nothing is impossible if we both want it. I have leased a house in London, we can be together—for a day or a week—as long as you can get away."

"I cannot—"

"Stop saying that! You can and you want to." His eyes burned with deep emotion that stirred her. "Can you tell me that you don't share my feelings?" He would not release her.

"I am a married woman," she whispered at last.

He shook her. "Damn it, then tell me you love him. Tell me you adore Francis and I shall walk away this instant and not bother you again!" His grip on her arms was like steel and she could feel the soft warmth of his breath on her face. She tried to speak, but no words came, and after a moment, Oliver bent his lips to hers again in a kiss more passionate than the first.

When at last he released her lips, he whispered, "The Duke has asked Francis and Anthony to accompany him to his estate in Sussex. Several other business associates are

274

to be there to discuss the railroad." He looked at her earnestly. "Find a way to spend the week in London while he is gone."

She was filled with yearning and with fear. "Will you not be asked to the meeting?"

"No. I am an employee who does not share in the decision-making." His voice held an edge of sarcasm. "But you can be sure Gwenn will play the hostess for her uncle and his friends."

It was like a knife twisting in her heart, but a two-edged blade that reminded her not only of her husband's infidelity but of the proposal that Oliver was making that she engage in similar deceit. She was torn between desire and conscience.

Oliver slipped her arm through his and began to walk as voices drifted to them from a group that had just entered the garden. Celia did not turn lest the flaming color of her cheeks betray the turmoil she felt. At the end of a path, they sat on one of the stone benches and Oliver pretended conversation each time the intruders in the garden glanced in their direction. They were people that Celia knew by sight but whose names she could not recall, friends of the senior Devys.

"I must return to the guests," she said at last when the group had moved on.

"You have not given me an answer."

"I cannot." She met his eyes and implored him silently.

Slowly, he rose and offered his arm again. "I'll take you back."

His silence was more painful than the conversation had been. Celia was terribly aware of the physical attraction she felt for him, the need, the desire. And when she glimpsed Francis laughing and chatting with Gwenn near the long table where the champagne bottles were being uncorked, pain stabbed her heart. A group of musicians had set up their instruments under a sycamore tree and music blended with the hum of voices. She thought of her first visit to Aylesford, the party where she had met and talked with Francis and been smitten with him. Where would she be at this moment if she had never attended it?

She mingled with the guests and pretended she saw nothing amiss in her husband's attentions to Gwenn, though the mood of the day was spoiled. The reception was set up in the sprawling gardens, with tables under canopies and chairs arranged in groupings so that people could sit if they desired. Servants moved about with trays of drinks and food, and people served themselves from the long buffet tables. And as dusk gathered, the musicians moved into the ballroom. The bridal couple had the honor of the first dance as a waltz was struck up; a radiant Theo, cheeks flushed and eyes sparkling, glided about the room in the arms of her groom. An hour or so later, Celia noticed when Theo and André slipped away from the party and retired to their apartment in the west wing. They would stay the night at Aylesford, then journey to the south of France for several weeks before going to Paris where they would live.

A servant threaded his way through the throng and bowed to Celia. "A messenger, ma'am . . ." He handed her an envelope, and when Celia saw the familiar script, her heart faltered. Her mother would not write unless— She moved toward the tall windows where a gaslight glowed in a wall sconce and tore open the envelope. She read the brief note quickly, biting her lip as her fears were realized. Her father was gravely ill and it was not thought he would survive. If she wished to see him she must come at once.

She stood a moment fighting back her grief. She turned to look for Francis but could not find him in the crowded room. She made her way to the hall, unmindful of several people who would have detained her, and rushed upstairs, calling to Alice as she reached the upper hall.

"I must go to London—at once. Please have Jennie pack me a bag."

"I'll tend to it myself." Alice glanced at her questioningly.

"I'll be several days—"

The old woman nodded and summoned Jennie to bring a valise from the storage room. By the time the girl returned with it, Alice had laid out dresses, stockings, undergarments and shoes and was collecting toilet articles into a small leather case. Celia sat at the writing desk and penned a note to Francis, then handed it to Jennie with instructions that it be given him at once. In less than an hour, she was ready and her bags had been carried downstairs by a side stairway. Francis did not come to the apartment, only sent word with Jennie that he wished Celia Godspeed. She crumbled the note and tossed it into the cold grate.

The carriage was waiting under the portico, the outside lights casting long shadows over it to give it a somber appearance. As the footman opened the door, a figure stepped from the shadows.

"Celia—what is it? Where are you going this time of night?" Oliver peered at her with a frown. He had seen her rush upstairs after receiving a note, and he knew from her face that the news had upset her; and when one of the servants had carried a note to Francis, Oliver accosted the girl and bribed her to tell him what had happened. The girl knew only that Mrs. Devy was packing for a journey, so he'd waited outside.

The tears she had been fighting overflowed. "My father is ill—dying—" she sobbed.

He handed her up into the carriage and climbed in beside her. At her surprised look, he said, "I planned to return to London tonight and you shouldn't be alone." He did not ask about Francis; he didn't have to. Hadn't he seen him barely read the note and speak to the maid before resuming his dance?

Celia was too miserable to protest. She sank back against the cushions and closed her eyes, giving herself to thoughts of her father and memories of happier days. Her father had been happy in Renfield; he loved the countryside, the green hills . . . but he was to die in a grimy London parish that closed around him with grey walls and crowded streets. He'd been damned to a small corner of hell because she had married Francis! All at once her hatred for the Devys struck her with full force. How could she ever have believed them kind and good? She shuddered and felt Oliver's touch at her arm.

She found him staring at her with love and did not resist when he drew her into his arms to rest her head on his shoulder. "Try not to think, not now," he whispered. He sat holding her comfortingly, and the pain within her eased a bit. He did not try to coax her into conversation, and she was grateful. From time to time she dozed, and

277

when she woke it surprised her that she could feel peace at such a troubled time.

She stayed a week at the parish house in Spitelfields. She could do nothing but sit by her father's bedside and listen to his labored breathing and wait for the end. She found a doctor who would come the distance from his home, but his only contribution was laudanum to relieve the Reverend Skerritt's last agonies. He would not venture a guess as to the cause of the final illness, not having seen the patient before, but it made no difference since the end was so definitely near. Celia realized that she should contact her brother Kevin in America, but knew of no way to reach him with so little time remaining. William Skerritt died on the fourth day of Celia's vigil.

Emma Skerritt took his passing without weeping, her eyes filled with pain and loneliness. Celia made the funeral arrangements with a neighborhood undertaker and was surprised, quite pleasantly, at the number of people who attended the brief ceremony at the graveside. The mourners were an assortment of ragged-looking men and women, with shabby clothes and hands soiled with years of hard work. A group of children Reverend Skerritt had taught in a ragged school walked slowly behind the wagon bearing the coffin, their faces solemn. The small cemetery was surrounded by the encroaching city. Celia would have taken her father to Renfield to be buried, but her mother refused. "William would want to lie here where his final work was. And when the time comes, I shall lie beside him."

A minister sent by the bishop said a brief service over the grave before the coffin was lowered. He had not known Skerritt and performed the final duty without emotion. It was as though he spoke of a stranger, not the man Celia had known all her life and loved so dearly. She stood without weeping, but her heart ached; and when it was over, she took her mother's arm and they walked slowly back to the shabby parish house where two women hired by the bishop had already set to clearing out Mrs. Skerritt's things. The new parson would take over immediately; Mrs. Skerritt had been offered a post as housekeeper-parish worker but Celia would not hear of it. Her

278

mother just as adamantly refused to leave the parish or allow Celia to provide her a small cottage in Renfield. With equal firmness, she refused to go to her sister Henrietta. Emma Skerritt did not fear death, only spending her remaining years alone and with nothing to occupy her time. She told Celia she would remain in Spitelsfield—she had friends to whom she could go—and continue to teach in the school and the Sunday school, if the new parson would permit; nothing Celia could say or do would change her mind.

Celia saw to the moving of her mother's personal belongings, which were pitifully few. There was no note from Francis, though she had written him of her father's death. When she remembered that both Francis and Anthony were scheduled to be at the Duke's estate in Sussex, she sent a second note there, telling Francis she planned to stay on in London for awhile. She could not bear the thought of being with the Devys when she held them responsible for her father's early death.

Mrs. Skerritt moved into a tiny back bedroom of a nearby house belonging to an elderly widow. Celia tucked several pound notes under her father's old Bible before she left, but she knew that her mother would spend the money to help others instead of herself. Sighing, Celia kissed her mother goodbye and promised to visit.

She emerged into the sunlight which seemed all the brighter for the gloominess of the small house and found Oliver seated in a hackney at the curb. He jumped down and took her hand, and she did not protest as he put her in the carriage and gave the driver an address.

"I went to the cemetery but you'd already left."

"The service was very brief." And cold, she thought with a hardening heart.

"Will you come with me now?" His eyes searched her face.

She hesitated, then answered quite simply, "Yes." He smiled and nodded, and she knew it was right.

CHAPTER SEVENTEEN

Oliver's house was in a fashionable section of Knights-bridge that had been abandoned by the very wealthy for the new elegance of Chelsea. It was a tall, narrow town-house, with high windows and a white-painted door with gleaming brass fittings. He unlocked the door with his own key, but a manservant appeared immediately to take their hats.

"Would you like tea?"

She shook her head. Now that she was actually here, doubts assailed her and her heart fluttered nervously. Oliver was watching her and she felt awkward all at once. She had avoided this moment so long, yet she had antici-pated it too. Since her first meeting with Oliver she had been drawn to him by some magnetism beyond her con-trol. She had lain with him in Malta and convinced herself it had been against her will, but that had been a lie to salve her conscience. She had wanted him then, as she did now.

"Then come with me. I've waited a very long time for this moment." He put his arm about her waist and led her up the stairs. Her fingers trailed on the polished bannister and she glimpsed her reflection in a long mirror over the entry table. She was wearing black but the dress did not seem like mourning against the gold and white stripes of the wallpaper behind her. There was color in her cheeks and the blue eyes that stared back at her were somehow changed—alive again and no longer afraid.

He opened the door of a bedchamber richly appointed in rust-colored velvets and satin. It was a masculine room, without frills, but pleasant and bright. He paused to slide the bolt on the door and the sound of the lock seemed loud in the sudden silence. He came to her and took her into his arms to kiss her with a fervor that was fiery and breathtaking. The emotions that had been buried in her so long sprang to flame and she clung to him breathlessly. His mouth was hard and when his tongue probed her lips, she welcomed it and their passions fused. She was swept headlong into a tide of desire from which there was no escape. All reason fled and she clung to him, savoring his caresses until she was weak and shivering.

He was whispering her name like a prayer, and his fingers found the fastenings of her dress and undid them quickly. She stood breathless while he stripped each garment as though unveiling a masterpiece whose beauty could be at last be shown. His fingers lingered on her flesh, touching a shoulder, moving over her breasts, smoothing a path across her body. He drew her to the bed and lay her against the russet spread so that she was an alabaster statue on display while he removed his own garments and came to her. He kissed her again, on the mouth, neck, breasts, gently at first and then with greedy desire. She felt as though a thousand fingers of fire burned at her and she whimpered when at last he spread her thighs gently and mounted her. She welcomed him and felt the wondrous surge of his strength within her. For a moment she was breathless with emotion, then blazing lights exploded in her brain and she was moving with him, meeting his powerful strokes with desperate need, clawing at his naked body as she cried out his name. She was caught in a whirlwind, sucked into a dizzying vortex of passion that erupted all at once. She cried out in ecstatic pleasure as his hot rush of love met her own.

She lay limp and quivering, unable to grasp the enormity of the emotions and physical pleasure she had experienced. He cradled her in his arms and held her close, her golden hair falling across his darkly patterned chest, as he stroked her cheek and brushed back an errant curl. She sighed tremulously.

"Say that you love me," he whispered and kissed the top

of her head. She was warm against his flesh and he never wanted to let her go.

Celia sighed again and could not deny him the words he wanted to hear. "I love you ..." The frustration that had built up over the months of Francis's indifference and infidelity vanished in Oliver's arms. She knew that she could not live without the fulfilling pleasure of being totally a woman whose name was dragged through the courts and ousness that was within her, the need and the desire. She did not realize she had sighed again until Oliver raised himself to peer at her.

"What is it, love?"

"I am happy ..."

"You were meant to be happy, my darling. We were meant to be happy together. When we are married—"

She bolted up, staring at him as reality washed over her. She tried to leave the bed but he grabbed her quickly.

"Surely you realize now that you cannot remain married to Francis. We must be together."

"That's impossible," she said flatly.

He pulled her about. "Impossible? Don't talk nonsense, of course it isn't. There are divorces. It will not be easy, but I'll find a way to arrange it."

She'd heard of divorce and the scandal it brought to a woman, whose name was dragged through the courts and degraded so that she would never hold her head up again. "I shall not suffer that disgrace!" she declared vehemently.

He glared at her, angry and slightly amused. "Would you expect me to play the gigolo? To chase you about and take you where and when you find a moment for me? No, my darling, I have more planned for us than that."

He was teasing her yet he was deadly serious. She saw the determination in his eyes and the firm set of his jaw. "Oliver, you must realize I cannot divorce Francis!"

"Why not?"

"Because—"

"Not because you love him. Not because you hold the Devys in such high regard that you would not disgrace them. Is it then that you don't love me enough?"

She flung herself into his arms and cried against his naked chest. "Don't even say such a thing in jest! I love you and want you more than anything—" She stopped and drew away so she could look at him. "I want you more than anything I have ever wanted before, but I will not give the Devys that final satisfaction of casting me aside. I wed Francis because I loved him and I thought he loved me. I was wrong and have become the laughingstock of Aylesford and London because I have been blind to the truth. They ruined my father and put him in his grave. My mother will not return home with me because they would make her life unbearable. And you ask me to tell them they can triumph over me as well? Never!"

He felt his anger surge, then wane. She was being a fool, and he wanted to shake her—or love her so passionately that she would change her mind. She was hurt and angry over her father's death, and she was ready to lash out at those who caused it, to her way of thinking. Nothing would dissuade her now but she would in due time see that her own happiness was more important. Instead of berating her, he took her in his arms and gentled her with kisses and soft words until she relaxed once more and lay willingly with him. Patiently and with loving tenderness, he banished thoughts of the Devys from her mind. He drew her close and stroked her trembling body until her anger was calmed. His lips nibbled at her ear and found the soft curve of her throat, passed down the silken valley of her shoulder to her breast. Shivers danced along her flesh as he teased the pink crest with his tongue.

"Oliver—" She was being drawn into an oblivion of passion again.

"Let me love you." They explored the heights and depths of mutual desire, and when at last they came together again, it was with total joy and awareness.

She spent five days with Oliver, and they were the happiest of her memory. Though he was gone several hours each day, the time passed quickly, and Celia found countless things to do. She went out to shop, browsing through Harrod's and other elegant stores along Knightsbridge and Brompton Roads. One day when Oliver had to be gone the entire afternoon, she took a hackney to Spitelfields and visited her mother, who seemed content in her new life. She also visited a physician in Mayfair who confirmed her pregnancy and said the child would be born about Christmastime, though she said nothing of this to Oliver.

Celia would not be seen publicly with Oliver lest gossip get back to Aylesford, so they dined alone each evening over a small candlelit table, enjoying meals prepared by the excellent staff Oliver employed. Sometimes Oliver retired to his study to work on pressing matters; Celia did not disturb him but met him eagerly when he emerged. The nights were idyllic and filled Celia with a sense of love and wonder that any man could be as perfect as he. When she told him this, he smiled indulgently and warned her that he was mortal and she must not set him upon a pedestal.

Oliver brought her the news that Lord Skeffington was back in London. He scowled as he spoke of several decisions that had been made that were not to his liking.

"It seems the Duke has made promises to investors that he means to keep," he said.

"That would seem an asset."

"Not if the promises are in the nature of bribes. He's assured several people that in return for their investments they can count on lines being run to the areas they favor. A fledgling company cannot build half a dozen spurs and hope to make a profit. Track costs the same whether it will be used heavily or only at the whim of a handful who see it as a novelty."

His face was tight with annoyance and Celia wondered at the seriousness of the matter. "Will the company fail?" Anthony and Francis had invested heavily hoping to bail out Aylesford from its pressing debts.

Oliver took a deep breath and let it out slowly. "Perhaps I can still convince them of the folly. But I've spoiled our dinner with such talk. No more of it." He tried to recapture their good humor.

Celia toyed with the chocolate mousse in the tall goblet before her. "If the Duke has returned, then I must go back to Aylesford. Francis will be home."

A tic of annoyance twitched the corner of Oliver's mouth. "He will not miss you." It was cruel, but he couldn't bear the thought of losing her now that he had discovered such happiness.

"I must."

"I don't want you to," he said angrily.

She looked up, surprised by his tone. "But we discussed it—we've both known all along that I must go back."

"*You* mentioned it, we never completed any discussion of the sort," he said, pushing aside his dessert glass and reaching for the coffee cup. "I let you ramble about your plans because I believed you would get them out of your system. Your anger with the Devys is understandable, but it's no reason to waste the rest of your life. Haven't you learned by now that happiness is at best an elusive thing that must be snatched up quickly?"

She wanted to agree, to throw herself into his arms and vow that they would never part but a cold, hard core of anger within her would not let her. "Yes, I have learned that lesson well, but I have also learned to be cautious where my emotions are involved. I fled headlong into romance once before."

He flung his napkin to the table and rose so abruptly that his chair rocked and almost fell. "You compare what is between us with the infatuation you felt for Francis Devy?" His face was dark and his eyes like lightning in a raging storm.

"No—I didn't mean that—"

"But you will not love me according to your heart, only according to the dictates of the Devys? I had thought you more sensible than to let money and name sway you. Perhaps I was wrong." He turned and strode from the room.

Celia heard the door of the study slam as he closeted himself. She bit her lip and swallowed a sob. Why did he persist in closing his eyes to the reality of her life? He *must* see that she could not divorce Francis, not when it would be on his terms and at his mercy. She sipped the coffee and pushed it aside when she discovered it had grown cold. She left the dining room and listened at the door of the study but heard nothing, so went upstairs to wait for Oliver. She laid out a traveling dress and packed her bag, collecting her things from Oliver's closet and chest where they seemed so right and natural. She would find a way to return, and though it could only be for brief visits now, her love for Oliver would not lessen. He had to understand.

She went to bed and lay waiting for the sound of his

footsteps. When at last he entered the bedroom, she saw that his anger had dissipated. He came to her with a need that was greedy, gentle, yet demanding, until he had sated them both. For the desperate hour of their passion, she forgot everything but her desire for him and his nearness. They slept locked in each other's arms.

Francis and Anthony returned in high spirits from the trip to Sussex and were full of chatter about the railroad. Squire Devy sat in a huge wicker armchair in the solarium and listened to the dreams and schemes his sons were taking part in.

"The Devys have never gone into business of that sort before," he said severely. "Seems the estate ought to keep us." He grimaced with pain and shifted his gouty foot on the stool.

Anthony paced the flagstoned floor. "Times are changing, Father. You know how hard it's been keeping cottagers when they can move to the city and double their incomes with factory work."

"Besides," Francis added, "there was never a Devy who didn't take opportunity when it came around. What's the harm of doubling our money if we've the chance?" He glanced significantly at his brother.

"Harrumph . . ." Squire Devy thumped his cane on the stone and shook his head. "You mean pay the notes Anthony has incurred this past year!"

Anthony whirled about, shocked that his father would state it so bluntly and unable to hide his guilt. "Gossiping tongues—"

"But truth, do you deny it? No, I see that you can't. Do you think me a doddering old fool that I haven't been aware of my own accounts? I've been forced to hand over the management of the estate because my health won't permit me to get about as I used to but I'm not deaf and blind. Lord Skeffington came to me with his talk of the railroad first. I will admit I didn't protest when he suggested discussing it with you, but I think you might have confided in me before investing as heavily as you've done. Do you realize what can happen?"

"Railroads are the coming thing."

"I'm not talking about railroads, dammit, I'm talking

about one company you've seen fit to invest our entire capital in! If one wrong judgment is made, one mistake, we can be wiped out! Your creditors already hold notes for more cash than we can raise." He turned an angry scowl to Francis. "And you've not helped matters much with your own spendthrift ways since your return. The trust fund from which you derive your income is all but depleted."

"More the reason for me to recoup my losses," Francis said, smiling but cowering slightly under his father's harsh gaze.

"I thank God that your sister has married well and at least is no worry to me. If you'd seen fit to wait for Gwenn Katon—but, too late for that, I suppose." He turned back to Anthony. "Time you looked about for another bride. I don't have to tell you that a good alliance between you and a woman of title and wealth would be most propitious."

Anthony's face clouded. "I have no wish to marry again," he muttered as he walked to the liquor cart and poured himself a stiff shot of whiskey.

Celia battled with her emotions in the days that followed. She longed for Oliver, to be happy and secure in his arms, yet her conscience troubled her that she had stepped out of her marriage bonds. No matter that Francis had done the same; it was different for a man. It was especially hard on her because of the strict upbringing she'd had. At times she lay awake nights wondering if the desire she felt for Oliver would ever subside. She was angry with herself for giving in to it, and angrier still for denying herself the pleasure of its complete fulfillment. She took from a trunk the carved ivory figure of a dancer Oliver had given her as a gift in Calcutta and set it upon her dressing table.

The household changed with Theo's departure. Mrs. Devy was more aloof than ever and paid scant attention to Celia. Unlike the Squire, who had turned over the management of the estate to his son, Mrs. Devy held the reins of the household in a tight fist so that Celia had no part in planning menus, daily schedules or social affairs. Francis seemed to occupy his time fully, though he, too, had little

287

to do. Sometimes he rode with her among the hills and in the woods, and at times they recaptured some of the joy of their marriage only to have it flee quickly when Francis set off for London or for destinations which he did not disclose. Their lovemaking dwindled to occasional times when he was restless and bored, and he seemed more interested in his own needs than hers. When she remarked on this one night, he reminded her that she was after all a woman married more than a year and had to expect changes. She knew that he saw Gwenn often, and she wondered if he told her the same thing! She said nothing of the child.

The business of the railroad progressed, and the Squire and his sons often discussed it over brandies after dinner. Celia tried to ask questions as they talked of the various sectors and spurs into the countryside. She recalled Oliver's annoyance at the pressure to please each investor without regard to financial considerations, but she dared not display more knowledge than she was supposed to have. The more she listened to the talk, the more she was sure Oliver was right. Obviously wealth and good business sense did not necessarily go hand in hand.

Summer descended on the countryside with balmy breezes and warm evenings. Mrs. Devy began talking about a garden party—she was bored since Theo's departure and needed something to fill her mind. When the Squire demurred that cost was prohibitive at this time, she pouted and sulked like a spoiled child until he gave in, still cautioning her about the expense. Agatha vowed she would economize, then put any such notion from her mind and planned as extravagantly as ever. The party would be held for Anthony's birthday in mid-August; it would be an outdoor fete, with a pavilion under the sycamores for dancing and dining, and the entire grounds and gardens would be festooned in a harlequin theme, since the party would be masquerade.

The prospect of costumes gave Celia an excellent opportunity to escape to London. Francis claimed business affairs would detain him but promised to join her in two days' time, and he reserved a suite at the Hyde Park Hotel. En route, Celia stopped to visit her mother briefly but found her poor company. Immediately on her arrival at the hotel, Celia sent a note to Oliver by messenger, but no answer from him was returned. Oliver was out and not expected until evening. She hadn't believed she could be so anxious to see him. Being in London, knowing he was somewhere within reach made her impatient with desire. She would go mad sitting in the hotel suite waiting to hear from him, so she spent the afternoon at the dressmaker's shop planning her costume for the harlequin party.

Madame Louvère's was located on Brompton Road two blocks below Knightsbridge. Since the day was perfect, Celia walked, dawdling and looking into shop windows along the way and enjoying the sun and solitude. In a tobacconist's window, she saw a cleverly carved pipe in the shape of an elephant's head, and she entered the shop on impulse to buy it for Oliver. As she emerged and stood in the doorway to put up her parasol, someone called her name.

"Celia!"

She blinked and squinted, then recognized Iris Beddington. "Iris—how wonderful to see you here, what a surprise!" The parasol forgotten, Celia hugged Iris and they laughed and chattered like schoolchildren.

"When did you come back? Where are you living? You look simply marvelous!"

"I thought I was seeing things. I hardly expected you'd be in London at this time of year."

"How foolish of us to stand here in the sun, though it's not nearly as warm as it was in India, is it? Let's have tea—there's a charming little shop just at the corner. You do have time? You're not rushing to some important engagement?"

Iris smiled. "It's nothing that can't wait."

"Good." Celia shook open the parasol and they walked together to the tea shop. "Now, for goodness' sake, tell me how you happen to be here. I am bursting with curiosity—and delighted of course!" Iris seemed not to have changed one bit since the first day they met. India had not sapped her vitality or attractiveness, nor had the harsh sun spoiled her milky white complexion. She was stylishly dressed in a pale green printed challis with a silk gauze collar edged with Irish lace, and Celia recalled seeing it in

Calcutta. Her own pink watered silk was new, but she occasionally wore dresses that had been made for her in India; many of them were still in excellent condition.

They settled over a small corner table and waited for the girl to bring their order. Iris fussed with the velvet ribbons of the bonnet that framed her face. "We returned just a few weeks ago. James grew restless in his position, and since neither of us enjoyed the heat or filth of India it seemed best that we return to England."

"He's found a new position to his liking?"

Iris hesitated. "He's considering several posts but has not yet made up his mind."

"I wouldn't be surprised if he couldn't stay with the Company here in London. The home offices are quite sizable and a man with experience must be a valuable asset."

Iris busied herself with the beaded reticule, searching for a handkerchief and pressing it to her lips as she coughed delicately. "Yes, but several other opportunities seem to offer more so he is considering the matter carefully. But enough talk about that." She smiled. "You look very well. Has Francis recovered completely from his wounds?"

The tea was brought and while they drank and ate tiny frosted cakes, pastries and scones, Celia told bits and pieces of her life at Aylesford. She avoided any suggestion that all was not perfect, and she was careful not to mention Oliver. When Iris did, Celia gave a guilty start.

"Did you know that Oliver Chadwick returned several months ago?"

Her first impulse was to lie but she did not. "Yes ... as a matter of fact he is working for a company that Francis and his brother have an interest in."

Iris looked at her quizzically. "I didn't know the Devys were in business dealings. The estate— Forgive me, it's none of my affair."

Celia shrugged. "They are convinced that railroads are an excellent investment and have joined Lord Skeffington in a company."

"And Oliver works for them?"

"The Duke was acquainted with his fine reputation over the years with the East India Company and asked him to take the post." Celia's face felt warm and she was afraid

290

to meet Iris's steady gaze. Just thinking and talking about Oliver brought her a rush of pleasure that would betray her, she was sure. They were silent a moment and Celia spread a scone with the thick Devonshire cream from a delft pot. "Are you living in London?"

"Yes," Iris said.

"Where? We must get together often."

"We've taken a temporary house until James decides on a post. But tell me, what are you doing in London in July? Everyone who possibly can has gone off to the seashore or the country for the hot months. I would think Aylesford would be delightful this time of year, far more so than the city."

"I've come for a costume. I was on my way to the dressmaker when we met." At the other's curious look, Celia explained. "Mrs. Devy has decided on a fancy dress ball to honor Anthony's birthday on the thirteenth next month." She smiled all of a sudden. "You and James must come to the ball! I am weary of people I scarcely know, it will be wonderful to have old friends."

"I don't think—"

"You must—unless you've another engagement?"

"No . . ."

"Then it's settled? Please?"

"I'll speak to James. Perhaps he'll agree."

"You must come as guests for the weekend. It will give us an opportunity to become reacquainted. You will love Aylesford, it is beautiful."

Iris laughed. "Yes, I'm sure I will, but the Squire and Mrs. Devy—?"

Celia didn't care, though she knew Mrs. Devy would raise some fuss at anyone Celia invited. "Francis and I are inviting numerous friends." Too late she had contradicted herself but Iris did not remark on it.

"I must be going," Iris said, setting aside the linen napkin and opening her reticule.

"No, you must let me pay." Celia removed several coins from her purse and handed them to the girl who came at her summons. "We're staying at the Hyde Park Hotel for several days. Do come by if you've time?"

"It was very good to see you, Celia."

"Be very persuasive with James so he'll bring you to Aylesford."

"I'll try."

They parted, and Celia felt lighthearted as she continued on to Madame Louvère's, where she studied sketches and discussed costume ideas with the proprietress herself and finally decided on a Grecian robe that was elegant in its simplicity and which could easily be finished in time for the party. She took a cab directly from the shop to Oliver's townhouse, anxious to be with him as soon as possible. The butler admitted her, and Oliver hurried from the study to take her in his arms.

"You should have let me know you were coming—I would have been here so we would not waste these precious hours!" He kissed her, sealing off her reply and instantly catapulting her into the heady emotion his presence brought. She was deliriously happy in his embrace and wondered how she had ever found the courage to part from him. She returned his kisses with ardor and let herself be led into the sitting room and to a small sofa close to the windows. The curtains had been drawn all day to screen the sun and now a gentle breeze ruffled them and stirred the air.

"Why did you not come directly here instead of to a hotel?"

She let him clasp her hands and draw her into his arms again. "Francis arranged it and will be joining me the day after tomorrow."

He muttered a curse, then pushed Devy from his mind for the moment. With Celia in his arms, he had thoughts only for her—and their being together. "You will stay the night, and I shall arrange matters at the office in the morning so I can have the day free to spend with you." He lifted her chin and brushed his fingertips across her red lips. "I have missed you more than I thought possible. You've made a madman of me. I pace the house wishing you were here, remembering the hours you were."

"I have been so lonely—"

"It seems months rather than weeks."

"Years."

"Then let us not waste a minute of our being together. Come, we'll go upstairs."

She smiled impishly as he pulled her to her feet. "Is that all you want from me?" she teased.

"There are not enough centuries left in eternity that I would ever tire of you. I hunger for your kisses and to touch your wondrous flesh, to have you—" He shook his head. "See, it's as I told you, I am a madman in my need for you."

Laughing, they climbed the stairs arms entwined, bodies close. When they reached the bedchamber, they had no need for words, but undressed and lay together in loving silence. In moments they recaptured the fever of their passion and found that their absence from one another had magnified it so they could not keep it in bounds. They climbed to lofty peaks, clinging to each other and speaking with their bodies in harmony. The crescendo was so breathtaking, that Celia lay weeping helplessly when it was over. Oliver held her close, and she could feel his heart beat in a tempo that matched her own. How wonderful to be with him, to experience such total joy and peace. They dined in the intimate fashion they had adopted on her first visit, and retired upstairs soon afterward to lose themselves in rediscovery.

True to his word, Oliver absented himself only long enough to arrange to have the day free. On his return, he insisted that they were going out, and though she protested, he refused to listen, nor would he tell her their destination. A carriage was brought about and the butler settled a large hamper onto the luggage rack; Oliver took the reins himself. They rode for an hour out of the city, crossing the river at Vauxhall and turning off on a narrow road that wound through the suburban countryside. The city houses were lost to sight and green hills lay as far as the eye could see, with only an occasional cottage or a field of pale grain to break the monotony. When at last Oliver halted the carriage, they were beside a placid lake bordered by hanging willows, nestled in a small valley that seemed cut off from the rest of the world. He lifted her down and began unloading the picnic basket.

"It's beautiful," Celia exclaimed as she moved to a grassy flat place beneath one of the low-hanging trees. A fresh breeze stirred the air, fanning the surface of the lake so it resembled a warped mirror. She took a blanket from the carriage seat and spread it, then knelt as Oliver set down the basket. His arms were around her instantly, pulling her down and holding her close.

"I hoped you would like it."

She pressed her face to his. "However did you find it?"

"I was driving in these parts and came across it. I've been waiting impatiently for you to return to me so that I could bring you here."

She nestled her head at his shoulder and stared at the fleecy clouds drifting overhead. "When I was a little girl I had a spot where I always went when I wanted to be alone. It was similar to this except there was no lake. But I'd lie and stare at the sky and think how someday my life would be different, someday I'd have more than the dull existence of the parsonage." She looked up abruptly. "It wasn't that I was unhappy—only that I knew there had to be *more*, that somewhere there was a freedom I didn't know."

"And have you found that now?"

She touched his cheek. "When I am with you."

He drew her close and pressed his lips to hers. The embrace erased all other thoughts and warmth flooded through her. "Then do not leave me again," he whispered.

She sighed and said nothing, and he did not pursue the matter. After a bit they spread the picnic things and lunched sitting close and chatting or falling silent as their mood shifted. She was at peace with him, and it was pleasant to banish all disturbing thoughts past and future. When they finished eating, they strolled along the water's edge and sat on an overhanging rock to trail their fingers in the cool water.

"I can't recall any more wonderful day in my life," Celia said. "I still marvel at my own emotions when I am with you. You make me feel whole, as though I've been only a part of a person all my life until now."

He smiled, wisely not pushing the matter of her remaining with him forever. She was coming to that conclusion, he knew. She would soon realize the impossibility of staying with Francis for whatever reason. "I own this land," he said, waving a hand to the valley and lake.

"Own it?"

"Yes. From my first sight of it, I felt as you do and

wanted to keep this secluded spot just as it is ... for us."
He shook the water from his hand and wiped it on a
handkerchief. "One of the Duke's investors is demanding a
spur line of the railroad to Upper Haven a few miles
north of here. It's absolutely impractical."

"A railroad through this lovely valley?! It would be
sacrilege."

He laughed shortly. "More than that it would be costly
and unprofitable. There is nothing to warrant a line here
at this time."

"Then you must tell the Duke so."

"*Tell* him? You make it sound a simple matter. He will
have my full reports, of course, but I've been overridden
before, and since I do not have a voice in the final decisions, I may well be overridden on this too."

"But they mustn't—"

He smiled at her vehemence. "Easier said than done. In
business, the man with the money makes the rules."

"But the Duke bragged that he had selected you to manage the company because you were an excellent businessman. Surely he won't disregard your advice?"

"I thought not when I accepted the post but I am no
longer so confident. He does as he pleases and the rest be
damned." Oliver scowled momentarily. "But he shall not
put this spur through, I guarantee it."

"How can you be sure?"

He laughed and took her hands to pull her to her feet.
"Because I have bought this land and I will not give him
access across it. It is impossible to reach Upper Haven
without it." He grinned. "So I shall have the last laugh."

Celia was delighted but also frightened. Lord Skeffington was not a man who would take such duplicity lightly,
and he was in a position to make considerable trouble for
Oliver or to dismiss him from his post. Oliver must have
considered that, but it seemed not to bother him.

"Come along, sweet, we shall ride about the valley. Perhaps I can entice you to pick a spot where you would like
our house to stand someday."

The fragile balance of her happiness was shattered as
she realized he was planning for their future again as
though it were assured. Was it a dream, nothing more?
No. Life without Oliver would be too bleak to contem-

plate. They returned to the carriage, packed the basket and stowed it, then set out at a leisurely pace to cover the miles and acres of the valley and hillside that Oliver claimed. He watched her with amusement as she exclaimed in glee over this stand of birch, that formation of rock or a gnarled oak. When at last it was time to go, they cast fond glances back as the carriage left the valley and gained the road again.

Halfway back to the city, Celia recalled that she had not told Oliver of her meeting with Iris Beddington and she did so in a rush of words. He looked at her strangely. "She said the decision to leave the East India Company was his?"

"Yes, of course."

"Perhaps . . ."

"Whatever do you mean?"

"I'd heard statements to the contrary."

"You mean that he was let out?"

"There was some trouble and his name was linked to it."

"I don't believe it."

"Celia, you are prone to see people's good points and not their faults. I can understand your friendship with Iris, to a degree at least, but you know nothing of James Beddington. Regardless of whether these rumors are true or false he's a man with an unsavory past and I would caution you against welcoming him as a friend."

"He was in a responsible position with the Company."

"Many unscrupulous men worked for the Company and many honest men who took employment with them were corrupted by the ease with which wealth could be acquired if a man looked the other way or encouraged someone else to do the same while he stole materials so he could sell them on the black market. The history of greed and corruption within the Company is legend, so much so that some day the Crown will be forced to take action—if the Hindus themselves don't revolt first. There has been increasing prejudice and conflict between the Company and some sections of Indian society over politics and education. These will not be solved readily. And men like Beddington don't help the Company image."

She saw that he was earnest, and she wondered that she

could be so fooled. Oliver was right, she scarcely knew James Beddington and she judged him through the eyes of her friendship with Iris. "I have invited them to the masked ball at Aylesford."

He turned and gaped at her. "Does Francis know?"

She shook her head. "It was impulsive but I was so happy to see Iris and I didn't want to lose track of her again." Oliver was silent and she looked at him defensively. "I'm sure James won't steal the family silver. He's not a common thief."

"Do you imagine that the Devys will welcome him even so? I would have thought you learned in Calcutta that the lines of social contacts are clearly drawn among people like the Devys."

"But you were at the wedding—" She flushed as his eyes darkened. "I'm sorry, I didn't mean—"

"Did you imagine that I was invited because the Devys thought me their equal? No, my pet, the Duke insisted I come along because he wanted me to explain some of the latest projections of cost to his fellow investors—half a dozen of whom would be at that one place at one time. It was convenient for him to combine his pleasure with business, and I was a necessity, not a chosen companion."

Her cheeks were flaming and she tangled her fingers in the skirt of her dress, then smoothed the wrinkles guiltily. She had to acknowledge the truth of what Oliver said. She herself was an outsider, a parson's daughter who did not belong. Mrs. Devy would be furious with her for inviting unsuitable guests.

"It might be a kindness to call on Iris and set the matter straight," Oliver said gently.

"I didn't get her address, I've only just realized."

"Then you shall make the best of it." He put an arm about her waist and held her. "Do not let it spoil the rest of our day."

She returned to the Hyde Park Hotel the following morning when Oliver departed for work. The night had been filled with gentle and desperate lovemaking, flamed by the awareness that they would have to separate all too soon. Celia vowed that she would return to London shortly and stay as long as possible. Oliver fumed that she spoke so casually of coming and going instead of being a permanent part of his life, but he bided his time. She would come to him of her own will, completely and expectantly, and she would never leave again.

The streets bustled with clerks and shopworkers en route to jobs; the stores were not yet open for business, and only a few hotel guests were about the hotel lobby and dining room. When she entered the suite, she was dumbfounded to see Francis standing in the center of the sitting room, arms akimbo, glaring at her.

"Where the devil have you been?!" He advanced and grabbed her shoulders, shaking her so that her bonnet slipped off and caught at her throat by the ribbons. "Answer me!"

She managed to twist out of his grip. "Stop it! You're hurting me!"

He scowled and dropped his hands, then turned to stride across the room and back. "I arrived yesterday to find the suite empty. The hotel staff informs me that you have not stayed a night since your arrival, nor have you been seen about the hotel. Madame Louvère says you spent one hour in her shop on Tuesday. Where have you been since then?"

She had never seen him so angry, and she felt her own temper rise. "You said you would not come from Aylesford until today. Had I known you would arrive sooner, I would have left word of my whereabouts."

"Would you?" His look was scornful.

Celia did not flinch. Her guilt was heavy but her anger outweighed it. He dared to accuse blindly when he joked of his own misconduct and declared it none of her business! "I visited my mother." She let the partial truth suffice and whirled to march into the bedroom, slamming the door behind her. Her hands were shaking as she undid the knot of the bonnet strings and threw it aside. She pressed her hands to her fiery face and tried to still her rasping breath. If he discovered her lie . . . but he would not, he had no reason to suspect she'd been seeing Oliver. They had been careful, still . . .

She could hear him stomping about the suite, slamming things. She took her time changing and when she emerged from the bedroom, Francis was seated at the writing desk studying some papers and scowling blackly. He thrust them aside with a muttered curse. She wondered what was upsetting him so but she would not give in and be the first to speak. She sat on a small blue settee and watched him. She was positive that her absence from the suite was not the cause of his anger, only fuel that added to the flames. Why had he come a day early, after so many protestations that he could not get away? The business of the railroad? It seemed likely. When he finally turned, she was pained at how he had aged this past year. The ravages of his wounds and long convalescence were clear, and his eyes seemed clouded rather than the clear dark ones that had so captivated her at first. Could his drinking be at a dangerous level? She thought of the Squire, and of Anthony, bloated and dissipated-looking. Was Francis following in the family tradition?

His anger had abated and he talked of other things. "Madame Louvère tells me you have chosen a Grecian gown, so I shall be Julius Caesar to accompany you."

She smiled. "He was a Roman."

Francis shrugged. "Then you shall be my slave. Besides, a Roman toga will be delightfully cool for a midsummer party." He came and sat beside her, smiling and clasping her hand. "Forgive my temper, darling. I should have guessed that you would stay with your mother a day or two." He squeezed her hand and she forced a smile to hide her guilt. "I have had bad news when I expected good, and I adjust poorly."

"Bad news?"

"I had expected a dividend from some investments but find they are faltering and my capital is dwindling rapidly."

"The railroad?"

"No, thank God I've still that to count on. While I was abroad, I left my finances in Anthony's hands. He has always been more business-minded than I—or so I thought. He bought stocks and bonds on the Duke's advice." Francis rose and resumed pacing the room. "They are failing rapidly."

"Can't you sell?"

"The market is glutted already and I'd get only a few pence on the pound. The Duke says to hold on and wait for them to come up, but in the meantime we are without funds."

"Without—"

He laughed. "Every penny of cash has gone into the railroad venture. We shall have to live on credit and the reputation of the family name to survive until the company is underway and profits begin accruing." He smiled wryly. "We might start by curtailing our stay here at the hotel. The Duke has invited us to stay at his place, or if we've settled what we came to do we can return home."

"I would prefer returning to Aylesford," she said.

"Fine, then I'll arrange the carriage and send word around to Edward while you tend to your packing."

She sat a long time lost in thought after he left. She didn't understand how the vast wealth of the Devys could vanish so quickly; perhaps it wasn't as bad as Francis believed. Squire Devy had done well over the years, the estate flourished. She had no idea what running expenses might be, but they had to be sizable, she was sure. There must be dozens of ways they could be cut. A good manager . . . but Agatha Devy was not. She was a spendthrift, wasteful. She would never change her ways, and she would never brook any interference from Celia, no matter how well intended.

When Francis returned, his mood had lifted and the trip home was enjoyable, though he was silent much of the time. Celia lost herself in thoughts of Oliver and wondered when she would see him again.

CHAPTER EIGHTEEN

Celia did not mention the invitation of Iris and James Beddington until the last possible moment. Mrs. Devy was flustered and harried with worry over details of the party, which she insisted had to be perfect for Anthony's birthday celebration. Celia made her announcement quite casually at dinner the night before, stating merely that she had invited two old friends she'd met in London. Agatha Devy accepted the addition with a show of impatience but no real dismay. It was Francis who questioned her.

"Which friends?" he asked.

"Iris and James Beddington."

Francis looked at her. "The Beddingtons who were in Calcutta?"

"The same. I met Iris by accident during our last visit to London."

"Why have you not mentioned this sooner?" Francis's voice had an edge of irritation, and his mother looked up sharply, studying first his face then Celia's.

"It slipped my mind. But surely two more guests will cause no problems. I told Iris they were welcome to stay here and I have spoken with Alice about readying the old nursery suite—"

"You invited them here?" Francis was aghast.

"What is it?" Agatha demanded. "Who are these people? Really, Celia, you might have consulted me."

"I saw no harm in asking *my* friends to come." It irritated her that they were all so ready to condemn her without a hearing. Besides, she had the right, even Francis must see that!

When his mother demanded to know more about the Beddingtons, Francis, still scowling, remarked that Iris had journeyed with Celia to Calcutta and the two had become friends.

"Was the chap in your regiment?" Anthony asked.

"No, with the East India Company—some kind of clerk."

"You've invited a clerk?!" Agatha stared at Celia. "Whatever were you thinking? What shall I tell people?"

Anthony seemed amused. "They may have the sense not to come."

"You may tell them that the Beddingtons are my friends!" Celia declared as she threw down her napkin and pushed her chair away from the table. She returned Agatha's steely look. "I am sure the Beddingtons will not embarrass you by a display of improper manners—and I can only hope that you have the decency to treat them the same way!" She wheeled and strode from the room to hide the trembling of her legs. How dare they treat her so? For all their airs, the Devys were contemptible and rude and— She rushed upstairs to her sitting room; the fury still roiled in her breast as she stood staring from the window. Oliver had warned her, still she was not prepared for the directness of Agatha's attack. Or Francis's and Anthony's wholehearted agreement!

She sighed. If Oliver's suspicions about James Beddington were true, she could only hope that he and Iris would not be shamed publicly by the Devys. She would have to keep them out of Agatha's way as much as possible. Hopefully Mrs. Devy would have enough to occupy her time and thoughts during the party.

The thirteenth dawned with a stillness that forecast heat. There was no breeze to flutter the green ivy clinging to the manor house, and dust clouds hung behind each carriage that came up the drive. Celia had slept badly, still chafing at Mrs. Devy's unwarranted attack and the lack of defense by Francis. He had remained downstairs late, and Celia feigned sleep when at last he came to bed. In the morning, she rose and went out riding among the hills to escape the trapped feeling that persisted each time she thought of what her life had become. As she walked the horse along the ridge and stared down at the valley, she thought about the peaceful afternoon she'd spent with Oliver in a similar valley. How wonderful it would be to know contentment all the time, to love Oliver and be loved. She could not live out her years in the cruel, tense atmosphere of Aylesford; it would be a living death. But would she be able to face the scandal of divorce? The Devys would blacken her name, or worse . . . and she had the child to think of.

By early evening, the halls of the house were filled with laughing, chattering people. Servants hurried about tending to last-minute details of wordrobe, colorful costumes were carefully hidden lest they be recognized. Near dusk, Alice rapped at the door and whispered to Celia that the Beddingtons had arrived. Celia hurried to the old nursery wing to welcome Iris and James. She was surprised at the change in James. At first glance, she thought it was only that he had shaven off the beard and moustache, but she realized he'd also grown thin and his eyes seemed restless and wary. His stare made her quite uncomfortable.

"I'm delighted you came!" Celia said, hugging Iris. She glanced about the room. "I'm sorry to put you into this part of the house but we're absolutely filled and bulging at the walls! When Mrs. Devy gives a party she does not stint on her guest list. If only I'd known you were in London sooner."

"No need to apologize, my dear Celia." James came forward and took her hand, bowing over it. His fingers were cold and Celia suppressed a shiver. "These accommodations are quite adequate—aren't they, Iris?"

"Of course . . ."

Celia looked about and saw the large canopied bed, a single chest and a dressing table with a tri-fold mirror. The wardrobe was a huge wooden affair that had been pushed into a corner of the square room when it had been converted from a playroom. The bare wood floor was covered only with an oval braided rug near the bed. She realized with a start that this was the same room to which she'd been brought when Francis found her in the storm the day of the fair. How elegant it had seemed to her then!

"If you've need of anything, Alice will see to it. She's in

charge of this wing." More accurately, Alice was the only one Celia dared ask to watch over her friends. Mrs. Devy would forbid the servants to answer bell calls from this end of the house. "And now I must run. I've still a dozen things to do before the party begins. What have you chosen as costumes—no, don't tell me. Everyone is supposed to guess! Most people are having supper trays brought up—there'll be food at the party of course, but if you're hungry—" She was babbling and she felt the color rise in her cheeks. She bid them goodbye for the time and returned to her apartment.

She spent hours dressing for the party, though her costume was deceptively simple. The gossamer white gown fell in soft lines from a gold clasp at one shoulder, unadorned except for narrow gold piping at the angled neckline and a gold corded belt which hung at her waist. The loose toga style hid the slight thickening of her waist and she was sure that no one would suspect her condition. The dress was tight across her bosom which seemed fuller these past weeks. She fastened the diamond pendant about her throat; it was incongruous with the ancient garb but the simple piece of jewelry added a decorative touch. She instructed Jennie to wind her hair high on her head and let it fall in loose curls at her crown, a style she had seen in drawings of women of early Greece. Among the curls, she pinned small clips of pearls set in gold that seemed to wink and reflect the highlights of her golden hair.

"You look beautiful, mum," Jennie said, smiling and clasping her hands.

When she entered the bedroom, Francis was just coming from his dressing room. He held out his arms and turned for her approval. "May I have this dance before I am off to the Forum, my love?" He swept her into his arms and whirled her about the room, their white robes flying like butterfly wings around them.

She giggled, pleased that he was in such good humor and excited about the party.

"You should have chosen to gown yourself as Cleopatra, since you are a sorceress who has stolen my heart," he said. He brought her to a halt and kissed her. Through the thin materials of the costumes, their bodies warmed to each other, and his kiss grew ardent. "You are an exciting woman, Celia." He gazed at her slightly breathlessly and she saw the rising desire in his eyes.

"Oh, Francis ... how happy we were those wonderful nights when I first came to Calcutta."

"And have we changed so much?" His gaze was serious, and she was instantly sorry that she had put her thoughts into words.

She shook her head. "No, we have not changed." She smiled and clung to him, trying to recapture the mood. "And after the child is born—"

He held her at arm's length. "Child?"

She had not planned to tell him but the words slipped out. She smiled. "Yes, near Christmas, I think. Does it please you?"

"Of course." He dropped his hands from her arms and frowned in concentration.

His reaction was quite different from the one he'd exhibited at the news of her first pregnancy, and she knew the spark of joy was missing, but she said nothing. He would grow accustomed to the idea, and he would welcome the child he sired when the time came.

"You must take care of yourself this time so you do not lose it as you did the first," he said.

It was the only time he'd mentioned her loss, but she did not pursue it now. He smiled and kissed her lightly. "Now, we'd best be downstairs with our guests." He turned back toward the dressing room, calling as he went. "Clive—where the devil is my laurel wreath?!"

She was puzzled by his reaction, but when he emerged from the dressing room again, he had regained his former mood as though it had never been disturbed. He was the Francis of old, and he would charm the guests and enjoy himself.

The ballroom was hung with garlands and paper ribbons to give it a carnival atmosphere. Along one wall, tiers of benches had been erected so guests could sit to view the entertainment Agatha had arranged. Celia had heard bits of conversation here and there, enough to know that Agatha had engaged a troop of players from London to perform, as well as several minstrels, a juggler and a Punch and Judy show. Celia's mind boggled at the thought of how much it all was costing for one evening's entertainment! Her mother could live out her years in comfort on such money!

The room was already crowded with dancers and people standing in small groups. The musicians were playing a lively quadrille, though the music could scarcely be heard above the chatter. Celia felt her face warm with excitement. Several others came down the stairs behind them, a man dressed as Wellington, a harlequin and a shepherdess with a jeweled crook, and Mary Queen of Scots and her lover, the Earl of Bothwell. Near the tall windows that opened to the court, Agatha Devy, her plump figure unmistakable in a costume of Elizabeth I, was holding court with a circle of men and women. She glanced up as Celia and Francis entered, and Celia was sure her own costume would have been deemed unfitting a Devy if Francis had not chosen to follow suit. Most of the costumes were elaborate, and the very simplicity of hers made it stand out. She looked about for Anthony who had let it slip that he was wearing the armor and tunic of Bertrand du Guesclin, and spotted him immediately. She marveled at his costume, which caught the light and reflected it from the metallic cloth that had been fashioned to resemble mail and plate armor without forcing him to bear excessive weight. A red, flying dragon was emblazoned on his chest mail, and atop his dark head, he wore a jeweled felt hat of scarlet with a small, jaunty feather at one side. Squire Devy had refused to masquerade and sat at the corner of the room with his leg on an ottoman; several portly men in garish costumes had pulled chairs close to talk with him.

The air was festive and Celia was caught in the spirit of the party. When the quadrille ended, she was immediately claimed by a man in soldier's uniform. She relaxed and enjoyed his chatter, free of the need to be anyone but herself behind the silk mask. She was claimed by partner after partner, once recognizing James Beddington's voice behind a jester's mask.

"You are quite lovely tonight, as always," he said gallantly. When she murmured a reply, he said, "Iris is delighted to renew the friendship you shared. She was quite desolate when she learned you'd left Calcutta."

306

"I'm afraid I had no thoughts for anyone save Francis when he was wounded."

"That's only natural. But you've met again now and all's well, eh? I hope you'll be able to see a lot of each other."

"I'm afraid I don't get into London as often as I'd like." She thought of Oliver and pain wrenched her heart. Every free moment in London would be spent with him, she knew.

"Iris tells me your husband has taken an interest in railroads. Sound investment, the coming thing."

"Yes, but I know little of his business." She had the feeling James was prying and she was uncomfortable.

"I'm considering going into it myself," he said, smiling as he inclined his head to peer at her. His eyes seemed like dark coals behind the mask. "Perhaps you might arrange an opportunity for me to talk with Francis before we leave?"

Oliver's warning cautioned her thinking. If James had left India and the Company under a cloud of suspicion, she would not be thanked for any effort to involve him in Devy business affairs. Even more, she was afraid that Francis would take no pains to hide the fact that he considered the Beddingtons beneath him.

"He's been so busy lately, I'm not sure—"

"Only if it's convenient, of course." James smiled as though to show her he was not forcing the issue, still her discomfort did not ease. She was glad when the dance ended and they moved to the sidelines. Almost immediately, a tall, thin, glittering-robed sultan bowed and extended his hand.

She glided to the floor with him and breathed a silent sigh of relief. The sultan had not said a word but was watching her with a smile. He wore a short neatly shaped beard and flowing moustache so that his face was nearly hidden, yet she sensed that she knew him. Then quite suddenly, the pressure of his arm at her waist increased and he spoke her name softly.

"Oliver!" She blurted it out before she realized what she was saying, then looked about quickly to be sure no one had heard.

"Shhh—" His fingers tightened on hers.

307

"But—"

"I couldn't bear being away from you any longer. I've seen enough parties of this nature to know that an uninvited guest has little trouble slipping in, especially when everyone is masked." His eyes danced. "Aren't you glad to see me?"

"Of course!" Her heart was racing so she could scarcely breathe. The ballroom seemed to blur and fade and there were only the two of them. He guided her toward the tall open doors that led to the court. Several couples were standing in the shadows but paid no attention as he took her down the steps to the garden. The night air was pleasantly cool on her flushed face and when Oliver slipped his arm about her waist, she trembled.

"This is madness," she whispered, glancing toward an elaborately attired nobleman who was standing close to a woman dressed as Marie Antoinette.

"It is madness when I am away from you." They moved along the path toward the lower garden. The glow from the Japanese lanterns faded and there was only the moonlight, pale and gleaming. Behind a tall privet hedge, he drew her into his arms and kissed her. She responded wholeheartedly but drew away quickly.

"If someone comes along—"

"Then let us find a place where we can be alone. I have not journeyed these miles to watch you from afar with longing."

"I can't leave the party—the entertainment is soon to begin—and the unmasking."

"Then promise you will meet me later."

"I—" With all her heart she wanted to say yes. She was weak with desire but what he was asking was insane. She could not meet him anywhere at Aylesford with Devys all about her.

"I shall wait until dawn if need be. My coach will be waiting under the great oak near the crossroad below the drive. You know the spot?"

She nodded mutely, and he kissed her before she could find the courage to refuse.

"Then come to me as soon as you can escape. There is something I must tell you and we can have a few hours together." He straightened and released her as the soft rustle of footsteps sounded beyond the hedge.

"I must go back," she whispered.

He took her arm and stepped around the hedge to the path. There was no one there, but Celia was certain she had a glimpse of pale skirts swishing into the shadows ahead. Oliver took her to the court, then vanished into the shadows without entering the ballroom again. Celia looked about but no one seemed to have noticed her absence. Dancers still filled the floor; she did not see Francis but in the press of the crowd it was not significant. She made her way to the punch table and accepted a glass of champagne to sip while she looked over the masked faces. As the musicians finished the selection, the maestro tapped his baton for attention, and Anthony stepped to the podium to announce that the entertainment was to begin. Immediately following it, the unmasking would take place.

Celia saw James Beddington motion to her and she joined him and Iris whose undisguised amber curls gave her away despite the Spanish mantilla draped over her head. She squeezed Iris's hand and had only time to whisper a few words before the curtains of the stage parted and the players appeared. The servants lowered the gaslights around the ballroom so that the stage was highlighted, and Celia was glad of the darkness which gave her a chance to sort her thoughts. She paid no attention to the voices and music from the stage but stared with fixed, unseeing gaze. Oliver so close—she could hardly bear the thought of not being with him. But she could not ignore the danger. Until now, her meetings with him had been apart from the setting of Aylesford and her responsibilities. That made it easier to push such things from her mind and to postpone any thoughts of the future save the moments she shared with Oliver. But for him to come here and ask her to meet him was something else! Suppose she were seen leaving or returning? Suppose Francis missed her and questioned her on her whereabouts? It was impossible, Oliver had to realize that.

Try as she would she couldn't still the throbbing of her temples or the trembling of her hands. An act finished on stage and the audience burst into applause; Iris made some comment to which Celia nodded absently. She glanced along the rows and saw Francis sitting with a woman in Marie Antoinette costume—the same she'd seen earlier in the court, she was sure. A troop of jugglers ran onto the stage and all eyes focused on them. Celia noted that Squire Devy had retired and Agatha was sitting with a group apart on special chairs which had been brought for them. Act after act came to the stage, each more exciting and lighthearted than those preceding until the guests were in high spirits.

When the entertainment was over, Anthony moved to the stage with upraised hands to still the chatter and announced the unmasking. The musicians sounded a loud chord, a drummer gave the signal. Masks were pulled off amid shouts of recognition and disbelief. Celia glanced toward Francis but his attention was claimed by Marie Antoinette, who smiled up at him intimately as she removed her mask. Gwenn Katon—Celia hadn't recognized her behind the mask and the huge powdered wig which covered her dark hair.

Beside her, Iris and James were suddenly confronted by a plump, red-faced and angry Duke of Arbel. He made no effort to keep his voice down. "You have the nerve to show your face here?!"

Iris backed away, pulling at her husband's arm, but he was too shocked to move. The Duke looked at Celia. "These people are imposters and must have stolen an invitation in order to come here tonight." His round face was almost purple and he waved one hand as though he would banish Beddington from his sight.

James looked sidelong at Celia and she came to his defense. "I think you must have mistaken my friends for someone else, Lord Skeffington. I personally invited the Beddingtons, so I know that they are not unwelcome."

The Duke sputtered and looked about; when he spied Agatha and Anthony hurrying toward him, he glared at Celia. "We shall see about that—ah, Anthony—"

"Whatever is the matter, Edward?" Agatha asked, though her malevolent look toward Celia spoke volumes.

"Celia tells me these people have been invited. Obviously she has been unwittingly duped into believing they are her friends, though why she would take up with the likes of them is incomprehensible to me. This man is a

thief and a liar." He scowled at James and poked a fat finger toward him. The look on James's face was frightening and the Duke backed from it. Anthony glanced from one to another in total confusion; it was clear that he wanted no part of the fight if he could avoid it. Around them, guests milled nervously.

"Perhaps we should settle this in the study," Anthony said with a show of diplomacy Celia had not thought he possessed.

"Best you ask Francis to join us," the Duke said.

There was no need to search for Francis since the commotion had attracted him and he was pushing toward them. A look around at the faces told him trouble was brewing and he paused to say a few words to the nearest guests. "The food tables are waiting and more champagne has been brought from the wine cellar. If the musicians will be so kind—" He signaled the maestro who hurried to the stage. Smiling and speaking a word here and there, Francis moved with the small group from the ballroom. Celia glimpsed Gwenn Katon's questioning gaze but she did not join them.

Agatha Devy sat beside the Duke on the sofa before the fireplace, her plump face pink and her eyes darting. "How terrible—my guests—please, Edward—"

He patted her hand reassuringly and accepted the brandy Anthony handed him. Francis poured a drink for himself but did not offer one to James, who stood glaring at the lot of them, Iris clinging to his arm, hatred and fear in her eyes. Celia wanted to reassure her but she sensed that such a move might make matters worse.

"Now, Edward, what is this about?" Anthony drank his brandy quickly and poured himself another.

"James Beddington is a thief and a scoundrel. He came to me several years ago with credentials from Colonel Jenkins in South Africa attesting to his character and worth. I was persuaded to put in a word for him at the East India offices, and they took the man on. Sent him to Calcutta." The Duke's gaze moved to James. "I learned some time later that the credentials were forged. Jenkins knew the man all right but only because he'd fleeced a diamond mining company of a quarter of a million pounds of raw gems and fled into the hills. There was talk of a mutiny among the natives he'd hired when he cheated them of wages, and Jenkins thought Beddington had been killed." He paused to sip at the brandy and Anthony paced impatiently.

Agatha fluttered nervously. "Oh, dear . . ."

The Duke seemed to relish his role as exposer, and he turned to look at Francis. "*You* have this man to thank for being almost killed, Francis."

Celia gasped and shook her head. "That's ridiculous—"

Francis silenced her with a quick gesture. He frowned at Lord Skeffington. "How so?"

Beddington shifted and Iris seemed to cower behind him. The boldness was gone from their eyes. Neither had spoken a word, and Iris could not meet Celia's gaze.

"I have it on reliable authority that James Beddington was engaged in stealing opium and selling it on the illicit market. I believe the patrol on which you received your wounds was one to quell a disturbance caused by a rift among the opium thieves?"

For a moment, Francis was rigid, then he whirled on Beddington and slammed a fist into his face before the man could collect his wits. The glass Francis had been holding crashed to the floor and splintered. Iris screamed and Mrs. Devy pressed a hand to her bosom. Anthony gaped in indecision and quickly swallowed the rest of his brandy before putting the glass aside. James had recovered from the surprise of the blow and came at Francis in a fury. Francis was not agile enough to sidestep the punch and staggered back, crashing into a chair and toppling it.

"Stop them—Anthony, do something!" Mrs. Devy screamed hysterically. Anthony moved between the two, watching Beddington warily while he helped Francis to his feet. Lord Skeffington had moved to the bell cord beside the fireplace and as the door opened, a maid took in the scene in a glance and rushed off; moments later Hobson and Clive hurried into the room. Francis had regained his senses. He glared at Beddington. "You have ten minutes to clear out of here or I'll have you run out!"

James would have had a last word but Iris yanked his arm to drag him from the room. She did not look at Celia, who was standing rooted to the spot. Everything had happened so quickly, she still could not believe it. James a thief ... and Iris—had she known all along? The door closed behind the Beddingtons and servants, and Mrs. Devy sighed tremulously.

"To think such people came into my house—" She turned to Celia almost snarling. "*You* invited them! Have you no decency at all? The man who almost killed my son—and you invite him into the house!" It was difficult for her to breathe and she sank against the cushions with a whimper.

"Mother—" Anthony rushed to her, kneeling and rubbing her wrists when he thought she would faint. The Duke poured brandy and hurried to her with it.

Only Francis did not stir. His dark gaze was fixed on Celia, his face twisted. Celia forced down the heated reply she would have given and met her husband's stare.

"I did not know."

His lips curled. "It would seem you do not choose your friends wisely, but perhaps I have no right to expect any more of a country parson's daughter."

Her rage exploded and she struck him a resounding slap that was loud in the abrupt silence of the room. The red mark of her hand stained his pale cheek but the sneering smile did not alter.

"Francis!" Agatha forgot her swoon and was half out of the chair. The other two men stared in confusion.

"It's all right, Mother. Celia is not herself. She has just tonight confided in me that she is with child." His voice was cold and without love.

Agatha gasped and sank back on the sofa again, white faced. Celia was shaking with fury that would not subside. Francis's announcement of her condition carried no personal pride, and she was astounded at his stinging words.

"Since the country parson is dead, perhaps my child will not suffer the same stigma as I in this house!" she declared. She turned on her heel and rushed from the room. A curious, staring Gwenn Katon stood outside the study but Celia paid her no heed as she rushed upstairs. She went directly to her apartment; she did not wish to say goodbye to Iris. There was nothing to be said. It was she, Celia, who had pushed the friendship, encouraged and invited Iris because she was lonely at Aylesford and did not fit into the Devy circle. Iris had been reluctant all along,

313

but James was an opportunist who used people in any way that suited him. Hadn't Oliver warned her?

Oliver! She walked to the window and stared out at the long drive that curved away from the house. He was waiting for her at this moment, waiting to hold her and love her as she longed to be loved. But she could not go to him, she must break off their relationship and never see him again. She would go to him, for a moment only, to tell him he must leave . . . and that she was carrying Francis's child. She should have told him long ago, but each moment she spent with him was so exquisite she could not endanger it.

She changed from the flowing Grecian robe and donned a dark dress, then threw a hooded cloak about her shoulders before running down the side stairs. It was several hundred yards to the bottom of the drive and another hundred to the crossroads where the old path, now unused, cut through the Devy woods to the highway. The night was quiet, the shadows lengthened as the moon passed its zenith and was partially hidden beyond the trees. She paused once or twice to listen to the rustle of leaves in the soft breeze, the chirp of crickets and other night sounds that were loud in the guilty silence of her mind. She'd seen no one, still her heart was hammering.

She made out the silhouette of the carriage under the large oak and pulled her cloak close as she raced across the road. Oliver had the door open instantly and pulled her up into his arms. He had removed the false beard and moustache.

"I knew you'd come!" His mouth was hungry on hers, his passion bringing her cold lips to life instantly. For several moments they clung together desperately as though to make up for the days they'd been parted. When she tried to draw away, he held her, peering at her in the gloomy light of the cab. "What is it?"

"I can't stay—I must go back at once."

"I shan't let you." He kissed her again and she was lost in the heady warmth of his ardor. How easy it would be to stay and pretend there was no other life, but she could not.

"You must tell him you want your freedom, no matter what. It is insanity to go on this way." He stroked her

314

cheek and kissed the hollow of her throat and the valley where the gown exposed the rise of her breasts. "I cannot live without you, my sweet."

She was dizzy with excitement and need. "I cannot—"

"You can and you will, or I shall tell him myself." His face was a pale mask.

"No—oh, darling, please—hear me out." She took a deep breath and shuddered uncontrollably so that he wrapped his arms about her with concern. "I am carrying Francis's child," she said flatly.

He drew back as though struck. His fingers gripped her wrist. "If you are with child, it could be mine."

She shook her head, biting her lip to keep the tears from overflowing.

"We have been together—"

She sighed uneasily. "I suspected before I first came to you but I couldn't be sure. Then when I was with you, nothing else seemed to matter."

He sat back and turned his face to the window. He was torn between his love for her and his hatred for Francis Devy. To think of Celia carrying the man's child— His fury smouldered as he stared at the darkness beyond the window. He had hoped to convince her to return with him to London tonight and turn her back on the Devys, but she would never do that now. He heard her soft sobs and turned.

"My purpose in risking this visit was twofold," he said.

She looked up and brushed at the tears.

"I have just learned that Lord Skeffington has paid out large amounts of cash to secure land at Upper Haven, though he knows that the tracks cannot possibly run through the valley that approaches it."

"Why would he do that?" Her curiosity made her forget her grief for the moment.

"I told you he promised his investors that the lines would accommodate them. It would seem the Duke owes this man a debt of money as well as friendship, and purchasing the land is little more than a bribe. The Duke is using the company's funds to bail himself out of a nasty situation."

"But he is a wealthy man!"

"It would seem so on the surface, but I have private in-

315

formation that convinces me he is using the Marlton Company in the hope of enough profit to stabilize his accounts. Like your charming husband and his family, the rich are not always wise."

There was an edge of sarcasm in his voice and Celia bit her lip. "Then the company may fail?"

"There is little chance we can lay tracks and get a profitable line going before the Duke bankrupts us all. I suggest you tell your husband to pull out his money as quickly as possible if he's to save anything."

She was frightened. "He will not believe me. What proof can I give? You forget, the Duke is his friend and will deny everything."

"Then he shall lose every pound he's invested. Do as you please."

She couldn't bear his anger but she was afraid to reach out to him. The moon passed from behind the trees and bathed the carriage in its cool light. She could see Oliver's face but the expression in his eyes was concealed by the shadows. She gathered her courage. "I must go—"

For a moment she thought he was going to take her in his arms but he drew back. Sobbing, Celia threw open the carriage door and stepped out. Almost instantly she was seized roughly and spun about.

"So you would betray me again!" Francis shook her so that her teeth rattled then pushed her away. "At least your taste has improved somewhat. You have risen above the level of a stablehand this time!" He reeled and grabbed for the carriage door. "Come out, you bastard—" He was still dressed in the Roman toga and looked ludicrous in the moonlight.

He was drunk; Celia almost retched with the odor of whiskey on his breath and the shock of seeing him. Oliver appeared in the doorway of the carriage, one arm extended to fend off the blows Francis tried to rain on him. Pushing Francis back, Oliver stepped down to face him.

"You filthy swine." Francis stumbled forward and Oliver caught him by the arm and turned him aside before he could punch. "I ought to thrash you—a duel—yes."

"Don't be a fool, man. You are drunk and I have no wish to fight with you."

"You toy with my wife and dishonor my name."

316

"You have done that yourself without my help," Oliver said coldly.

Francis lunged at him again. "You're not worth fighting, you scum." He raised his hand and Celia saw the pistol he was carrying. "I shall kill you on this spot!"

"No!" Celia cried and grabbed for his arm but he flung her aside with a blow that sent her sprawling to the ground. A sharp stone cut her hand and she whimpered with pain and tried to roll away from the foot he kicked at her.

Oliver was upon him like a demon. He grabbed his wrist and twisted sharply, pulling back at the same time so that Francis stumbled off balance. The gun went off suddenly and Oliver grunted with pain as the ball grazed his shoulder and slammed into the carriage door. His anger exploded. He drew his arm back and pulled Devy upright as he crashed his fist against Francis's jaw. Francis fell heavily, striking his head against the carriage wheel, then lying unconscious.

Celia stumbled to her feet and Oliver grabbed her. "Did he hurt you? Are you injured?"

"No . . . only frightened." She glanced at her husband's motionless form. "Is he all right?"

"I hope to hell he's dead!"

"Oh—my God—no!"

Reluctantly, Oliver bent over Francis to examine the head wound caused by the iron rim of the wheel. "He has a nasty cut but he will live."

The sound of running feet and shouts came from the drive. Several men, one holding a lantern high, rushed toward them. As Oliver rose, Celia saw the crimson stain of blood at the shoulder of the silk sultan's robe he wore. She could not control the shuddering sobs that tore from her throat. "You're hurt—"

"It's nothing." Her fingers were cool on his arm and he shook with rage as he thought of how Francis had struck and kicked at her. Drunken fool deserved worse than he got.

"What's going on here? We heard a shot— Good Lord!" Anthony bent over Francis quickly. Anthony had removed the knight's armor but still wore a tunic with a

317

red dragon on its front. Behind him, Edward Skeffington and two other men shifted awkwardly and stared at Celia.

"Your brother attacked me with a gun," Oliver said in a tight, hard voice. "I think you'll find him none the worse for wear once he sobers up."

Anthony faced him. "What the hell are you doing here?" His gaze took in the sultan's robes. "You were not invited to the party." He turned to look at the Duke who shook his head, denying any part of it. One of the other men picked up Francis's pistol and handed it over; Anthony recognized it as Francis's.

They turned as Gwenn Katon approached and ran to Francis's unconscious figure, murmuring over him and stifling a scream when her hand came away bloodied from his head. "We must get him to the house."

"I want some answers," Anthony insisted as the two men began to lift Francis.

Gwenn whirled to Celia. "This is your doing! You and your lover have—"

"Lover!" Anthony stared at Oliver, his face darkening.

"They don't dare deny it!" Gwenn snarled. "I told Francis I had seen them in the garden but he was amused to think that Celia would flirt with one of the guests. But when she left the house to meet him, he believed me."

"You—" Celia flung herself at Gwenn and would have torn her apart except Anthony came between them. It had been no accident that Gwenn had overheard the conversation in the lower garden—she had deliberately followed them because she recognized Celia. And after the scene in the study, Francis was only too willing to rage at her again.

The two men moved off with Francis's limp form and Gwenn stepped to her uncle's side as though seeking his protection and support. Anthony was watching Oliver with wary eyes.

"I think under the circumstances you'd better clear out of here at once," he said.

"Let her go with him," Gwenn said icily. "Francis will want no part of her after this."

Celia clenched her fists so that her trembling would not be evident. She wanted to strike out with physical blows or to retort in kind to Gwenn's remarks, but to do so would

318

create more trouble for herself and for Oliver. He was standing tight-lipped, eyes scornful.

"Celia will stay," Anthony said.

"The company will no longer need your services," Lord Skeffington said flatly.

"The Marlton Company will need a miracle to survive," Oliver answered wryly. He turned to Celia. "I bid you goodbye, *Mrs. Devy.*" With that he climbed into the driver's seat of the carriage and snapped the reins on the horse's flank.

Celia stifled a sob. Watching the carriage vanish in the darkness, she felt as though part of her were going with it. She wanted to run after it, call to Oliver to take her with him—but it was too late. His cold farewell left no doubt of his anger. She would never see him again.

"We'd best get back to the house," Anthony said nervously. He was confused by all the sudden events and accusations. Lord, what a night! It was too much to try to sort now with his brain fogged from partying and weariness. Besides, it was Francis's affair and he was welcome to it. The exchange about the Marlton Company puzzled him but he had not the head or energy to pursue it now.

Gwenn and Edward started for the house and Anthony held back until Celia preceeded him. He supposed he should speak to her, but what the devil was there to say? She'd been caught *in flagrante delicto*—

Celia's thoughts were in a turmoil, her emotions as well. What a mess she'd made of things! She hastened up the drive and entered by the side door so that she might avoid the guests who were now descending to carriages as the party broke up.

Francis had been taken upstairs and laid upon the bed. Alice was cleaning his wound, a basin of bloodied water on the night table beside her. When she saw Celia's pale face, she tried to reassure her.

"He's had worse as a young 'un and it never knocked any sense into him." She patted the cut dry and lay a bandage over it. She began collecting her supplies. "I doubt he'll feel the pain at all, sleep right through. I'll send Clive to undress him."

Celia stared down at Francis and wondered what was to become of them. How could she bear staying under a roof

319

where there was no love, or even respect? He was like a stranger lying in heavy drunken sleep. There was no resemblance to the charming man who had captivated her and promised her eternal happiness.

When Clive came, she retired to the dressing room and readied herself for the night. She stood before the long glass, hands over her slightly rounding belly and the child it held. The child would be born into a house of hatred; what chance would she have to guide him against the influences of the Devys? She wished that she might miscarry as she had before, but her conscience twinged with remorse at the thought. The child was innocent.

She looked in again at Francis who seemed not to have stirred except that Clive had undressed him and put him under the covers. One arm flopped across the pillow at Celia's side of the bed and she turned and retreated to the sitting room. The thought of lying close to him was abhorrent to her and she could not bring herself to do it. She took a blanket from a shelf in the dressing room and made herself a bed upon the chaise.

CHAPTER NINETEEN

Francis woke and thrashed in the darkness. The bed beside him was empty and his head ached with a roaring pain that made him dizzy when he tried to sit up. Lord, his brain was a soggy sponge and his mouth foul with stale brandy. He didn't recall going to bed.

He sat up more slowly and found a glass of water on the night table to ease his thirst. Where the devil was Celia? He remembered then and anger flooded him anew. First the business with James Beddington, then Oliver Chadwick! He swung his legs to the floor and steadied himself until the dizziness passed. There was truth to Gwenn's story that Celia and Oliver were lovers, else why would she have gone to meet him—or why had he come uninvited in the first place!? By God, the woman had no shame! She would disgrace him, fling her infidelity in his teeth and make him a laughingstock. She had gone off with Oliver Chadwick and was probably at this moment in the blackguard's arms or bed. Well, she wouldn't get away with it! He stood, gingerly at first, then finding his strength. He walked to the window and drew back the curtains to let the moonlight fill the room. He found fresh clothes hung over a chair and donned them in a minute's time, then rummaged about in the dresser until he found the second of the dueling pistols he'd left there when he stormed after Oliver and Celia. He slipped it in his belt and let himself out. As he went out through the empty ballroom, he snatched up a half-empty bottle of brandy, taking a swig to help ease the pain in his head.

At the stable he poked the boy awake and demanded his horse be saddled at once. The sleepy groom scurried to do his bidding and Francis paced and had another drink from the bottle. When the horse was brought, he swung himself up and clattered off into the darkness. He would catch them together, and this time he would kill Oliver Chadwick. He would make sure Celia knew that he would not be cuckolded! He was still holding the brandy, and he lifted it to his lips and let the liquor pour down his throat. He cast aside the empty bottle and heard it smash against a rock. He swayed in the saddle, reining in at the crossroads where Chadwick's carriage had stood. He would have taken the old road—shorter—

He wheeled the animal sharply and slapped the reins against its flank. Frightened, the horse bolted and galloped into the black woods. Francis was almost unseated and clutched the pommel to right himself. The wind was cold against his face, clearing his head momentarily so that he realized he could not see the path. He pulled back on the reins but the frightened stallion did not respond. The animal stumbled once, gained its feet, rushed on. Cursing, Francis jerked so the bit cut cruelly into its mouth. The horse veered and plunged from the narrow road and into the trees. Branches slapped against Francis's face, lacerating his flesh and stinging his eyes. He roared with outraged fury and beat the running horse mercilessly. He had only a glimpse of the thick tree branch before his head crashed against it and he was thrown to the ground. He knew nothing more.

Celia woke and realized that someone was shaking her gently. The room was gloomy with predawn grey and it took her a moment to recall she was in the dressing room. Alice was bending over her, coaxing her awake.

"There's been an accident, ma'am—"

Celia sat up. Through the open door of the bedroom, she saw the cluster of activity near the big bed. "What is it?" she said, rising quickly and slipping on the robe Alice held for her.

"Mr. Francis—" The old woman's voice caught.

"He was sleeping soundly." Celia hurried to the bedroom. Clive, hastily dressed in trousers and a worn sweater instead of his impeccable black uniform, looked up as she approached the bed. The other was Samuel, the stable boy, who stood nervously twisting his cap and staring at the floor. On the bed, Francis lay atop the rumpled covers, fully dressed but his shirt torn and bloodied. A huge gash across his forehead had poured blood over his face and matted his hair, and his face was waxen.

"My God!" Dizziness assailed Celia and she gripped the bedpost. "Call the doctor at once!" she whispered, but she knew it was useless. Francis was dead. Her knuckles were white on the bedpost, her eyes fixed on Francis's motionless form as she tried to deny what her mind saw. No one moved and the three servants stared and waited.

"What happened?" Celia whispered. Where did one begin with death? She shivered and Alice came to put an arm around her.

"He woke and went to the stable," the old nurse said.

Celia looked at Samuel, who bobbed his head. "Demanded his horse. In a fair temper he was and drinking from a bottle, if you'll excuse me, ma'am." He was thoroughly frightened and could hardly get the words out.

"But why—where was he going?"

"I don't know, ma'am. When the horse came back to the stable with an empty saddle, I roused Clive." He glanced at Francis's body. "We found him in the woods just beyond the crossroads."

Celia closed her eyes and breathed deeply. Beyond the crossroads. Had he tried to go after Oliver? What madness had driven him to his death? She was numb with shock. "Have—the others—been told?"

Alice shook her head. "I thought you should be the first, ma'am."

"We'd best wake them."

Clive and Samuel left the room and Alice led Celia to a chair. "I've sent the girl for hot tea. You need something—"

The door was flung open and Anthony rushed in, hastily tying the sash of a crimson robe around his middle. His feet were bare, his hair tousled from sleep and his eyes bloodshot and red-rimmed. He glanced at Celia, then at his brother on the bed.

"What the hell!" He touched Francis's hand and drew back quickly at the shock of cold flesh. For a moment he looked as though he would be physically ill; he turned away from the bed and leaned his head in his hands. "My God—"

Mrs. Devy could be heard screaming as she rushed along the hall toward the apartment. "Francis—my boy— oh—Francis!" Two maids scurried behind her awkwardly, trying to help but being pushed roughly away one moment and clung to the next. Anthony came out of his stupor and moved to his mother's side as she neared the bed. Mrs. Devy's face drained of blood and her eyes went round with horror. "Francis!" She shrieked and would have thrown herself across the lifeless form except that Anthony restrained her. Squire Devy hobbled in on his walking stick with Clive gripping his arm. He said nothing but went straight to the bed. Agatha was screaming incoherently and weeping against Anthony's chest. The Squire's face was livid when he turned to Celia.

"What happened?" he demanded, his fists clenched and his body shaking.

"I don't know," Celia said softly. "Samuel found him."

"I know that. Tell me what happened between you to send him out in the night that way?" He was glaring at her so that she wanted to cringe. She forced herself to sit still.

"He was drunk and abusive." She was sure the Squire had been informed of the scene in the study and the later one at the crossroads. "I chose to sleep in my sitting room so as not to disturb him. I knew nothing until Alice woke me."

Agatha Devy turned and ceased her weeping long enough to scream at Celia. "You killed him! He is dead because of the misery you brought him." She sprang upon Celia, raking and beating at her.

Stunned, Celia tried to push the heavy woman from her and to cover her face from the clawing attack. She felt the pain of Mrs. Devy's fingernails across her face, and the breath was knocked from her as the woman fell onto her.

After a stunned moment, Anthony and Clive ran to pull

Mrs. Devy away. Celia put a hand to her face and felt warm oozing blood as she stumbled from the chair. She was trembling and could hardly stand. Jennie appeared in the doorway with a tea tray which she set down on the dresser before quickly backing from the room.

Squire Devy glared, still unsatisfied by Celia's answer but knowing to pursue it would upset his wife further. He spoke to Clive. "Take my wife back to her room, then see to what must be done."

"Yes, sir." Clive and Anthony led Mrs. Devy out. Her wailing faded as they went down the hall to the master wing and ceased when the door closed behind them. The Squire moved to the bedside and touched the hand that lay across Francis's breast. Then without looking at Celia, he hobbled from the room.

Celia moved like a marionette when Alice led her back to the dressing room and brought the tea tray. She poured a steaming cup of strong brew and forced her attention on Celia. "Try to drink it, it'll ease the ache a bit."

Celia accepted the cup. She felt no pain—and it surprised her. Her husband lay dead in the next room and she felt nothing, no loss, no sorrow—only pity at what had become of the man she once loved so desperately. Alice shuffled back to the bedroom and shut the connecting door so that Celia could no longer view the bed. Alice would tend to cleaning up Francis this final time, readying him for the undertaker who was probably being summoned this very moment. A funeral. She sighed and closed her eyes, remembering her father's funeral and how none of the Devys cared enough to attend. Only Oliver, and now she had lost him too.

She remained in her sitting room throughout the day. Carriage wheels crunched on the drive as guests left in the sudden pall of sadness that covered the house. The gay party atmosphere that had made the halls ring with laughter only yesterday was gone; workmen hurriedly took down the bunting and streamers that decorated the ballroom and dismantled the tiers of benches near the stage. The gardeners removed the Japanese lanterns along the paths and restored the court to its customary barrenness. The sounds of coming and going in the bedroom were definable and Celia knew that Francis's body was being taken downstairs to one of the rooms where the coffin would be placed. Alice brought her a tray but she could not eat, though the old servant coaxed and pleaded. And when it was finally dark once more, Alice made up a bed on the chaise, as though she knew that Celia could never lie in the big bed again. Alice also brought her a draught of tincture of laudanum and stood over her until she downed it. A physician had been called for Mrs. Devy and Alice had taken it upon herself to ask the man for a sedative for the young widow.

"You'll need the sleep," she insisted. "You must think of the child if not yourself."

The day of the funeral was grey, with clouds threatening along the horizon. Celia dressed early and sat staring at her hands in the lap of the black dress, turning the gold band on her finger. She had not been consulted on the funeral arrangements but Alice informed her Francis was to be buried in the cemetery behind Ascension Church, the same that Celia had viewed from her bedroom window as a child. The service would be held at the chapel, though the parson there had never known the Devys as part of his flock. Alice said many people from London were expected, and the service had been scheduled for mid-afternoon to allow time for the drive.

"Will Theo be coming?" asked Celia.

"We sent a messenger to France," Alice answered, "but our message was returned as undeliverable."

The Devys had not spoken to her since the morning of Francis's death; when it came time to descend to the waiting carriages that would follow the hearse to the village, Celia found herself seated with Alice in a second coach, the three Devys in the one ahead ignoring her as though she did not exist. It was just as well. There was nothing to be said, and Celia had no more desire to be with them than they did with her. They would be forced to sit together in the church, and to stand together over Francis's grave, but no more. Celia stared ahead blankly as the carriage moved slowly down the drive and along the highway toward the village. Each cottage, each tree along the route was a reminder of a life past.

There were dozens of carriages already pulled up before the church, and villagers stood with solemn faces to watch the Devys walk into the chapel. Celia was glad of the heavy veil that hid her face and masked the anger that took the place of sorrow. She sat through the service, not hearing the words the parson spoke but instead an echo of her father's voice. And when the service was over, she walked beside Anthony to the cemetery and watched the coffin placed in the newly dug earth. Mrs. Devy was weeping loudly and the Squire leaned heavily on the crutches he chose to use rather than be aided. The parson completed the final prayers in a low voice, then picked up a handful of dirt to drop atop the coffin. Mrs. Devy screamed and would have fallen except for Anthony and Clive rushing to support her and lead her back to the carriage. Celia accepted the dirt the parson held out and dropped it into the grave. It was finished. The restless crowd began to disperse. She walked wearily back to the carriage and was surprised to find the Squire waiting for her. As soon as the door closed, the driver set out. Squire Devy didn't speak until they were past the village.

"Mrs. Devy does not wish to see you. It upsets her to have you about the house. We have discussed the matter and decided you will leave immediately."

She looked at him. "Leave?"

"You are no longer welcome at Aylesford."

"No longer welcome! You seem to forget that I am—was Francis's wife. Am I to be hidden away like some poor relative?"

His dark eyes were obsidian. "If there were some way I could prevent you from claiming the Devy name, I would do so! You have never had a right to it and have been tolerated because of Francis's whim and his desire not to scandalize the family by divorce."

His words fell like a physical blow, so filled with venom that she was stunned. Her voice shook. "I will not speak ill of my dead husband but to listen to you mouth such platitudes tries my patience sorely, sir."

His face clouded and he drummed his fingers on the crutches beside him. "Your patience or lack of it is of no interest to me. The servants were instructed to pack your things while we were at the service. I will arrange for the carriage to see you as far as London."

She could scarcely believe what she was hearing. "And what am I to live on?" She had a cold dread in her heart.

"That also is no concern of mine." He fastened his gaze on the window as though he had already erased her from his mind.

"The child—!" Had he forgotten she was to bear Francis's child, who must certainly be considered a Devy no matter how conveniently *she* was cast aside.

He turned to her and his dark eyes smouldered. "You dare to speak of the bastard child you carry! It is not enough that you have disgraced us with unsuitable conduct but you would have us believe the child you will spawn is Francis's and not your lover's? Take the bastard to Oliver Chadwick and ask him what you are to do with it!"

"That's a lie! The child was conceived before—"

He laughed cruelly. "Your stupidity is overwhelming, Celia, or should I say your craftiness? You surely cannot expect us to accept your lies and deceit. Now I will hear no more of it." He looked to the window as the carriage turned into the drive.

She sat rigid with fury, her jaws clenched, her hands trembling. They had conferred in secret, and she was to be banished without being given a chance to prove the truth. Prove? How could she hope to do such a thing? To admit that she and Oliver had been lovers since June would only convince them of the truth of their claim. She could do nothing, nothing at all!

The carriage halted under the portico and the footman swung open the door and helped the Squire out. Celia climbed out unaided and rushed past the hobbling Squire into the house. Her trunks and valises were lined along the wall near the foot of the stairs. Anthony emerged from the drawing room and carefully closed the doors behind him. Undoubtedly Mrs. Devy was inside, waiting for Celia to leave.

Anthony flushed and his gaze could not meet hers. "I'm sorry, Celia. I tried—"

"Anthony!" The Squire pounded his crutch on the marble hall floor. "These blasted crutches are chafing my flesh raw. Come and help me into the drawing room."

"Yes, sir." Anthony's glance slid past Celia as he helped his father and once more closed the doors of the room behind them. Celia had only a glimpse of Agatha sitting erect in a chair, her gaze unwavering. Infuriated, Celia rushed up to the apartment. She was shocked at the sight that met her eyes. The apartment had been stripped, all the bedding removed so that the bare mattress was exposed. The wardrobe doors stood open, the drawers of the chests as well. Every piece of clothing, hers and Francis's, had been removed, all traces of their presence gone.

A weeping Alice, standing by the window in the dressing room, shook her head sadly. "What's to become of you?"

For a moment, Celia was close to tears but her anger dried them before they were shed. "I will manage," she said tightly.

"But the baby—oh, you poor child—" Alice covered her face with her apron. "To think they could be so cruel, and Mr. Francis not cold in his grave." She wiped away her tears and looked at Celia. "When the shock passes, they'll reconsider. Mr. Anthony tried to convince them." She shook her head and sniffled.

She was heartened to hear that Anthony had come to her defense in some small manner but she wondered if he too believed that the child was Oliver's. No matter, he was too weak to be much of an ally in a house of hatred and vengeance.

Alice dug in her pocket and pushed some pound notes into Celia's hand. "From Mr. Anthony, but the Squire's not to know."

Celia wanted to throw the money aside, but she could not afford such foolishness. She had nothing, and she would need money to find a place to stay.

Alice was clucking. "He says he's sorry it's so little but it was the only cash he had."

Celia looked at the notes. Eighty pounds. How long would that last? She'd never had to manage before, but she'd learn quickly or starve. "Tell him thank you for me—no, I'll write a note." In the misery of the past few days, she had forgotten Oliver's warning about the Marlton Company. If she warned Anthony, he might be able to salvage some of his investment before it was too late. She wondered what the Squire would say if he knew that his friend the Duke was bringing about a ruin far worse than that which fate had already dealt.

She sat at the writing desk and penned a few lines:

> *Anthony: Alice has conveyed your message and gift. I thank you. Perhaps I can return the favor by advising you to remove your money from the Marlton Company at once. I have excellent information that poor management will soon see it in bankruptcy.*

She frowned, wondering what more to say and finally scrawled her name and sealed the envelope. With a last look about the empty apartment, she descended with Alice following close behind her. The baggage had already been loaded onto the carriage and the footman waited at the door to hand her up. No goodbyes. She sat on the hard leather cushion and did not look back as the carriage clattered down the drive.

Alice stood in the doorway until she could no longer see the coach behind the trees. Turning, she saw Anthony emerge from the drawing room and with a quick glance past him to be sure his father was not in sight, she handed him Celia's note. He started to tear open the envelope but pushed it hurriedly into his pocket as his mother appeared suddenly.

"Is that from *her?*" she demanded icily.

"It's personal, Mother."

"I have suffered enough, Anthony, do not wound me by continuing to defend that little snippet. Give me the note."

"I am not a child——"

"Give me the note!"

Sighing, he handed it over and watched as she tore it into tiny pieces which she let flutter to the floor. "Now, darling, please help me to my rooms. I am exhausted with grief. My poor darling Francis . . ."

Anthony took her arm and silently led her upstairs.

CHAPTER TWENTY

August 1840, London

Celia found a tiny flat on a crowded street not far from Piccadilly Circus. She was determined not to go to her mother, who had no room for her anywaly, but set about establishing a new life at once. It would do no good to weep or moan—that would give the Devys the final victory. And she had the baby to think of. She would not let him be born into squalor and grow up an urchin of the street! Each time she saw the ragged crossing sweepers who scurried about the intersections, cleaning up mud, horse droppings and refuse, she renewed her vow. She would neither beg nor starve, nor would her child.

She was turned away at every establishment she approached about work. She had no skills and jobs were scarce, and those that were available had dozens of girls seeking them. The eighty pounds Anthony had given her was dwindling rapidly, though she tried every means to economize. Lying awake at night she stared into the darkness; she had no tears left—except for Oliver. Memories of his arms about her, holding her close, loving her as she longed to be loved, set her tossing and turning through the nights. If only it had been possible not to hurt him and turn him away ... but he wouldn't accept Francis's child. She should have told him her suspicions right from the start and given him the chance to end the affair before it began. No! She would not have missed the brief interlude of their love for anything in the world. Without that, she would have nothing now. She bit her knuckle and turned her face to the pillow. The walls of the tiny room seemed to close in on her in the darkness, and the lumpy cot offered no comfort. How ironic that she should wind up alone in London where her dreams had first begun.

The following morning she chose a simple dark gown and bonnet. The tiny flat was hot and airless as she prepared tea and toast for her breakfast which she ate standing at the window that overlooked a grimy alley behind the buildings. No sunshine penetrated the canyon among the bricks. A barefoot child paused to inspect some bit of garbage the night foragers had missed, then hurried on with his tray of matches that might bring him sixpence for ten hours of hawking along the streets.

The church bells at St. Stephen's were tolling the hour of nine when she climbed the steps and rang the bell of Miss Claredon's School for Ladies on Marley Row. She tucked a vagrant wisp of hair under the edge of the Dunstable straw bonnet and clutched her purse as the door opened and a scrubbed-faced girl in grey calico peered at her.

Celia smiled. "I would like to see Miss Claredon, please."

The girl curtsied politely and stood back. The child was no more than fourteen, a slim brown-haired gamine who looked as though the stiff collar of the school uniform were chafing her spirit. How well Celia remembered her own impatience with the school and with life.

She stood by a narrow table flanked by two straight-backed chairs with dimly patterned tapestry seats while she waited for the girl to return. The school had not changed. She glimpsed the shabby sitting room where evenings were spent listening to Miss Claredon or one of the instructresses read aloud from Shakespeare or Milton and interminable Sundays passed listening to scripture until she had begun her weekly trips to Aunt Henrietta's and the rides with Joseph. So much had happened since then, it didn't seem possible that she was the same wistful child.

The girl returned to tell her that Miss Claredon would see her. Solemnly but with covert glances at the fine muslin lace-trimmed gown, the girl led Celia along the familiar corridor to the head mistress's office. Miss Claredon was sitting behind a large table that served as her desk, the top neatly arranged with several stacks of paper, a pen, ink well, blotter and a small prayer book. She waited until the girl had closed the door behind Celia, then inclined her head toward a cushioned chair at one corner of the desk.

"How very nice to see you again, Celia. I must say, I did not expect such a familiar face when the girl told me a lady was calling. Do sit—"

Celia lowered herself into the chair, unconsciously sitting on the edge as she always had when called here as a student.

"Now, to what do I owe this pleasure?"

"It's kind of you to see me. I hold very dear memories of my year here."

"Yes . . . your young man? The parson?"

Celia lowered her gaze. "I never saw him again after leaving London."

Miss Claredon was silent but Celia felt the woman's eyes on her. She offered a partial explanation. "I am Mrs. Francis Devy."

Though there was no change in Miss Claredon's expression, Celia knew she was surprised. "The young Army officer who brought you home the day of the coronation?"

"The same. We were neighbors in Renfield, you know, but we'd never met."

Miss Claredon was silent for a moment then returned to her polite but direct line of questioning. "Are you visiting from Renfield?"

"No, I am living in London. I am a widow. Francis died a very short time ago and . . ." It was difficult to say what had to be said.

Miss Claredon sensed her discomfort and eased her over the rough spot. "I see. It is often difficult to live with the family after such a tragedy."

Celia smiled gratefully. "Yes. My own family is no longer together. My father is dead and my brother in America. My mother lives very simply but it is not convenient for me to stay with her. I find it necessary to support myself." She looked up and met Miss Claredon's grey eyes directly.

For several moments the woman was silent, and Celia

began to fear that she had come on a fool's errand. She was not trained to teach academic subjects, and Miss Claredon knew only too well her limitations in social graces. But the head mistress nodded and smiled again. "You have come at precisely the right time, it seems. I have just had word that Miss Tollinger who has been instructing the girls in history is to be married and will not be returning to us after her holidays. Is there a chance that your knowledge of history has improved since I saw you last?" There was a hint of amusement in her eyes.

"I could not have chosen a better subject myself," Celia said. "I spent a year in India while Francis was with his regiment there."

Miss Claredon picked up the pen and drew a sheet of blank paper toward her. Celia was silent as she made several notes before looking up. "As you know, our instructresses live at the school and must do duty as chaperones and sleeping hall monitors. Is that satisfactory?"

"Yes, of course."

She made more notations on the paper. "We have a new quarter beginning in a week's time and I shall expect you to be settled in by then and have your lessons prepared. Your students will range in age from thirteen to eighteen and can be classified according to their previous schooling as you see fit. The salary is four shillings a week."

Four shillings ... a pittance, but she would have no expenses. "Thank you." She wished she could avoid the next truth, but she could not deceive anyone who was being so kind. "I am to have a child ... near Christmas." She did not flinch from Miss Claredon's hard gaze. The office seemed very still all at once, and Celia's heart skipped a beat.

"I see." Miss Claredon returned the pen to the holder and settled her fingers along the edge of the desk as though preparing to play the pianoforte. "It would be patently impossible for one of our mistresses to conduct classes while obviously with child, you can understand that."

"Miss Claredon—please—I don't know where to turn." A sob choked her and she quickly rummaged in the small tapestry-cloth reticule for a handkerchief to wipe away the spate of tears that came to her eyes.

Miss Claredon sighed, and her eyes were kindly once again. "I suppose you might teach for awhile—it would take me some time to find someone else. When your condition becomes ... ah ... noticeable, perhaps we can find work for you of a different nature. We'll see."

"Thank you."

"I shall expect an honest day's work from you at all times, there'll be no excusing you on the grounds of your ... indisposition."

"Of course, I understand, and I shall do a good job, I promise." She felt almost the schoolgirl again, promising to attend to her lessons and obey the rules. It was a pose she had once vowed never to assume again, but she had no choice.

"As I recall, you had some talent in art. It might add to your lessons if you could sketch the flora and fauna of India. There are too few illustrations in our texts."

They talked a few minutes more, then Miss Claredon rang for the student monitor and asked her to show Celia the room she would share with Miss Framington. Several of the teachers Celia had known in her time at the school were still there, but Miss Framington had replaced Miss Janeau who had accepted a position as private governess with a family in Sussex. Celia would have a cot, a small chest, and several pegs behind a curtain on which to hang her clothing. She thought longingly of the huge dressing room and wardrobe at Aylesford. However would she manage her clothes? She would have to select only the most suitable and sell the rest, there was no other way. Miss Framington was in class, so Celia did not have the opportunity to meet her but it didn't matter. Miss Claredon said she could move in on Saturday, and that would be time enough.

On the street again, Celia walked toward the river. With a determination that surprised her, she closed the doors of her mind to the past and accepted her new life. The anger and bitterness she'd experienced at the Devys after Francis's death was still a raw wound, but it would do no good to brood over it. Once the child was born, she might be able to find someone to care for him and be able to resume her duties as a teacher. Miss Claredon had made considerable concessions already and might keep her on. Another bridge to cross in time.

She walked along the embankment, past Villiers Street; the Duke of Arbel's house was only a block away. She wondered if Anthony had accepted her advice and managed to recover some of his funds. At the Tower, she turned from the river and found herself in Knightsbridge, on the street where Oliver lived. Her cheeks flushed with the desire to see him, but she turned resolutely away. To have him refuse to admit her would be more than she could bear.

Her life at Miss Claredon's school settled into a dull routine that was both comforting and boring. She found the teaching of history more interesting than she had the learning, and the pupils in her classes were enthused by her first-hand knowledge of India; she devoted more time than strictly necessary to that Eastern country during the first weeks while she studied and read at night to better acquaint herself with other facets of her subject.

Maria Framington proved to be a pretty young woman, with wide green eyes and copper-colored hair that glinted in the sunlight. She was so different from what Celia expected, she found it difficult to believe that Miss Claredon had actually engaged such a delightful person—not the usual schoolteacher type at all and so vivacious that she was sure to find herself a young man quickly and leave her post in favor of matrimony. Obviously, Miss Claredon was hard pressed to keep the school operating with the sudden growth of competing schools about the city.

Maria was delighted that Celia would share the back room on the second floor with her. She was full of chatter—and interest—about Celia's adventures in India, and properly sorrowful when Celia told of the death of her husband and of the child she was carrying. Maria was from a large family and was well acquainted with some of the blessings and horrors of babies and the burden of a woman's bearing them. Three of her sisters had more than a dozen among them, and Maria said it was as though there was always one or more squalling all the time.

"Father says he has had enough and so I must be educated and secure a job in London where I have the chance to meet men who are not farmers!"

She was also a compassionate girl and did everything she could to help Celia when she tired or her back ached from standing all day and from climbing the stairs. Celia was grateful to have a friend so close at hand. She was allowed Sunday afternoons free and usually spent them walking in the park when the weather was pleasant. At least once a month, she went to visit her mother, who soon questioned her about private matters.

"I read an account of Francis's death," she said one day early in fall. "Why did you not tell me you were widowed?"

"I didn't want to worry you."

"Why are you not at Aylesford?" Her mother's gnarled hands picked at bits of lint on the dark skirt. The hands were rough and red, the knuckles so swollen that she could not bend three fingers. She continued to work at the ragged school and help at the church, though she spent every penny she earned on those who received her charity. It would have saddened Celia to see her in such circumstances except that she knew her mother was happier than she would be elsewhere.

"Aylesford is no longer my home." She would have let it go at that but her mother prodded and would not drop the matter. "You are a Devy."

"In name only. The Devys despise me—as they did you and Father. They have driven me out just as they did you."

Pain crossed her mother's face and she looked very old suddenly. "I wanted so much for you . . ."

Celia went to her and put her arm about her. "No one is to blame but me. I was a foolish child reaching for a dream that was never meant to be. It's over now and we must forget it or it will cause more pain."

They never spoke of the Devys again, but Mrs. Skerritt noticed quite soon that Celia was with child. She asked how Celia would manage; Celia said she hoped to stay on at the school after the birth of the baby, though she was not sure Miss Claredon would consider such an arrangement. Her mother said she could bring the child there and she herself would tend it, but Celia refused. Spitelfields was not where she would wish any child to grow up. She

337

had a tentative plan but would not speak of it until she could put it in action. Tucked in the bottom of a small leather case, she still had the emerald ring and diamond pendant Francis had given her, and the Aylesford crest ring which had sealed their engagement. The jewels would bring a decent price, she was sure, though she might not get their full value since she was inexperienced in such matters. But it would be enough for a small cottage away from the grime and dirt of Spitelfields where her mother might care for the child.

She never spoke of Oliver but he was not far from her thoughts. It would have been easy to let her yearning for him overpower her emotions and drag her into self-pity and depression, but she would not let them. But she woke often at night and stared at the ceiling where shadows played as tree branches fluttered in the moonlight, and she remembered what it had been like to lie in his embrace.

During the last months when her condition could no longer be disguised by letting out the waist and seams of her gowns or adding petticoats, Celia stayed to her room and the teachers' sitting room on the second floor, helping Miss Claredon with the accounts, grading papers, sewing for those students not yet adept enough at tending their own wardrobe repairs and fixing tea for the other teachers each night after the girls were abed. Most of the girls went home for Christmas and the teachers took holidays, but Celia stayed on through the recess. Maria fussed and worried but in the end went home to be with her family and to introduce her prospective bridegroom. So Celia was alone when she woke with the tight pain across her back. She turned heavily, knowing the pain portended her time. She waited for it to pass, then strained to listen for the sound of Big Ben so that she might have some idea of the interval between pains. She had talked with her mother and Maria enough to know that the pains had to be close, and that might be hours in the case of a first child. When the clock struck the quarter-hour, she sighed and tried to relax.

By dawn, the pains were quick enough that she knew it would not be long. She struggled from the bed, pulling on robe and slippers. Another spasm gripped her and she

338

grasped a chairback to hold herself up until it passed, then went quickly along the hall and rapped on Miss Claredon's door. A sleepy voice answered, and when Celia gasped with a fresh pain, Miss Claredon was at the door immediately, helping her back to her own bed before leaving her to go downstairs to send one of the kitchen maids around for the doctor. When he arrived, Miss Claredon had already made Celia as comfortable as possible. Celia was amazed at the compassion of the woman and she was grateful for the cool cloths on her brow as she thrashed and gripped the sheets. Miss Claredon had readied a basin and fresh cloths on the table so that the doctor nodded with satisfaction.

The wracking pain engulfed Celia's body and she clenched her teeth to keep from screaming. She would not scream, she owed Miss Claredon that much for allowing her to stay on at the school so that her child would not be born in a hovel. Her whole body was aflame with the hard pressure of her muscles. She was dimly aware of the doctor bending over her and of Miss Claredon beside him. She was drenched in sweat though the room was chilly; Miss Claredon had lighted the gas burner but its warmth did not reach beyond a small circle. Pain blurred her mind. There was no end to it. She seemed to swirl in talons of grey fog that pulled her into an abyss of agony, letting her surface only momentarily before sucking her down again. Suddenly her body erupted in a peak of torture; she felt strong hands holding her down, felt the hot rush of searing pain . . . then it was gone.

For several moments she was too dazed to believe it was over. She lay panting as Miss Claredon wiped her face with a cool cloth. When she opened her eyes, she was surprised to see the sun high beyond the window. The doctor moved about the room like a figure on a shadow screen, and the world seemed muted by the pounding pulse in Celia's breast. She tried to speak, but her tongue was thick and dry, her lips bloody.

"A healthy girl, Mrs. Devy," the doctor said.

Miss Claredon smiled and arranged the covers over Celia; then placed a swaddled bundle in her arms. "A perfect child," she said almost reverently.

Celia looked down at the tiny face under the soft cloth.

Red and wrinkled, it hardly seemed human, but her heart swelled with a fierce pride at her firstborn. How small and perfect the tiny fist that closed instinctively around a finger when she pressed it to the babe. The child was fair, with soft downy blonde hair that was like spun gold and long velvety lashes that lay upon her tiny cheeks.

Miss Claredon said, "She will favor you, Celia, and grow up as strong and pretty as you have done."

The little speech surprised Celia; it was as close as Miss Claredon had ever come to any kind of intimacy, and Celia wondered that she had never noticed the genuine love of children that motivated the woman. Celia had always thought of the headmistress as an efficient business-woman, but one without particular talent for the work she had chosen. But she was wrong, she saw that now. Miss Claredon's face when she looked at the baby was soft and yearning, full of wonder at the mystery of a new life.

"Have you thought of a name?"

Celia sighed. "Emmaline, after my mother, I think."

"You must rest now." Miss Claredon lifted the sleeping child from her arms.

"Yes." She was very tired and in moments she drifted into peaceful sleep, more peaceful it seemed than any she had known for a long time.

When she woke the room was warm and cheerful, despite a cold rain at the window. The doctor was gone, and for a moment she thought she was alone but then saw Miss Claredon sitting in a small rocking chair near the gas burner. At her feet a tiny cradle moved in rhythm with her foot on the rocker, and she was humming softly as she stared into the glowing coils. When she saw Celia was awake, she came to the bed.

"I've tea and hot soup waiting. You'll be hungry."

Surprisingly, she was. Celia sat propped in the bed and devoured the thick vegetable soup and buttered bread from the tray Miss Claredon set before her. When she glanced at the cradle, Miss Claredon said, "I brought it down from the attic. It was mine when I was born. My father carved it so that generations of Claredon babies might sleep in it." Her eyes veiled and she forced a smile. "Since there never were any, your daughter shall have it."

"You're very kind—"

"Hush. A babe's the right to start life right, even without a father. Life is hard enough for each of us without beginning among strangers." She poured tea into two cups from the pot under the cosy and gave one to Celia, then sat beside the bed with the other. Celia felt at peace, and the months of dread vanished. Emmaline would not know a father, but she would know happiness. Celia vowed silently that somehow she would find a way to give the child what was rightfully hers. She would find a way to furnish her with the things that had never materialized except briefly in her own life. And she would give her love.

A small mewing sound from the cradle brought Miss Claredon to her feet instantly. She lifted the child and brought her to the bed. "I suspect she's hungry. The doctor said you are to let her suckle, though it will be a day or two before your milk comes in." She lay the tiny bundle beside Celia and unwrapped it, unfastening the wet napkin and changing it from a stack of folded cloths on the table. Then she wrapped the child again and placed her in Celia's arms. Celia bared her breast and put the child to it. The crying gurgled to a stop as the infant rooted and tried to find nourishment. Smiling, Celia raised the tiny head so the nipple brushed the baby's mouth and she caught it greedily, clamping gums and lips about it. Celia shivered at the feeling of warmth and love that filled her. The baby's eyes were open wide and such a deep blue to be almost black. Celia brushed her fingertips over the downy hair and tiny features, but the babe was not in the least distracted.

"Her eyes will be blue, like yours," Miss Claredon said.

"How can you tell?"

The head mistress shrugged. "They are all born with blue, you know, and those with that shade stay blue. She'll have your fairness, mark my words."

It amazed Celia that Miss Claredon was so knowledgable in these matters and she so ignorant. She thought about the child she had lost and wondered what he or she would have been like. The child would have carried the Devy name and they would not have been able to deny it. And she would still be at Aylesford. She pushed the disturbing thought aside and refused it space in her heart.

"The Cumberland fairness ..." She looked up. "My

341

mother's family. I do believe Emmaline resembles Mama—" She touched the silky cheek again and smiled. "Mama will be proud."

The baby had fallen asleep once more but still held the nipple tight in her tiny mouth so that Celia had to release it forcibly. Miss Claredon returned the baby to the cradle and picked up the tray. "You should sleep again if you can. The day's about gone."

"I'm not at all tired," Celia protested.

"Then read a bit and I'll look in on you later. I have promised Millicent Harcourt to read Christmas stories in French. She's lonely, poor lamb, with her parents off in Paris and all alone on the holidays." She moved to the door and opened it softly, smiling back as she left and pulled it shut behind her.

For some time, Celia lay staring at the cradle. A mother . . . how strange it felt. She rose, surprised at the weakness of her legs, and donned a warm robe and slippers, then sat before the fire and watched the sleeping child. If only she could share such a precious moment with Oliver, her life would be whole again. If it were Oliver's child he would not have gone away. She remembered their times together, the gentle yet passionate lovemaking. A child of such a union would be conceived in love. Instead, her baby had been born of indifference on Francis's part, then denied. All the more reason she herself would lavish as much love as possible on the child.

The steady droning of the rain at the window was mesmerizing, and her eyes grew heavy. She stirred and went to the bed, sitting on the edge to brush the snarls from her hair diligently before tying it back with a ribbon and once more crawling under the blankets. She slept soundly, wakening when the baby cried and finding that Miss Claredon had moved the cradle to the side of the bed so she did not have to rise. And after she nursed Emmaline again, she fell asleep with the baby in her arms.

CHAPTER TWENTY-ONE

Celia regained her strength quickly. The babe was strong and healthy, a placid quiet child who lay content in the cradle except to squall when hungry. Celia resumed her teaching duties and ignored the curious stares and whispers of the girls—who had undoubtedly heard about the child but who dared not ask questions. She slipped to the bedroom between classes to feed Emmaline and each evening sat in the rocking chair Miss Claredon had supplied and hugged the child in her arms, speaking soft words of love, as though the baby could understand. The bright blue eyes looked alert and knowing.

January was raw and wet, with driving rains that filled the streets with rivers and huge puddles and caused mudholes among the cobblestones. Celia sent word to her mother of the baby's birth and asked her to visit one Sunday if she were able. Mrs. Skerritt came during church hours early in February; she had no desire to shame her daughter by visiting when the school was filled with young girls who would gawk and gossip about her shabby clothes. Celia was delighted to see her and displayed the baby proudly. Mrs. Skerritt sat by the gas burner with the babe in her lap, rocking and crooning softly, declaring that Emmaline did indeed favor the Cumberlands and would be a beauty. It was evident that she was proud that the child did not resemble the Devy family which had disowned her.

Celia was horrified at the threadbare coat that provided so little warmth for her mother against the chill. She knew her mother's wardrobe was meagre but she had expected better than this. She was sure the coat was one her mother had worn in Renfield, which meant it was at least five years old. She sat watching her mother with the baby, and decided that she would see about finding a cottage as soon as she could.

Maria Framington moved into a small spare room beyond the classrooms so that Celia and the baby could have the bedroom to themselves. She assured Miss Claredon that she did not mind in the least—and confided to Celia that it would only be for a short time since her young man had already asked her to marry him and was impatient for her to set a date. She hated to leave Miss Claredon in mid-term, so had chosen June for her wedding.

Celia's first step in setting her plan in action was to sell the diamond necklace so she would know how much money she could afford to spend on a cottage. One blustery Saturday early in March, she tucked the piece of jewelry in her purse and set out for a small shop she remembered just off Bond Street. Francis had taken her there once while he arranged for a rope of pearls to be restrung for his mother. She walked, ducking her head into the wind and pushing her hands deep into the muff that matched her fawn-colored coat. She was thankful that so many of her clothes were of such fine material that they would last. It relieved her of having to supplement the wardrobe for a long time.

The shop was in a small arcade where windows formed a solid wall for browsers and buyers. A small brass bell above the door tinkled as she entered, and an elderly man with a jeweler's loop at his eye looked up from behind a glass-partitioned table. He removed the eyepiece and slid from the stool to come forward.

"May I help you, madam?"

Celia smiled nervously. "I would like to sell a piece of jewelry." She dug in her bag and brought out the tissue-wrapped pendant and laid it on the velvet pad on the counter. The man picked it up and held it aloft, then stepped to the partition to retrieve his loop so that he might study the diamond more closely. He held it to the light, turning it and looking at it from all angles. When he looked back to her, he nodded.

"A fine stone, I remember when I sold it."

"It came from here?" She had not considered that possibility.

"Yes ..." He frowned in concentration. "Francis Devy, as I recall. Yes, I'm sure it was. A gift for his betrothed, I believe."

She felt her cheeks flame. "I am Mrs. Devy."

"Ahhh ..." He seemed undecided for a moment, then said, "I was most distressed to hear of your husband's death last year, Mrs. Devy, and even more so to learn of the disaster which has befallen the family since then." At her look of astonishment, he shook his head and let the diamond swing from the thin gold chain. "A pity that a proud family is reduced to— But then, you want a price, not empty words that remind you of your recent sorrows." He studied the pendant again.

She started to exclaim that she didn't know what he was talking about but stopped lest he begin to suspect her ownership of the diamond. "It does not pain me to discuss it, Mr.—?" She glanced at the window where a name was lettered in gold.

"Yarby," he supplied before she could decipher the reversed letters.

"Mr. Yarby ..." She smiled encouragingly. "I did not know that our family news was commonplace."

He shook his head as though lamenting what he told her. "The newspapers carried the notice of the bankruptcy of the Marlton Company and its debtors. A shame, I'd say, in these days when railroads are springing up so fast."

So the Duke had ruined the Marlton Company as Oliver predicted. "And the story of the Devys?" she asked, more curious than she wanted to let on.

Mr. Yarby looked at her pityingly. "Only that they had lost heavily and were being forced to sell their estate to pay creditors. A man should be allowed time to recoup his losses and not be treated like a beggar, I think." He realized he was touching on subjects that were none of his concern and he brought the subject back to business. "Are you sure you want to sell this, Mrs. Devy?"

"Quite sure, and since you know its original cost, I'm sure you will give me a fair price for it."

He looked apologetic. "Of course, but I cannot give you a retail price, you realize."

She said nothing as he considered and finally set a figure. "Four hundred pounds—that's two-thirds the original cost. I'll have to reset the diamond . . ."

Four hundred pounds seemed a fortune to her right now, though she suspected Mr. Yarby would double his price for the stone and get it easily. Still, she might be forced to take less elsewhere; it was a stroke of luck that the piece had come from here. "Very well, I'll take it."

He went to the cash box to count out the notes. She folded them and put them in her purse with the decision not to ask for a price on the emerald ring now. If she couldn't make the four hundred pounds do, she would come back.

She was elated. Four hundred pounds would lease a decent cottage, perhaps in Camden Town or Islington. It would mean a lengthy carriage ride for her each week, but it would be worth the airiness and less crowded conditions that prevailed closer in. Already the baby was moving about more, kicking her tiny legs and waving her arms as though to break loose of the confines of the cradle. She would be crawling about in several months, and there was no way she could be left unattended. Celia decided she would begin searching for a cottage the following Sunday if she could prevail on Miss Claredon or Maria to keep Emmaline for a few hours.

At the school, she looked in on the baby, whom Maria was watching, before going downstairs to the pantry where the trash was kept until it could be hauled away. She went through the papers week by week until she found the stories to which Mr. Yarby had made reference. She tore the sheets out and took them upstairs. It was as the jeweler had said—the Marlton Company collapsed because it had been unable to meet its bills. There was a detailed account, some of which Celia did not understand, full of words such as receivership, notes and promises to pay. It mentioned the Duke only to say that he had announced the dissolution of the company and regretted the losses of his investors.

346

She threw the paper aside impatiently and turned to the other, reading it quickly first, then going back over it more slowly to be sure she had not missed anything. Stated in simple terms, the Devys were being forced to sell Aylesford in Renfield parish because of heavy losses incurred in the failure of the Marlton Company in which they had invested heavily. The Devys had petitioned Her Majesty's court to be allowed time to make restitution to their numerous creditors, but it had been denied. Though the news story did not say it outright, the implication was that the debts were of monumental size. She let the paper drop to her lap and stared at it. Why hadn't Anthony heeded her advice? Surely there should have been some way he could have done so in spite of his parents' attitude toward her. They need never have known it was she who told him.

A soft tap sounded at the door and when Celia opened it, Miss Claredon came in with a pot of cocoa. She had fallen into the habit of coming up to sit with Celia a bit each evening, holding the baby and talking about school matters. Celia handed the clippings over for her inspection.

"Yes, I saw the stories."

"Why did you not say anything to me?"

"Would it have helped? I think it best you put the Devys out of your mind completely. You have a new life now, and their troubles are no concern of yours."

Celia sighed. Miss Claredon was right; still it upset her to think of Aylesford being sold off. It had been part of her own dreams so long, it seemed strange to consider the future without it. She realized that she had been harboring a vague dream of returning someday and taking her rightful place as mistress. Now that dream was shattered like so many others.

Celia had mentioned finding a place where her mother could care for Emmaline, but when she told Miss Claredon that she planned to begin her search immediately, Miss Claredon frowned.

"So soon? But she's only an infant and she is no bother—"

Celia smiled. "You've been kind, it is difficult to think of moving her. Emmaline will miss you. Though some say a child cannot recognize people at such a tender age, I think she knows you and looks forward to your visits."

Miss Claredon's face flushed; Emmaline chose that moment to wake and begin to stir. Miss Claredon was at the cradle instantly, lifting the baby and carrying her to the bed to change her while Celia bared her breast. When the baby was nursing comfortably, Miss Claredon sat again. "You're right, of course. A single room in a middle-class school is not a proper home for a child. She needs space to grow. Where will you go?" She frowned. "And the cost? I know it is not my business but I have a great interest in both you and the child."

"I have just this day sold a piece of jewelry and realized a good price. I'm sure I'll be able to locate a pleasant cottage. I was thinking of one of the northern areas that is not yet overrun with factories."

Miss Claredon looked thoughtful. "I have a friend in St. John's Wood. I could speak to her, she might know of something. It's quite pleasant and clean in that area."

"But not cheap, and I'm afraid cost must be one of my first considerations."

"Let me at least ask. You never know what may turn up."

Celia nodded. How could she refuse such an offer? She knew that Miss Claredon was hoping to have Emaline in a place where she could visit, and if she made frequent trips to St. John's Wood, it was ideal. They drank their cocoa and the talk turned to other things and the hour passed quickly. Emmaline was put down for the night and Celia went down to the laundry to wash out the day's accumulation of baby garments and hang them to dry in the long narrow drying room behind the big stove.

Miss Claredon's friend located a small cottage, and Celia was enchanted with it at first sight. It could do with a good scrubbing, but she'd see to that. It had a small parlor, a kitchen and a bedroom with a large sunny alcove that would be perfect for Emmaline. The funiture was neat, though shabby, and a small yard where the baby could play opened off the kitchen door. Most important, the rent was within Celia's means; the money she had secured from selling the diamond paid it for the year and left enough for Celia to hire a scrubwoman to come in and right the place and a man to put a fresh coat of whitewash on the walls. Celia also found a young girl who would come in a few hours a day to help with some of the heavier work, and a wet nurse for the months until Emmaline could be weaned.

Mrs. Skerritt and the baby moved into the cottage on a balmy day in May. Miss Claredon gave Celia time off to take the child to the new home, watching sadly as the carriage pulled away from the school. She had grown so accustomed to visiting with Celia each evening and Emmaline, she would miss the companionship. Still, with Celia staying on to teach at the school, it would keep a bond between them.

Celia hired a carriage for the trip to St. John's Wood, detouring by way of Spitelfields to pick up her mother and her meagre belongings. Emma Skerritt seemed reluctant to leave her friends in Spitelfields but also pleased to settle into a more easy life. She never complained, but Celia knew that it was increasingly difficult for her to get about or to handle any but the simplest tasks without fatigue. The tiny cottage and the responsibility of one small child would not tax her unduly. She was impressed with the cottage, staring about wide-eyed as though she had never seen anything so elegant. It pained Celia to think that the happier days of Renfield had faded so far from her mother's memory.

They walked through the cottage with her mother exclaiming over furniture, the pleasant view from a window, and the bright, sunny bedroom she and Emmaline would share. When she looked in the wardrobe closet and saw the four new dresses Celia had bought for her and the crisp aprons to cover them, her eyes filled with tears. Celia pretended not to notice but went to the kitchen to put the kettle on and busy herself with the teapot.

Her mother joined her as she poured the boiling water over the leaves, set two cups on the small table and opened a tin of biscuits. She had laid in a supply of food and other items her mother would need.

"She's asleep, poor lamb," Mrs. Skerritt said. "Tuckered from gawking at every sight across the city. Such an alert and wondering child." She had changed into one of the new dresses, a blue poplin with white collar and cuffs, and she looked as though she had shed years with her old garments. Her eyes sparkled and a touch of color came to her cheeks as Celia smiled approvingly.

When the tea was steeped, Celia poured and added milk from a small blue and white pitcher. "I shall come every Sunday," she said, "but if you've need of anything between times, you must promise to send a message."

Her mother nodded.

"And I've arranged with the greengrocer at the corner to deliver fresh vegetables and fruit twice a week. Whatever else you need you can get at the shop around on Finchley Road."

"I'll manage, child. I was running a household long before you were born and I've not become so addled that I can't do it now."

Celia hid her smile. It was good to hear spunk in her mother's voice and see her eyes so alive. They had not discussed money and for the time being, there was no need to limit her mother's spending. Mama was frugal by nature and would manage the house on less than what Celia could herself, no doubt. There was still the emerald ring ... and after that money was gone, she would find some other way to make do. She might be forced to seek another job that would pay her better, though she was reluctant to leave Miss Claredon after the kindness the woman had shown when she needed it most.

When they finished tea, Celia beckoned her mother to follow her outside. Wondering, Mrs. Skerritt walked into the yard and watched wordlessly as Celia opened a small shed built against the wall of the cottage. It was the type of structure generally used for garden tools and the like, and she exclaimed in surprise and delight as Celia pulled out a wicker pram.

Celia smiled lovingly. "So you can walk with Emmaline on mild days."

Emma Skerritt clasped her gnarled hands, then examined the baby carriage, rolling it back and forth to test its mobility. She nodded her approval. "If you think you might bring some yarn, I will knit a pram robe ..."

Celia smiled, "Of course." No matter that her mother's hands were stiff with such a task of love before her.

350

Her mother was happy and Emmaline was thriving. By the middle of June, the baby had begun to creep about on the cottage floor, dragging her long skirts across the Axminster rug of the parlor like a mermaid's tail. She gurgled and made cooing sounds that seemed so intelligent she looked surprised when no one understood. She was a happy child, and a delight to her mother and grandmother.

The school term was nearing its end and Miss Claredon promised the girls an outing to the Surrey Zoological Gardens. The girls were excited and chattering, much the way Celia and her schoolmates had been the day of the Queen's coronation. They fussed and spent extra minutes with hair and bonnets though they wore their everyday grey calico dresses at Miss Claredon's insistence. The girls would have chosen not be branded as schoolgirls by everyone who saw them, but Miss Claredon was adamant. To her, the excursion was part of the curriculum, a learning expedition, but privately she smiled at the excitement the day generated.

They rode by omnibus to Walworth Road and Celia and the other instructresses struggled to keep the impatient girls together as Miss Claredon paid the one-shilling admissions at the gate. Once inside, the girls followed decorously, though they could no longer suppress the giggling and whispering. When Miss Claredon did not shush them, Celia relaxed and felt her own excitement growing. It had been such a long time since she'd had an outing of any sort, she was looking forward to the day. With the three girls that were assigned to her charge, Celia entered the gardens. The animals were housed in various buildings constructed to resemble the countries from which the animals had been brought. Native attendants in long flowing robes and turbans fed tall-necked giraffes and impala. The girls screeched with delight when the huge elephants trumpeted and bellowed.

"Oh—Madame Devy—just like the pictures you drew!" Millicent Harcourt exclaimed.

"Not quite, dear. Indian elephants have small ears while these have large. See there—" She pointed as a huge beast lumbered toward the glass enclosure of the walkway, his huge ears flapping like fans. Around her the girls chattered

351

and Celia was lost in the bittersweet memories that seeing the beasts stirred. She had glimpsed similar beasts in Alexandria and in Cairo on her way to India, and the ugly camels as well. She felt a stab of pain at recalling the turbulent emotions that gripped her as she'd tried to avoid Oliver then. She had refused to allow him to show her any of Egypt in the hope of forgetting what happened in Malta. To be given a chance to change the past— She turned abruptly as one of the girls called her name impatiently and she realized they were ready to go on.

They had tea at an outdoor garden. Miss Claredon managed to commandeer several tables close together so that they were not separated in the crowd, and the girls found almost as much pleasure in watching people stroll past as they did in the sights they had come to see. How vividly Celia remembered her own enthusiasm and curiosity as a student. She smiled when Rachel Thackery nudged the others and pointed out a woman in an elegant silk gown with full, swishing skirts and looped rows of lace about the peplum, who twirled a silk parasol as she went by on the arm of a gentleman in pale buckskin trousers with a gold watchchain across his waistcoat.

"How grand!" Rachel whispered, her eyes wide. "Someday I am going to be rich and have a hundred dresses like that—and a beau to escort me everywhere!"

The others giggled and huddled to whisper over some new delectable bit of girlish conversation; Celia let her gaze move about the garden restaurant idly. It slipped past a woman in yellow-flowered muslin who was staring curiously at her. Suddenly she recognized the icy blue eyes under the yellow bonnet. Her heart clutched and she felt the blood drain from her face as Gwenn Katon murmured to the man seated beside her, then rose to make her way between the tables to where Celia was.

"Celia Devy—or is it something else now?" She glanced at the children who gaped, and the surprised faces of the other teachers. When her eyes came back to Celia, they were malicious. "I have often wondered what became of you when you left Aylesford."

Celia felt a tic at the corner of her mouth. Quickly she gathered her reticule and gloves, pushing back her chair and getting to her feet.

"I think it is time to go, girls—" She looked pleadingly at Miss Claredon, who got to her feet at once and began shepherding the group from the restaurant. But when Celia would have passed, Gwenn blocked her way.

"A schoolmistress? How unexpected! I would have thought you would have wed your handsome lover and be living in the grand style you always pretended to." She made no effort to keep her voice low, and people were turning to stare. "Or did he too deny the bastard child you carried?"

Celia was outraged and her face flamed. "How dare you speak to me in such a manner!" She would have struck the woman, but the schoolgirls had paused at the far side of the walk, out of earshot of the dialogue but staring and whispering despite Miss Claredon's efforts to divert their attention.

"How should one speak to a murderess—I've never known one other than you!"

"Murderess?" Shock made Celia blurt the word.

"You are nothing better than one for driving Francis to his death!" Gwenn's face was pale and her lips drawn tight against her teeth. She dropped her voice to a hard whisper. "How often I have wished that he never set eyes on you! Francis would be alive today, and we would be together! My only pleasure lies in the knowledge that your lover deserted you!" She laughed cruelly. "How very fitting. I could only wish that he had been reduced to the same level as you instead of building a new success for himself in Scotland. But then he's back now, and about to marry another if one can believe the gossip." She looked triumphant.

Celia was conscious of dozens of eyes on them and she was cold with anger. "And your uncle, the Duke? Did he get away with his thievery after ruining all of his friends?"

Gwenn was taken aback and for a moment was speechless. Then she said icily, "Such talk is slanderous and you'd best watch your tongue unless you've a mind to see the inside of a jail. My uncle is not a man without influence."

"I know that only too well," Celia said. "Now if you'll excuse me, I have friends waiting." She stalked past Gwenn and dared not look to left or right as she moved between the tables amid stares and whispers. She felt as though she had been plunged into a pit of fire; her body burned with fury and with the embarrassment of being a public spectacle. The students gawked and fell silent as she approached. Miss Claredon clapped her hands sharply.

"We must be on our way to the other exhibits if we're to complete our sightseeing. Come along now, girls, here then, Isobel—put your hat on properly." Her stern eye swept over the group and they followed her bidding meekly.

No one spoke of the incident but Maria Framington squeezed her arm and smiled sympathetically as they made their way to the glass conservatory where the lions were housed. The girls were fascinated at once by the huge roaring, pacing beasts, and Celia had time to collect herself. She was badly shaken by the encounter with Gwenn. But Gwenn would feel as the Devys had—that everything was Celia's fault and no blame could be laid to Francis himself. She sighed inwardly. Gwenn had not said where the Devys were now. More than likely she had severed relations with them after Francis's death. With a stirring of memory, Celia thought about Bradford Katon and how kind he'd been to her—and how aware of his wife's indiscretions. Gwenn had soon found herself another man to occupy her time and bed after Francis was gone.

More disturbing than anything was having reference made to Oliver after all this time. She had convinced herself she'd erased his memory from her mind and heart, but the mere mention of him set her pulse racing and her emotions churning. He'd gone to Scotland, according to Gwenn, and been successful in some new venture. And now he was back in London and about to be married. She bit her lip and tried to conceal the misery the thought evoked.

They continued their tour of the animal buildings. The girls were disappointed to learn that the balloon ascent which had been publicized was canceled because of some functional difficulty with the heating apparatus that would carry it aloft. Miss Claredon curtailed their complaints by saying they would be permitted to see the panorama instead, and the girls whooped with glee. The panorama was displayed after dusk, which meant their holiday would be extended and they would be out after dark—a rare luxury. Celia, too, found herself looking forward eagerly since the excitement of the panorama would occupy her thoughts and help her forget the incident with Gwenn.

Miss Claredon inquired the way to the panorama and herded the girls in that direction as soon as dusk fell. Long shadows crept across the park grass and walks as gaslights were lit. A street musician with a hurdy-gurdy and a small monkey on a leash ground out a merry tune as they approached the small lake which served as a stage for the evening spectacle, which was a representation of the siege of Gibraltar. The background canvas was skillfully painted to show the huge rock of Gibraltar. From either side of the lake, ship replicas to represent the French and Spanish fleets began to move toward each other, amid great noise of the firing of guns, the shouting of sailors and billowing clouds of smoke. For several minutes the battle seemed to rage as the beseiged returned the fire in the mock fight. All at once, an immense quantity of crackers and other fireworks burst into the air at the center of the panorama, and delighted cries and applause went up from the audience. The girls danced about and clapped wildly; the spectacle surpassed anything they had imagined! As the throng finally began to disperse, Miss Claredon did not try to quiet her charges as they made their way back to the omnibus stop. During the long ride back to Marley Row, Celia was aware of the covert glances the headmistress sent in her direction, but she knew Miss Claredon would not ask for any explanation of the scene with Gwenn. The incident was over and forgotten ... except that the knowledge that Oliver was somewhere close by in the city haunted Celia and left her sleepless that night.

The days that followed were strangely restless ones for Celia. The incident at the Surrey Gardens disturbed her and she could not put Oliver from her thoughts. She tried to busy herself with the dozens of tasks that marked the closing of the school term and the departure of the girls but could not fill her mind. It was as though the scene with Gwenn had opened an old wound healed only on the surface. She pored over the newspapers in search of any mention of Oliver, and when she found one, it made her more heartsick than ever. The story described Oliver as successful in property management and real estate, with a company of his own that was prospering as he handled huge parcels about the countryside for the growing railroads and industrial enterprises. There was no mention of his pending marriage.

Miss Claredon planned to close the school for four weeks in July while she went on holiday, and she asked Celia to stay on to answer inquiries that might come and to oversee the reduced household staff. She would have ample free time to spend with Emmaline, yet still have some income over the summer months. The cash supply from the sale of the diamond had dwindled and she had already visited the jewelry shop again, but came away with less than expected from the sale of the emerald ring. The two hundred pounds was top price, Mr. Yarby assured her. Soon she would have to seriously consider looking for other work; she could not support Emmaline and Mama on the tiny salary she made at the school. There seemed to be so many unexpected expenses, it taxed her talents to make ends meet. And from Miss Claredon's books, she knew it was out of the question for the woman to pay her higher wages. The school was barely getting by as it was.

The last of the students was departing and Celia stood in the hall watching the hackney driver carry out a trunk. Miss Claredon was bidding Rachel Thackery goodbye, with last-minute reminders on her deportment and manners during the coach ride to her parents' home in Essex.

"Do not strike up conversations with strangers, and do not wander from the posting station during stops."

"Yes, Miss Claredon."

Miss Claredon worried about the fifteen-year-old traveling such a distance without proper supervision, but her parents had not been able to come for her and had entrusted her to the supervision of an elderly woman who lived in a neighboring village and was returning from a visit to London. The woman seemed preoccupied and was most certainly deaf, hardly the strong hand a child like Rachel needed.

"I shall come back in a few months," Rachel said solemnly to Celia. "And I shall hate every minute I am out of London! I find Essex so dull."

"Hush, that's no way to talk when you're about to see your family after so many months."

Rachel sighed. "I shall be glad to see them—I've honestly missed them. It's just that ... oh, why must life be so dull in some places and so exciting in others when I am not able to choose which I want?"

Celia smiled and hugged the girl close a moment. "Someday you will, and until then you must be patient and learn all manner of things so you'll be ready to make the right decisions when the time comes. Now, Mrs. Sharp is waiting, you must be off. Remember to stay with her until your family meets you."

"Yes, ma'am ..." Rachel curtsied and flew down the steps, her blue gingham skirt flying out behind her. As she climbed into the carriage, she turned to wave a last farewell and impulsively blew a kiss from her fingertips toward Celia. Then the driver closed the door, climbed to his seat, slapped the reins against the horse's flank and rattled the coach from the curb. Rachel peered from the window until the carriage rounded the corner and was out of sight.

Celia did not see the man until he was almost to the top of the stairs. He was a short plump figure, with spectacles that gave his eyes an owlish quality. He tilted his head and studied the brass plate at the side of the door and nodded with satisfaction.

"May I help you, sir?" Celia said.

"I am in search of Mrs. Celia Devy. I am informed that she is employed in this establishment."

Celia's mouth went dry. She had never had a visitor of any kind since her arrival almost a year ago ... and this man did not have the appearance of a casual caller. He was dressed in a dark suit, with a stiff-collared shirt and cravat that seemed too tight for his thick neck, and wore a tall silk hat.

"I am Mrs. Devy," she said unsteadily.

He removed his hat and bowed. "The name is Fields, Mr. Edgar Fields, and I am a representative of Ashley, Fitzhugh & Morton, solicitors." He looked about and Celia recalled her manners tardily.

"Please, come in." She stepped back and ushered him into the hall. Miss Claredon had gone elsewhere, and Celia opened the door of the parlor to lead Mr. Fields inside. "You say you wish to see me?"

"Yes ... ah ..." He reached into his pocket and withdrew a long envelope. "You are Celia Devy, widow of the late Francis Devy of Aylesford in Renfield parish?"

She nodded, suddenly afraid that the Devys' creditors had somehow found a way to exact some measure of payment from her.

He handed her the envelope. "You are requested to appear in the offices of Ashley, Fitzhugh & Morton on Thursday this week at two o'clock."

"But why—what does this concern? I have no connection with any dealings—"

The plump man stared at her with round eyes. "I was asked to locate you and deliver the enclosed. All questions will have to be asked of the proper people at the proper time. Good day, Mrs. Devy." He walked to the door and Celia was behind him immediately, still holding the envelope and staring until the front door closed behind him once more. Her hand trembled as she studied the formal rendering of her name on the heavy parchment. She summoned her courage and unsealed the flap to draw out the thick sheet of paper and read it quickly. It did little more than confirm what Mr. Fields had said—that she was requested to be at the solicitors' offices on a matter of "considerable importance." A carriage would be sent for her to facilitate her arrival, and on giving her name, she would be shown to the proper office. It was signed George R. Fitzhugh, Esq.

On Thursday, she was glad the term had ended so she had plenty of time to ready herself before the carriage came for her. She'd pondered the summons, examined it from every angle, but had not come up with any possible answer to the riddle except that it boded trouble. She had considered her life with the Devys past, and to receive a legal notice so unexpectedly unnerved her. She showed the letter to Miss Claredon who was as bewildered as she but advised her to present herself at the proper time without fear.

"You have done nothing and cannot be held accountable for family debts, no matter what. Besides, you have

358

so little, what possible good could it do the Devys to try to take it from you. It would not be worth their effort to try. Solicitors cost money, and the Devys have lost every penny of theirs."

The carriage that called for her was fashionable and well appointed. The driver needed no instructions but set off the moment she was seated. She stared out at the street and tried to keep her mind clear. No matter what came, she would face it, she told herself. She would not let the Devys defeat her now!

She recognized the area along the Strand and Fleet Street and saw the dome of St. Paul's only a few blocks away as the carriage halted before a tall, grey stone building with carved pillars flanking an ornate door. The driver helped her down and indicated that this was her destination, then hurried to ring the bell to announce her. A thin, bent man admitted her, and immediately upon hearing her name, asked her to come with him. The business establishment was most impressive. The parqueted floors gleamed in the diffused light from tall windows. A wide stairway curved as it rose to the upper floors, each step carpeted to deaden the sound of their steps. As she climbed, Celia glanced into the two large rooms visible on the lower level and saw half a dozen clerks busy at desks, and several copyists working at a long table to the rear of one office. The place seemed a beehive of activity but in a very restrained and hushed way. There was no sound except the occasional shuffle of papers or the scratch of pens and the whispered footsteps of Celia and her guide.

The upper floor was even more surprising. Several doors opened off the long hall; she was led to the one nearest the front of the building where the man tapped softly, before opening the door and letting her precede him. A woman with grey hair and bright eyes, wearing a high-necked lace-edged blouse and a dark skirt, looked up from behind the desk.

"Mrs. Devy," the man almost whispered.

"Thank you, Clarkwell. Please come in, Mrs. Devy, I'll tell Mr. Fitzhugh you're here." She rose and entered another office behind a richly paneled door. When she reappeared, she said, "You may come right in, Mrs. Devy."

Mr. Fitzhugh was a solemn-faced elderly man; when he

smiled his skin wrinkled into an intricate web. "How good of you to come, Mrs. Devy. Please sit down ... may I have some tea brought for you?"

"No, thank you ..." She was much too nervous to sip tea as though this were a social call.

"Ah, very well." He resumed his seat behind a large desk with mounds of papers almost covering the surface. The office was very large and very elegant, with heavy velvet drapes at the windows and a thick carpet under her feet. The chairs were leather and two walls were lined with bookshelves containing leather-bound volumes. Ever since she had entered the building, Celia felt awed by the richness of the establishment—and confused. Certainly if the Devys had found some way to threaten her, they would not be able to afford to do so in such grand style. Had they recovered their losses? Then why seek her out?

Mr. Fitzhugh was watching her, still smiling; she knew he was trying to put her at ease. "Bradford has spoken of you often, I almost feel as though I am already acquainted with you."

"Bradford?"

"Bradford Katon. I believe you met him about a year ago at Glen Oaks?"

"Yes, but—" It was so totally unexpected that she hardly knew what to say. What had Bradford Katon to do with the Devys?

Mr. Fitzhugh selected a file of papers from one of the stacks before him and went through it until he found what he was looking for. He laid a long document in front of him and leaned back to look at her again. "Bradford Katon was a friend as well as a client. We have known— knew each other almost sixty years. He died a few weeks ago after a long illness."

She felt a wave of pity. "I'm very sorry to hear that." She remembered the old man's quick smile, his sharp eyes and mind.

"Yes ... we were all most grieved." He seemed to pull himself together and assume a businesslike air once more. "As his solicitors, we are executors of his estate. He has left you a bequest in his will."

"Me? But I scarcely knew him."

Fitzhugh smiled and tilted his head to wait until her

protest faded. "Nevertheless, he remembered you. As I said, he spoke of you often. If your meeting was brief, it made a lasting impression."

Celia thought about the camaraderie she'd shared with the old man, the smuggled brandy and cigars that had delighted him so, highlights in his world of gloom and illness. The enjoyment those times had given her were reward enough, but he'd felt moved to remember her further.

"I am flattered that he remembered . . ."

"Bradford Katon was an extremely wealthy man, Mrs. Devy, extremely wealthy. The bulk of his estate goes to his wife, of course."

How delighted Gwenn must be! And how strange that she had not mentioned her husband's death when they'd met at Surrey Gardens only a week ago—ah, but she had alluded to it and Celia had missed it. Gwenn said if Francis had never met Celia, *she* would be Mrs. Devy! Her long-awaited hope of being rid of her husband so she could marry Francis had been destroyed by Francis's death. The old man had outlived the young lover—how ironic—and how delighted Bradford must have been with the knowledge he had the last laugh.

"There are numerous bequests to others." Fitzhugh looked at her kindly. "And to you he left the sum of three hundred thousand pounds."

"Three hundred thousand—" She gaped at him, sure her ears had deceived her.

"Yes, my dear. You are a wealthy young lady."

"But that's impossible—" The sum addled her mind and she could not think. So much money—there had to be some mistake.

Fitzhugh pressed a bell on the desk and the woman who had admitted Celia to the office appeared in the doorway instantly. "I think Mrs. Devy could do with a spot of tea now, Miss Rogers."

She nodded and vanished.

Mr. Fitzhugh said, "You seem a little pale, can I get you something stronger perhaps?"

"No, I'm quite all right . . ."

"It is always difficult to break such surprising news to one totally unaware, though the fact that it is good makes it much easier," Fitzhugh said. "I deliberated sending the news in my letter once our investigator had located you but thought that might leave you even less prepared and able to cope. Besides there are papers to be signed."

The door opened and the secretary returned with a tea tray which she set on her employer's desk. She had everything in readiness so it took only a moment to pour the water into the pot. Young Mrs. Devy looked pale and confused. No wonder, finding herself a rich woman in the twinkling of an eye. She looked like the type who would enjoy her new wealth sensibly, unlike the greedy Mrs. Katon who was infuriated that any part of her late husband's estate had gone elsewhere. How the woman had screeched and ranted three days ago when informed of this bequest to Mrs. Devy! Lord, the whole building echoed and shook with her temper. It had taken Mr. Fitzhugh some time to calm her *and* to convince her that she could not interfere with the conditions of her husband's will. Bradford Katon had been very careful to take precautions against just that possibility.

Miss Rogers poured the tea then retired from the office; Celia sat holding the cup and marveling that her hand was not shaking. She felt strangely apart from her body as though viewing it from afar and not part of it at all. Three hundred thousand pounds was more money than she had ever imagined she might have in a lifetime, yet to Bradford Katon it was a small token of thanks. The solicitor had said the major portion of the old man's estate went to Gwenn. How rich she must be! She could have her pick of handsome young men now—rich or poor!

"That's better," Fitzhugh said, sipping his tea then setting aside the cup. "You've some color back in your cheeks. Now, the details—if you're ready?"

"Yes . . ." She sipped the tea while listening. The money was to be paid into an account established in her name with Lloyd's Bank. She had full and complete control of it with no accounting to anyone save herself. Katon had requested that the names of several good brokerage, real estate and investment houses be made available to her in case she chose to use them but she was under no obligation to do so. Mr. Fitzhugh drew another paper from the folder and handed it across to her. It was a receipt for the deposit of the sum of three hundred thousand pounds in her name. She need only sign the form and the transaction would be complete.

She wrote her name in bold script where he indicated but still felt dazed. Mr. Fitzhugh walked with her as far as the outer office, taking her hand briefly before she departed and saying she must feel free to call on him if he could be of assistance. She declined the carriage he offered for her return to Marley Row. She wanted to walk and to think and bring order to her jumbled thoughts.

She headed toward the river and then along the grassy embankment where children played under the watchful eyes of governesses and couples strolled leisurely. She was *rich!* She would never again have to worry about money! As her mind finally absorbed the fact, her steps grew lighter and she would have run or danced except for the stares such behavior would bring from passersby. *Rich!*

She sat for a bit on a bench in a tiny park just before she reached Waterloo Bridge. What would she do now? Find a more suitable place for Mama and Emmaline—that was first. And herself too. She would not have to work at the school or be separated from her child any longer. She could live anywhere she wanted—even Aylesford! The thought struck her and she frowned at a laden barge moving slowly in the sluggish stream of the river. She could live at Aylesford if she chose. She had no idea what price was being asked for it, or if it was still for sale, but she could find out. And why shouldn't she? Was it not by right hers, and Emmaline's? The Devys had lost it through their own stupidity and mismanagement, but it could once more be made into a productive estate which afforded work for dozens of families in Renfield. Mama would like being back, she knew. And Emmaline would grow up in a pleasant atmosphere away from the noise of the city.

She began to grow excited over the idea and she was unable to sit still. She wished she had asked Mr. Fitzhugh for the name of a real estate agent who might handle such a deal— She cautioned herself to move slowly. She could not take on Aylesford unless she was sure it would be good business to do so. She would begin making inquiries at once. In the sycamores along the path, birds trilled a summer song as Celia smiled and turned onto Lancaster Place, which would bring her to Marley Row. How very different the world seemed when one had money!

CHAPTER TWENTY-TWO

Miss Claredon was amazed at her good fortune but sad to know that Celia would be leaving the school. Celia promised to stay over the weeks that Miss Claredon would be gone on holiday; it would take her considerable time to make the necessary inquiries and decisions. Besides, she was so grateful to Miss Claredon for all the help she had given when Celia needed it most that nothing would induce her to leave without decent notice.

She said nothing to Mama; she wanted to wait until everything was settled, then surprise her. With school out for the summer holiday, Celia had plenty of time to drive out to Renfield and hire a carriage to take her to Aylesford. How desolate it looked! The gardens were unkempt, the walks overgrown with weeds. The ivy clinging to the house had not been trimmed and it straggled over panes and stone alike. The fences were down and squatters were living in many of the abandoned cottages. The agent Mr. Fitzhugh had recommended offered to accompany her but she insisted on making the first visit alone. She wanted to walk the familiar paths and gardens and sort her memories. She wanted to wander through the house and see if the ghostly memories would permit her to once more live here, or would she see Francis in every shadow, feel the pain the Devys had caused her?

The driver halted the carriage at the portico and jumped down to lower the step and help her out. "Would you like me to open the door for ye, mum?" He tilted his cap toward the house.

"No, that won't be necessary. Please wait here."

"Aye ..." The man climbed back to his seat and watched her with a curious expression as she went up the steps and fitted the key into the brass lock. The door creaked open and musty air assailed her nostrils. Much of the furniture was gone, sold at auction, she supposed. The rooms had a barren look that made it difficult to envision the gaiety that had once abounded here. It saddened her to walk about remembering the past. How different life might have been if only Francis had not changed. No, that wasn't true. He had not changed, it was she who had. She had not recognized his faults nor her own childish fancies for what they were until it was too late.

She stood in the vast, empty ballroom and thought about Anthony's birthday party almost a year ago. It was the last time she had seen Francis alive—and the last time she had seen Oliver. The two men she had loved, one dead, one gone from her forever. It surprised her that she could view the room without feeling the pain anew. To ascribe sorrow to a place was as silly as blaming it on the stars or the moon. Sorrow was inside a person, to be carried about forever or forgotten by force of will. Now that she was within reach of the goal she had always dreamed of, she felt strangely calm. In her lay the knowledge that Aylesford meant nothing to her any longer—at least not as a symbol of life as she had yearned for it to be. It was only a house, and without love, it was no different from any other house.

She went upstairs and wandered along the long halls, opening apartment doors, peering at empty rooms—the rooms she and Francis had shared, the nursery that had never known their child. She wondered what had happened to Alice. Dismissed to eke out her last days in poverty when the Devys departed? She would find her and bring her back to be nurse to Emmaline and to spend her last days here where she belonged.

She stood at the tall mullioned window of the upper hall and looked out across the stables and fields. She would concentrate first on restoring the grounds, putting fields into production to attract cottagers back. With Aylesford once again a great manor house, there would be a steady income to sustain it and help build the economy of the parish. For the time being, she would refurbish and furnish only the rooms that she and Mama and Emmaline would require; the rest could be done as needed. She would be on guard against spending money recklessly as the Devys had done.

When she had been through the entire house and satisfied herself that it was not just a whim that made her want to buy it, she returned to the carriage and rode back to London deep in thought. There was talk of a railroad line passing through Renfield. The London & Birmingham Railway Company was expanding rapidly and it was said the new route might be completed within a year's time. She wondered again about Edward Skeffington's scheme and the friends he had bilked. Bradford Katon had told her he had turned the Duke down when asked to invest in the Marlton Company. A wise man, but for every wise man there were twenty foolish. Why did men rush headlong into any scheme that promised quick riches with no effort on their part?

She had promised Mr. Fitzhugh to discuss her own investments with him soon. It amazed her that she had so quickly become accustomed to her new wealth and could plan so rationally for her future. She resolved that Emmaline would have a good life and learn more than only frivolous pursuits.

The real estate agent said he would make final inquiries into the purchase of the property and would have the papers drawn up for her signature within a fortnight. He foresaw no problems; the price had been quoted at one hundred thousand pounds but he thought she might bargain for a bit less, since the property had been on the market for close to a year with no offers. There were few people with the money to buy it who cared about living so far from the city, he thought. But when the railroad came through, it might be another matter. Mrs. Devy was very wise to invest now.

When she returned to the real estate office on the appointed day, Mr. Cornwall met her with an apology and ushered her into his office. "I should have sent a message round—"

"Has something happened?" She could tell by his expression that he was worried.

"A delay . . . I'm sure we can work it out very soon. I'm afraid I do not have the papers ready."

She frowned, annoyed but sensing at the same time that he was not speaking of a simple clerical problem. "What has caused the delay?"

He wet his lips nervously. He was a slight man with a perpetual smile that was meant to keep clients at ease. She had never seen him flustered before. His fee on a sale of such magnitude was considerable—was he in fear of losing it?

"As you know, our company is not handling the property directly. When it was put up for sale, it was taken on by Messrs. Daniels and Coburn of Oxford Street. When I approached them to act as your agent, they assured me that the property had not been spoken for and they welcomed your inspection of it."

"And now?" Would the man never get to the point?

"I conveyed your offer to purchase as instructed. I had a return note from Mr. Coburn saying that there had been another offer and the buyer wished to discuss the matter with you personally."

"A buyer? Isn't that highly irregular? If someone else wants Aylesford let him make an offer so that I can deal with it or not as I see fit. I don't know much about these affairs, Mr. Cornwall, but I'm sure that is the proper procedure."

He nodded, the smile widening as though to reassure her. "Exactly my reply to Mr. Coburn, but he says his client is most insistent and does not wish to enter into bidding on the property if he is convinced that you are more deserving of it than he."

"More deserving? How extraordinary. The man must be an eccentric of some sort."

"Yes, but I did not close the door on our compliance since it might well be to your advantage to hear the chap out. If he will withdraw his bid, you can buy Aylesford at a better price than if he competes with you. Sound business . . ."

She saw the reasoning, though the other client's logic eluded her. But now that she had committed herself this

368

far, she was anxious to have the matter settled. Miss Claredon would be back in ten days, and if Celia was to move to Renfield before summer's end, she must begin readying the house soon.

"All right," she conceded. "Can you arrange the meeting as soon as possible?"

He nodded and opened a folded sheet on his desk. "I took the liberty of making tentative plans, subject to your approval and convenience." He handed the sheet over to her and she read the name and address. Arthur Tomkyns, 24 Cadogan Place, Belgravia.

Mr. Cornwall cleared his throat and his smile seemed to waiver for an instant. "Mr ... ah ... Tomkyns asks that you call on him at your very earliest convenience, today if possible."

Her head came up sharply. "Call on *him!* Surely—" The presumption of the man!

"I believe Mr. Tomkyns is an invalid of some sort, unable to get around. Mr. Coburn hinted as much. I thought ... that is, since the property at Renfield seems so important to you, you might humour them in this instance."

"I'll do more than that," Celia declared. "I shall call on him at once and set the matter right before the day is out. I will not be pressured or taken advantage of because I am a woman. I have made an offer on the property and it can be accepted or rejected on that basis. I will not indulge in games with this—Mr. Tomkyns." She rose and gathered her gloves, parasol and reticule. "You may send a messenger around this evening for my decision in the matter, Mr. Cornwall. Good day."

She marched from the office and to the carriage. She was puzzled and annoyed by the peculiar change of events and delay. She gave the carriage driver the Belgravia address and sat back impatiently to endure the ride. She had not been in Belgravia before but had heard that it had become the most fashionable area to reside. Mr. Tomkyns had wealth then. If he was an invalid, what interest did he have in a country estate? She shrugged off the thoughts. She would know soon enough.

The house was three storys, attached to its neighbors in a row of similar townhouses facing a quiet square. The grey stone was freshly scrubbed, the door painted a soft grey and trimmed with white, with a gleaming brass doorknocker and bell pull. Celia studied her reflection in the brass, tucked a stray curl under the green print lawn bonnet and straightened the silk bow under her chin before pulling the bell. She heard no sound as the bell pealed in some deep recess of the servants' quarters, but in moments, a butler in impeccable black, with stiff collar, opened the door.

"I wish to see Mr. Tomkyns. I believe he is expecting me. I am Mrs. Devy."

The man bowed and ushered her into a narrow hall with marble floor and crystal chandelier. The wall at her left was adorned with a black marble table with gilt legs; atop it, two elephants carved of ivory gleamed in the soft light and were reflected in the large mirror that stretched from table to ceiling.

"My. Tomkyns has asked that you be shown in at once," the butler said.

Celia was again struck with the presumptuousness of the man. He requested a most unorthodox meeting, then assumed that she would do his bidding without question. She followed the servant along the hall to a set of double doors, where he tapped softly before opening them. "Mrs. Devy has arrived, sir."

"Show her in." The deep voice was scarcely audible.

The butler stepped back and Celia entered the room. The shades were partially drawn and the room was dim and cool. It was a man's room, a study or library, with large comfortable chairs and ottomans, a fireplace screened by a low triptych of delicate silk, painted with elephants and tigers against a jungle background on the side panels and an intricate domed palace on the center one. The walls of the room were shelved with books and the air was tinged with the faint aroma of leather. A thick carpet covered the floor so that her footsteps made no sound.

The butler withdrew and closed the door. She glanced about for the man who had bid her enter. At first she did not see him; only his legs showed from the depths of the big chair that was partially turned from the door. His voice was barely above a whisper.

"Mrs. Devy . . . Celia?"

"Yes . . ." She started toward him, then stopped. She

370

was nervous all at once, as though the strangeness of the situation had become overwhelming. Her anger dissipated all at once and she peered toward the figure rising from the depths of the chair. Her heart stopped, then raced erratically. It couldn't be—

"Celia, is it really you?" Oliver was coming toward her, his hands out.

She was dumbstruck, unable to move. She felt weak and almost faint with surprise—and with delight. She took a step toward him but stopped in confusion. She no longer had any claim on his love.

"I—I was expecting Mr. Tomkyns ..." She looked about helplessly.

He laughed softly and closed the distance between them, taking her hands in his and pressing them to his lips. "Can you forgive my deception? There is no Mr. Arthur Tomkyns, there is no one but me."

"I don't understand—" She wanted to fling herself into his arms and forget everything but the love they had once known. Didn't he realize what torment he was causing her?

"I was afraid you would not come if I allowed Mr. Coburn to use my name."

"*You* are Mr. Tomkyns?"

When he nodded, she exclaimed, "*You* want to buy Aylesford!" Again he nodded and she could only stare in surprise. She could not bear the thought of Oliver taking his bride there, living with another in the place she had always considered her own. She pulled her hands from his and fussed nervously with the lace edging of the green and white muslin dress. He was watching her with amusement and some surprise. Her legs were trembling and she walked toward the fireplace to hide her discomfort. She studied the screen, recognizing now the scenes of India it portrayed. She forced herself to take a deep breath. "Mr. Cornwall said you were willing to talk the matter over and relinquish the property to me if I am deserving of it. Pray tell, how are we to come to such a decision?" She turned to face him. He had not moved, and the muted shadows of the room partially hid his face. His smile made her weak all over.

"Your husband is dead." It was not a question, but she

nodded. "I learned that fact only a short time ago, and also that the Devys' money went in the collapse of the Marlton Company. A pity you did not see fit to warn them."

"I did, but they paid no heed."

"Then they richly deserve their fate and I can find no sympathy for them. But you ... ah, that's another matter. They banished you from Aylesford, I'm told, immediately after Francis's funeral."

She flushed. "You seem very well informed of my affairs, but then you were from the first time I met you. I would think you would find them boring to say the least." She drew off her gloves and absently twisted them as she avoided his gaze, which had the power to unsettle her just as it always had done. "You know, too, then that I have come into some money from another source and am now in a position to buy Aylesford. I wish to do so in order to take my mother and child there to live. Do you consider that a worthy cause?" She looked at him defiantly.

"The child—?" His face altered but she could not read the expression.

"A girl, born just before Christmas last year." She did not lower her eyes though she would have gladly escaped the steady, piercing gaze he fixed on her. He had left her because she was with child—Francis's child.

"No heir to the Devy name then?"

"Should that concern you?" She was beginning to regain some of her composure now that the shock of seeing him was wearing off, but she could not control the wild pulse that fluttered each time their eyes met. It was she who looked away now.

"Does the child resemble her mother?"

"I am told so."

"Then she must be beautiful indeed."

The room was very quiet for several moments and Celia felt her nervousness grow again. He seemed content to spend time on chitchat and not the business that had brought her here. "Has your wife seen Aylesford and expressed a desire to live there?" she asked.

"My wife?" He sounded genuinely surprised. "I am not married."

She could not hide her surprise. "But I thought—I'd heard you were engaged—"

He smiled and came toward her, taking her hands so that her knees trembled and her heart raced.

"I could never wed anyone but you, Celia. I have never stopped loving you."

"But you left—" She stopped, unable to blame him for her own folly.

"You sent me away and I went because I was angry and hurt. How could I take another man's wife when she carried his child?" He shook his head. "I had no idea Francis was dead or I would have come for you long ago. I was out of the country and did not know until quite recently that you were no longer at Aylesford in the bosom of the Devy family."

She stared at him and could not speak. He was saying words that she had waited so long to hear that her heart had given up hope.

"I went to Scotland the very morning I left you last August. I vowed to forget you, and I threw myself into a new job with the fury of the damned, but it did no good. Memories of you haunted me night and day. Love another? I could not, though I tried and there were enough willing women around—even one presumptuous enough to announce our engagement without waiting for me to ask her." He smiled and took her in his arms. "But my heart was with you and I could not give it to anyone else. Tell me that you feel the same ..." He bent his lips to hers gently, and for a moment the world stood still. Celia felt a surge of love that shook the fiber of her being and flooded through her with delicious warmth. She could not control the hunger for him his lips aroused, and she answered his kiss fervently. She clung to him and gave herself to his embrace.

"Celia ... my love." His lips were hungry and eager and the wounds of the past were erased in a moment of time. They were together at last, and nothing would separate them now. "Say you love me," he whispered, his breath warm at her neck.

"I love you ..." She loved him with a need that surpassed anything she had ever experienced.

Wordlessly, he led her upstairs to a large elegant bedchamber. Smiling, Oliver laid aside the pale shawl that covered her shoulders, ran his hands over the bare flesh of her throat, then carefully undid the fastenings of her dress. She shivered with delight as he caressed her, drawing off the cambric chemise and leaving her to stand naked before him so he could feast his eyes on her beauty. He discarded his own garments, and they came together in an urgency born of desperate love. The fires of their passion were rekindled and they explored new heights, murmuring endearments or lying wordlessly, staring at each other until their need brought them into a new lovemaking that transcended all that had gone before. And when they were sated and could only lie helplessly happy in each other's arms, they were silent a long time.

Oliver brushed the golden hair from her cheek and kissed her. "If all my business conferences were so delightful and lengthy, I would have time for little else," he teased.

She stirred reluctantly as she was reminded of the purpose of her visit. She was surprised to see the light beyond the window fading with evening. "You still haven't explained why you engaged in such a ploy." She pretended to frown, and he laughed.

"You sent me away once, I did not know if you would willingly see me now."

She raised her brows in surprise. "I have thought of nothing else this past year!"

"I know that now, but I could not be sure. When I returned from Scotland a few months ago, I tried to find you but you had dropped out of sight. Your mother was no longer at Spitelfields and Aylesford was empty and on the market block. Everywhere I asked I drew a blank. It was as though you had dropped out of sight and did not wish to be found. My only hope was to maintain an interest in Aylesford and hope that you would return like a moth to a flame."

"Was I so apparent in my love for the place?"

He nodded. "More than that, I knew that your pride would not take kindly to being thrown out by the Squire and his wife. Did I mention that I even sought them out to ask about you?"

"You did?"

"Yes, not that they had anything to tell. Anthony is dead." From the pain that crossed her eyes, he realized she had not known. "A fall from a horse. Some called it suicide but that can't be proven, of course. He'd become a pitiful thing with his drinking, and the rumours were that would have killed him if the horse hadn't trampled him. The elder Devys are living with relatives in Wales."

She felt nothing. "Will they realize some cash from the sale of Aylesford?"

He shook his head. "Their creditors have already claimed every penny of income they're likely to see in their lifetimes. They are finished and must content themselves with existing on the charity of others." He lifted her chin and touched the corners of her mouth to make her smile. "Tell me of the child."

Celia smiled. "She is fair and blue-eyed and growing so fast that Mama can hardly keep up." She told him of her work at the school and her struggle to create a home for the baby. His face was somber as she related how she would have failed except for Miss Claredon's kindness and her mother's willingness to help. And when she spoke of the huge sum of money Bradford Katon had left her, Oliver laughed aloud.

"So the old man had the last laugh, just as you triumphed over the Devys. By God there is some justice in this life after all!" He took her in his arms again and looked earnestly into her eyes. "Yes, there is a justice who has brought you back to me." They kissed, and once again the dizzying passion they'd thought at rest came into being once more, and they feasted on it until they were surfeited.

CHAPTER TWENTY-THREE

June 1842, Aylesford

A steady stream of carriages stopped under the portico, one barely emptying before another nudged it from place impatiently. The sound of music drifted into the warm summer afternoon, and the smell of honeysuckle clung in the air. People paused to exchange greetings, exclaim over a gown or renew acquaintances. The huge carved doors were thrown open; a butler and two maids took wraps and showed ladies to the dressing rooms that had been set aside for them.

At the door of the ballroom, Celia and Oliver greeted guests. Most were people whom Oliver knew from business, only some of whom Celia had met. His real estate enterprises had expanded steadily, and he was well known and respected as a man who could be trusted to buy or sell at a fair price, and to locate exactly the property a client wanted. Though he spent considerable time in London, he also traveled about the counties or worked from the offices he had set up at Aylesford. The estate had prospered the past year, and Oliver was proud of the business acumen Celia showed in running it. He was confident to let her manage when he was away.

He smiled and introduced some new arrivals. "Celia, darling, this is Sir Hillary Owens, the Earl of Suthbay, and his wife, the Countess Madelaine."

Celia offered her hand and the Earl bowed over it. The

Countess babbled a greeting which Celia answered properly. How vast Oliver's circle of friends was! It never ceased to amaze and delight her. She found it gratifying that everyone liked him with a genuine warmth. She gazed sidelong at him and her heart swelled with pride. The procession of guests continued endlessly. Had Aylesford ever had such a party? When at last the carriages dwindled to occasional late arrivals, Celia and Oliver joined their guests in the huge ballroom and the gardens below. Celia had insisted on waiting until the weather was warm and perfect for an outdoor party. It was their first since their marriage, except for small intimate dinner parties or gatherings that could be accommodated in the less pretentious rooms of the house. The refurbishing of the ballroom had been completed less than a month ago. The great crystal chandeliers that had belonged to the Devys had been repaired and polished to hang over the dance floor once more, but otherwise the room had been changed considerably. The stage was gone, replaced by a curtained alcove for the musicians; the smaller alcoves which the musicians had used previously were now fitted with satin sofas where guests could enjoy small conversation groups. New gas lamps in gold sconces lined the walls so that the brightness of the room could be carefully controlled according to the mood of the party. The walls were papered in gold and white stripes, accented by gilt coping to round the line of the white ceiling. Celia had insisted on a simple Grecian carving for the coping, though the wood craftsman who did the work tried to influence her toward the more modern, ornate styles that were coming into vogue. She was pleased with the overall effect of the room; it had a simple grandeur that set a proper mood for any festivities. She had chosen not to decorate it further for this party but to leave its uncluttered lines to speak for themselves. The gardens, on the other hand, had been richly decked with umbrellaed tables in gay colors, garlands of flowers twisting around tree trunks, and huge arrangements of flowers in white wicker stands or large tubs set along the edges of the grass. The corner of the upper garden nearest the house had been converted to an outdoor nursery; a white trellis screened the sun and banks of flowers formed walls to surround the cradle. No babe could ask for a more elegant christening celebration.

Celia and Oliver moved arm in arm among the guests.

"When are we to see the guest of honor?" Paul Richmond, who was an official of the Birmingham and London Railroad Company, asked, handing Celia a cup of punch from the tray on the table behind him.

She smiled. "His nurses will bring him down as soon as he wakes. I'm afraid he is not impressed enough with the party to alter his sleeping schedule for us."

Richmond laughed and raised his punch cup in a toast. "To your son and heir—Oliver . . . Celia . . ."

They drank and Oliver said, "When is the line through Renfield to be started, Paul?"

"Present plans call for the first September, but the work will be done from both ends to meet at Charles Court, so we are projecting a three-month completion date."

"So soon! How marvelous it will be to be able to reach London in an hour's time." Celia still found it difficult to believe she would be able to journey into the city for a day's shopping and be home in time for supper. Still, she had ridden the wondrous new trains with Oliver several times, and she knew the remarkable speeds they attained with complete safety.

Paul Richmond nodded. "The company has considered an easterly route through Upper Haven but one parcel of land is unavailable, so the Renfield line received priority. Land acquisition remains our largest single problem, as you well know, Oliver."

"Proporty becomes more valuable every day, it seems," he said noncommittally. He winked at Celia and she suppressed a smile. A pretty red-haired girl with flashing green eyes claimed Paul's attention and he led her off to the garden. She reminded Celia slightly of a younger Iris, and for a moment she wondered what had become of the Beddingtons. Then she turned to her husband and grinned impishly.

"So the land was not available to Upper Haven? Was this some of your doing, pet?"

His smile was enigmatic. "I am still hoping that someday you will agree to escaping to that pleasant little valley with me, so I cannot bear to give up the property."

"But we have a lovely home here—and a townhouse in London. How many more can we use?"

"A cottage, perhaps, just big enough for the two of us when we want to flee the rush and pressures of life." His dark eyes held hers and she felt herself go weak inside. After a year of marriage none of the excitement or ardour of their being together had diminished. It was as if they would never see or have enough of each other. She looked away with a sigh.

"I think it best if we change the subject for the moment. It would hardly be proper to absent ourselves from our guests so soon—as we surely will have to do if you put thoughts of passion in my head!" she chided.

"And what of my body? Have you no pity for the passion trapped there?" He slipped his arm lightly to her waist and brushed his lips to her cheek.

"Oliver! Our guests—"

"Let them know how much I love you," he murmured, but released her and forced his attention to an approaching couple. "Ah, Mr. and Mrs. Golding. We were so sorry that we could not accept your invitation to Royal Ascot week, but as you know, my wife has recently presented me with a son, our second child . . ."

Celia felt a surge of pride, not only for their son but for the fact that Oliver spoke so easily of Emmaline as his own. He had accepted her without restraint, loving her and spoiling her as any father would. And now, Celia had given him a son and heir.

She mingled with the guests, chatting and making everyone feel welcome. She took special pains with the vicar of Renfield, who had conducted the christening services this morning and who had been surprised at his invitation to the party but accepted eagerly. His family, a wife, two daughters and a son, stared about in awe and looked frightened out of their wits, despite Celia's attempts to put them at ease. How well she recalled her own first party at Aylesford under similar circumstances!

When she was informed that the baby had wakened and was being brought down, she signaled Oliver. He crossed to the musicians, and they struck several chords. Oliver stood with hands raised. "Ladies and gentlemen, if you will retire to the upper garden, the guest of honor is about to make his appearance."

Applause and a murmur of excitement eddied as people drifted toward the tall doors opening to the court and along the side of the house toward the garden. Celia went through the drawing room and exited directly to the trellised outdoor nursery, where her mother and Emmaline sat on a gilt rosewood sofa while Alice fussed over the infant in the cradle, petting a cover just so, straightening the white lace bonnet on the tiny dark head.

"Mama, Mama—" Emmaline rushed to her and threw her chubby arms about Celia's legs. Her golden curls caught shafts of sunlight and glittered like gold; her blue eyes were large and wondering.

"Here, child," her grandmother coaxed.

"It's all right, Mama," Celia said, bending to lift Emmaline and hug her close. "This is a grand day for all of us." Oliver came beside her and held out his arms as Emmaline squirmed to escape to him.

"It is supposed to be your brother's moment of glory, you little vixen, but all eyes will be on you." He hugged the child, and she squealed with pleasure and planted a wet kiss on his lips.

"Such a fuss over a christening ..." Mrs. Skerritt pretended annoyance but her eyes shone with pleasure. She had never been happier than this past year at Aylesford, and seeing Celia so happy at last. Celia and Emmaline sat beside her on the silk upholstered sofa as guests began to press forward for a glimpse of the baby. A smiling Oliver stood beside the cradle, beaming down at his son. "Oliver William Chadwick ..." he said in answer to someone's question of what the child's name was.

Celia smiled and caught his glance. Her life had been a quest that led her to this moment. She had no need to search further.

ON SALE WHEREVER PAPERBACKS ARE SOLD
— or use this coupon to order directly from the publisher.

BARBARA CARTLAND

4277-01	**AGAINST THE STREAM** $1.25 £ (68) 0-515-04277-3
3908-01	**AGAIN THIS RAPTURE** $1.25 £ (#36) 0-515-03908-X
3831-01	**ARMOUR AGAINST LOVE** $1.25 £ (#64) 0-515-03831-8
4157-01	**THE AUDACIOUS ADVENTURESS** $1.25 £ 0-515-04157-2
3991-01	**THE BITTER WINDS OF LOVE** $1.25 ‡ (#76) 0-515-03991-8
3792-01	**BLUE HEATHER** $1.25 £ (#54) 0-515-03792-3
3992-01	**BROKEN BARRIERS** $1.25 ‡ 0-515-03992-6
3491-01	**COIN OF LOVE** $1.25 £ (#3) 0-515-03491-6
3828-01	**THE COMPLACENT WIFE** $1.25 £ (#53) 0-515-03828-8
2921-01	**DEBT OF HONOR** $1.25 £ (#16) 0-515-02921-1
3473-01	**DESIRE OF THE HEART** $1.25 £ (#1) 0-515-03473-8
3996-01	**DESPERATE DEFIANCE** $1.25 ‡ (#73) 0-515-03996-9
4118-01	**THE DREAM WITHIN** (#62) $1.25 £ 0-515-04118-1
3537-01	**A DUEL OF HEARTS** $1.25 £ (#8) 0-515-03537-8
3907-01	**ELIZABETHAN LOVER** $1.25 £ (#28) 0-515-03907-1

7